I0669987

JUDAS GUNN AND HANGIN' PARDS

Two Full Length Western Novels

GORDON D. SHIRREFFS

WOLFPACK
PUBLISHING
— EST 2013 —

Judas Gunn and Hangin' Pards
Paperback Edition
© Copyright 2022 (As Revised) Gordon D. Shirreffs

Wolfpack Publishing
5130 S. Fort Apache Rd. 215-380
Las Vegas, NV 89148

wolfpackpublishing.com

This book is a work of fiction. Any references to historical events, real people or real places are used fictitiously. Other names, characters, places and events are products of the author's imagination, and any resemblance to actual events, places or persons, living or dead, is entirely coincidental.

All rights reserved. No part of this book may be reproduced by any means without the prior written consent of the publisher, other than brief quotes for reviews.

eBook ISBN 978-1-63977-048-9
Paperback ISBN 978-1-63977-049-6

JUDAS GUNN AND HANGIN' PARDS

JUDAS BUNN AND HANGIN' PARDS

JUDAS GUNN

JUDAS BUNN

CHAPTER ONE

A DRY DESERT WIND soughed softly through Dragoon Pass, feeling its way through the thick darkness of the Arizona night. Ken Sturgis led his tired roan across the right-of-way of the Southern Pacific. A horseshoe struck the rail and it rang like a cracked bell. Ken shoved back his battered hat and looked up the rough slope just north of the tracks. He caught a faint glimmer of light high on the slope. The boys had reached the rendezvous ahead of him. As he led the roan up the rough trail that slanted transversely across the side of the deep pass he scented the faint odor of bittersweet woodsmoke and the delicious aroma of coffee.

He cursed as stinging catclaw raked across his right hand. There would be a good moon that night, but it wasn't due up for at least another hour or so. They could continue their hunt by moonlight if the boys weren't too tired. It had been a long, dry day with little success.

He heard voices as he reached the broad shelf that had been neatly sliced by nature along the rugged face of the pass. Shadows moved against the face of the upper portion of the pass, grotesque in their length and movement, as one or the other of the boys passed between the fire and the rock wall behind it.

"Hello, the camp!" called out Ken. It didn't pay in that country to walk up on a man's fire without identifying yourself, even if one of the two men at the fire was your younger brother.

"That you, Ken?" called out Roy Sturgis. "We've been here for hours!"

Ken led the roan to where the other horses were picketed. His eyes narrowed as he saw three horses. Two of them were from the ranch he and Roy owned down on the San Miguel. The other was a fine-looking coyote dun he had never seen before. Ken unsaddled the roan. Water trickled into a rock pan from a crack in the side of the cliff. As far as Ken knew it was the only water in a full day's ride in any direction. The railroad had built a tank down in the pass to store up the overflow. It was likely that a man who knew that country would camp in the pass near the water, but in the times Ken had used it he had never seen anyone else there. The pass had had a bad name for years. First, because of the predatory Chiricahuas, and later because of the outlaws who would lie in wait for the Abbott-Downings and freight wagons that had used the pass before the railroad came through.

Ken placed his saddle on a flat rock next to the two saddles there. The dun was still saddled. Ken removed his Winchester from the saddle sheath and walked toward the fire.

Roy was placing the spider over the glowing embers. He grinned up at his brother, white teeth shining in the ruddy light. He was a slender, handsome kid, more like his sainted mother in appearance than rough, tough Slade

Sturgis, whom Ken resembled. "We've been waiting for you, Ken," he said. "Got a pot of Mex strawberries buried in the coals. Bobcat says he got the receipt from a Yankee he knew in Huntsville Pen. He was a Maine man, says Bobcat, and he didn't want to leave this world of sin and tears without he'd pass on the receipt his maw had given him to a worthy recipient."

"Like Bobcat," said Ken dryly. "Where've you been getting those twenty-dollar words?"

"Out'n books," said Bobcat Bates from the far side of the fire. He handed Roy a greasy handful of sliced bacon. "All the time books! Almanacs, feed catalogs, mail order catalogs them medical books old Doc Deatheridge left your maw afore she died."

"Hello, Ken," said a man who stepped out from the darkness beyond the firelight. He placed a filled water can beside the coffee pot. "I didn't know you Bar S boys were up in this country."

Ken stared at him. "By God!" he said. "Marl Meyner! I didn't recognize you for a minute. You've changed."

Marl smiled. "It's the Mex mustache," he said. "Learned how to trim one down in Sonora."

Ken stuck out a hand. "It's more than that! When we rode the Rio together you were just a kid!"

Marl smiled again. "How old were *you*, Ken?"

Ken grinned. "About the same age, Marl. Last time I saw you was in Bisbee. You were a mine guard then. That was at least three years ago. What are you doing around here?"

Marl looked down at the other men and shook his head slightly.

Ken nodded as he hunkered down beside the fire and felt for the makings. Marl had been ambitious to be a lawman. He had worked as turnkey for old Matt Bali in San

Miguel, then later as town marshal, although God knew there wasn't much to be done outside of throwing Saturday night drunks into the bullpen and making Luz Hernandez' girls stay off the front porch of her "establishment" so they wouldn't solicit the passersby. After that he had worked in the Bisbee area as a mine guard, and they were as tough as whang leather on high-graders, ore thieves and troublemakers. It wasn't the sort of job Ken would have wanted, nor did he ever figure it was the right niche for Martin Meyner.

Ken tossed the makings to Marl who began to fashion a smoke. "Came up here on business," he said. "Heard down in Tres Cabezas that you and the boys were south of here looking for horse thieves. Any luck?"

Ken caught the makings as Marl tossed them back, and began to roll a cigarette. "Not unless the boys found out anything."

"Forget it," said Bobcat sourly. "I'll swear to God them thieves painted them damned cayuses with invisible paint or something."

Ken lighted his cigarette. He blew a smoke ring. "Lost ten good horses," he said quietly. "One of them was the best stud Roy and I ever had. Took us two years to build up the cavy we had. Just getting the business rolling when we got cleaned out by a bunch of Mexes who got across the border ahead of us and vanished. Damned rurales wouldn't give us any help. They said it was an even-up deal all the way around. We steal from them and they steal from us. When we got back to the Bar S we found out we had been hit again and the bastards had headed toward the San Pedro. We've been tailing them for a week."

"Mexicans again?" said Marl.

"No," said Ken. "By Godfrey! They *know* this country.

Maybe Bobcat is right. Maybe they did paint them with invisible paint." He looked about. "We figured they'd *have* to come this way for water."

Marl shoved a brand back into the fire with the toe of a boot. "They didn't," he said.

"What makes you so sure?" asked Bobcat

Marl looked down at him. "I know," he said.

Bobcat spat a stream of tobacco juice at a rock, hitting it neatly. "Seems like you know a lot, mister," he said.

"I know you're taking a hell of a chance camping here at night."

Roy looked up. "Why so?"

"Because of the railroad."

"They don't own this damned water hole," said Bobcat. "Even if they did, they wouldn't stop me and the others from stopping here for a drink or two."

"That's not the point," said Marl quietly. "The Southern Pacific was hit back at San Simon six months ago and lost plenty out of the Express. Twenty thousand I hear. Bandits tried it again west of here, near Pantano but got driven off. They got into the express car and couldn't open the big through safe. By the time the gunsmoke cleared there were two dead bandits and a dead Wells Fargo guard."

Ken looked thoughtfully at Marl. "So the Espee has been keeping an eye on the right-of-way."

There was a message in Marl's eyes. "You boys better get out of here before dawn," he said.

Roy took the spider from atop the coals. The odor of the sizzling bacon was tantalizing. Bobcat dug the clay bean pot out of the fire and pried off the lid. The delicious odor of beans, fat pork and molasses drifted out to mingle with the odor of the bacon, and in a minute the coffee began to bubble in the pot.

"Get the plates, Ken," said Roy. He looked up at Marl. "You're staying, of course?"

"Sure thing, kid."

The four of them ate silently. Bobcat hadn't been joshing. "Damned shame they had to hang that Yankee," said Roy.

"What's the difference?" said Bobcat. "I got the receipt, didn't I?"

Marl forked bacon into his mouth. His dark eyes studied Bobcat. "Huntsville?" he said. "That's the Texas State Pen, isn't it?"

"Yup."

"Were you a guard there?"

Ken looked at Roy. Roy looked at Bobcat. Bobcat laid down his fork. "No," he said quietly, but in such a way a man wouldn't push the question if he had the sense God had given him for a starter.

Marl drained his coffee cup and refilled it. "You didn't answer my question, Bobcat," he said.

"No," said Bobcat. He wiped his plate with a piece of bread and popped the bread into his mouth.

It was very quiet in the pass except for the whispering of the wind. One of the horses whinnied. A brand popped in the fire.

Bobcat stood up and took out a lint-specked chunk of wedding cake. He began to whittle a chew. "I was a 'con' in Huntsville," he said. "That answer your question, *mister?*"

Marl nodded. "Serve your time?"

"*All* of it, mister," said Bobcat. He looked at Ken. "I'll take a look at the hosses," he said. He walked off into the darkness.

Roy finished his meal. "You shouldn't oughta kept after him like that," he said.

Marl put down his coffee cup and reached for the makings. He rolled a cigarette and lighted it. Then he slid his right hand inside his coat and withdrew it, holding out something in the palm of his hand so the firelight shone on it. It was a badge. Ken didn't recognize it.

"Special agent, Southern Pacific Railway," said Roy quietly.

Marl nodded. He looked at Ken. "Ever seen one of these before?"

"No."

Marl looked at Roy. "Not many of them around," he said. "Few people have ever seen them unless an arrest is made."

Roy flushed. He looked quickly at Ken and then looked away.

Ken rolled a smoke. "Roy was just a kid then," he said. "Fifteen years old and wild as a young mocky. Paw paid off the bill."

Marl nodded again. "It's still on the record," he said.

Again, it seemed to be inordinately quiet.

Ken blew a smoke ring. The kid had been mixed up with a bunch of yahoos from San Miguel. They had gone on a two-day drunk up north around Benson and had run out of *dinero*. Three of them had busted into some freight cars on a siding, making so much noise they could have been heard in Tombstone. It was more of a lark than a stealing. The S.P., tough as its agents were on thieves, had not pressed charges against Roy, although the others had served time for the escapade because of their ages. That had been more than five years ago. No one ever mentioned it around the Sturgis boys.

"You know a lot," said Ken quietly.

Marl smiled pleasantly. "It's my job to look for trouble before it starts. I know you boys aren't aiming to cause any trouble, but, Ken, you're camping here in the pass with an ex-con from Huntsville, and a kid who got into trouble with the S.P. five years ago. Might look bad if anything happened."

"Got anything on me?" asked Ken dryly.

Marl stood up. "Have to move on," he said. "Thanks for the grub."

Ken stood up. "I asked you a question," he said.

Marl dusted off his pants with his hat. He looked directly at Ken. "Nothing the S.P. might hold against you," he said.

Roy stood up to one side of the agent. Somewhere in the darkness beyond the flickering pool of firelight a stone clicked against another. Bobcat was somewhere out there, and he wasn't looking at the horses.

Ken dropped his cigarette into the fire. The light shone on the hard planes of his tanned face and Roy had the uncanny feeling that old Slade Sturgis, the man who had sired Ken and Roy, had come back to life in the form of his elder son.

Marl put his hat on his head. There was no fear on his handsome face. Marl Meyner had faced too many hard-cases in his life to show fear now. The mines wouldn't have hired him as a guard, nor would the Espee have taken him on as a special agent if they hadn't known what caliber he was, for they hired men of Big Fifty caliber.

"Are you talking about 'Red' Lopez?" said Ken quietly.

"You rode with him, didn't you?" countered Meyner.

"He was a *revolucionario,*" said Ken.

"And you were a hired gun with him."

"I wasn't alone," said Ken. "A lot of Mexicans, *and*

Americans, thought Lopez was a patriot, not a bandit chief."

Marl smiled. "But he *was* a bandit, Ken."

"You're talking about his brother Eduardo," said Roy.

Ken waved a hand. "When I rode with Lopez," he said, "he was a *revolucionario*. I never knew Eduardo until later. *I* left Lopez when he got out of line in Cascabeles."

"Lopez sent his Dorados after Ken," said Roy. "Ken beat them to the border."

"With a burro-load of 'dobe dollars," added the agent.

"A sackful," said Ken. "Wages."

Marl shrugged. "It's no concern of mine."

"Isn't it?" said Ken. "You've made an issue out of it, Marl."

The agent smiled. "I'm on my way," he said.

"Here's your hoss," said Bobcat out of the darkness. "Nice bit of hoss flesh." He led the dun forward.

Marl mounted the fine animal and looked down at Ken. "Take my advice," he said quietly. "Get out of this pass before dawn. *Vaya con Dios, amigos!*" He rode off into the darkness.

They heard the dun's hoofs striking the rocks on the steep trail. It took an expert to ride a horse down that ribbon in the darkness.

"Well, I'll be dipped in manure!" said Bobcat angrily. He spat a stream of juice.

Ken sat down and slowly rolled a cigarette, his eyes far away. "He knows a helluva lot," he said quietly. "Too much maybe."

"We ain't done anything," said Bobcat.

"Just the same, we'd better light out before the dawn," said Roy. "When's the next train due through here?"

"About dawn," said Ken thoughtfully. He looked at

the others. "You don't suppose Marl knows something we don't know."

"Knows a helluva lot mor'n he should," snarled Bobcat. "I done my time!"

There was a faint trace of moonlight in the pass when Ken emptied his coffee cup. "I'll take a looksee north of here," he said. "Moon ought to be bright as day in an hour or so."

"You won't find anything," said Bobcat.

Ken looked down at him. "I might as well tell the both of you now," he said. "The Bar S is about busted. I planned to sell off all those horses but the stud, to pay the mortgage. The money would just about meet the debt for a few months anyway, long enough for us to figure out some way of raising *dinero*. Boys, if we *don't* find those stolen horses, there won't be much sense in even going back to the Bar S."

"I didn't know it was bad as all that," said Roy.

Ken grinned wryly. "That bag of 'dobe dollars was enough to make the down payment on the Bar S and get some good stock. If we can last until next year I might land a government contract for army horses. Major McCudden was interested in our stock. That contract would pay the way for the Bar S and anything over that would be sheer profit."

"Then, by God," said Bobcat, "we'd better *all* go look under the light of the moon like little fairies."

Ken shook his head. "Sit tight. Get some shut-eye. I'll be back as soon as I cut sign, if any. If not, I'll be back in time to get you up and out of here before the Express comes rattling through."

He saddled the roan and rode along the broad shelf to the east end of it, then dismounted to lead the horse through the twisted, rugged notch that opened onto the low mesa north of the railway line pass.

He led the roan out onto the mesa just as the moon tipped the eastern mountains, shedding a pale, silvery light across the hills and the desert. He squatted beside the roan, smoking steadily, until there was enough light to cut for sign, He didn't have much faith in his search, but he had wanted to get away from the others for a little while. Somehow he could best clarify his thoughts when alone in the desert, or in the mountains.

Marl Meyner puzzled him. There had been no antagonism in his manner. He and Ken had been riding partners for a time on John Slaughter's spread and later had worked in the Baboquivari country and along the Santa Cruz. Ken had liked him then. He was a good man in a fight, a drunk or a poker game, and his last dollar and last shirt were yours for the asking. Likely Marl had information known only to the Espee, and didn't want to let any of it out, but he had, at least, warned Ken and his boys to get out of there. Maybe his conversation regarding the pasts of all three of them had been merely to point out that if anything did happen, they'd be suspect until the real malefactors were caught. *If* they were caught—

"By Godfrey," said Ken as he ground out his cigarette and rolled another, "I'm acting as though all hell were going to break loose around here and us right in the middle of it."

When the moon was fully up, he moved out, and half a mile from the pass he cut sign. He studied the tracks that crossed a little playa which spread out fan-shaped from several flat-topped hills almost in the exact center of the mesa. There had been at least six to eight horses in the group. He trailed the tracks across rough and rocky ground, losing the scent now and then, only to pick it up when he cast about, back and forth, with the patience of a bloodhound or a Chiricahua scout.

Two miles from the pass, under the clear light of the moon, the trail divided two ways. Half of the horses had gone due east, and the other half southwesterly. He lost the southwesterly trail in twenty minutes on treacherous malpais. They'd have to pick it up in daylight. Meanwhile he'd try to follow the other trail as far as he could.

It was past midnight when he reached the bottom of the mesa. Several times he had lost the trail, only to find it here and there, in fits and spurts. He was getting tired. It had been a long day in the saddle, and the roan was more tired than he. But it was the best indication he had found as yet in the long trail north from the San Miguel country.

He led the roan down into an arroyo and out toward the flat desert country. He stopped short as he saw a fieldstone house squatting on a level shelf just beyond the arroyo. It was a big place, but time had not dealt kindly with it. He was puzzled. It wasn't ranching country, and there were no mines hereabouts, and it certainly wasn't a trading post, for there wasn't anyone for miles with whom to trade.

He saw the sagging remains of a large corral to one side. The building was square-shaped, with an open court in the middle. Centered in the front wall was a large, high gateway, half filled by a sagging wooden gate.

"By Godfrey," said Ken. "I'll bet that's the old swing station on the Southern Overland!"

He led the bay toward the old stagecoach line station. The Southern Pacific had reached this area from the west in '80 and had connected with the Santa Fe at Deming, New Mexico in '81, and there had been no further use for stagecoach stations in that area, the swift Abbott-

Downing "Concord" coaches being relegated to the back areas of the growing Territory.

He could see the line of track stretching to the east across the flat, sterile country beyond the pass. It wasn't more than half a mile from where he stood. He circled the old station. The well had long dried up. The wind scrabbled gently at the eroding walls of the place.

Near the gateway he found sign again. Horses had been there, and recently. He raked fingers through the droppings. They had been there some time that day, and not long before the sun had gone down. He eyed the silent, brooding station. He ground-reined the roan and drew his Winchester from its sheath.

Ken worked his way in through the gateway. On the hard-packed earth in what had been the courtyard of the station he found more droppings. In an angle between two walls, he saw the remains of a fire. He scraped aside the ashes and felt the ground. It still held a faint trace of warmth. Slowly and carefully, he went over the area. He found several cigar butts, an empty sack that had once contained Pride of Durham, and a broken bottle that had once held Bacanora. Here and there he found piles of coffee grounds, like little ant heaps.

Ken shoved back his hat as he surveyed the building. Anyone could have made a temporary camp there. Soldiers, cowpokes, drifters, herders or maybe railroad men. He poked into the building, padding from room to room, wrinkling his nose at the stench of some of the rooms where chance visitors had relieved bladder and bowels.

In the room nearest the gateway, where a battered zinc-topped bar still dominated one side of the room, he found a curious thing. Lying in the dust and debris of the floor, unmarked by dust or time, was freshly shattered wood, from a stout box. He picked up the pieces and carried them to the nearest window. In the clear light of the moon he read aloud the lettering: " 'Kepauno Chemical Company Giant Blasting Powder.'"

From the size of the pieces he estimated that the box had contained half a dozen good-sized cans of the powder, enough to blow the whole station clean off the face of the desert. He leaned against the wall, feeling for the makings. He rolled a cigarette and lighted it. There was something damned curious about this. There were no mines in that area, but it was possible a railroad maintenance or building crew might have used the powder, and yet there were no signs of fresh blasting in the pass area, for he had been clear through it from one end to the other earlier that day.

Ken shook his head. He walked outside and looked about. His eyes narrowed as he looked east. In the moonlight he could see a trace of something alien against the clear night sky, hanging just above the great dip in the desert that led down toward the distant, unseen Willcox Flats.

Slowly Ken took the cigarette from his lips. It wasn't a cloud. It was smoke.

His boot kicked a bottle as he walked toward his horse. He picked it up, eyeing the blue and white label. " 'Abyssinian Desert Companion,'" he read aloud, with some amusement. " 'Good for wind colic, flatulent colic, botts, diarrhea, scouring, dysentery, inflammation of the bowels, bladder and kidney trouble, colds in the head, congestion, fits, the mad staggers, looseness of the bowels, inflammation of the brain and general debility. For botts, in both man and beast, it has no equal.'"

Ken placed the bottle on the windowsill behind him. It still had an inch or two of dark-looking liquid in it.

"Too damned bad that Bacanora bottle couldn't have had an inch or two in it," he said.

He looked at the smoke. It was thicker, rising in a steady column against the night sky. He led the roan toward the railroad line and looked again at the smoke. It was still rising. He took off his hat and placed an ear on the rail. Faintly, ever so faintly, he caught the tremor that indicated the coming of a train.

Ken wet his lips. He put on his hat and looked again at the smoke. There was no train due through there until around dawn, and that was at least five hours off. There was something wrong. Ken ran back to the roan. Marl Meyner had warned them to be out of there before the dawn. He had known something; something he could not divulge to Ken. But he *had* warned them as much as he could.

There was no time to take the easier route up the pass and then up the trail, and furthermore, after Ken remembered those shattered bits of wood back in the station, he didn't want to go into that pass, parts of which were still in shadows, places where the moon could not throw its clear light. There was something alien about the pass that night; something brooding and evil.

He turned the roan back the way he had come and then urged it up the mesa side, between the right-of-way and the abandoned station. The roan was tired. He flagged constantly but Ken kept at him with the cruel spurs until the blood ran down his hide.

He reached a point where he could see down into the pass. He looked east. The plume of smoke still hung against the sky, but much closer now, and he could swear that he heard the faint puffing of the exhaust.

Ken touched the roan with the bloody spurs. The horse floundered on loose rock and before Ken could throw himself from the saddle the roan went down heavily, landing on Ken's right leg, and he heard the dull snapping of bone. He sickened as the horse moved spasmodically and then lay still. For a moment he managed to maintain his senses and then he lapsed fully into unconsciousness.

CHAPTER TWO

I t WAS the thudding of the locomotive that drew Ken Sturgis back into the land of the living. He could smell the smoke as he opened his eyes. The roan still lay on his leg. He forced himself up on his elbow and saw that the horse was dead, its neck twisted at an awkward angle. Ken's sheathed Winchester was pressed cruelly into his right inner thigh. He tried to free it but it was impossible. Cold sweat ran down his face as he tried to work free but the pain in his broken leg was agonizing. He looked down into the pass. The locomotive, a Standard, was moving slowly up the grade from the desert, laying a trail of smoke behind the hardworking engine. There were half a dozen cars behind it, none of them passenger cars, all baggage and express.

Ken looked the other way. The water hole was around a spur of the pass but the camp was not out of his sight. They'd hear the locomotive, but the sound of it would drown out Ken's voice. He'd have to wait until it passed through and then try to free one of his guns to fire a distress signal. His six-gun was in its holster, but it had worked around almost to the middle of his back and he could not reach it to free it.

He closed his eyes, fighting to keep his consciousness. He got a grip on himself and opened his eyes. The locomotive was almost below him now, and then he saw something else. A man lay flat on a broad-topped rock which jutted out into the far side of the pass, just above the level of the engine cab.

The moonlight glistened from the water in the open-topped water tank that had been placed on a rock shelf high enough over the tracks so that water could flow down into the tank of a tender. Ken stared at the locomotive as it slowed down and then ground to a halt just below the water tank. The fireman dropped from the cab and started up the crude steps that had been cut into the rock. He was reaching for the hose when a man stepped out from behind the tank and fired just once. The fireman pitched down the steps and lay still.

Ken saw the man on the rock drop atop the cab and poke a gun into it. The gun flashed twice. Seconds later the engineer fell backward down the steps of the locomotive. There were other men moving along the side of the train. A gun flatted off near the end car. A man's scream rose above the sound of the steam escaping from the Standard. More guns flatted off.

A man ducked under the second express car and another man handed him something from which the moonlight glistened. Powder cans! Ken had a damned good idea where they had come from. There was nothing he could do but hope Roy and Bobcat had cleared out when they had heard the coming of the train.

Ken tried to work his leg loose. The horse slid a little down the slope but Ken was still firmly trapped.

He watched with morbid fascination as the men scattered from the express car, leaving on the ground a faint sparking of light that moved swiftly beneath the car. There was a brilliant, eye-searing flash of orange-red light and a thundering explosion that rocked the pass like the crashing of heavy artillery. Smoke and bits of debris sailed up through the air, and part of the express car roof went with it, to land with a crash atop the locomotive.

Before the smoke cleared, the men broke from cover. Axes flashed in the moonlight and a man yelled in triumph. Three of them climbed into the smoke-filled interior of the car. Two other men passed in powder cans. In a matter of minutes the three men dropped from the wrecked car, scattering into cover an instant before there was another explosion, though much smaller than the first one. Again, before the smoke had cleared, three of the men were inside. Other men led up horses and burros.

Ken wiped the icy sweat from his forehead. The stench of powder smoke filled the pass and flames had begun to lick at one end of the shattered express car. Something was passed out to the waiting men and the burros were loaded. Then the three men jumped from the burning car. Every man mounted and in a matter of a few minutes they were out of sight down the pass. There was another explosion and then the flames leaped from the burning express car to the next car, a baggage car, and then that, too, started to blaze.

The flames were roaring, casting giant flickering shadows on the rugged, blast-scored walls of the pass, while a thick cloud of smoke swirled in the updraft up into the clear moonlit sky. Nothing moved in the pass but the flames. The locomotive crew must be dead. There was no sign of any other of the train's crew.

Ken worked his sheath knife free and managed to cut the girth of his saddle. Slowly and painfully he worked the saddle free, giving his leg a little more room. It was likely the bone had been cracked instead of snapped clean through. There was no bleeding that he could feel. The moon was on the wane when at last he pulled himself free from the dead roan, scrabbling at the cruel ground with bleeding fingers.

He lay still for a long time, his face pressed against the ground, trying to regain his strength. There was no use in yelling for help, for the noise of the crackling flames would drown out his voice, and he didn't want to fire his six-shooter. Not yet anyway. The Winchester was still pinned beneath the roan.

A man can do impossible things at times; things he will wonder at for the rest of his days. Ken Sturgis did such a thing that smoke-filled night above the pass. He tied grease-wood branches to his broken leg, using his scarf and thongs from his saddle for lashings. Slowly, foot by foot, he dragged himself along the ground, wincing as he passed jumping cholla or plowed inadvertently into clinging, stinging cat-claw. His pants were in tatters when he at last reached the broad shelf whereon was the water hole and the camp. Here the going was better. He bellied along the ground, pulling himself with bleeding hands, coughing in the thick, acrid smoke that shrouded him now and then.

He crept to the edge of the water pan and thrust his head into the cool water. He looked toward the camp but there was no sign of Roy and Bobcat. Likely they had pulled out in a hurry, looking for him.

He found a length of pole that would serve for a crutch and hobbled over to the camp. They had pulled foot all right. Bobcat had likely given the orders, old owl-hooter that he was, for there wasn't a trace of the camp. The fire had been covered with dirt, raked smooth with a branch of brush.

Ken looked down into the pass. He could see the bodies of the fireman and the engineer lying there. The engineer's overalls were smoldering. Flying embers hissed into the water tank. It was an eerie sight to see the cars burning and not a sign of life anywhere about.

Ken knew he'd never make it through the notch. He'd have to go down into the pass and hobble along the level right-of-way. Maybe he could help a wounded man if there were any of them still alive down there.

The moon was low in the west when he reached the bottom of the pass. The fire had begun to die out at the end of the third car. The express car that had been blown up was a huge mass of embers and red-hot iron. The heat in the pass was stifling, and the vagrant wind did little to ease it. Ken staggered as the full blast of heat hit him. He worked his way toward the engineer and fireman. Their smoke-blackened faces looked up at him, the sightless eyes bright from reflected firelight. He rolled them further to one side, out of the way of the hungry, reaching flames. The sweat of heat, exertion and pain began to drain his lean body of strength.

He hobbled past the burning cars, the intense heat searing against his flesh, and almost fainted several times until he reached the end of the train. A man lay face downward on the ballast. Another had been under a car and the burning car had collapsed on him. Only his legs protruded, and the fire had thoroughly cooked them. The stench of the burning flesh drove Ken off.

He rounded the last car. A man lay between two rocks

beyond the ballast. Ken hobbled over to him and found himself looking into the set, blue face of Bobcat Bates, his green eyes staring fixedly up at his boss. Ken knelt beside him and raised his head. Blood stained his fingers. A bullet had struck the little man in the back of the skull, likely killing him instantly. A rifle lay beside him and his six-shooter was still clutched in his right hand.

Ken stood up, looking down at Bobcat. The little man had worked for him for two years, through fair weather and foul, and Ken had owed him six months' wages; but Bobcat had known few other employers would take on an ex-con, alumnus of Huntsville Pen. He had been more like a relative than an employee, and a damned good friend.

"Roy!" yelled Ken.

"Roy! Roy! Roy!" echoed the pass.

Ken rubbed his burning face. There was a mystery here. Maybe Roy and Bobcat had pulled foot and had been caught in the cross fire. But where was Roy? He might have seen there was no use in staying with Bobcat and gone to look for Ken. Yes, that was it!

Ken wiped the sweat from his face. He'd have to get a horse, although he didn't know whether he could straddle one or not. He'd have to have water until he was found by Roy, or until he could get to a doctor. It wasn't going to be easy. If his leg stayed the way it was too long, it would be agonizing when it was set, if complications didn't set in. *Where the devil was Roy?*

"Roy! Roy! Roy!" yelled Ken desperately.

"Roy! Roy! Roy!" echoed the pass. "Roy . . . Roy . . . Roy . . . Roy . . . Roy . . . Roy . . ."

It was no use. Ken worked his way back through that trough of imitation hell to the water tank beside the tracks. One of the cars collapsed behind him, sending a blast of heat and a shower of fat, soaring embers through the gathering darkness. Ken winced as sparks stung his skin and burned through his shirt and pants.

He worked his way up the steps cut into the rock and bathed his face in the soot-covered water of the tank. He looked up the trail and winced within himself. The heat was terrible in the pass. He'd have to get above it. He could stay by the water hole until help came. Those flames and the smoke could be seen for miles and the sounds of the explosions would have carried across the desert. Someone would certainly have heard them. By Godfrey! Marl Meyner couldn't be far off. He'd come back. It was his job. Or maybe he had taken off after the bandits.

It was fully dark when he reached the camp area. The bottom of the pass still glowed with huge beds of embers and red-hot, twisted ironwork from the cars. Ken got to the water pan and bathed his face again. He lay down, leg stretched out in front of him and rolled a quirley. He wished for a bottle of good Bacanora, or *aguardiente,* or maybe a good belt of sotol. That would put the spirit back into a man, but it certainly wouldn't reset a broken leg. Maybe he'd have to do it himself. . . The thought made him shudder.

The wind shifted before the dawn. It grew cold. Ken Sturgis groaned in his sleep. He didn't see or hear anyone near the water hole. It was a sixth sense, honed by years along the border, that caused him to open his eyes. He saw pale, gray light in the sky. He looked up at a big, broad-shouldered man, whose hard-hewed face was half shadowed by the brim of his dusty black, flat-crowned hat. A star glinted dully from his coat. A Winchester was in his left hand, and the rifle seemed dwarfed by the size of the hand.

"You didn't get far," said the big man coldly.

"I didn't try," said Ken quietly.

The man poked Ken in the belly with the butt of the rifle. "Get up," he said. "Keep your hands away from that cutter."

"I've got a busted leg," said Ken.

"I said, Get up!" The rifle butt pushed against the pit of Ken's lean belly.

Ken felt cold hate pour through him, but there was no use in antagonizing the big bastard. He struggled to his feet. "Give me a hand," he said.

"I'll give you shit," said the lawman.

"*Gracias,*" said Ken dryly.

"Where are the rest of them?" asked the lawman.

"Who?"

"Don't play foxy with me! I'm Max Fremar, deputy sheriff of this county. Which way did they go?"

Ken could hear voices down in the pass and the chuffing of an engine coming from the west. He glanced past the officer and saw it, pulling several passenger cars, and two flatcars loaded with horses. The smoke hung against the sky.

The rifle muzzle prodded Ken's belly, almost pushing him off balance. "We found one of your boys down there. Your pals left him like a dead dog. My posse is rounding up another one on the far side of the pass. He's been wounded. Blood tracks all over the place."

Ken narrowed his eyes. "My brother?"

"Is he your brother?"

"I won't know until I see him."

Fremar spat. "Which way did the others head?"

"I don't know anything about the holdup, sheriff. My brother, one of my hands and me camped here yesterday.

I'm Ken Sturgis, from the San Miguel country, tracking stolen horses."

A thin man came through the thorny brush. "Listen to him, Max," he said with a loose grin. "We got the other one."

Max Fremar nodded. "This one is a tough nut He don't want to talk, Harry."

The lean one grinned again. "He don't? My, my. . ."

Fremar's right hand cut backward across Ken's face, driving him back against a boulder. He felt the salt taste of blood in his mouth. Fremar smiled coldly. "Tracking stolen horses, eh? That's the best one I've ever heard. Which way did they go?"

The backhanders drove Ken along the side of the boulder until he fell heavily on his broken leg. Blood leaked from his mouth. A tooth was loose.

Fremar stood over him, big and impassive, and cold as death. The rifle butt rested on Ken's crotch, and Fremar pushed it up and down, pressing heavily as it came down. "I'll give you a couple of minutes," he said, "while I talk to this other one."

Two men came along the trail, with a man between them, his boot toes dragging in the dirt as he was pulled along. It was Roy. The left side of his head and face was dark with dirt and drying blood. He raised his head and looked at Ken with glazed eyes, and did not see him. The two men let him fall heavily at Fremar's feet.

"This your brother?" said the sheriff to Ken.

"Yes."

Fremar rubbed his broad jaw. He hooked a foot under Roy and rolled him over on his back. "You," he said. "Where are the others?"

Roy slowly wiped a hand across his bloody mouth. "All I know is they shot Bobcat and creased me. They left me for dead. I crawled into the brush, hoping my brother would find me."

Fremar smiled. "And we found your brother."

Ken sat up, resting his back against the boulder. He slowly dropped his hand to his holster. The six-gun was gone. He saw it lying on a rock beyond Fremar. He looked at the three men with the deputy sheriff. Their faces were impassive.

"Nice friends you've got," said the lawman. "They pull foot outa here with all the loot and leave three of you behind. Well, it was the biggest mistake they made. Should have killed off you two as well. The dead do not talk."

"Look, sheriff," said Ken. "He doesn't know any more about this than I do."

Fremar turned slowly. "Listen, you," he said. "No one but the railroad officials and me knew the Express was coming through here hours early with gold coins from the Denver mint and a helluva lot of folding money. How did you know?"

"I said we didn't know anything about it!"

Fremar shrugged. "Tim," he said to one of the men. "Have the boys make fires and cook up some breakfast. I'll have the information by that time. Glen, you go down and get that Papago breed tracker and tell him to work along the pass looking for sign. Harry, you stay here."

It was very quiet after the two men left. Fremar took out his cigar case and carefully selected a cigar. He cut off the end with a silver cigar cutter attached to the chain across his solid belly. He lighted it and puffed out a satisfying cloud of bluish smoke.

Ken shifted a little, easing his leg. "Look," he said patiently. "Marlin Meyner saw us here yesterday evening.

He knows who we are. Find him and he'll tell you we didn't have anything to do with this robbery."

"Who's Marlin Meyner?"

"Special agent for the Southern Pacific."

Fremar looked at Harry. "Go down and see Jim Castleman. Ask him to find this Meyner."

Roy groaned. He tried to wipe the blood from his face.

"Roy," said Ken. "Who killed Bobcat? Who shot you?"

"I don't know. They were masked. They came up on us after you left. Took away our guns. They shot Bobcat near the tracks. I made a break for it and got creased. I guess they thought they'd killed me."

"They took Bobcat's guns away?"

"Yes."

Ken narrowed his eyes. There had been a rifle lying beside the little man and a six-gun had been clenched in his stiffened grip. A cold feeling crept through him. Whoever had planned this thing had planted Bobcat beside the tracks and had tried to kill Roy, to throw evidence to the law that both men had been mixed up in the holdup, and had been killed in the attempt.

Fremar squatted, the rifle across his muscular thighs, his eyes flicking from Roy to Ken and back again, while a cloud of smoke hung in front of his broad face.

Boots grated on the trail. Harry came through the brush.

"Well?" said Fremar.

Harry grinned. "Castleman never heard of no Marlin Meyner."

Fremar looked at Ken.

"Who's Jim Castleman?" said Ken.

Fremar took the cigar from his mouth and inspected

it. "Just the Chief Inspector on this division of the Espee is all."

Ken stared at him, and then at Harry. "You're sure about what he said?"

Harry began to fashion a smoke. "Sure thing, *hombre.*"

"But Meyner was here," protested Ken. "He had the badge."

"You take a good look at it?" asked Fremar casually.

"My brother recognized it."

"How did he know what it was?"

It was very quiet around the water hole. The faint sound of voices came up from the pass. A locomotive whistle sounded from the east. Smoke drifted against the lightening sky. They would be arriving to clear the pass of wreckage and open the line. They never wasted much time that way. The trains had to go through.

"Eighty thousand dollars," said Harry softly. "My God, the likker, clothes and whores a man could buy with that kind of *dinero* in his jeans."

Something came creeping uneasily into Ken's mind. Meyner had been fooling around the pass the day before. If he had really been an Espee agent he would have spotted any strangers around there, over and above Ken, Roy and Bobcat. He had been damned positive the horse thieves had not passed that way, which indicated he had been in that area for some time. He had warned Ken and the others to be out of the pass *before dawn,* but the Express had come through hours early, and he couldn't have been far enough away from the tracks not to have known it had come earlier. You could hardly miss hearing it, or seeing the smoke and sparks from miles away. If he had been an Espee agent he would have known *exactly* when it was coming through. Meyner was a skilled enough lawman to have noted any strangers in the area over and above the three men from the San Miguel. How could he have missed seeing those men at the abandoned stage station?

Fremar blew a cloud of smoke. "Which way did they go?" he said, almost as though to himself. He looked at Ken. "North?"

"I don't know."

He looked at Roy. "West, or east?"

"I don't know," said Roy huskily.

"South?" said Fremar to Ken.

"You know we don't know."

Fremar stood up, rifle in hand. "No," he said, almost patiently. "I don't know that *you* don't know, but I aim to find out. We haven't got much time, *hombres*. Every minute we fool around here they are making tracks. I got a jumper wire on the telegraph ready to alert posses up and down the line, to go either way on the railroad, hauling their horses, food and water, to the place closest to where those bastards took off, but I don't know which way they went. Now, you *hombres* must of made *some* plans. This job was engineered by an expert. He knew when the train was coming through. He knew it was carrying gold coins from the Denver mint. He knew how to blow open that car and blow that safe. If he was smart enough to meet the Express and get away with the loot, he was smart enough to plan a damned good getaway. Relays of horses cached at hidden water holes. Supplies cached. Changes of clothing. So on and so on."

Ken shifted his throbbing leg. The pain was getting worse.

"Who's going to talk first?" said Fremar. He looked at Ken. "Not you. I know your breed. You're brothers, eh? *Bueno!* You ain't goin' to see little brother get hurt worse than he is, are you?"

Ken looked up. "You hurt my brother worse than he is now, Fremar," he said coldly, "and I'll kill you."

Fremar smiled. *Will* you now? Harry, watch this fighting cock."

The big man walked over to Roy and pulled him to his feet. "Start talking," he said thinly. The hardhanded slaps snapped Roy's bloody head from side to side. He broke loose and staggered back. Fremar closed in on him, striking savagely and steadily, like a man chopping wood, or meat on a butcher's block. "Talk, you ornery sono-fabitch! Talk! Talk! Talk!"

Roy spat bloodily, full into Fremar's face. Fremar cursed. He tore the cigar from his mouth, cast it aside and swung the rifle horizontally. The barrel slapped heavily just above Roy's left ear, right where the cruel track of the bullet had made its mark. Roy fell to one side and lay still, his face a mask of running blood.

Ken tried to get up and Harry struck him down with the butt of his rifle. Ken looked at Fremar. "I told you what I'd do," he said.

There was a thoughtful look on the deputy sheriffs face, and for the first time he felt a slight trace of fear as he looked into the eyes of the man lying at his feet.

The man named Glen came through the brush, looked curiously at Roy, then back at Fremar.

"Made a break for it," said Harry. "Had to buffalo him." "The breed found sign near the west end of the pass," said Glen. "Horse and burro tracks. Heading north."

Fremar nodded. "Tell Joe Evans to take ten men and follow the tracks. Tell him to take the breed along. Get some horses up here. I want these boys down at the tracks. They can ride back, in comfort and style on the train."

"The wrecker train just pulled up at the east end of the pass. They're starting to clear the right-of-way. Anything you want to look at first?" "I'll be down."

Ken rolled a smoke and lighted it, never taking his eyes off the big man. The sun was up, casting bright light across the mountains and desert to the east. Smoke wreathed up from the two locomotives down at each end of the pass.

Fremar lighted a fresh cigar. He looked at Ken. "Six dead trainmen down in the pass, not counting your boys," he said. "We've got you neatly. Murder, robbery and destruction of railroad property. We've got you in a sack and can pull the drawstring tight, right around your dirty necks. Now, if you talk, turn state's evidence against your *amigos,* you might get off with a short stretch in Yuma Pen." "Nice place," said Harry. "Ever seen it, *hombre?*" Ken nodded. He knew that country. He knew Yuma. He knew enough about Yuma Pen to know it was Hell on the Colorado; the Devil's Island of the Desert.

"Maybe three to five years," said Fremar. He inspected the end of his cigar.

"Lotsa *hombres* prefer a hemp necktie to that place," said Harry.

Fremar spat. He looked at Roy and then back at Ken. "You might last three to five years in there, tough guy, but *he* won't. You remember that."

"I'll remember a lot of things," said Ken. "I'll remember what you did to him. After we're cleared, Fremar, I'll settle a score with you."

Fremar looked at Harry. "After they're 'cleared,' he says."

They were still chuckling now and then as Ken and Roy were placed aboard a car of the westbound train.

Roy was still unconscious when the train pulled out, bound for Benson.

Ken looked down at his shackled wrists. Something churned in his mind. Marlin Meyner must have been in on the train robbery. There was no question about it. If he had been, he was responsible for the death of Bobcat Bates, and the cruel injuries of Roy. He was responsible for Ken's predicament. *"Judas,"* said Ken to himself.

CHAPTER THREE

A FAINT BREATH of the desert wind crept toward the dark pile of buildings atop the hill overlooking the dark waters of the Colorado. It felt its way between the thick stone walls and along the passageways into the dark cells, stirring the noisome stench of the arched cubicles into each of which six men were crammed. The mingled foetor of sanitary buckets, sweat-soaked mattresses and striped prison suits was too heavy for the wind to move out of the cells.

Ken Sturgis lay in the top bunk on the right-hand side of the narrow cell, staring up at the smoothly plastered ceiling several feet over his head, fingers interlaced at the nape of his neck. He was praying, as he had almost every night for the past month.

Men coughed and snored. Bunks creaked as toil-worn bodies heaved about on the thin, lumpy mattresses made in the prison shops, and as they did so the chains that shackled them to the ring set in the cell floor clanked dismally.

It was quiet except for the soft scrabbling of the wind and the sounds of sleeping men.

Thank God, thought Ken. It won't happen tonight.

The scream shattered the brooding quiet. It rose from a scream into a maddening howl, like an insane coyote baying at the moon. It echoed along the cell blocks and penetrated into the stinking cells. It carried down from Prison Hill across the Southern Pacific tracks to Yuma. When the wind was right it would carry clear across the leaden-colored waters of the rushing Colorado to the quarters of the soldiers at Fort Yuma on the California side.

"My God," said a hoarse voice from the lowest left-hand bunk. "There he goes again."

Big Nose George Schmidt, the man beneath Ken, shifted. "I been here two years," he said. "I've heard them screaming in the Insane Cell at night, but never night after night like he does."

"They oughta take him outa there," said lower right-hand bunk. "Ain't no place for a crazy man. No one can sleep with that goin' on."

"What'd you expect in Yuma Pen?" said middle left-hand bunk. "It's part of the treatment, Jerry."

The cell quieted down. The screaming kept on.

"How old you say he was, Ken?" said lower left-hand.

Ken closed his eyes. "Just twenty, Carl." My God, he thought. Twenty years old and hopelessly insane. Roy, Roy...

There was a grating that filled the center of the cell structures and ran from one passageway to another, like an arched tunnel, and on the far side of the crossbarred iron bars were six more bunks, three in a tier, just as there were in Ken's cell, and six sweating men lying there listening to Roy Sturgis scream his heart out in the

Insane Cell, with the whole prison to listen, and a good part of Yuma town as well.

"Wait until he wakes up Bill Savage," said a man from the other cell.

Cold sweat worked down Ken's sides. Bill Savage was the worst screw in the place. An expert at laying his iron-wood club over a man's kidneys without leaving a mark. The only mark would be excruciating pain for the recipient and bloody urine that night. Savage by name and savage by nature. No jungle had more of a beast in it, and Yuma Pen was a human jungle.

The heat was almost intolerable. All day long the August sun, sending the temperature into the 100's at times, would beat down on the rock that composed Yuma Pen, sitting atop a ten-acre naked hill without a shred of shade, storing up the heat like a sponge stores up water; and at night, the furnace winds would sometimes blow across the desert to add to the misery. Hell on the Colorado.

Roy began to scream again. Ken closed his eyes. The Insane Cell was not really a cell, but rather a hole gouged into the side of the highest part of the hill that had been leveled and used for special cells. The Snake Den was near it, buried inside the hill, hewn from the living rock, and reached by a narrow passageway hardly wide enough for a man to breathe, with heavy iron-barred doors at each end. At the east end were the Tuberculosis Cells, exposed to the blasting heat of the sun a good part of the day, crammed with six or eight and sometimes as many as twelve coughing, blood-spitting consumptives. At the other end of the hill were the Women's Cells, overlooking the right-of-way of the Espee. Bad as they all were, it was the Insane Cell that made every con in the place shudder. To lose control of one's self was to end up first in the Snake Den, chained to the floor in the darkness, sleeping on the bare rock, a haven for rattlesnakes which the careless guards let in, perhaps on purpose. Men had been bitten to death in there by sidewinders and diamondbacks. A dose or two of the Snake Den was enough for even the most vicious and recalcitrant of prisoners, but eventually they would be removed and returned to the dubious comforts of their "home" cells. Not so the lone occupant of the Insane Cell. He stayed there, in a roughhewn hole not high enough to stand in, not long enough to lie down in, not wide enough to turn around in, exposed to the blasting hell of the afternoon sun, *and never let out, for any reason,* except his death.

The screaming rose again. Somewhere in the building a metal door clanged shut.

"That'll be Bill Savage," said lower right-hand.

The screaming rose higher, although it seemed impossible that it could be any higher, or more nerve-wracking.

No one spoke.

Metal grated and clanged. There was a moment of silence from Roy and then he screamed, just once. ... In the quiet that followed, the sound of the club came to the rest of the prisoners. Ironwood against flesh. Further torture for a poor, deranged kid who had never done anything wrong except to bust into an Espee boxcar five years before, and to happen to be in the vicinity of the biggest Express robbery in the history of railroading in America.

There had been two faces in Ken's dreams and thoughts all the time he and Roy had lain in Bisbee, county seat of Cochise County, waiting for trial. The handsome face of Marlin Meyner and the broad, impassive face of Deputy Sheriff Max Fremar. Since Roy and Ken had been in Yuma Pen, Ken had added yet another face to the two he had never let out of his thoughts for the past six months. The brutal face of prison guard Bill Savage, whose proud boast was that he never started a day's duty without clubbing at least one prisoner into unconsciousness.

"It was him that set the kid off, wasn't it, Ken?" asked Shorty Stiber, middle left-hand.

"Yes."

"He wasn't right when he come here," said Pablo Mendez, upper left-hand. "Poor *hombre! Madre de Dios,* why do they not take him away from here?"

"He's got an edge on us," said Carl. "At least he ain't never quite sure what's going on."

Metal clanged against rock. Booted feet thudded on the hard-packed earth. A door clanged shut. Then it became quiet except for the soft sound of the night wind and the constant coughing, spitting, snoring and thrashing of the hundreds of men who lived atop that hill of hell.

"Ain't no use in trying to sleep," said Carl. "It'll be light in a couple of hours."

Pablo laughed softly. "So we talk about the escape, *no?*"

"We talk about the escape, *yes,*" said Shorty. "Christ! At least it helps to keep a man's mind sane. God knows, I never pass that cell Roy is in without sweating blood thinking I might slip some day and wake up finding myself in there."

"Take it easy," said Big Nose George. "That ain't no way to talk in front of Ken."

"Go ahead," said Ken. "I feel the same way. We all do."

Carl shifted on his bunk. "Yuma Pen Chapter of the Lifers' Escape Society will now come to order."

Ken closed his eyes. "You're all loco," he said. "You haven't got a chance and you all know it. You can't get over the walls. You can't beat the desert. You can't swim the river. Even if you do, the Yuma or Mohave trackers will run you down, and the guards here don't ask questions about your condition when the trackers bring you back. You ever see a Mohave or a Yuma playing with a knife on a helpless white man?"

"We got to take a chance," said Shorty stubbornly.

Carl hissed for silence. Boots thudded in the passageway.

A guard checked the metal bar that actuated the inner and outer cell doors together, and the heavy padlock that held it fast, peering into the dark cell as he did so. "You bastards stink worse than usual tonight," he said.

"It's your breath blowing back in your face, Kelly," said a muffled voice.

"Who was that?" demanded the screw.

There was no answer. No one would talk. They had better not. Cell mates could be more dangerous and vicious than any punishment meted out by the screws.

Kelly spat. "We need a new grave-digging detail," he said. "One con died yesterday from sunstroke and another went loco. We'd of had trouble fitting him in with young Sturgis, but he made a break for the river." He paused. "By God, he swum pretty far out before the current got him. Didn't even waste a shot on him. Now, you boys can take over for a week or so. Gettin' to be a hell of a note around here. Get prisoners to dig graves for other prisoners and then we have to let 'em fill the graves they dug themselves. No profit in that. Good night, boys. Sweet dreams." His boots thudded off.

"There just might be our chance," said Carl. "We can beat the walls that way."

Ken shifted and looked over the side of the bunk. "With a Gatling gun overlooking you from the water tower? With guards armed with Winchesters along the walls? With guards right there in the graveyard with you? The only place is the river and it will be broad daylight. How many of you are expert swimmers? How many of you can swim at all?"

It was quiet for a minute or two.

"Listen, Ken," said Shorty. "The way we figure it is this: Sure, we can't *all* escape. But if enough of us break at one time, some of us might just make it."

"So you get across the river with a whole fort full of troopers looking down on you. How far could you get across the desert without water? By God, Shorty, there isn't a well for thirty miles or more west of here, unless you stay on the road, and they'd pick you up within twenty-four hours along there."

"By Jesus, Ken!" said Shorty fiercely. "What about Mexico? The border ain't more than five miles south of here on the California side of the Rio, is it?"

"Same thing," said Ken dryly. "No water for miles."

"The Colorado's there, ain't it?"

"So are the rurales," said Ken.

"Ain't you with us?" said Jerry to Ken.

"Sure, but I'm not making a break."

"Why?"

Ken did not answer.

"Because of his *hermano*," said Pablo softly. "He will not leave here while his brother is alive."

"You better not talk about us," said Jerry quietly.

"Look," said Ken angrily. "I'm not making a break. I'm not going to turn you in. All I know about this country is yours for the asking. Let it go at that. And another thing: Don't *threaten* me, *hombres.*"

None of them spoke. They had seen this cold-eyed man in action when he had first come to Yuma with his addled brother. A Mex *bandido* by the name of Bustamente had made the mistake of hazing the kid with the staring eyes and scarred skull. Bustamente had been a big man, as mean as a sidewinder and hating all gringos. Ken Sturgis had caught him in the laundry when one of the guards had called the other outside for a few minutes. The story was that one of the heavily laden laundry carts had somehow run over Bustamente's face. Bustamente had been cock of the walk around Yuma Pen at that time, in a prison full of hardcases the like of which was unknown in other state and territorial prisons throughout the United States. Ken had not taken over his mantle, but after that no one bothered Ken, or the kid.

"Which way, Ken?" asked Carl.

Ken closed his eyes. "Listen for the screws," he said. "Some of them have taken to wearing gum-soled shoes, the bastards."

"North of here," said Shorty.

Ken wet his cracked lips. "No water right inland from the Colorado for almost a hundred miles as the crow flies, until you get to Ehrenburg, or what's left of it. If you go that way they can send a boat up the river and be waiting for you there."

"Inland?" said Jerry.

"Northeast, about fifty miles, past Castle Dome Peak, in the Kofas, is Deep Well. Ten miles northeast of that is Alamo Springs, if it isn't dry. Sometimes it dries up in a bad summer."

"What about the other side of the Rio?" said Big Nose George.

"Water at Middle Well, about thirty-five miles from here, northwest, as the crow flies. About eight miles south of Arroyo Seco, about ten miles in from the Colorado. Due west of here, past Fort Yuma, is Gray's Wells, but that's on the road."

"East of here," said Carl quietly, "is plenty of water, but it's along the Gila. You'd never make it that way."

"What about south of here?" said Jerry.

"Pablo knows that country better than I do," said Ken.

The Mexican nodded in the darkness. "Away from the Rio, on either side there is not much water. The rurales watch the Mexican banks for smugglers. The Cocopahs get paid for capturing escaped prisoners. They are very good at it, *amigos*. East of the river there is the Yuma Desert. No water. Maybe thirty, forty miles to the mountains."

"There any water there?" said Jerry.

"Beyond the Fortuna Mine, which has water, but many guards, there are the Gilas, with *no* water. Southeast of the Gilas are the Tinajas Altas Mountains and on the east side of them is the place called Tinajas Altas Tanks. The 'tanks' are deep holes eroded in the rocks, filled with rainwater a good part of the year."

"Beyond that?" said Shorty.

"Further southeast is Mexican Sonora. The Lechuguilla and Sierra del Viejo Mountains. A country like hell, or the moon, for there is no water, and that place is the anvil of the sun."

"What about along the border?" said Jerry.

The Mexican laughed dryly. "El Camino del Diablo," he said.

Ken nodded. The Highway of the Devil, and well named. The Spaniards had a knack for such names. A hundred miles of burning desert, where one depended on water from *charcos* scooped in clay basins, *pozitos* dug in sand washes, or *tinajas* eroded in the granite mountains.

Pablo leaned over the edge of his bunk and spat accurately into the filthy, reeking slop bucket. "If thirst does not get one, or heat, there are always the Sand Papagoes, or maybe wandering Apaches or their Sonoran cousins the fierce Yaquis."

There were a few minutes of silence.

"We have to try anyway," said Shorty softly. "I can't stand this place much longer."

"We've got a week," said Carl. "Somehow or another we got to break for the river. Maybe just about the time it's beginning to get dark. We'll need all the help we can get."

Ken looked up at the dim ceiling above him. You sure will, he thought, you poor damned fools. No one, *but no one* escapes from Yuma Pen.

The gray dawn light slowly sifted into the gloomy, stinking cells. Whistles blew. Boots thudded in the passageways. Levers on Winchesters were worked to load chambers as the guards went to their posts, working in teams of two, one to open the cell doors and unchain the inmates from the huge ring set deep into the rock floor, the other to stand watch with ready Winchester.

Men coughed and hacked as they shuffled out into the dim passageway, scratching and yawning, with another day of hell ahead of them. They lined up as roll was called. The "junior" member of each cell carried out the overflowing, reeking slop bucket, filling the passageway with its foul stench.

The sun was not up as they shuffled into the mess hall, to sit silently at the tables, eating lumpy mush and drinking foul coffee, gnawing hardtack that had been baked maybe twenty years before for the Army of the Potomac or the Army of the Tennessee and bought as surplus by the prison contractors for a pittance.

Thirty-one cents a day, thought Ken as he looked at the gray, unappetizing mess on the tin plate. Thirty-one cents a day to feed a grown man who was expected to do the work of two well-fed men every day, under the gentle stimulus of an ironwood club laid over his kidneys. Roy was wasting away to a shadow, he had heard. He would not, or could not eat. He had always been a choosy eater, and even in his derangement he was the same. Maybe it was just another way to keep control over the prisoners. Most of them hardly had the strength to work, much less make a break for the river or the desert. How far could they get? *How far?*

When the prisoners were through with the slop that was called "breakfast" they'd be marched to their duties for the day. Mattress Shop, Laundry, Tailor Shop, Blacksmith Shop, Bakery, Library, Mess Hall or other workshops. The unfortunates, the ones whom the screws desired to hammer into line, worked outside in the searing sun. Graves had to be dug on the flinty slope overlooking the junction of the Colorado and the Gila. An hour swinging a pick, mattock or shovel in that sun was enough to fell the strongest of men, but, as guard Kelly had said: "Gettin' to be a hell of a note around here. Get prisoners to dig graves for other prisoners and then we have to let 'em fill the graves they dug themselves. No profit in that."

"I saw the kid this morning," said Big Nose George out of the side of his mouth, convict style. "Blood all over. Blood all over the walls of the cell. He ain't come to yet. The doc is over there now."

There was no expression on Ken's face. He looked up

to see Bill Savage watching him across two rows of tables. If Ken opened his mouth it would be an invitation to the sadist to come after him. He did not even dare look at the man for fear he'd attack him then and there, and there'd be no profit in that.

"Savage said the kid attacked him," said George.

"For Christ's sake, Big Nose!" said Jerry Riley. "Savage is watching us! You think he knows something?"

Three hundred men arose as one at the whistle command. They shuffled silently out of the mess hall, heads down, lips compressed, looking like huge caterpillars in their yellow-and-black-striped suits and round caps. Ken passed within a foot of Bill Savage and the smell of evil seemed to exude from the man.

From seven a.m. to five p.m. was the working day, with half an hour for lunch, such as it was. If there was no work to do, one idled away the time in sheer boredom within the high walls, eighteen feet high, eight feet thick at the base, tapering to four feet thick at the top, with guard towers at each of the four corners and a tower built over the humped shape of the water cistern, with a Gatling gun mounted there which could sweep the interior of the prison and two of the walls, as well as the gateway, with soft-nosed .45/70 slugs at the rate of 350 per minute.

Ken and his cell mates drew their tools and were marched through a side gate to the sloping graveyard. The August sun was just coming up but already the heat of the day was beginning to be felt. As Ken worked he looked now and then across the mesquite and greasewood-stippled desert to the east, or at the shimmering expanse of the mighty Colorado flowing unchecked down toward the Gulf of California. Eddies swirled in the powerful current. Sandbanks were deceptively firm-looking, but if a man stepped on one of them he'd find himself in a more deadly grip than that of the current. Heat waves shimmered up from the far side of the Colorado, on the California side, as the sun began its day's work in fury.

As the day dragged on, wind-devils played back and forth on the sterile land about the baking prison, swirling about here and there in a mad and aimless dance, appearing and disappearing. Now and then one of them would sweep across the graveyard, scouring the head-boards, raising the stinging grit, battering at the sweating prisoners, but bringing no cooling relief to them. It was like standing before an open blast furnace.

Shorty Stiber lasted until noon. Big Nose George lasted until two in the afternoon. Jerry Riley was next. Only Pablo Mendez, Carl Mason and Ken Sturgis worked on. There were other prisoners working in the graveyard and on the road that wound up from Yuma, crossing the right-of-way of the Southern Pacific, and cutting into the flat-topped bluff upon which squatted Yuma Pen. Now and then one of them would fall over. The clubs of the guards did little good. They were dragged into the dubious shade of the heat-soaked walls and allowed to lie there until they stirred, and there was no use in trying to fake it.

For five days Ken worked in the graveyard, and only his hate kept him going when other men fell. Big Nose George died of sunstroke the third day and was buried in the grave he had been digging. A man named Diaz took his place. Every night the rambling escape talk went on in the cell, and soon the inmates of the cell beyond Ken's were in on the deal. They too were working in the grave-yard or on the road.

By Friday morning there were twelve cons in on the

plan, and eleven of them planned to escape. Plans had been worked out to the last-minute detail. Nothing was to be left to chance but getting across the river, or down the river. None but intensely desperate men would have made such plans, but they were all long termers or lifers, and each of them knew what the future would be. They could hear Roy Sturgis each night until a guard, usually Bill Savage, would quiet him down. Every man in the prison wanted Roy to die. The bullet wound in his head, and the buffaloing given him by Max Fremar, had addled his sanity, and Bill Savage, like a cat playing with a mouse, was evidently trying to see how far he could go with Roy.

Saturday morning, in the mess, Diaz, who had been placed in Ken's cell, and who, as "junior" member, was required to empty the sanitary- bucket, tipped Ken off. "Your *hermano* is no longer in the cell, *amigo,*" he said out of the side of his mouth in Spanish. "He is in the hospital, and they cannot stop the bleeding from the inside. You understand?"

"*Si,*" said Ken. He looked up at Bill Savage. He knew every detail of the man's cruel face, the unblinking blue eyes, the sensual mouth under the thick yellow dragoon mustache, the deeply cleft chin. He knew the muscles that bulged the sleeves of the blue coat, and the granite-like fists, looking as though they had been roughhewn from mahogany wood and stippled with coarse reddish hairs, like copper wires. He knew every detail. Every detail except one. *How* and *when* he would kill the man.

Ken was told the news at noon mess. Roy had died in the surgery. He was asked if he wanted to see the body and he refused. He wanted to remember Roy as he had known him before Yuma Pen, and before Max Fremar had beaten out the kid's sense.

Ken's detail was a punishment detail. No Saturdays

off for them, or the other cell as well. Back to the graveyard. There was one difference. Only half the guards were
on duty. One on the water tower, leaning on the brightly
polished Gatling gun. One on the tower at the other end
of the wall and two in the graveyard. A dry, searing wind
had been making up all morning and by four o'clock in
the afternoon it was sweeping sheets of grit over Prison
Hill, battering at the graveyard detail and the guards who
stood there, clubs under their arms, cursing the prisoners
as though it was their fault that the guards had to stay
with them.

Carl Mason climbed out of the half-dug grave he had
been working on. "Your turn, Ken," he said. "Rocky as
hell. Use a bull point."

Ken nodded and dropped into the hole. He took a
bull point out of a burlap sack and set to work on the
rocks. It was almost time.

A guard strolled over, shielding his face from the
gritty wind. "Make it nice, Sturgis," he said with a smile.
"It's for your brother."

Ken did not look up while the guard was there. The
sledge was in his hand and it would have been too easy to
smash that grinning face to a shapeless pulp.

Carl scraped at the pile of harsh earth with his spade.
"Gettin' dark," he said out of the side of his mouth.
"Dust blowin' like hell. You can't see the mountains. The
far side of the Rio is half hidden by it. Swirling over the
Rio, too. You sure you won't make a try for it, Ken? We
could partner it. You and me could make it. Remember
they got Roy."

"I'll remember," said Ken.

"You won't come then?"

Ken shook his head. "Good luck, *amigo.*"

Dust swirled high over the graveyard. It was like a dry

fog. The guards in the towers had their backs to the wind. It would be now or never for the escapees.

"Now!" yelled Carl Mason. He struck with savage fury and the guard went down. Carl dropped the spade and snatched up the guard's rifle. He fired twice at the other guard, who fell backward into an open grave.

"Yieee!" shrieked Jerry Riley as he snatched up the other guard's rifle.

Ken peered between the mounds of harsh earth, watching the yellow and black figures plunging toward the half-hidden river, crashing through the brush and willows. The Gatling stuttered spasmodically into life. Two prisoners fell. Rifles cracked. A guard stumbled and went down. The Gatling chattered again, tearing into the trees and brush, trying to search out the half-seen prisoners.

No one paid any attention to the one man who still crouched in the open grave, half hidden by the swirling dust. It was getting darker by the minute. He reached out and dragged the dead guard into the hole. Swiftly he stripped the still warm body and then pulled off his sweat-soaked prison garb. He dressed the guard in it. He was sickened at the sight of the guard's face, for Carl Mason had put his full weight behind the spade blow, and even the guard's own mother wouldn't recognize him now.

Ken placed the guard's pistol and club in the bottom of the grave. He peered between the mounds. The grave-yard was empty except for the sprawled figures of two convicts and the legs of the other guard sticking out of the open grave. The Gatling was silent now, but the wind picked up shooting and yelling from the riverbank.

Ken heaved the dead guard out of the grave. He rolled partway down the slope and lay still, his bloody face matted with dirt. Ken took the burlap sack. He lay down in the half-dug grave and pulled earth down over his body, up to the neck. He placed the sack over his face and pushed earth partway over it, then drew his dirty, blistered hands beneath the sack. He lay still, getting used to breathing through the meshes of the coarse sacking.

The shooting died away. The wind increased in fury. There was no sign of life in the darkening graveyard, which was as it should be.

CHAPTER FOUR

THE MURMURING OF VOICES came to Ken Sturgis. Boots grated and scraped on the harsh earth. They were close. It was dark, and the moon was not yet up. Sweat worked from Ken's forehead and trickled into his eyes, stinging them. He felt an intolerable thirst and suddenly his breathing became increasingly difficult. He could have sworn they could hear him.

Gravel pattered into the grave. Some of it struck the burlap sack and a stone rebounded stunningly from Ken's rather prominent nose. His eyes filled with quick tears and he could feel the trickle of blood start.

"Here's one of them," said a hard voice. Boots grated again. Gravel pattered into the hole. Dear God, thought Ken, *they know I'm in here*. They were playing with him. He could almost feel their hard gaze down into the half-filled hole. It was all he could do to keep control of himself.

"Must be Sturgis," said a familiar voice. It was that of Bill Savage.

"Is he the only one unaccounted for?" asked another man. It sounded like Kelly.

"We ain't sure," said another guard. "We got all of 'em from the other cell. Two killed. Two drowned. Two in the Snake Den."

"Diaz was killed," said Kelly. "Riley and Mendez drowned. I saw both of them go down. Helped Riley along with a bullet in the head."

"What about Stiber and Mason?"

"Tim Ord said he saw Mason get out on the far side of the Rio. Headed northwest." He laughed. "The sonofabitch is likely trying to make Middle Well. Doesn't know it's been dry for a month. Thirty-five miles of hell and then a dry well. Hawww! Some of the boys are going up-river on the *Cocopah* to wait for him at Arroyo Seco. Hawww!"

"What about Stiber?"

"Some say he drowned. Some say he drifted down-river. It was too dark to see. Anyways, we warned the rurales and the Cocopahs. There's a steamer going down-river at dawn. They'll keep an eye out for him."

"You sure it was Stiber and not that bastard Sturgis?" said Bill Savage.

"Ain't that Sturgis lying there?"

Ken heard a scuffling sound. "It's his con number all right," said Kelly. "Jees, look at his face! Slug musta cut right acrost it. Musta been the Gatling."

"Throw him in the hole," said Savage.

"Do it yourself," said Kelly.

"One of these days—" warned Savage.

"I ain't no con," said Kelly. "You can't bully me." There were a few moments of silence.

"Well, maybe we better get him over to the surgery," said the other guard. "They'll want to make sure."

Icy sweat poured from Ken's face. If they had dumped the guard's body into the hole and covered him, that would have been the end of Ken Sturgis.

Ken heard the snap of a match. In a moment the odor of cigar tobacco drifted down to him.

"Wish this damned wind would stop," said Kelly. "Can't see mor'n fifty yards away. I'll go get some cons to haul Sturgis to the surgery for examination." Boots thudded on the ground.

"Sturgis," said Savage quietly. "I used to *want* that cold-eyed bastard to make a break. Wasn't much fun beating that crazy kid. Well, maybe I done him a favor at that."

"The older Sturgis woulda been hell to break," said the other guard.

Savage laughed and it was not a pleasant thing to hear. "I broke Dan Gary, didn't I? And Libertad Sanchez. Sturgis would have been an interesting problem. Well, he's beyond me now, but there's a few others I can work on. Sorta like a hobby of mine, Joe. Only regret I got is that Roy Sturgis wasn't all right in the head. The way that older brother worried about the younger one would have made it a pleasure to break both of them at the same time."

Boots scraped on the ground and then Ken was left with only the moaning wind for company; that, and the cold hate he had in his heart for Bill Savage.

It was an hour before the body of the guard was removed to the prison and another half an hour before Ken dared to move. He pulled the gagging burlap from his face and drew in deep, grateful breaths of the dry, dusty air. The sky was still dark, stippled with stars dimly seen through the dust haze in the air. He sat up and peered over the mounds. Here and there he saw yellow lights in the prison, not more than two hundred yards away. There were still guards in those towers. There would be guards and deputies searching the river banks on both sides.

He brushed off the dust and crawled out of the hole, then lay flat on the mound on the far side of the hole. He checked the guard's pistol, a heavy-barreled Schofield-Smith and Wesson revolver, caliber forty-four. He released the spring catch, tipped up the barrel and checked the chamber. It was fully loaded. He holstered it and picked up the ironwood club, fitting it into the ring that held it swinging at a guard's side, although most of them kept it ready in their fists, and used it whenever possible.

He put on the cap, then bellied down the rough slope between the mounded graves marked by plain wooden headboards. He slid down the southern slope of the hill, through the mesquite and greasewood, until he was in a deep hollow, screened by scrub trees and fringed with brush. There was no use in going east along the valley of the Gila. By daylight they'd spot him and they'd know well enough no guard would be wandering out in the heat on foot. The moon would soon be up and he'd be seen if he tried to swim the river, or drift across on a makeshift raft. If he walked due south he'd soon be walking in clear moonlight, and by dawn he'd be seen and picked up.

He was so exhausted and confused he had to fight to keep his mind on his plans. They'd find out that the battered body in the surgery wasn't Ken Sturgis. A guard would be missing in the morning and if they thought that Ken had killed him there would be short shrift for him, and a life of unholy hell under the clubs of the other guards until he went insane or died. No one kills a prison guard and lives long in that same prison. Ken hadn't killed the man but they'd never believe him. Bill Savage would make it his personal task to subdue and punish Ken. He was an expert at drawing out torture to the last gasp of breath of the tortured.

He wanted a smoke, a drink and a bed. There was only one possible solution for him. There would be guards in the streets of Yuma and if he could pass for one long enough to find a place to hide and get rid of the guard's uniform, there might be a shot, a long, long shot that he might eventually get out of Yuma.

He knew Yuma fairly well. He had been there in years past. He had to get into the streets before the moon caught him walking down Prison Hill into the town.

Ken crawled out of the hole. In the dimness he dusted the uniform and cap as well as he could. The dust would pass for the results of a guard's search for escapees. He'd have to bank on that. He knew one thing for sure—they'd never take him back to Yuma Pen alive. There were six rounds in the Schofield, and one of them would be for him if the gamble was lost. He knew what would be waiting for him up on the hill. Hell would be a pleasure after that.

Swiftly, before the moon rose over the eastern mountains, he worked his way south, keeping well back from the unseen riverbank. The river flowed south toward Yuma, then turned sharply back on itself, forming a loop which flowed below Prison Hill, then flowed west, turning south again far down the river, below the town. He kept to the shelter of the willows and then headed toward the right-of-way of the Espee, lying down in the ditch while he studied the lay of the land. The wind swept billowing sheets of gritty dust toward the prison and over the town.

There were some railroad cars sitting on a siding.

Cars that quartered the Mex laborers who kept the right-of-way in good repair. Yellow lights showed in the windows. The drifting odor of highly-seasoned food came to the man lying in the ditch and he almost got sick at the tantalizing odor. Six months, at thirty-one cents a day, is hardly good fare for a man like Ken Sturgis, who had always been top-hole grade with a knife and fork.

He hurried across the right-of-way beyond the cars, and turned to look back. Something whipped across his face. He whirled, drawing the Schofield, to find himself looking at a line of laundry whipping in the wind. He sheathed the pistol, and walked down the line of laundry, selecting a shirt here, trousers there, socks further down. Maybe they'd blame it on the wind.

He walked quickly into the shadows of the first buildings and looked back at the hill, clouded in sheets of whirling dust. Ken found it hard to believe he had indeed escaped from the prison proper, but he knew there was a bigger prison to escape from before he knew real freedom. The desert was waiting for him, armed with thirst, heat and death in half a dozen varied and uncomfortable forms. He glanced to the south and east. It was there he'd have to make his bid for freedom, across the Yuma Desert to the Gilas and the Tinajas Altas, where Pablo Mendez had said there *might* be water. Beyond that was waterless Sonora, and to the east, along the border, the Highway of the Devil. "A country like hell, or the moon, for there is no water, and that place is the anvil of the sun," Pablo had said.

There was a faint suggestion of moonlight in the east, through the dust haze, as Ken walked through the darkened side streets. It was Saturday night, and the town would be lively, but the dust storm might slow down the liveliness. One suspicious person—one cry of alarm—and

Ken would be hunted down like a mad dog in the streets. He thought of going to the river and stealing a small boat, to drop downriver on the swift current, but that too was dangerous. Both banks would be patrolled at dawn. The Cocopahs had already been alerted for escaping prisoners, and no one would be able to pass through their country unseen. The Gulf of California was about a hundred miles downstream but it would do Ken little good to get there. Strangers would be spotted instantly down there. A steamer was leaving at dawn from Yuma, and even if Ken managed to hide from it, the word would be passed clear down to the gulf.

He turned into a side street and saw that it was deserted. A mangy dog rooted in the gutter. The tin sign of a little cantina battered back and forth in the gusty wind.

He started up the street and when he was almost even with the cantina he saw a familiar figure pass into the opening at the end of the street. There was no mistaking the uniform of a prison guard. There was no choice for Ken. He pushed open the door of the cantina and closed it behind him.

Dim lantern light sketchily illuminated the interior. A drunk sat at a table, his bloated face resting in the stale liquor slops. A Mexican leaned on the end of the zinc-topped bar, his steeple hat pulled low over his dark face. The bartender waddled toward Ken. *"Si, senor* guard?" he said politely. "There are no escaped prisoners here."

Ken looked about the place. "Anyone in the back?" he said.

"See for yourself."

Ken walked into the tiny, greasy-smelling kitchen. A door opened into another room. He pushed into it. A young woman, hardly more than seventeen or eighteen, slept on a rumpled bed, her naked breasts dewed with sweat. She opened her eyes to look at Ken. "It is too early, *senor* guard," she said sleepily. The odor of whiskey drifted from her, mingled with stale sweat and cheap perfume.

Ken walked back into the kitchen and opened the rear door. He stepped into a small, walled courtyard, littered with stinking garbage and empty tin cans. He closed the door behind him, looked about, then climbed over the wall to land in a narrow, refuse littered passageway that led to the street he had just left. Even as he landed he saw the guard pass the street opening.

Ken walked to the street and peered around the corner just in time to see the guard walk into the cantina. Ken ran swiftly to the next street and stepped into a deep doorway. The street was fairly well lighted with the lamps shining through shop windows. A player piano tinkled off key somewhere down the street. A sagging buckboard was driven past. A horseman cantered the other way, face muffled in his scarf.

He wasn't sure what to do. The guard uniform was a good disguise for Ken to wear for almost anyone but the other guards. They'd know he was a phony right off. But, if he wore the cheap Mex clothing, he'd be suspect. His walk, his mannerism, his appearance would belie the cheap laborer's clothing. He was damned if he did and damned if he didn't.

He felt in the pockets and brought out the guard's wallet. He whistled softly. There was sixty dollars in it. Ken stepped into a cheap store run by an incredibly aged Chinese who asked no questions; indeed seemed hardly aware that Ken was there, although his clawlike hand swiftly swept the money into a cash box, leaving Ken with the bottle of Bacanora, half a dozen sacks of Bull

Durham, a box of cartridges for the Schofield and razor, soap, extra socks and a good clasp knife.

He rolled a quirley and drew in the smoke with a deep hunger. The streets were being lighted by the rising moon. The wind was dying down. He had to make his initial moves. A thought struck him. There was *one* place a man could hide, if he had the money, at least for the night, with no questions asked.

He remembered a drunk he had been on in Yuma years past, when he had been a kid sowing too many wild oats. He remembered, too, whom he had been with, a *companero* by the name of Marlin Meyner. Marlin had liked the girls, the younger the better, and Yuma had had more than its share of young *putas* saving up for their dowries. About all Ken could remember about the place was that Marlin had lived there off and on for three days, while Ken had waited for him. One night's hell-raising had been enough for Ken.

"Encarnacion!" said Ken as he walked through the filthy side street. The girl had liked Ken. She had been hardly more than fifteen then. If she hadn't saved enough money she might still be in business at the old stand.

He walked into a filthy courtyard behind an empty house and stripped off the uniform, putting on the Mex clothes he had stolen from the laundry line. They were tight, the pants legs too short, but there was no choice for Ken. He buried the uniform and cap beneath a pile of trash, took a good belt from the bottle, rolled another cigarette and walked back down the deserted street.

A drunk lay in the gutter at a corner, plastered with the manure into which he had rolled. Ken looked up and down the dusty street. There was no one in sight. He snatched up the man's hat and darted into an alleyway. A man without a hat was too conspicuous in that country. Even the Indians had taken to wearing them.

No one noticed him as he walked up the next street to the narrow lane where the girls plied their trade, mostly from one-room 'dobes and jacales. Yuma was a town where men minded their own business as a rule, but an escaped con was anyone's business.

The moon was up high, shedding a clear light through the thinning dust haze. A rider passed Ken, looking curiously at him. He turned in his saddle, resting a hand on the cantle, to watch Ken pass out of sight. Ken ran to the next corner and climbed over an eroded adobe wall. He squatted in the darkness, rolling a cigarette. He'd have to have shelter of some kind. By daylight the streets would be full of Mexicans heading for the Catholic church and Protestants heading for the other churches, with bright-eyed kids staring at everyone. The prison stamp was on Ken Sturgis. The thin face from lack of grub; the shaven head; the fetter scars on his ankles. The very look of Prison Hill.

Encarnacion had lived in the end jacal at the far end of the street, but that had been years ago. There was no choice for Ken. He had to take a chance on the *puta* if she was there. There was no one else he could turn to. In an hour the streets would be lighted, almost like daylight, from the full moon.

Ken worked his way over wall after wall, for each shack and 'dobe had a small, trash-littered yard behind it, with the inevitable stinking privy in a corner. Now and then he heard voices and once the sound of a guitar. It was still too early for the lane to fill up with drunks and half drunks looking for their favorite whores.

He reached the end shack. The yard was just like the others. In fact, it seemed to Ken that it hadn't changed a bit, except for a more powerful stench than it had had years past.

He walked softly to the rear door and pressed an ear against it. He heard nothing. Ken climbed over the last wall and walked up the narrow street, turning into the lane. There were two men at the far end and he stepped quickly into the deep-set doorway, cold sweat breaking from his body, for one of the men had on a guard uniform and the other had a rifle resting butt down on the ground.

Ken rapped on the door.

"Quien es?" called out a muffled feminine voice.

"Open up," said Ken in Spanish.

"It is too early, *hombre*."

"Encarnacion?" asked Ken.

There was a moment of silence. "Who calls Encarnacion?" asked the woman.

By God, she wasn't there! Ken had been a fool to think she would be. He peered around the side of the door. The two men were talking to a young woman who leaned indolently against a wall, letting her brightly colored shawl hang loosely from a bare brown shoulder.

The door creaked behind Ken but he heard the tightening of a chain lock as it did so. "Let me in," he said.

"Who is it?"

Ken plucked a five from the wallet and passed it through the crack, half expecting the door to slam shut as he withdrew his fingers.

The chain dropped and the door swung open. Ken walked in and closed the door behind him, hooking the chain lock. It was dark in the room. The mingled aura of feminine flesh, perfume, sweat and stale booze hung in the place. He could dimly see the woman standing in the middle of the room, half naked, a wrapper hanging from her shoulders. "You asked for Encarnacion," she said quietly.

Ken snapped a match on his thumbnail and looked at her. She was pretty. Most of them were. But she had been in the business quite a few years from the looks of her. Maybe too long to get a dowry and find a husband. He narrowed his eyes. It was her all right, but the passing years had been added to by the profession she served. "You don't remember me?" he said.

She looked him over from head to foot. "You're dressed like a tramp," she said scornfully. "I don't do business with such as you."

"Ken," he said quickly. "You remember me? And the one who was always with me. The handsome one who always laughed."

She stared at him. *"Madre de Dios!"* she said at last. "It is like seeing a ghost. Take off your hat! Let me see your face."

Ken hesitated. Yet there was nothing she could do if she saw his shaven head. He could keep her quiet until he could get out of town. At least he thought he could. He pulled off the battered hat.

She gasped. *"Jesuscristo!* You are from up on that accursed hill!"

He moved closer to her and she did not move away. He gripped her by her slim wrists and her wrapper fell away from her full, red-budded breasts. "Keep your voice down," he said.

"They are looking all over town for escaped prisoners," she said.

"Have they been here?" he asked.

"Not yet. *Madre del Diablo!* What a chance you have taken!"

"There was no other place to go."

She searched his face. "And you came here? To the house of a *puta* you had not seen for many years?"

He nodded. Slowly he released her and pulled the wrapper up about her breasts and shoulders. One outcry and he'd have to knock her cold.

"Gracias," she said quietly.

He walked past her into the tiny kitchen and checked the rear door. He placed a bar across the rests and then looked into the bedroom. A lamp guttered on a wooden table. The calm, Indian-like face of a *santo* stared back at him from a wall niche, below which flickered a votive candle. The brass bedstead sagged, covered with rumpled bedding. A bottle of whiskey stood on a side table with several dirty glasses beside it.

He walked back into the living room, if one could call it that. Most of the living in that jacal was done in the bedroom.

She sat down on a hogbacked couch. "It is said that some of them were killed and others were drowned in the river, while others were brought back to the prison. It is said that a guard was killed and another was badly wounded."

"I had nothing to do with that." Ken sat down on a chair and pulled out the cork of the Bacanora bottle with his teeth. He drank deeply. He looked at her with his hard eyes. "You will be quiet?"

She shivered a little. It was like having a lobo wolf look at her, She nodded. "How will you escape from the town?" she said.

"I don't know. There was no place for me to go without an outcry being raised. They are not sure yet that I escaped. Right now they think I am dead, shot down in the graveyard."

She shivered again and crossed herself. "You look like the *espectro,*" she said. "A ghost. . ."

"When will your customers come?"

She shrugged. "Within the hour. It will be busy tonight."

"And tomorrow?"

She drew herself up, almost haughtily. "Tomorrow is *Sunday,*" she said.

Ken almost grinned.

She searched his thin face. "You are hungry? *Bueno!* I will make food. I have just gotten up and I am hungry too."

He looked up at her as she stood up. "No tricks," he said.

She shook her head.

"There will be payment enough for you," he said.

She shook her head. "My brother died up there," she said. "I have no love for that place."

"My brother died up there too," he said.

The look on his face frightened her as she walked into the kitchen. It was the same *companero* she had known years past. The voice, the eyes were the same, but something had changed him a great deal. But then something had changed her as well. Both of their lives were hard, but death was stalking that man through the moonlit streets of Yuma. She knew they'd never take him alive, and that he wouldn't go to hell alone.

She spoke of her brother Sebastian as they ate. He had been hardly more than a boy, goaded into a fight with a man who had meant to kill, but Sebastian had been too fast for him, and his *cuchillo* had found its mark. Sebastian had been an excellent dancer, a fine guitarist, with a future. None of his skills had helped him on Prison Hill. He had died within the year.

"What will you do now?" she said.

"Get out of Yuma," he said.

She shook her head. "Where will you go? It is summer. The deserts are like hell itself. The water holes are few, and far apart, and many of them are dry. Never has there been such a dry summer. The Yumas, Mohaves and Cocopahs get fifty dollars a head for bringing in escaped prisoners; to them fifty dollars is a fortune. They hate white men anyway. I have seen them bringing in the recaptured prisoners, a rope noosed about their necks, more dead than alive. Wrecks of men."

He pushed back his plate and rolled a cigarette. "There is always the river," he said.

She shook her head. "It is said steamers are going up and down the river, with armed men on them, looking for some of those who escaped today. The *Cocopah* is going upriver and the *Mohave is* going downriver."

Ken lighted his cigarette. The river was likely his only chance to escape from Yuma.

She took the cigarette from his lips and placed it between hers. "And the handsome one, the one who was always laughing. Where is he now?"

Ken fashioned another cigarette. "I don't know," he said quietly.

She studied him. "You are no longer *companeros?*"

He lighted the cigarette. "He killed my brother," he said.

"But you said your brother died in the prison."

Ken nodded. "The handsome one; the one who always laughed. He started him on the way to his death. There was another one who helped him along the way. The final part of the deed was done up on the hill."

The murmuring of voices came to them through the

walls. A man laughed. Someone rapped on the door, waited, then rapped again. Then it was quiet.

"The street is getting busy," she said. "As long as the door is closed and they see no light in the front room they will think I have a customer."

"We can't sit here all night," he said.

She looked at him sideways. "We do not have to *sit* here," she said. "You cannot leave while the moon is up."

"How much do you make on a Saturday night?" he asked.

She shrugged. "Ten dollars is a good night," she said.

He placed a limp bill in front of her. She looked at it and then at him. "I do not take money for nothing," she said.

"It is not for nothing, *mi vida*."

She smiled. She picked up the bill and placed it within the loose bosom of her dress. *"Gracias,"* she said.

They sat in the hot darkness of the living room. Now and then Ken nipped at the bottle, his mind teeming with thoughts. Occasionally they would hear footsteps in the street, hesitating and sometimes stopping at the door, with a tentative rapping, or a low calling. Encarnacion would open the door when it was quiet, and peer up and down the street.

Ken dozed off. She watched him for a long time. It would be so easy. She could pick his pocket, then call the police, and fifty dollars would be hers in addition to what she could glean from him. But she remembered him too well. A big gentle man, hardly more than a boy, who had treated her like a lady so many years ago. He had come to her for help. Yet, she would never see him again, and it was a hard life. There was a little shop she wanted to buy, a place that would keep her for the rest of her life, and perhaps bring in a husband who would not be critical of her past profession.

A hard fist battered at the door. The echo fled through the jacal. Ken's head snapped up and he placed his hand on the butt of the Schofield.

"Go away!" said Encarnacion. "I am busy!"

The fist hammered harder. "Come on, Encarnacion!" yelled the man. "It's your best customer! Bill Savage!"

Ken stood up, cocking the pistol.

She looked at him. "He will not go away," she said. "If he comes in he always throws out whoever is in here."

Ken stepped back. There was a high wardrobe in the room, with just enough space between it and the side wall for him to cram into. The room was dark and Bill was likely too eager for Encarnacion to look for another man anywhere but in her bed. Ken worked his way into the space. He felt the sweat trickling down his body. Of all the whores on that street, Ken had picked the very one who had taken Bill Savage's fancy.

CHAPTER FIVE

THE DOOR SWUNG OPEN, crashing against the wall. "Who's in here with you?" demanded Bill, a little thickly.

"No one, *mi vida*," she answered.

"You said you was busy."

She laughed. "Getting ready for you, Bill."

"Yah?" His boots thudded on the floor.

She closed the door behind him and dropped the chain into its socket. "I did not expect you tonight," she said.

"No? Why not?" he demanded suspiciously.

"The escaped prisoners," she said.

Bill spat. "We got 'em all except two," he said.

Despite his predicament, Ken felt a twinge of relief. They evidently did not know as yet that the battered corpse in the surgery was not Ken Sturgis.

Ken saw the big man standing with his back toward the wardrobe. All he had to do was turn and he'd see Ken. The big guard was out of uniform, but no man went unarmed in Yuma at night.

Bill picked up the bottle of Bacanora from the table. He sniffed at the mouth of the bottle. "What the hell is this?" He said. "My drink is whiskey."

"Someone left it here," she said carelessly.

"Who?"

She shrugged. "I do not remember."

He gripped her by the arm. "Whyn't you keep Saturday night only for me, like I asked before?"

"I thought you would be busy this night looking for prisoners."

"I got plenty of time after I'm through with you."

She winced in pain as he twisted her arm. He passed a thick hand through her hair, then gripped the hair and twisted it sideways. She grunted in savage pain. The bastard was a sadist with women as well as with men. He slowly forced her to her knees, then pulled her loose dress back from her upper body. "I told you," he said coldly, "that you was to keep Saturday nights for me. For Bill Savage. *El Toro!*"

Sweat broke out on her face as he increased pressure. "No, Bill," she said. "Not tonight! The last time I could not work for days."

"So much the better. You'll be saved for me."

She shrieked suddenly.

Ken had all he could do to keep from rushing the big man. He couldn't afford to be found out.

She was groveling on the floor now, thrashing in silent agony.

Bill laughed.

The laugh triggered Ken's hate. He stepped out. He swung the pistol side arm, to buffalo him with the barrel, but just as he did so, Bill moved sideways and the pistol glanced off his broad shoulder. He cursed, releasing the woman, spinning on a heel to face Ken. He stared for a fraction of a second. Ken swung the pistol again, but he was dealing with Bill Savage, expert at defense and murderous on offense. Bill gripped the pistol and twisted it hard, pulling it free from Ken's grasp. Ken slammed a left into the man's thick belly and it almost seemed to bounce. He slammed a right at Bill's jaw and it skidded past his ear. The big man laughed. His laugh was a chilling thing.

A rocky fist bounced from Ken's jaw. He went back against the wardrobe. Bill laughed again and dropped the Schofield. "I thought you said you was alone, *mi vida*," he jeered over his shoulder.

A startling thought came to Ken. Bill had not recognized him as yet.

Ken went under a left hook and hit Bill in the belly with a driving one-two that staggered him. Bill was a little drunk and Ken wasn't in the best condition, because of his imprisonment, but even so Ken knew the big man could whip a man like Ken any day in the week and twice on Sundays. He hadn't earned his nickname because of his prowess with the *putas*.

Bill hit Ken twice, driving him back against the table. The bottle fell but did not break as it struck the floor. Encarnacion ran toward the kitchen, pulling open the door. The lamplight showed full on Ken's bleeding face.

Bill stopped in midstride and stared at Ken. "Well, I'll be double-damned," he said. "Sturgis!"

Ken raised his fists. He'd have to kill the big man now. He didn't know how, but there would be no choice. It was him or Bill now and the devil would take the one who went down at last.

"You bitch," said Bill over his shoulder. "I'll take care of you after I take care of him."

Bill moved in swiftly and his fists slammed Ken

around the room like a shuttlecock. He went back against the wall, his face a mask of blood, his breath coming like a steam engine exhaust. Now and then he got in a good punch but it was like hitting a brick wall. He kneed the big man and caught him flush on the jaw, driving him back onto the couch. He dived on the big man and gripped for his throat but it was like gripping a cable of wire rope. Bill laughed as he dumped Ken on the floor. Ken's strength was going. It would soon be over.

Ken rolled sideways, picking up the half-empty bottle as he did so. As Bill dived at him, he struck with vicious fury. The bottle shattered on Bill's cropped head, the liquor splashing into his eyes. He gripped Ken and began to throttle him. There was no escape.

Encarnacion ran from the kitchen. Something glittered in the lamplight and the knife went deep between Bill's shoulder blades. He let go of Ken and got slowly to his feet, his eyes wide in his liquor-stained face. He felt for the knife with his left hand. He turned. His right hand swung out, catching the woman alongside the head, driving her back into the kitchen. She fell into the bedroom.

Bill turned. Ken narrowed his eyes. No man in the world should be standing with a knife in his back like that, *but Bill was.*

Bill opened, then closed his mouth. He tried to say something and then he fell like a huge pine, and the jacal seemed to tremble with the fall.

Ken rolled him over. The man was dead. Ken pulled out the knife. He checked the door lock, then ran into the bedroom. She lay on the bed where she had made her living for so many years, her head askew, and her eyes staring sightlessly at Ken.

Ken picked up the whiskey bottle and drank deeply.

He wiped the blood from his battered face. He had to get out of this place; if anyone came into it, they'd set up a hue and cry for him. A double murder, they'd say, and God himself couldn't bear witness that he hadn't done it.

His eyes caught the guttering light of the votive candle. These shacks were always burning down. Fire was a cleanser, a concealer. Fire could effectively cover a man's tracks.

While the moon waned he worked swiftly. He dressed in Bill's pants. The boots were an excellent fit. The coat was a little large, but satisfactory enough. He ripped out the manufacturer's labels. Bill had thirty dollars in his wallet, which Ken appropriated, as he did the money that belonged to Encarnacion. She'd no longer need it. He took Bill's double-barreled derringer and cigar case.

Now and then someone would tap on the door, and cold sweat would run down his face until they went away. He could hear drunken laughter now and then, and the voices of men and women.

He slid a full whiskey bottle into one pocket and a packet of food into the other. Then he opened the rear door. The moon was gone. The wind scattered old papers across the yard. The wind would swiftly spread a fire. He hauled firewood into the jacal and scattered it near the bed. It took all his strength to haul the dead guard into the bedroom and to dump him on the floor. He didn't have the heart to put him in the bed with the woman.

He scattered coal oil throughout the place. Everything was dry. It would burn well.

He looked at Encarnacion. God help her soul, he thought. Be merciful to a sinner, O Lord.

He lighted the clothing in the wardrobe, the stuffing of the hogbacked couch, the scattered firewood, then waited until the flames caught well. It would be a little time before anyone noticed the smoke and flames. Just enough time for him to get out of the neighborhood.

He walked to the back door and opened it. When he was outside he wedged wood inside the doorway so that anyone who tried to get in would lose time.

Ken padded across the filthy yard, wrinkling his nose at the privy stench. He looked back at the jacal. A wisp of smoke had crept through a crack in a rear window. He scaled the crumbling adobe brick wall and ran swiftly up the side street, turning into a lane, down that to an alleyway and up that to the next street. He stopped and lighted one of Bill's excellent cigars, pulled the hatbrim low over his battered face and walked casually across Third Street.

He was beyond First Street, in the shadows, when he heard the first distant cry of alarm. He ran toward the dark river. A fire bell began to ring.

Yuma Landing was at the foot of Main Street, about two blocks from the railroad bridge. He'd never get across the bridge. He darted into the shelter of the trees close to the riverbank. He could see the white superstructures of two steamers at the river's edge, moored side by side, the inner one pointing upstream and the outer one downstream, their tall black stacks silhouetted against the star-stippled sky.

There were lights on in several cabins of the inner steamer.

A man ran down the slanting gangplank. "Hey, fellas!" he yelled. "Big fire in the red-light district. Streets full of screaming whores! Come on! See the fun!"

Boots thudded on the decks and on the gangplank and four men ran toward the town.

Ken wet his lips. The inner steamer seemed deserted now. He ran silently up the gangplank to the deck. He saw someone step out of a cabin and turn to lock the door. Ken stepped behind one of the big piles of cordwood piled on the bow of the steamer. Boots thudded on the gangplank.

Ken looked up at the nameplate of the steamer. It was the *Cocopah*. She was due to go upriver at dawn. He went around to the port side of the steamer and looked at the other steamer, a much larger one. The nameplate showed the name *Mohave*. She was due to go downriver at dawn. Ken stepped across to her and padded aft to the stern wheel, looking for a place to hide. He knew well enough that the steamer must have been searched for prisoners several times that day. The stern wheel was housed neatly in white-painted timbering. He tried the door that led into the housing. It opened easily. He stepped into the dark interior. The huge wheel was within several feet of him. On each side of it were huge beams that held the axle of the wheel. The actuating arms were on either side of the wheel. The area where he stood had been planned just big enough for a man to inspect the wheel or do repairs. The steamer was too small for a man to find a secure hiding place. Perhaps they wouldn't bother to look in the stern wheel housing. It was the best he could do.

He closed the door and took a belt of the whiskey. It was quiet along the river, except for the murmuring of the current along the sides of the boats. When the wind shifted he could hear the town noises, and once he thought he scented smoke. By now the jacal would be a tumbled ruin of embers with two charred bodies in it.

Some hours after midnight he heard stumbling feet on the deck of the steamer, and the sounds of men's voices. A door slammed. Somewhere on the nearby shore two men argued drunkenly until a harsh voice from the *Cocopah* made them shut up.

Ken sat down. He couldn't sleep. His face ached from the blows Bill had dealt it. He was tired, almost to exhaustion, but he couldn't sleep. The whiskey was of little help. It didn't relax him, and he could have emptied the whole bottle without getting drunk. He dared to smoke a good part of the night. He had to have some consolation.

Something creaked and groaned. Ken's left hand was struck by something hard. He awoke with a start. The big wheel was beginning to turn and he lay on a narrow shelf hardly a foot away from the metal-tipped blades. He jumped up, cold sweat breaking from his face, just saving the half-empty whiskey bottle from tumbling into the river. It was cold. He could hear the muted *sssoooo hhhaaaa* of the steamer's slow-speed, cross-compound engine as she slowly moved out into the strong current in the middle of the Colorado. By God, he had slept all through it! He must have been exhausted. If anyone had opened that door they could not have missed him.

He peered past the slowly revolving wheel. It was still dark on the river, but it must be just about dawn. He could just see the tracery of the railroad bridge against the sky, and beyond it something else. The flattened hump of stark land with Yuma Pen atop it.

The *Mohave* creaked and groaned with the thrust of the wheel and the liquid grip of the muddy river. Ken wedged himself in between two vertical beams. He couldn't be seen from the doorway unless a person leaned far out, dangerously close to the wheel, and looked his way. Yet he didn't dare stay anywhere else. He watched the wet, dripping blades passing within two feet of him.

It was a long way down to the gulf. A long, long way, and he'd have to stay where he was until darkness came.

Hour after hour he stood there, keeping his eyes closed to keep from being hypnotized by that eternally turning wheel. If he did become hypnotized, or dropped asleep, and fell forward into that wheel, it would kill him, or injure him so that he could not swim, or perhaps force him under so that he might never come up.

The *Mohave* was likely headed for Port Isabel downriver, near the Gulf of California, to pick up cargo from the oceangoing steamers that ran up the gulf and deposited their cargoes and passengers there for transshipment upriver by river steamer. Ken would have to get off the steamer before then, but where would he go? There was nothing but waterless desert east of the river, with waterless mountains backing it up, except for the chancy water supply at Tinajas Altas. This was the driest time of the year.

The steamer would travel swiftly downriver, aided by the current. Somewhere along the heat-soaked route Ken would have to make his break. If he was seen leaving the steamer the searchers would be alerted. The Yumas lived in that Godforsaken stretch of country. A mouse couldn't move across their bailiwick without being seen.

Hour after hour he stood there, stiffening by the minute, his clothing soaked to the skin by the dripping water. That was one blessing at least. Beyond the revolving wheel he could see the murderous sun glinting from the water, and when the steamer rounded a bend he could see out across the sterile land he would have to cross, a heat haze shimmering and dancing, creating a distorted view of that land of hell.

Some time in the afternoon the *Mohave* stopped for wood. Ken could hardly move, but he had to fight off the maddening desire to jump ship then and there. He'd certainly be seen.

Now and then the whiskey seemed to give him enough strength to hang on, watching that wheel revolving over and over, almost in his face; the steady, throbbing, thudding of the engine and the monotonous washing of the water against the sides of the steamer acting as a soporific to put him to sleep. To sleep ... to sleep...

Time and time again his head snapped up. He knew it was only a matter of time before he would fall.

Somehow he slept. He snapped open his eyes. The wheel was dimly seen, but turning at a slower pace. He could hear driftwood thudding against the hull. The steamer creaked as she turned. Ken moved stiffly from his hideout. He checked his Schofield. He eased open the door a crack. He could see land, fifty feet away. The *Mohave* was stopping for the night, short of Port Isabel, for some reason or another. He didn't know where they were. But he knew for sure he couldn't put in another hour in that place of confinement.

He waited until the *Mohave* was moored, not right against the muddy bank, but somewhat out, for the Yumas would steal the pennies from a dead man's eyes. There was a huge pile of wood on the shore, beside a rickety wharf.

He watched the crew starting to load the wood. It would keep them busy for hours. Lights flickered on board the steamer.

Ken walked aft, past the port actuating beam, to stand at the very end of the steamer. He let himself down into the muddy water and his feet struck bottom in armpit-deep water. He held his Schofield high out of the water as he pushed his way ashore and then crawled into a thicket. He didn't want to shoot, but if he was seen he would have to.

He peered out at the steamer. A line of men were trotting up the swaying gangplank to load the cordwood on the decks. The yellow light cast glimmering paths on the muddy waters. On the upper deck, below the stack, he saw a man in a familiar uniform watching the loading. Now and then the man looked up or down the river. Another man in uniform walked along the side deck, past the end of the gangplank. and opened the door that led into the stern wheel housing. He walked inside the housing.

Ken rested his head on the stinking mud. It had been so close. Too damned close!

Ken bellied out of the thicket and behind a low fold of ground. He emptied the whiskey bottle, then crawled over another fold of land to the river, where he filled the quart bottle with water. He drank his fill of the silty water until he thought he'd heave it all out. He found a rusted gallon can and filled it with water, fashioning a sling for the can, and covering it with part of his shirt to keep it from sloshing out.

In the thick darkness away from the lighted steamer he looked up at the stars, then he trudged east, through the hummocky sand crowned with thorny brush. Somewhere east of him were the mountains, perhaps the Gilas, or the Tinajas Altas, where the natural granite tanks were. God help him if he had come too far south, and the mountains ahead of him were the Lechuguillas or the Sierra del Viejo, for there was no water there. None at all. And between Ken and the mountains would be not the Yuma Desert, but the larger, more deadly Gran Desierto of Sonora—the Anvil of the Sun, as Pablo Mendez had called it. Even the *zopilotes,* the great buzzards of Sonora, avoided *that* place.

He had until daylight to make time. There would be no resting for him, stiffened and weak as he was. The darkness would be his friend, and he would be far enough away from the river for the moonlight to make his path easier, if he wasn't spotted by the Yumas.

He walked on like a drunk, forcing himself to plant one foot in front of the other, knowing full well that each step took him farther away from the river and possible disclosure, and closer to the distant mountains.

Once he was away from the river it was very quiet. It was a lifeless place. His boots grated steadily on the harsh soil that had replaced the soft, clinging sand. It was better footage, but hell on boot leather. Thank God Bill Savage had worn low-heeled boots, and that Ken had been lucky enough to find his size in them. He grinned. "Walking in a dead man's boots," he said to himself. He laughed. There was no echo. Nothing. Nothing but the darkness of the night and the steady shuffling of his feet against the ground, while high overhead the ice-chip stars stippled the dark sky.

On and on. Hour after hour. On and on.

He saw the first faint suggestion of moonlight. In a little while the moon tipped the humped mountains and shone down their rugged western flanks.

He looked back toward the distant river. He could see the lights of the *Mohave.* He was dismayed at how close it looked. He turned his head and slogged on. Now and then he looked to the south, trying to get an idea of how close he might have been to the mouth of the river.

The ground sloped slowly upward. About midnight, when the moon was low in the western sky, he stopped to sip a little water and as he raised the can he saw something far to the south. He narrowed his eyes as he lowered the can without drinking from it. There was a faint sprinkling of lights down there. It could only be one place. Port Isabel. Port Isabel was almost on the gulf itself.

Ken slowly recovered the can without drinking from it. He knew where he was now. The *Mohave* had traveled faster than he had thought. Beneath his feet was the Gran Desierto. Due east of him was El Camino del Diablo, many miles across the hell of the desert. Those moonlighted mountains must be the Sierra del Viejo. There was no water there. No water at all.

He stood there for a few minutes. He thought of the rushing Colorado. Thousands upon thousands of gallons of fresh water being poured each hour into the salty Gulf of California. He could go back. The *Mohave* would not chance the river until dawn.

Ken lighted one of Bill Savage's cigars. He slanted his hat to the back of his head, drew in the good smoke, and started walking. East. East toward the Sierra del Viejo.

CHAPTER SIX

A COOL, DECEPTIVE WIND crept across the Gran Desierto. It was the forerunner of the dawn. The moon was long gone. The mountains didn't seem much closer, but they had to be, for Ken Sturgis had not stopped walking all that night, sipping a little water now and then, rinsing out his mouth, then squirting the water back into the whiskey bottle. The gallon can was still full, although he had lost a little of the water by slopping.

There were no lights to be seen. No one lived in that country. No white men crossed it. Few Indians would cross it in the wintertime, and it was now the very core of the summer, the blazing heart of it. Still, the Yumas would chance it if they knew a prisoner was crossing toward the mountains. They had a habit of racing across the deserts to hide near the few water holes, knowing full well that an escapee would have to head for the water holes, if he knew where they were. All travel in that country depended on water holes. The only reason the dreaded, almost waterless El Camino del Diablo was used was because some travelers preferred chancing death by thirst rather than by the hands of the Apaches along the Gila Trail further north.

There were hostiles along the Camino. Sand Papagoes, less dangerous than wandering Apaches or Yaquis, but treacherous enough if they found a weak party, or *one man* crossing to water. There were bandits too, both American and Mexican, some of them as rapacious and cruel as the Indians, some of them worse. It was a country of death and without law, except the law of the strong.

There are some things stronger than fear. Hate is one of them. Even a frightened man can overcome his fear if he hates enough. Such a man was Ken Sturgis. His fear was not that of one who ventures into the unknown. He *knew* what he was up against. It was that knowledge that could save him, if he made the next water hole. If he didn't it wouldn't matter. They'd never take him back to Yuma Pen. Of that he was positive.

The false dawn faintly touched the dark eastern sky.

The wind died away fitfully, coming and going, but weaker by the minute.

It was very quiet, almost deathly quiet except for the husking sound of the boots on the harsh earth.

The mountains were dim, humped shapes, sleeping out the dying night.

The stars paled.

The wind was gone, fleeing toward the unseen Gulf of California.

Ken began to notice his hard breathing. The last rest he had had, had been the last night he had spent in that stinking overcrowded cell back on Prison Hill. He laughed. He had forgotten the time he had spent in the grave, waiting to make his break.

The sky was much lighter now.

The mountains were closer. Or were they?

He had the feeling he was on a treadmill, the harsh earth running back beneath his thin boot soles, the nearness of the mountains naught but a cruel delusion, or a painted backdrop.

Suddenly it was light. He could see the great folds of the mountains. Each scant desert bush stood out clearly on the ground like a plant in a tank of clear water. The very air seemed like water. He had the illusion he was walking on the sand in the bottom of a great tank.

The eastern sky turned from dark gray, to light gray, to pearly gray. The tops of the rounded mountains stood out starkly.

He stopped and lighted a cigar. They seemed to help. When he raised his head the sun struck at his eyes. It was still cool.

By the time he had walked another half mile the heat of the sun was already flowing down the western side of the lead-colored mountains to meet him.

Then it was full daylight. The air was very quiet. The sun seemed to explode silently as it fully cleared the mountains.

The rays of the sun touched his face and the skin drew a little in anticipation. He stopped and checked his water. He could feel the sun groping for a hold, driving invisible rays into his clothing, feeling for the skin, the moisture within the envelope of skin.

It would start with his face and hands. Searing the flesh. Cracking the lips. Burning the eyes. Striking through the cloth.

The ground began to heat up, feeling its way through the thin soles and worn socks, touching the soles of the feet. Soon it would start reflecting the sun and the heat up into his face. The faint puffs of dust which had been rising from each footstep all during the night, faintly acrid to the smell, now gathered together about him, or so it seemed, coating his sweat-streaked face through which fresh droplets of sweat cut new courses, only to have them filled up again. The sweat and the dust worked together, stinging his eyes, coating his cracked lips, working up into his nostrils, trying to get into his mouth.

Several times he looked back over his shoulder. He could not distinguish the river, although it must be there, hidden by folds of the ground. To his right, far off, he caught a faint metallic glittering, the reflection of the sun upon the gulf.

He passed the last of the scant growths and faced an expanse of crusted earth, whitened by salt deposits. Perhaps the bed of a lake dried up before man had appeared on the Gran Desierto. It was cracked and interlaced by furrows where rains had beaten on the thin crust in times past, perhaps even covering the harsh earth with a thin sheet of water for a very short time. Then the sun would have had its way, as it always did, drying up the water, then the mud, then driving what little moisture was left deep down into the ground, cracking the dried upper crust.

There would be no escape for him this day. No rest. No going back. He was committed. As long as he kept on his feet he would survive as long as the water lasted. He could not rest until the sun was gone. He was fully committed.

He looked up at the glaring sun. "I've been committed since Roy died," he said. "You won't stop me."

The sun struck back with savage fury, lancing deep into his reddened eyes, trying to reach the brain, to weaken it and destroy it, to turn this gaunt lath of a man into a screaming wreck who would tear at his clothing, and then start to run, as they always did, until exhaustion struck them to their knees, and the sun drove them belly flat onto the burning earth, to dig senselessly into the arid ground with broken, bleeding hands for the water that was not there.

Ken tied his dirty scarf about his nose and mouth, pulling down his hatbrim, so that only his eyes showed. It was hot, but it was better than the stinging dust.

He began to think of water. He remembered the steady pumping of the old Halladay Standard windmill on the ranch, near the San Miguel. Of the clear water that welled into the tank and often overflowed. He remembered the water at Hueco Tanks and at Tonto Springs. He remembered the water in the railroad pass where the Express had been held up. He thought of the tap in the mess hall at Yuma. They never rationed water at Yuma. It was the only thing they didn't ration. He remembered the hours he had stood on that narrow beam, with the big stern wheel turning slowly a few feet from his face, dripping gallons of water back into the Colorado. It had been like standing in a cave beneath a waterfall.

He tried to force thoughts of water from his mind. He thought of Roy, and of how he had died, and the hate welled up within him, for a time at least. He could see the lean, handsome face of Marl Meyner and the broad, impassive visage of Max Fremar. He envisioned the hard face of Bill Savage, and remembered how he had fallen, with the knife sticking out of the middle of his broad back like some alien growth.

"Pagosa Springs," he said clearly.

He stopped in astonishment and pulled the filthy scarf from his face. He looked about in wonderment. He looked back along the trail and saw the mountains. He was looking down the long, heat-hazy slopes toward the unseen Colorado, while off to his left he saw the faint, metallic light reflecting from the Gulf of California.

He stood there stupidly. He shook his head and touched his cracked lips with his swollen tongue.

The mountains were *behind* him.

The Colorado was *ahead* of him.

The Gulf of California was to his *left*.

"Jesus God!" he said.

The mountains should be *ahead* of him.

The Colorado should be *behind* him.

The Gulf of California should be to his *right*.

He must have turned in his walking, perhaps in a semiconscious condition, and headed back toward the river. How long had he been walking that way?

He looked up at the sun. It was directly overhead. It didn't mean anything. He had forgotten how long he had been walking. Everything ran together in his mind.

The full, blasting heat of the day was on him now, in the time of summer when the very core of heat has come, in a country where there was no shelter and no water, other than that which he was carrying with him.

Once more the decision came up. There was never any peace out here. To go back to the river or to strike on toward the mountains.

He sipped a little of the gamey, silty water. The Sierra del Viejo seemed to rise and hover from the baking ground, veiled in shimmering, distorting haze. A dust-devil arose from the flat ground between him and the shimmering mountains, whirled swiftly into towering height and swept toward him, only to vanish as suddenly as it had appeared. Further south another one appeared, or was it the same one? It whirled toward the distant Gulf of California and then it, too, vanished.

The sun felt like a hot flatiron pressed against the nape of his neck. He ripped off the tail of his shirt and hung it down the back of his neck from beneath his hat. In the short time he stood bareheaded, the sun seemed to strike through the shaven skull into the very brain.

He literally aimed himself toward the haze-filled notch that indicated the way between the Sierra del Viejo and the Lechuguillas. The third range to the left must be the Tinajas Altas. Beyond them, somewhere on their rugged eastern flank, must be the place that had given the mountains their name. The great potholes eroded by time into the very granite. Holes, or "tanks," which held rainwater most of the year. But this had been the driest year in many years.

He put one foot in front of the other and marched like an automaton. "The journey of a thousand miles begins with but a single step," he said. He laughed. "That damned ol' Chinee who thought that one up, was smart enough not to say you'd ever *get* there."

The sun was slanting on his back. He felt as though his guts were bubbling and fermenting because of the heat. The baking ground struck up through his boot soles so that each step was like placing his foot atop a hot oven.

"Dripping Springs," he said.

He remembered the stock tank back on the San Miguel and how he and Roy would strip, their bodies incredibly white against the tan of their hands, necks and faces, and splash about like kids after a hard day in the saddle. You could bet your boots you'd never get Bobcat Bates into the tank. Roy had thrown him in one time, and only Roy's youth and speed had saved him from being caught by the old bastard. At that, Bobcat had ripped Roy's shirt from neck to tail in the effort. Ken laughed at the memory. He winced as a lip cracked.

He saw creosote bushes here and there, but the shade beneath them was hardly enough for a kangaroo rat. He toyed with the idea of cutting enough of them to make a sunshade, then dismissed it from his mind. The effort would be too exhausting. He would have to last out the day. If he fell, he'd never get up.

Smoothly rounded pebbles grated beneath his boots. Salt bush and ocotillo began to show among the scattered creosote bushes. The ground was no longer level, but slightly uneven, broken by hardly distinguishable ridges, and shallow areas where rains of the past had swept away the harsh soil to the bedrock.

He looked back over the tortuous trail. The river was far away. "I'll beat you yet," he said to the shimmering desert. His left boot toe caught on a large pebble embedded in the ground and he fell heavily, bruising his hands as he tried to break his fall. There was a sudden gushing of warm wetness along his left side, soaking through his clothing. The empty gallon can rang hollowly as it hit the ground. He grabbed at it, but it was no use. The thirsty ground had swiftly swallowed the water. For a few minutes he dabbled foolishly at the still damp earth.

He checked the whiskey bottle. It was half empty. "Or half full," he said. He laughed. "Depends on how you look at it."

He got unsteadily to his feet. He slanted toward the notch. Maybe the sun wouldn't go down. Maybe he had entered a place of eternal sun. Maybe it was a suburb of hell.

He fell again as he slogged through a drift of yellow sand. He opened his mouth and tasted the grains that coated his cracked and bleeding lips. The sun was torching his back. It was the end. He hoped he would lapse into unconsciousness and die without regaining consciousness.

There was a great lump in his gut, pressing upward into his rib cage. A hard, rounded thing that he had to get rid of somehow. He opened his eyes. It was dark. A cool breeze played along the warm sand and whisked dust into his scorched face. Slowly he felt his belly and he grinned as he felt the rounded shape of the bottle.

Ken sat up and uncorked the bottle. He sipped a mouthful of water, recorked the bottle, then looked up at the stars. "You took a hell of a time coming," he said with a grin.

He looked down the great, gradual slope that eventually reached the Colorado. Far to the left he saw the faintest of lights. Perhaps a steamer on the gulf, or perhaps it was Port Isabel. It was a long way off.

The mountains seemed to have moved in closer for the night, as though to inspect the mite of humanity that had been cast by the desert at their deeply buried feet.

Ken took stock of himself. He had a little food left but there was no hunger within him, except for water, water and more water. He selected one of Bill Savage's half-dried-out cigars and lighted it while he pulled off his boots, wincing as the blood-glued socks clung to the inside of the boots. He felt a huge blister break. The socks seemed like a second skin, so soaked and glued with blood and lymph were they to his raw feet. He patiently opened the blisters, then wrapped his burning feet in rag strips from the rest of his shirt.

There would be a moon again. He didn't know how long he had lain unconscious, but he would allot that time for rest. He had no desire to lie there all night and go through the hell of the next day.

It was dark, except for the winking stars, when he started toward the notch. From somewhere, along with the night breeze, there came an uplift in spirits and in strength. He forced each leg forward, swinging along with a steady, distance-eating stride, listening to the irregular gurgling of the water in the bottle and the husking of his boots on the ground.

He passed the notch, despite his desire to cut through it, for he knew it trended away from the Tinajas Altas. He would have to take the long way around the outthrust flank of the Lechuguillas, for somewhere to the northeast was the rugged gap that led between the western side of the Lechuguillas and the overlapping, eastern side of the Tinajas Altas. If he missed the gap in the dark, or walked up a box canyon, he'd live to see the next day, but certainly not the next night.

There was another factor he did not like. The border between Arizona Territory and Mexican Sonora slanted up from the vicinity of Nogales, many miles to the east, to a point somewhere below Yuma. Therefore, somewhere in the gap between the Lechuguillas and the Tinajas Atlas he would pass the unmarked border line. In Sonora he might have a chance of avoiding capture; the rurales were more interested in smugglers than they were in escaped prisoners. In Arizona Territory he would be fair game for anyone who wanted to make fifty bucks. But the water was on the Arizona side, and so were Marlin Meyner and Max Fremar.

The moon arose and lighted the desert. Ken Sturgis slogged along between the great shoulders of the mountains. By the time the moon was fully up he had reached a place where he could look partway along the eastern flank of the Tinajas Altas. Far to the northeast he could see the humped shapes of other mountains, likely the

Cabezas Prietas. There were supposed to be "tanks" there too, but he wouldn't take a chance on them.

Somewhere he crossed the border. He wasn't sure, but as a gesture he emptied his bladder before he slogged on. He had to salute the occasion with some sort of a libation.

The Tinajas Altas loomed to his left. By the time the moon was on the wane he had stumbled onto a faintly rutted road. It trended along the eastern side of the mountains, but to his left, drifting through the scattered greasewood and ocotillo, was another faint trail, not marked by wheels, but by the hoofs of animals and the boots of men.

He sipped a little water and tightened his belt for a Spanish supper. He walked up the steadily rising slope, higher and higher, with the moon shining on his battered, sun-scorched face. There was no sign of life. Nothing but the brush, standing still in the now windless air, and a few smoke trees in lower areas.

He was now walking on rock still warm from the beating of the sun. The heat seeped up through his boots. They were full of holes now. The heat hung about him, for the rocks held it like a sponge holds water. "Water," he said. He shook the bottle. There wasn't enough in it to keep him alive through the next day, no matter in which direction he went.

The rocks were humped now, with huge boulders thrusting themselves up through the harsh flank of the mountain. The ground leveled. He stopped and looked back. He could see across the Lechuguilla Desert, dreaming in the silvery moonlight.

Where was the water? It had to be near him somewhere.

He bent his head and prayed for the first time since

he had prayed for the death of his brother, to release his poor, tortured soul. Minutes ticked past. He prayed again, trying to keep faith. It wasn't easy, for shallow doubt kept creeping into his mind.

A faint wind crept down the side of the mountain and rustled the brush. Ken raised his head. "It has to be here, Lord," he said to the night sky.

Something moved. Something *splashed*.

Ken ran awkwardly toward the sound. Some creature flashed past him, running for the shelter of the rocks and brush. Ken cast aside his hat and stared back and forth. Then, he looked down the slope. Right at his feet was a great hole in the living rock. It was rounded, and deep, and covering the water in the hole was a thin film of algae, dust and pinkish bladders.

He dropped to his knees on the warm rock, but before he bent his head to drink, he bent his head to pray.

CHAPTER SEVEN

Something warned Ken. He opened his eyes and raised his head. It was still dark, but there was a faint trace of dawn light in the eastern sky over the Cabezas Prietas beyond the Lechuguilla Desert. The rocks were still warm beneath him but a cool breeze was stirring along the flank of the Tinajas Altas. He sat up and immediately reached for his filled water bottle. He had had his fill the night before, and several times during the night he had sipped more of the slightly gamey water. He peered into the clinging darkness. He had heard nothing, but there was an uneasiness in him.

He walked softly up the rocky slope. Before the moon had gone, he had scouted the area. There was a place above the tanks where he could hide and yet see the tank area. He worked his way in through a cleft and then pulled himself up higher. He cached his water bottle and then looked down toward the tanks. It was very dark down there. He imagined he could see the irregular shapes of some of the tanks. He had left no trace of himself down there. There was little chance that anyone who came there might be looking for him, but if he was seen, they might wonder who he was, and perhaps they might know there had been a break at Yuma. Word traveled fast by telegraph and by mouth when there was a break.

The wind stirred the scant brush. Ken wet his cracked lips and looked further down the slope from the tanks. His heart seemed to leap against his ribs. Something had moved. Something that seemed to have materialized from the darkness of the night and the star glow. Ken lay flat. It was a man. He did not wear a hat, in a country where a hat was the mark of a man; a *white* man, at any rate. Two more hatless figures silently materialized.

Ken rested his hand on the big Schofield. One was beyond the law here. All sorts of people came to the Tinajas Altas for water, but usually only in the cooler weather. The Indians avoided traveling in the core of the summer, but they were better at it than any white man. If they had come to Tinajas Altas Tanks, it might be because they had been sent there to look for someone, unless they were just nomadic Sand Papagoes.

The intruders padded softly to the tanks and stood there. It was slightly lighter now, enough for Ken to see their heads moving from side to side and up and down as they scouted with their keen eyes. Their ears and nostrils would be alert as well. He hoped to God they couldn't detect the stink of his sweat-soaked clothing.

There was a soft bird call. A moment later it was repeated down the darkened slope. A horse whinnied softly in the darkness as it smelled the water.

Ken's skin crawled. If they were looking for an escaped prisoner, they would know that if he had come that way he would have to stop at Tinajas Altas Tanks for water. There would be no escape for him. They could sit at the tanks and look out across the heat-soaked Lechuguilla Desert toward the hazy Cabezas Prietas, and nothing could move out there during the day without being seen by those keen eyes of theirs. Or they could wait for him to stagger up to the tanks, too weak to resist, and likely not caring whether they recaptured him, just so he could drink his fill.

The main thought in Ken's mind was that they would likely *stay* at the tanks. He had just enough water in the bottle for one day under that blasting sun. There would be no chance for him to get to the tanks without being heard or seen. He cursed himself for not driving on to the east as soon as he had had his fill of water, but he knew well enough he would not have made it.

The sky was grayer now as the sun slowly rose behind the easter mountains. Now, from the Tinajas Altas, El Camino del Diablo could be seen threading its way through the mesquite and dull, metallic-looking creosote bushes, with here and there a senita or organpipe cactus standing like a signpost.

With Indian trackers, if they *were* trackers, at Tinajas Altas Tanks, it would be likely that telegraph messages had been sent in all directions from Yuma, warning people that there had been a break. Everyone would be on the lookout for ragged, thirst-crazed strangers. To the people in that country the Yuma cons were dangerous animals and nothing more. Their human semblance concealed the animal savagery within them. If these were trackers, then the messages must have been sent along the Gila, thence south toward the border.

He could see some of them leading their tired mounts to the water. Now and then one of the Indians would glance up at the dark rocks beyond and above the tanks.

In a little while the full dawn light would strike across the desert and reveal the eastern flank of the Tinajas Altas.

He couldn't run now. Behind him and above him were the rugged heights of the Tinajas Altas, and on the western side, between the mountains and the river, was waterless desert. If he struck for the Camino he would likely be seen and run down. Even if he managed to remain unseen on the Camino, reaching the wide gap between the Tules to the south and the Cabezas Prietas to the north, he wasn't sure about the water supply at Tule Tank, or that there would be no Indian trackers there, or perhaps lawmen from further east, alerted by the telegraph.

Ken rested his throbbing head on his crossed arms. Beyond Tule Tank was Tule Well, and beyond that was the Tule Desert and the barren and waterless Pinacate Plain. There was a place called Las Playas there, but he had never heard if it had water, or if it was a place at all, beyond just a name. Due east were the Cabezas Prietas, and there were tanks in those mountains, but their water supply was never sure. If a man reached them and they were dry, he would have to head south to either Tule Tank or Tule Well, for there was no water north of Cabezas Prietas Tanks, until one reached the Gila—perhaps fifty miles of waterless, scorching desert. They would be keeping their eyes peeled for escaped prisoners along the Gila Trail.

Faintly, now and then, as the wind shifted, he heard the low voices of the Indians and the occasional whinnying of a horse.

He saw the dawn light tip the Cabezas Prietas. What was beyond them due east? More desert, with several long mountain barriers rising like dislocated bones from the sere desert floor, leaden-hued and veiled with the ever-present heat haze. Few people ever traveled that country, even in the wintertime when the heat was gone and the need for water was not as demanding. In the summer, if thirst did not kill, the heat would; and the combination of the two was more than enough to dissuade the hardiest of men. Even the Indians would not go near it.

The sun tipped the Cabezas Prietas. It picked out the thread of El Camino del Diablo, twisting its deadly way east, just north of the border. Seventy miles or so of that hell and one would reach Quitobaquito, and beyond that, Sonoita. Before one reached Quitobaquito, there was a place called Agua Dulce—Sweet Water—and from there on it was easy going to Sonoita. It was a well known place. Travelers filled their bellies, canteens and kegs with the sweet water before traveling further west along the Camino. A stranger would be noted at Agua Dulce. Questions might be asked.

The sun began to send its heat down into the Lechuguilla Desert and against the eastern face of the Tinajas Altas. There was no sign of the Indians down at the tanks. They would not travel during the day. They could rest like snakes, curled up in the hot shade. Perhaps one of them would be the lookout.

Ken crouched lower in his shelter. He would have to save his water. He had already finished the greasy, dried-out food he had taken from Encarnacion's jacal. He could last for some time without food, but once the water was gone he'd be through. Maybe they'd leave when the sun went down.

As the sun rose higher and the full fury of its heat was felt on the land, it was almost as though nothing living existed there. The only movements on the baking surface of the desert were the swiftly spiraling dust-devils.

As the heat of the day gathered, Ken retreated deeper into the jumbled rock formations, but always the heat would find him out. By midafternoon his water was gone, poured into his dry mouth and then out of his pores. He tried not to think of those natural granite tanks, and the gallons upon gallons of water in them, within a few minutes' walk from where he lay hidden.

At last the killer sun slanted around the southern end of the Tinajas Altas, and slow shadows began to form on their eastern flank. There was a little movement from the Indians down at the tanks. It was hard to believe they could not feel that hawk's gaze peering down at them from the rocks above the tanks.

The wind rose a little, sweeping from the north, and as it did so, a sound came with it. Two of the Indians looked to the north. Hoofs were striking against rock and hard earth. One horse, from the sound of it. Already much of the mountain flank was in shadow. The Indians faded into it. They knew their business. Ken felt uneasy as he thought of how his arrival at the tanks had almost coincided with theirs.

Ken gingerly touched his cracked lips. Whoever was approaching the tanks would be no friend of his. Indian, lawman or traveling stranger would offer Ken Sturgis nothing but trouble, and perhaps death, or the living death of Yuma Pen.

In the dying light a man appeared, slogging up the rocky slope, leading a horse whose flanks were spur-lashed. Yellowish foam had hardened about its mouth and on its chest. It was almost as though the man was dragging the blown horse up the slopes by sheer strength. He knew he had to have that horse to continue along El Camino del Diablo, and the only way to keep the horse and himself alive was to reach the water of the Tinajas Altas.

Ken quickly made his decision. There would be excitement, and perhaps action, when the stranger reached the first of the tanks. Perhaps time enough for Ken to reach the farthest tank, deepest in the shadows, to drink his fill and replenish his bottle. He worked his way down the dark slope, cursing as sharp-edged stones cut his hands and knees.

He was belly flat in a clump of scanty brush when he heard the first sounds coming from the stranger and the Indians. A horse whinnied sharply. A man shouted. Boots thudded on rock. Ken squirmed his way past two of the tanks. He'd have to get down into them to reach the water. He looked back over his shoulder and saw dim figures struggling near the first of the tanks. There was a heavy splash as something fell, or was kicked into the water.

He reached the last of the tanks and bellied down the smooth rock to reach the warm water. He drank just a little as he forced the bottle beneath the water to fill it. The bubbling sounded like Niagara Falls to him. He lay flat, keeping the bottle in the water, right hand holding the cocked Schofield. He didn't want to kill any of the Indians. He had killed no one, despite the fact that he had been named an accessory in the killing of the Express train crew, and he had killed no one in his escape from Yuma Pen. He only wanted to reach Marl Meyner and Max Fremar, and then let fate take its course.

A gun blasted the quiet and the echo fled along the dark flank of the mountain. Ken's head jerked and the bottle slid from his hand, to bubble quietly down into the murky depths of the tank. He felt about for it. Something moved in the brush near the next tank. There was no time to rescue the invaluable bottle. He rolled over and over into the brush and broken rock and lay still, watching an Indian pad past, moving silently toward the last tank—the one he had just left.

Ken worked his way further back in to the brush, and then up the slope. He could hear the muttering of voices from near the first tank, but he could not recognize any of the words. He knew one thing: they were not speaking English.

The mountain was in thick darkness when he reached his hideout. Despair came to roost with him. He had paid too high a price for his drink of water. If the Indians stayed at the tank he'd never last through the next day, and even if they left, he'd have to make it to the next tank or well without carrying water with him.

A light flickered up in the darkness. He saw an Indian moving about, the shifting light revealing the flat planes of his face. In a few minutes a fire showed a winking eye through the darkness and then it flared up. The white man lay on his face on the rock, his wrists tightly bound behind his back, blood staining his dirty hands. His horse stood to one side, spraddle-legged, head hanging low, too far gone to care, perhaps too weak to reach the water.

The fire had died down into a thick bed of embers about the time the moon swung up behind the Cabezas Prietas and lighted the desert. The smoke hung in rifts in the windless air. Some of the Indians lolled about the fire, far enough back to avoid the heat. Now and then one of them would lazily pick up a stone and toss it at the white man, who moved very little. On the rock was a dark stain that had slowly spread from the man's mouth or nose.

One of the Indians came from the tanks. He looked at the broken horse. He walked to it and pulled up its head. Another Indian moved in swiftly. His knife flashed in the firelight as he ripped the keen edge across the taut throat of the horse. It fell heavily. The two Indians squatted on each side of the dead animal, carving out the choice pieces of meat. They tossed bloody chunks back to the other three Indians who lolled about the fire. Soon the smell of roasting meat drifted up to the famished white man who watched from above the tanks.

The Indians ate well of the partially cooked meat, the blood and juice running down their chins and onto their naked chests. They paid no attention to the white man. By the time the fire had died down to a bed of ashes, with here and there a winking eye of flame, like a ruby on velvet, the moon had flooded the eastern flank of the Tinajas Altas.

The Indians were in no hurry. Idly they tossed stones at the helpless white man and Ken felt his hate and anger rise within him. They rolled the man over on his back. His face was masked with blood. Two of the Indians brought up the horses. A reata was noosed about the white man's neck and he was pulled to his feet. He was very short. The moon shone fully on his face. Despite the blood, Ken knew him. It was Shorty Stiber! The little man had made it then. He had seemed the most interested in making a break to the south, toward the Tinajas Altas, and then the border. He and Carl Mason had made it to the river, and Mason had made it to the California side, they had said. Stiber? Kelly, the guard, had mentioned him while standing near the grave in which Ken had been hiding. "Some say he drowned. Some say he drifted downriver. Anyways, we warned the rurales and the Cocopahs. There's a steamer going downriver at dawn. They'll keep an eye out for him."

One of the Indians shoved Shorty. The little man staggered. His eyes were wide in his blood-masked face.

The Indians mounted. One of them jerked the reata, almost pulling Shorty off his feet. The sorry cavalcade rode slowly down the moonlit slope.

Ken could have raced through the brush and reached the side of the down trail in minutes. Time enough to ambush those bushy-haired bastards. He could get a couple of them before they knew what hit them. It would be a fifty-fifty chance maybe to rescue Shorty. If he failed, however, he'd never be able to clear himself; he'd never make Marlin Meyner and Max Fremar pay the blood debt for Roy.

He hung on his decision. He was damned if he did and damned if he didn't. The little man was a thief, a potential killer, a cheat and a scoundrel. A convicted felon. Ken shook his head and bit his cracked lower lip. It was now or never if he wanted to bring Shorty Stiber back from the gates of a living hell. The little man had almost achieved the impossible in getting as far as Tinajas Altas Tanks.

The group was almost out of sight. Ken stood up and fingered the Schofield. Then he shook his head. He couldn't risk it.

Shorty Stiber screamed just once, more like a stricken animal than a man. He knew what was ahead of him all that moonlit night and the fiery, waterless hell of the next day, that at the end of that trail of hell would be Yuma Pen, and most likely the Insane Cell, conveniently emptied for him by Roy Sturgis.

Ken waited half an hour. He walked slowly down the slope to the almost extinct fire. He fed it, restoring the bed of coals. He roasted enough meat to carry him for a few days. He tried to find his lost bottle in the murky water of the last tank and gave it up. He was wasting too much time. There was one other way for him to carry water. Apache style.

The moon was swinging far toward the west when he left Tinajas Altas Tanks, walking with long strides down the slope toward the Lechuguilla Desert. He had enough water to sustain him as far as Cabezas Prietas Tanks, and somewhat beyond them, *if* they were dry. Slung over his shoulder, like the blanket roll of a Civil War foot slogger, was the large intestine of the dead horse, sketchily cleaned, but full of water, the ends tied with gut. It was something he had learned along the border. Apaches would ride one horse almost to death while leading another. At the last possible moment, just before the first horse died, they would dismount, cut its throat, carve off the best of the meat, remove the large intestine for an improvised canteen, and ride the other horse to the nearest water. No wonder the troopers hardly ever caught up with them.

Dawn would find him in the naked Cabezas Prietas. He would hole up there during the day, and strike out at dusk, to descend the eastern slope of the mountains, onto the Tule Desert. Beyond that he knew nothing; nothing more than that he would have to keep on, with death in the desert a better choice than being brought back to Yuma with a rope about his neck.

Something haunted him as he crossed that dark desert under the glittering stars, aiming for the far notch in the Cabezas Prietas where the tanks should be. Something haunted him. The last, despairing scream of Shorty Stiber as the Yumas led him off into the desert.

CHAPTER EIGHT

THE SYCAMORES, cottonwoods and willows formed cool walls along the shallow, winding creek, letting through the warm, dry wind but tempering it in the process. The water was inches deep in the pebbly shallows, flowing into wide pools hardly more than a foot deep, upon which floated little argosies of drifting leaves swirling lazily in the eddies. Trunks and branches of dead trees littered the wide, damp banks of the creek, draped in dried moss and dead vines. Magpies fluttered through the treetops, calling raucously to each other. A brown towhee hopped along a log, tilting its head from one side to the other in a bright-eyed search for grubs beneath the scaling bark. A whiptail lizard shot from the shadows and scooped up a waddling beetle, then fled for cover again.

Water splashed. The towhee vanished. The magpies grew quiet. The stream made hardly a sound. The wind soughed softly through the trees.

A shadow fell across the dappled sunlight. Ken Sturgis walked toward the nearest pool, then stopped to look up and down the deserted creek. He looked at the water and shook his head. It didn't seem possible there could be so much water for the taking in the world that he had known for the past weeks.

The magpies looked curiously at the caricature of a man who stood there so quietly. His feet were covered with split-seamed boots that seemed held together by the thick dust that covered the cracked leather. His shirt and trousers were rags and his hat was a complete wreck, with no jaunty tilt to the brim, but just a hopeless, shapeless sagging to it.

He looked up at the treetops with reddened eyes that peered fiercely from a sun-blackened face covered heavily with a dusty beard. His lips were dried and cracked, thrusting themselves out from his mouth as though he were perpetually whistling.

Now that he had reached a fork of the San Miguel he didn't quite know what to do. Beyond the low ridge that bordered the creek valley was the Bar S. It was no longer his. It had been repossessed. He hadn't come back to the San Miguel to see the old place, but to hide until he could go out again into the world of men, to try to pass unnoticed among them until he found two particular men.

He walked slowly through the dappled sunlight, staring uncomprehendingly at the wealth of water beside him. He had reached the San Miguel the night before and had slept close by it, reveling in the sound of the water. This was the first time in weeks he had walked by day. The last of August and all of September had crept by as he had slogged over two hundred miles on foot over the deadliest desert in the southwestern United States. From the tanks at Tinajas Altas to those at Cabezas Prietas and from there across the Tule Desert and through the Sierra Pinta to walk across the immense Growler Valley to Bates Well in Growler Pass. He had traveled on, always by night, holing up by day, across the vast Papago Reservation, as big as the state of Connecticut. He had stolen water from Quijota, the Covered Wells, avoiding the Papagoes. He had ridden a stray burro as far as Chukut Kut, and it had died beneath him, but in death it had helped him as well, for he had hidden near water in the Baboquivaris, sustaining himself on the tough, stringy, tasteless meat of it for a week until he had the strength to leave the shelter of the aged mesquites and oaks and strike across the Valley of the Santa Cruz, again at night. All night long he would walk easterly, hiding at the first light of the dawn. He had driven off a hawk from its fresh kill of a long-legged jack so that he might eat. He had stolen stale food from a closed-up shack. Then suddenly he had splashed into the San Miguel.

The magpies stopped chattering. They had started in again when they had gotten used to him. Now it was quiet again in the creek valley. A jay squawked once and flew off. Ken vanished into a tangle of tree trunks, silvery-looking driftwood and tangled brush. The Schofield was in his hand by instinct.

A tall shadow fell across a sunlit pool. A horse and rider. The rider was a woman, not more than nineteen or twenty years of age. Her dark hair was braided. Her hat hung at the nape of her neck. The butt of a Winchester showed from beneath her right thigh. She looked from side to side as the mare walked slowly along the bank of the stream. The mare suddenly blew and shied. She had caught Ken's scent. It would have been hard to miss.

The young woman rested a hand on the saddle cantle and looked back upstream. The mare whinnied sharply.

The woman turned to ride on and at that instant she found herself looking directly into a pair of the fiercest human eyes she had ever seen. For a moment she couldn't believe that she really saw them. The man did not move. Perhaps she could ride on, pretending she had not seen him.

The mare whinnied sharply. "Quiet, Dancer," said the woman. The mare would not move on.

Ken stood up. "Don't touch that rifle," he warned.

"I didn't intend to," she said.

This was a hell of a mess for Ken. For weeks he had drifted east, not being seen by a single human being, and now that he had reached his goal he was saddled with a young woman. He couldn't take her with him and he couldn't let her go to tell about him. There was one alternative, but he could never do that, and anyway, in time they would come looking for her, and find *him*.

"Who are you?" she said.

There was something familiar about her. "Never mind," said Ken.

She eyed the gaunt lath of a man who stood up in the brush. There was hardly enough flesh on him to cover his bones. He seemed to be existing on sheer will; a will that would drive him to his death before it would let him quit.

The mare whinnied again. The young woman slid from the saddle and watched the mare trot over to Ken. She nuzzled him. "She knows you," said the woman.

"Are you alone?" said Ken.

She smiled. "It's obvious, isn't it?"

"You're not afraid?"

"Should I be?"

"I don't know yet," he said. "Is this your place?"

"In a way," she said.

"What does that mean?"

"My brothers and I have leased it, with a condition that we can buy it at the end of a year. We don't live on it, if that's what you mean." She looked at the mare. "Her name is Dancer. She isn't mine. Not yet anyway. She belongs to this ranch."

There was no expression on his face. "Who are you?" he asked.

"Ruth Harper. My brothers and I own the Triple H across the San Miguel."

He stroked the mare's velvety nose. He knew the young woman now. She had two brothers, Al and Jonce Harper, whom Ken had known by sight. He remembered her, too. It had been a good two years since he had last seen her, a long-legged, freckle-faced kid who thought she was a boy instead of a girl. Times had changed. She was no knockout, but there was something about her that appealed to Ken. Maybe it was her coolness in the face of possible danger. Maybe it was because he had not been with a woman for so long a time.

"I was looking for strays," she said.

He started a little. His mind had a bad habit of wandering off.

"Are you hiding from someone?" she asked.

"No," he said, and he knew well enough she'd never believe that whopper.

"This place used to belong to two brothers named Sturgis," said Ruth. "They were sentenced to Yuma for robbing the Southern Pacific Express."

She knew who he was! She was playing with him. She was stalling for time. There was no time for him to rest along the San Miguel. He was doomed, like the Wandering Jew, to travel on and on and never reach his goal.

"You're safe," she said. "As far as I know I'm the only one, outside of you, on the Bar S."

He stroked the mare again. "I'll buy her from you," he said.

She looked at his clothing.

He grinned, cracking a lip. "I can pay for her," he said. "I'll throw in twenty dollars for the Winchester."

She studied him. "There's food and some clothing over at the Bar S house. You're welcome to them."

He shook his head. He was utterly weary. He could leave her there on foot and take the mare, but he wasn't sure how far he could get. He knew those hills better than any man along the San Miguel, but they'd catch him in time. There would be no hope for him then. He couldn't shoot at them.

"Some say the Sturgis brothers were innocent," she said. "My brothers never really believed they were guilty. It doesn't matter now."

The wind shifted a little. A swirl of leaves drifted down toward the stream. A wren swooped overhead.

"Why doesn't it matter?" he said in a faraway voice.

"Roy Sturgis died in prison. His brother was killed in a jail-break," said Ruth. "It was in all the Territorial newspapers."

"Do you believe it?"

"There isn't any question about it."

A man has to gamble on pure instinct at times. Sometimes, he loses and sometimes he wins, but he has no other choice but to gamble. Ken had gambled from the instant he had hidden in that empty grave on Prison Hill so many weeks past. But then he had gambled on himself. How long could he go on playing the lobo? He looked at her. There was no guile on her face.

"I'm a little hungry myself," she said.

He smiled. "Show me the way," he said.

"We can ride double."

He looked down at himself. "Lady, I wouldn't ask a self-respecting pig to ride double with me."

She mounted and he walked beside her as they left the creek bottom and rode toward the ridge. They crossed a sloping field of dry grass, toward the unseen buildings hidden in a swale looped by a fork of the creek. The only sign of the place was the top of the old Halladay Standard turning to face into the shifting wind, the shaky vanes slowly rotating.

His eyes darted from side to side as they topped the ridge. There was no sign of life at the old place. There was a faint air of decay about the place. He missed something until he realized he had expected to hear old Luke's welcoming bark. Likely the old hound was either dead or had strayed off into the hills long ago.

She had asked him only once who he was and when he had not told her she had not mentioned it again. He helped her down from the saddle and walked with her toward the house. He tethered the mare to one of the porch posts and looked at the Winchester. She opened the front door and walked in. "We keep food here for emergencies," she said over her shoulder. "Some of the boys use it when they are riding fence or looking for strays. We've been running stock on the place for some time."

He looked back over his shoulder as he walked inside the house. There wasn't a sign of a human anywhere around the place. The Triple H was a good five miles away, on the far side of the San Miguel, and the ranch buildings were three miles beyond that, closer to the town of San Miguel. Still, he'd have to keep an eye peeled.

He looked about the old, familiar living room, now hazy with dust. Most of the furniture was still there. It would have hardly paid anyone to haul it away. A thick bed of ashes was in the big fieldstone fireplace. Dust rose about his feet as he walked to a window and pulled back one of the dusty, faded curtains.

"Al left some of his tobacco on the table," she called from the kitchen. "Help yourself."

He rolled a cigarette from the bag of Ridgewood and lighted it with a lucifer he found on the stone mantel of the fireplace.

"There's some coffee left from this morning," she said. "I'll reheat it if you want a cup."

"What's coffee?" he asked with a grin.

"You sound like you just landed from the moon."

"More likely the sun," he said. The memory of his trek across more than two hundred miles of burning deserts and mountains was like a living flame.

"There are some clothes left by the former owners in a closet in the bedroom," she said.

He sucked in the tobacco smoke and felt his senses swirl. It had been such a long time. He walked into the room he had shared with Roy. Dust drifted from the floor. Mice and rats had played havoc with the mattress stuffing. He opened the closet door and whistled softly through cracked lips. Some of his and Roy's clothing still hung there and on the floor were three pairs of boots, two of his and one of Roy's. A melancholy twinge crept through him as he looked at Roy's boots. Ken's escape from Yuma had driven almost every other thought from his mind. There had hardly been time to mourn Roy, or even to think about him. All that had been left had been the urge to escape and to find the two men who had helped kill Roy. The fire had never died out. Now the wind of hate and vengeance was fanning it into a bright glow.

He was clean despite his filthy rags. He had bathed in the Santa Cruz and later in the San Miguel. He stripped and then dressed himself in the faded, but fresh clothing. The wind would drive off the dust of months. He felt his ragged bush of a beard and the shaggy fringe of untrimmed mustache. A little trimming would do the trick. He found a pair of scissors in a dresser drawer, along with a half-full bottle of rye. He took a good belt of the juice before he began to shape beard and mustache. He studied himself in the cracked, gold-flecked mirror. It was no wonder he had scared that girl half to death. He'd never look quite the same again. His experiences in Yuma and on his escape had placed a lifetime mark upon his visage. It didn't matter. It was all to the good.

He rolled another cigarette and lighted it from some matches he found in his shirt pocket. He slowly slid up the loose window and climbed outside into the afternoon sunlight. The sun was slanting toward the west. The mare was hipshot, dozing at the front of the house. The windmill was grinding steadily away.

The urge came over him to take what food he could get, the rifle and the mare and to head for the shadowy hills. He would not be taken alive, and yet he could not kill to escape. Still, there was no sign of other humans about the place.

He stepped back into the room and took another drink. It hit him harder than the tobacco had, but it gave him temporary strength.

He did not speak while they ate and she talked only in generalities but now and then he caught her studying him. She couldn't have recognized him, and yet why had she helped him? Why was she not deathly afraid of him?

They had their coffee in the dusty living room. He studied her through the wreathing tobacco smoke. What was her game?

"The boots and clothing seem to fit rather well," she said.

"Luckily," he said. "Tell me. Why do you and your brothers want to take over this place?"

"Why not? We had been thinking about it some time ago, but it was our Uncle Jim who sold us on the idea. He had spent some time here earlier this year."

"Thinking of buying it?"

"No. He was searching for something."

He narrowed his eyes. "Like what?"

It was very quiet except for the faint humming of the windmill.

"Like about eighty thousand dollars' worth of mint gold and some paper money," she said. "The money taken from the Express was never found. The Sturgis brothers were captured almost right away, but some of their gang got away. Just vanished into thin air. No trace of the money ever showed up. The Southern Pacific, the federal government and local lawmen hunted all over Arizona, as well as New Mexico and parts of California for it, but not a trace was found. Not a trace, mind you."

"You said your Uncle Jim," he said quietly. "Was he hunting for the loot for himself, or for the reward?"

"Neither," she said. "It was his job. He's Chief Inspector for the Southern Pacific on the division where the Express was blown up and robbed. His full name is James Castleman. He's my mother's oldest brother."

What was he to do with her now? Once again she had forced him to think about what he would do with her. If he let her go she might tip off Jim Castleman, and that worthy would burn up every trail in the country looking for Ken Sturgis.

She refilled their coffee cups. "Uncle Jim never fully accepted the guilt of the Sturgis brothers," she said. She looked at Ken.

"How do you feel about it?" he asked quietly.

She shrugged. "I know my Uncle Jim well enough to know that he never lets up on a case, day or night, until he proves it, or disproves it. As late as six weeks ago, when the news of the death of the Sturgis brothers was in all the newspapers, I heard him say that he had never been sure they were guilty."

He slowly rolled a cigarette. "Do you know who I am?" he said quietly.

"I'm quite sure who you are," she said.

"How did you know?"

She smiled. "My uncle is not the only detective in the family. You might not have remembered me, but I had a terrible crush on you the first time I saw you years ago. You looked terrible when I saw you there at the creek, and yet I seemed to know you. The mare clinched it. She's not the friendly sort."

"Go on."

She stood up and walked to the ancient rolltop desk in the corner. She took a picture from a drawer and brought it to him. It had been taken of him and Roy in Nogales one time when they had been playing the bottle and the fargo tables. "You've changed," she said. "But not that much."

"Maybe it's you who should be working for the Espee," he said.

"I told you I believed you and Roy were innocent."

"What happens now?"

She looked at the holstered Schofield and the rifle

leaning against the wall near the door. "You hold all the aces, Ken," she said quietly. "I knew you needed help. God alone knows how or why you came back here, but it's about time someone believed in you and wanted to help you."

It had been a gamble and he was sure he had won it.

"What do you intend to do now?" she asked.

"I want to clear my brother, Bobcat Bates and myself."

Her clear gray eyes studied him. "Is that all?"

"Isn't that enough?" he said harshly. "It has cost the life of my brother and one of my best friends, not to mention this ranch. It took away my liberty. All I want to do is find the men who robbed that Express and bring them to justice."

"Is that all, Ken? No hatred? No vengeance?"

"Yes."

She looked deeply into his eyes and he knew she knew he was lying. "Let the law take care of them, Ken."

"Like it did with Roy and me?" he said dryly.

She stood up. "You can have most of the food and the mare," she said. "We'll have to leave enough food so that no one suspects anyone was here today but me. I can say the mare strayed on me."

He watched her clear the table and walk into the kitchen. He followed her to the doorway and stood there watching her. "You're taking a chance," he said. "If I'm caught, you might be arrested for aiding and abetting me."

She turned and looked at him. "I don't go halfway," she said simply. "I said you needed someone to help you. I know you are innocent. I believe in you. The odds are terribly against you, Ken. I wish I could do more. What will you do now?"

"Hide out in the hills until I get back my strength. I'd raise suspicion wherever I went the way I look now. I think I've changed enough to fool most people. The last thing I want to do is to draw attention to myself."

"Where will you hide?"

He hesitated. "Follow the fork of the San Miguel southeast five miles to a place where two canyons meet it. The right one is a box canyon, but there is a trail up the side of it. On the top there is a little mesa and a small water hole. I doubt if anyone but the Apaches ever knew it was there. No one can approach it any other way than by that trail. One man could hold it against a hundred."

"I hope that won't be necessary."

He did not answer. He had not told her everything.

"I ride alone a lot," she said. "Uncle Jim will be at the ranch this weekend. I'll try to find out anything I can about new developments in his search. I'll come to you Monday afternoon."

He nodded. It was getting late. The old uneasiness came over him. They did little talking as he gathered together the things he needed. Late afternoon shadows were falling as he rode along the fork of the San Miguel, with her behind him, her arms about his lean waist. The feeling of her and her faint fragrance did things to him. He had to force himself to think of the business at hand.

She slid down at the beginning of the Triple H home range. "I'll just tell them the mare strayed, with the rifle as well. Shall I bring you anything next Monday?"

He did not answer for a moment or two and then he smiled, but there was no mirth in his smile. It was grim enough to make her feel uneasy. "Just bring me news of the men who robbed the Express. Bring me news of *Marl Meyner. That, most of all.*"

She nodded. "I'll do everything I can, Ken." She smiled. *"Adios,* Ken!"

"Vaya con Dios, Ruth," he said. He kneed the mare into the shadows of the trees and was gone.

She stood there for a long time before she struck out for the ranch. "It is *you* who must go with God," she said.

CHAPTER NINE

THE CLEAR OCTOBER AIR seemed to lend distance to the eyesight. From his eyrie Ken could see west for miles across the rolling country that sloped toward the distant San Miguel. In the early mornings and late afternoons he could see the faint streamers of smoke from unseen habitations rising in the quiet air to stain the sky. In the middle of the morning the cloud puffs would form somewhere to the east, above the castellated mountains, to drift steadily westward, while their shadows dipped down into the deep hollows and climbed swiftly up the steep and rugged slopes in their hopeless pursuit. To the south, across broken country, was the border, and the distant mountains, always shielded by haze in the afternoons, were in Sonora itself. But it was the east that always caught and kept his attention.

In the morning the eastern mountains would be shapeless, colorless and mysterious in their varying shades of gray, until the sun rose, moved across them and then slanted golden light down upon the rock fantasy far below. It was then that a subtle change came over the mountains. The dark blues and greens of the trees stood out against a wilderness of cracked, eroded and weathered rock, hued in yellow, buff, salmon and pink. The rock itself had been shaped by a master hand into spires, pinnacles, turrets, towers and needles, with here and there the dark mouths of many caves.

Between Ken's rather barren eyrie and the dreamlike eastern mountains were great swales of country, heavily forested in evergreens, sloping down to the river valley far below. Pines, firs, spruces and white-stemmed aspens grew in profusion. Ken could not distinguish them from where he was, no matter how clear the air, but he had been there many times before, hunting deer, or cattle, and sometimes men.

It was the time of early fall, approaching that time which the Apaches call Earth-Is-Reddish-Brown. It would not be too long before Ghost Face, the winter, closed in on those magnificent heights to the east. Before that time Ken must be on his way in his manhunt, while he, himself, was a hunted creature. Certainly it was thought that he was dead, but the young woman had recognized him despite his appearance, and he had been pretty well known in the very country where he must hunt down Marl Meyner, while Max Fremar, the local deputy sheriff, kept his eyes peeled for lawbreakers. It wasn't likely that he'd let Ken Sturgis, beard and all, get by his hawk's gaze. A lawman develops a phenomenal mental file of wanted men as part of his equipment.

The days that had drifted past since he had left Ruth started to run all together so that it was hard to distinguish one from the other. His strength returned swiftly, with regular meals, plenty of water and plenty of rest, but perhaps most of all because he was comparatively safe, and could sleep at night with both eyes closed, and his hand loose from the cocked Schofield. He had a bed of brush and dusty blankets in a shallow cave near the little water hole. The water trickled down the face of rock like lacework, to collect in the shallow *tinaja*, as clear as the bright air, sweet and cool to the taste. His fires he made only at such times of the day so that the faint bluish smoke mingled with the early morning haze, or the shadows of late afternoon. He cooked every other day, and ate lightly, though well,

A drifting puzzle floated through his mind time and time again no matter what he was doing, or what he was thinking. Now that he had escaped, and was thought dead, and had reached the country where the Express has been robbed, he did not know where to start. It would take time and he had precious little to go on. His luck had been good since he had dropped into that empty grave on Prison Hill, but he had parlayed it into success, of a sort at least. Time was important now. Marl Meyner had had a long head start on Ken. But there was one thing he did not know: Ken Sturgis was still alive, and looking for Marl. The catch was that Ken wasn't sure that Marl had been in on the Express deal. That was circumstantial, as had been the evidence against Roy and Ken. But Ken was sure of one thing: Marl Meyner had meant no good the night he had been in the pass over-looking the Espee tracks. Marl must be the key to the puzzle.

He was restless Monday morning, looking often toward the top of the box canyon trail, but knowing full well she had said she'd come Monday afternoon. It was a long, slow ride from the San Miguel, and she was clever enough to make sure she was not being followed. That alone would take time. She'd have to double back, wait in hiding, and be careful not to leave obvious tracks.

He saw her long before he could distinguish her features. She appeared and disappeared in the scrubby woods far below the cliff face, then disappeared altogether as she followed the narrow fork into the place where the two canyons faced each other across the gap that the fork had cut through the softer stone between the opposing heights. He studied the way by which she had approached, but there was no sign of anyone following her. A hawk hung low over the scrub timber, indicating that there were no other humans in that area.

He picked up the rifle and walked to the head of the trail to look down into the deep box canyon. He saw her leading the horse toward the sheer stone wall that closed the southern end of the canyon, while she scanned the forbidding walls looking for the threadlike trail that seemed tacked to the stone. He walked quickly to the heights that overlooked the fork and once again looked for anyone who might be following her, but, as before, the place was deserted.

He walked back to the head of the trail and threw a rock down into the canyon. She turned quickly to look toward the place where the rock had struck the canyon floor, then looked up toward him. He waved the rifle and pointed to the trail.

She came up very slowly. It was no place for the faint of heart or the weak of will. Now and again he saw her white face as she looked up toward him. Thank God she didn't look down. Bits of crumbling rock dropped from the edge of the trail and plunged far below. The horse whinnied in fear. She stopped and tied her scarf about his eyes and he was docile again, long enough for her to lead him to the top.

"I should have come down for you," he said.

She shook her head. "It is all right. He might not have become used to you. I hope he does though. I brought him for you."

He shook his head. "I can't ride a horse with the Triple H brand, or the Bar S, for that matter."

"He isn't branded," she said. "I rode into San Miguel with a neighbor this morning, in his buckboard, saying I had to go to the dentist. I bought this roan from Charley Bodwell who owns the livery stable."

"Wouldn't he think that was odd?"

She shook her head. "Charley worked for us for years. I helped finance him when he wanted to buy the livery stable. I just asked him for an unbranded horse. Said it was a gift for someone. He looked at me rather oddly, and I told him it was between him and me. That was enough for Charley. He doesn't care much for my brothers anyway."

He looked at the roan. He was broad-chested, solid looking, maybe not good for a quick burst of speed, but likely good for a long steady run if a man had to leave somewhere in a hurry.

"I'll ride Dancer back," she said.

"What about your brothers? Won't they get curious how you found her?"

"Let me worry about that. She's still Bar S property. I didn't keep her on the Triple H range." She slapped the full saddlebags and the thick cantle roll on the roan. "I picked up extras for you. Here's something you might need." She handed him a pair of field glasses, rather worn as to finish.

He raised them to his eyes and held them on the dreamlike mountains to the east. They swam mistily into view. He focused the glasses and the mountains stood out in sharp relief. He whistled softly.

"My father used them when he was an officer in the army during the war," she said. "I've taken care of all his effects. I thought they might be of value to you."

He led the roan to the water hole and picketed it. "I owe you so much," he said.

She took off her hat and looked out across the vast panoramic view in front of them. "No," she said. "I believe in you, Ken. I said before that someone had to help you."

"Did you learn anything from your uncle?"

She sat down on a rock and handed him a fresh bag of Ridgewood, almost as though she knew he was dying for a smoke and had run out of smoking material two days before. He rolled a quirley and lighted up. She thought of everything.

"He's been pretty busy," said Ruth. "Other things besides the Express robbery, but that hasn't lost his interest. The money hasn't been found as yet, but a man was observed in Naco, just over the border from Bisbee, throwing five-dollar gold pieces around as though he had an inexhaustible supply of them. He was 'stinkin' drunk,' as Uncle Jim said. He got into a fight with a Mexican over a bar girl, was cut up about the face, killed the Mexican, then got back over the border into Arizona. He paid gold for a fast horse and vanished toward the Swisshelms."

"Doesn't mean much," said Ken. "Gold pieces don't have serial numbers on them."

"They were freshly minted pieces from the Denver mint," she said.

He took the cigarette from his mouth and looked thoughtfully at her. "How long ago did this happen?"

"Two months ago," she said.

He put the cigarette back into his mouth. "He could be plumb up to Canada by now," he said.

"He told a bartender he could get all the gold pieces he wanted," she said.

Ken flipped away the cigarette, then rolled and lighted another. He was mentally working out the terrain northeast of the Naco-Bisbee area. It was rough and mountainous, much like the country he could see to the east beyond his hideout, but east of the San Pedro and of the Swisshelms. He blew a smoke ring. Due north of the Naco-Bisbee area, perhaps sixty miles, more or less, was where the Express had been blown up and robbed.

"His nickname was Shorty," she said. "That was the only name."

"I wonder how many Shortys there are wandering throughout Arizona Territory," he said. "I had a cell mate with that name. It's a cinch it wasn't him."

"Have I been of any help?" asked Ruth anxiously.

"It's a start. Trouble is I'll be back in Cochise County."

She looked at him curiously. "What difference does that make?"

He ground out the cigarette and looked to the east. The mountains he could see over there were in Cochise County. "Max Fremar is deputy sheriff of Cochise, in charge while John Slaughter is on leave. Bisbee is the county seat. I was known in Bisbee before the robbery. I spent the time before and during the trial in Bisbee jail, and was tried and sentenced there. The courthouse was always full. I sat up in the front of that courtroom throughout the trial, and was led through crowds of people every day, to and from the *calabozo* and the court-house. Wasn't hardly a soul in or around Bisbee that didn't know me and Roy."

"You'll have to go back to Cochise County to solve the robbery," she said. "There's no other way out of it, Ken."

He was quiet for a long time and then he looked at her. "I know," he said.

"When will you leave?" she asked.

"In a week. I'll cross the border south of here and head toward Naco. If I'm lucky enough to get a string on Shorty I'll head out of there without going into Bisbee. Trouble is, all that country east to the New Mexico line and north to the Winchesters is Cochise County. If Max Fremar gets an idea that I'm on the loose and in his baili- wick, he'll burn up the trails looking for me. There was never any doubt in *his* mind that we were guilty."

"He got the reward for capturing you and Roy," she said.

"He's like a damned bounty hunter," he said viciously. "He's even worse than that. He's like a scalp hunter. I knew some of them. They were paid for Apache scalps. The Army never questioned whose hair it was just as long as it was black, coarse and there was plenty of it. Man, woman or child, Apache, Yaqui or Mexican. It was all gathered up and brought in for pay, like the ears and tail of a mountain lion. That's Fremar! Some of the others at Yuma told me about him. By God, he had sent plenty of them there!"

She studied his hard face. He seemed to have forgotten she was there. "Why do you hate him so much?" she asked.

He looked at her, and his glance seemed to strike at her. "He never gave us a chance. He condemned us before he knew anything about us. He made no effort to try to find the others who were in that pass the night the Express was robbed. My brother was badly wounded.

Creased alongside the head, within a hair of having been killed. Roy was just about out of his head but that didn't stop Fremar. He struck him repeatedly about the head and face with hands the size of hams and as hard as ironwood. He struck Roy with the barrel of his rifle, *right on the place where Roy had been wounded. . ."* His voice trailed off.

She placed a hand on his shoulder. "You don't have to tell me about it, Ken."

He shook his head. "You might as well know the truth. I promised Fremar then and there I'd settle the score. He said Roy would never last in Yuma Pen and he was right. God, *how right he was!* Night after night in Bisbee jail I'd listen to Roy moaning, and sobbing, talking out of his head. The kid might have pleaded insanity, but he seemed to know he'd get out of going to Yuma if he did that, *and he didn't want me to go there alone.* He played it smart in the courtroom. That's not the word, for he went to his death at Yuma by acting sane during the trial. It was at night that he'd break down."

"Go on, Ken."

He looked at her. "And all the time Fremar knew the kid wasn't in his right senses. He could hear him at night. The whole jail could, and part of the town. Fremar could have stepped in and had the kid committed rather than sent to Yuma, but he didn't. He wanted *both* of us in Yuma." Ken slowly rolled a cigarette and lighted it, blew out a smoke ring, and watched it drift off with the afternoon wind. "It was hell at Yuma. Hell on earth. Roy was twenty years old with his whole life ahead of him. If he had been all right in the head he might have lasted out his sentence, but there wasn't any hope for him. They got to him at last."

"Uncle Jim has told us about that place," she said quietly.

His eyes seemed to strike at her again. "No one who has not been sentenced there, and spent time there, can tell you a fraction of anything about that place. When you are behind those walls a feeling of hopelessness comes over you. The worst thing is to think about cracking up and being put into the Snake Den, or worse than that, if such a thing is possible, into the Insane Cell. It pushed Roy all the way. A brutal guard helped him along the way."

She narrowed her eyes. There was something hidden in what he had said.

Ken grinned, almost evilly. "That guard won't ever have another chance to send a half-crazed kid to his death," he said softly.

She wanted to ask what had happened to the guard, but she did not dare.

Ken stood up and looked to the west. "You had better leave," he said. "I don't want you riding after dark."

"I don't mind," she said with a smile.

"I do," he said harshly.

She stood up and watched him walk to the mare. He saddled it and led it to her. She looked up at him, searching his face. "You will be careful?" she asked.

He nodded. He didn't want her to go, but she certainly couldn't stay. He had not realized how lonely he had been and how easy it was to talk to her.

"You will be back?" she asked.

He put a hard hand beneath her smooth chin and raised her head a little. "I hope so," he said.

"Is there anything else I can do for you?"

Minutes flicked past before he spoke. "You can wait for me," he said softly.

She came close and slid her arms about his lean neck. Her soft full lips met his cracked, dry ones, and for the first time in her life she knew what love was.

"You'd better go now," he said.

She clung to him. "Isn't there any other way? Can't you ask for a re-investigation?"

He laughed bitterly. "What chance would I have? They haven't found the men who really did it. They haven't found the loot. I participated in a prison break in which guards were killed. I didn't kill any of them but that won't make any difference. You couldn't convince Max Fremar that I might be innocent. No. I'll have to do it myself."

She knew he was right. Her pride in him and her love for him was offset by the thought that he was walking to his death, or back to that which was worse—the living death of Yuma Pen.

He led the mare down the trail and waited for her at the bottom. She came to his arms, but did not speak. He helped her mount, and stood there looking up at her as though committing to memory every detail of her face and the love in her eyes. He stepped back and slapped the mare on the rump. *"Adios, mi vida,"* he said quickly, as though afraid to trust his emotions.

She did not look back until she reached the mouth of the canyon, and when she did, he was gone, as though he had vanished into the thin air. She shivered a little with the loneliness. Not the loneliness that she herself felt, but that which she knew he faced, for all men's hands seemed turned against him.

CHAPTER TEN

H E ENTERED Naco at dusk, although he had waited patiently, some miles out of town, before riding into the *placita*. He no longer rode the roan Ruth had bought for him in San Miguel. Maybe Ruth trusted Charley Bodwell, but liverymen are not like bartenders, who tend to be closemouthed in their business. Liverymen always did have a tendency to run off at the mouth. "Sold that blocky roan to the Harper girl today. Said she wanted an unbranded hoss. Now, I wonder why? You boys don't suppose she takes them long and lonely rides of hers to commune with nature, like it says in the book. Well, she can't fool ol' Charley. I'd know that roan anywheres, branded or not."

Ken had ridden as far south as Bacoachi, then had followed the dry valley of the Rio Moctezuma to Nacozari, where he had traded off the roan to a Mex smuggler headed south as far as he could go because the rurales had been sniffing at his heels. Ken had taken in trade a dusty burro and twenty 'dobe dollars. He had bought an unpretentious coyote dun from a drunken *vaquero* who had run out of money before the cantinas of Nacozari had come anywhere near running out of tequila.

In Fronteras he had picked up a few worn prospecting tools which he loaded on the burro. He sold his boots and bought a pair of flat heels in order to carry out his guise of prospector. He had looked for "color" now and then in his life and knew the jargon of the trade.

All this had consumed more than a week, but he hadn't been in any hurry. He couldn't afford *one* mistake. He knew Sonora well enough from his days with "Red" Lopez. His stories had to tally. He himself could pick out a phony after a few minutes' talk in a bar, and he didn't want to have himself picked out by some sharp, half-drunken inquisitor. He'd have to bank on his harsh, withdrawn attitude and weathered face to stave off foolish but revealing questions.

He entered the plaza, which was graced by a sagging, weather-beaten bandstand with a drunk lying asleep on the splintery floor. The town was dull, gray-looking and dusty, but it was a little too early and still too hot for the evening's festivities. A *vaquero* cantered past Ken, the silver *conchas* on his saddle and bridle shining dully in the gathering darkness. He looked curiously at Ken, then raised a hand in casual greeting. Two half-naked children ran for cover when they saw the dusty, bearded gringo, and, from the shelter of a sagging *carreta,* they peered at him with bright, liquid eyes.

Two months or more had passed since Shorty had scattered largesse, in the shape of freshly minted five-dollar gold pieces, in Naco, but he would be remembered for that as well as for having killed one of the local boys. Life was cheap along the border, stories and legends were long in the keeping. Perhaps some local guitarist and composer had already worked out the verses of an interminable *cancion* about the jealous gringo, laden with golden wealth, who had fought and treacherously killed the chivalrous and courageous Mexican over the love of a cantina girl who cared not a centavo for either one of them, beyond that which they spent on her.

He swung down from the dun, then tethered both horse and burro to a rack in front of a grocery. He slapped the dust from his clothing, eased his crotch, then walked toward the nearest cantina. One was the same as another, and he could see only five of them in Naco, slightly less than the standard number for a border town of only a few hundred souls.

He looked up and down the street and across the plaza before entering the cantina. He'd have to live as though he were suspect at all times. It wouldn't be easy. Still, it was better than lying on a stinking mattress in Cell Number Six at Yuma, sick to his gut at the combined smells and night noises of the cell block, knowing there was no escape, feeling the weight of the chain that bound one ankle, as well as the ankles of five other hopeless men to the great iron ring set deep in the floor of the cell.

The bartender dozed at the end of the bar. A peon sat at a table, staring with blank eyes at an empty beer bottle, surrounded by a dully buzzing swarm of flies. Ken tapped on the sticky zinc. The bartender opened one eye, then waddled down to Ken.

"Beer," said Ken. "Cold?"

The Mexican smiled proudly, revealing one gold tooth. "*Si, senor!* We have the only ice machine in Naco. The others must buy from us."

Ken sipped the beer. It was good. Most Mex beer was better than the slop sold on the American side of the border, and cost a great deal less.

"You are traveling south?" said the bartender.

"North, *amigo*. No luck in the Sierra Madre."

"That is too bad."

Ken nodded. "Besides that, my partner was wounded by a man near Soyopa. He died sometime later."

"A bandit perhaps?"

Ken shrugged. "He was not a Mexican, if that is what you mean."

"An American?"

"Yes. By the time my partner died, weeks had passed and I had just about run out of *dinero*."

The bartender looked quickly at the half-empty beer bottle.

Ken grinned. He plucked out a 'dobe dollar and placed it on the zinc. "Not that broke . . . yet."

The bartender smiled. "The rurales? They caught this man?"

Ken shook his head. "He came north. By God! If I catch up with Shorty I'll kill the sonofabitch."

The peon raised his head and looked at the bartender. The bartender slowly mopped the sticky zinc with a filthy rag. "Shorty?" he said.

Ken nodded. He emptied the beer bottle and shoved it toward the bartender. "The ornery sonofabitch," he repeated. "Cleaned out a good part of our grubstake when he left. By God! Gold pieces they were! Five-dollar gold pieces."

The bartender placed a fresh bottle in front of Ken. Ken looked back at the peon. "Give my friend a bottle too," he said.

The peon doffed his battered hat and stood up, bowing deeply. "Cipriano Ortega," he said in the politest of tones. *"Servidor de usted."*

Ken grinned. "Mike Webster," he said. "Your servant too, Cipriano. Belly up to the bar, *amigo!*"

Cipriano wove a little as he walked to the bar. He drank the beer as though it were mother's milk, which, in a sense, it was to Cipriano Ortego, *servidor de usted.*

Ken looked at the bartender. "Help yourself on Mike Webster," he said.

"Gracias."

Ken passed the makings to Cipriano and when he was finished with the Ridgewood, Ken rolled one for himself. "Yessir," he said, blowing out a cloud of smoke. "I ever get my hands on Shorty I'll make him a helluva lot shorter than he is!"

The bartender eyed Ken. "This Shorty," he said. "A troublesome man, without a doubt?"

"Very," said Ken.

"He likes the girls?"

Ken nodded wisely. "Very much."

"There was a Shorty here," said Cipriano gravely. He hiccupped. "How long ago did you say this thing happened?"

Ken cocked an eye at the flyspecked ceiling. "Couple of months ago."

"This 'Shorty,' as you call him?" said the bartender. "He had much gold? From you, I mean?"

Ken looked down at his beer bottle. "Perhaps."

Cipriano hiccupped. "It was my cousin Hernan," he said.

Ken looked at him. "Your cousin, *amigo?*"

The bartender leaned close to Ken. "Hernan was killed in here in a fight over a girl. A *puta.* You understand?"

"Yes," said Ken with a puzzled look.

"This girl, you understand, was Hernan's fiancee. This

Shorty came in here, throwing *dinero* around as though he were sowing a field. He wanted Delicias, the girl, to come north with him, into the States. Hernan did not like this, you understand, for Delicias had almost saved up enough money for her dowry. Hernan was quick with the knife, quick enough to scar this man Shorty for life, but not quick enough to escape the bullet, you understand."

"He was very fast," said Cipriano gravely. He looked uncertainly at Ken. "Very fast."

"A tragic story," said Ken. He looked at the three empty beer bottles. "Replace those, my good friend. There is tequila?"

The bartender's gold tooth shone in the lamplight. "We have the best supply in Sonora."

"Fill a glass for my friend here. A *big* glass. He has had much sorrow."

It was dark outside. Now and then voices came to the trio in the cantina. A horse trotted by on the hard-packed *caliche* of the street.

"This Delicias," said Ken after a time. "She is here in Naco now?"

The bartender shook his head. "She has gone to Bisbee," he said. He looked at Ken. "There is more money there; more business. You understand?"

Cipriano raised his sagging head. "The *puta!* It is said she followed the man who had killed her lover."

"This Shorty?" said Ken.

"That is so."

"Maybe he is not in Bisbee now," said Ken. He reached over and filled the tequila glasses of Cipriano and the bartender.

"That is not so," said Cipriano. "Miguel Ortiz, a cousin of mine, saw him there several weeks ago. Jesus Padilla, a cousin of mine, saw him there only last week."

"You have many cousins," said Ken.

Cipriano bowed politely. "My uncles and aunts are blessed with great fertility," he said.

"Next to great wealth, what more could one ask?" said Ken.

Cipriano tried to focus his eyes on Ken. "You are a man of great wisdom ... for a gringo."

"Gracias," murmured Ken.

"You will perhaps not know him as he looks now," said the bartender. "Hernan, Cipriano's cousin, marked him for life."

"I will know him," said Ken.

Both Mexicans looked at him. Cipriano shivered a little. Ken filled his glass. "It gets chilly when the sun dies," he said. "This Delicias? Where does she work?"

"Who knows?" said the bartender. "There are many such places in Bisbee, you understand."

Cipriano drained his glass. "You will know her," he said. "A she-devil! She thinks of nothing but gold and men, and only of men because they bring her gold."

"You have Bacanora?" asked Ken of the bartender.

"The best in all of Sonora."

"A bottle then, my friend."

As the bartender waddled into the back room Ken filled their tequila glasses to the brim.

He placed five 'dobe dollars on the zinc and took the Bacanora bottle from the bartender. "Good night, my friends," he said.

Both of them nodded. "A *caballero,"* said Cipriano.

Ken turned as he reached the door. "Perhaps I may revenge Hernan," he said.

Cipriano raised his head. He flung out his arms. *"Viva Mexico!"* he shrieked. He fell flat on his back and lay still. The bartender drained his glass and refilled it. He shook his head as Ken closed the sagging door behind him.

Ken left town the way he had come, tracking east along the border toward Agua Prieta, but by the time the moon arose, he had slanted northerly to cross the unmarked border back into Arizona. An uneasy feeling came over him. This was Arizona all right. *Cochise County,* Arizona.

The moon was on the wane when he reached Bisbee. He saw the yellow glow of the lights long before he could distinguish the houses, buildings and close-in mine headings. He sat his dun for a long time, smoking, taking an occasional nip from the bottle of Bacanora before he rode on toward the town. Mule Pass Gulch rose high on each side of the thriving town, with houses clinging to the sides of the canyon, terraced tier upon tier. Here and there in the darkness he saw the mine headings, the dirty windows showing yellow light. Steam and smoke drifted from some of them, and the sound of a stamping mill came dully to him from the distance.

He left the dun and the burro at a run-down livery stable, cleaning himself up with the help of a bucket and water from the stable. He changed his shirt and put on a dark coat he had found in one of the well-filled saddlebags of the roan Ruth had brought him. He put on a hat he had bought in Nacozari. He studied himself in the cracked mirror nailed above the washing stand. Strangers came and went in Bisbee. Ken almost had a hard time recognizing himself.

He walked toward Post Office Plaza, the center of the town. Delicias would likely ply her trade in or about Brewery Gulch. It was Friday night, and pretty lively, for the day shifts had been paid that day. Brewery Gulch was alive with miners, gamblers, a few cowpokes, and a great many whores. Carefully, so very carefully, Ken drifted from saloon to saloon, until he got a line on Delicias. She wasn't working that night. A high lonesome had started her off the night before, and she had been at it all morning. A two-bit piece paid a twelve-year-old Mex boy to lead Ken to the sagging, stilt supported shack she shared with several of the other *girls*.

Ken looked up and down the street before he climbed the creaking, sagging steps to the dangerous porch that seemed to have been lightly tacked to the front of the shack. He tapped on the door and after a time he heard her grumbling in the darkness. A light flickered up inside and she opened the door to stare suspiciously at him.

"I'm looking for Shorty," he said with a winning smile.

"Who isn't?" she said bitterly. She pushed back a hank of dark, uncombed hair from her olive face. She was pretty, except for some pockmarks and the beginning marks of dissipation. She shook her head as though trying to straighten out her senses.

"Say," said Ken. "You need a drink!"

She shrugged. "I haven't got the guts to walk down and get one."

He took the Bacanora bottle from his side pocket.

She looked curiously at him. "Who are you?" she asked suspiciously.

"Mike," he said. "How about some glasses?"

"Mike who?"

He grinned. "You know *Shorty's* last name?"

She spat over the railing of the porch. "Who does?" she said. "Come on in. You look all right."

The odor of greasy food, unwashed bedding and unwashed femininity mingled with the aura of stale perfume and tobacco smoke. She lighted a cigarette and blew a ring of smoke toward him, surveying him with avid interest as she watched him fill the glasses. "I'm not working tonight," she said.

"I was looking for Shorty," he said.

She took the glass and tossed down the Bacanora. "*Jesusita!*" she gasped. "I needed that!"

He refilled the glass.

"You a lawman?" she said as she sat down and moved the bottle closer to her.

"You're a great one for jokes," he said.

She tilted her head to one side. "What do you want with Shorty?"

He sipped at the Bacanora and took a chance. "A little matter of gold pieces," he said.

She narrowed her eyes and looked toward the door. "There are a lot of people around here interested in gold pieces."

"Including you?"

She laughed carelessly. "Why not?" She emptied her glass and refilled it.

Ken rolled a cigarette and lighted it at the lamp. "Cipriano Ortega said Shorty was around Bisbee."

"That drunk?"

Ken looked at her. "He said you had followed the man who killed your lover."

She laughed again. "Hernan? A boy. He had no money. He was so quick with the knife."

Ken looked about. "And this Shorty? He lets you live in this place?"

She fiddled with her glass. The hangover was getting dulled, the temporary easing from added alcohol. "He will be back," she said bitterly.

"With more gold?"

"What is it to you?"

"Some of that gold is mine."

It was very quiet in the shack. The sound of drunken voices carried to them. An odd feeling came over Ken. It was though he were back in Yuma with Encarnacion, hiding from the Yuma guards.

"And what will you do with all that gold?" she asked.

He grinned. "I can come back to Bisbee."

She shrugged. Once again she filled and emptied the glass.

Ken took out his wallet. Ruth had put a hundred dollars in one of the saddlebags. She had forgotten nothing. "Where is he?" he asked softly.

She was silent for a long time, and two more drinks.

Ken rustled two tens together. She paid no attention to him. He upped the ante to fifty dollars.

"You will be back?" she asked in a thick voice.

"Assuredly, *mi corazon.*"

She looked unsteadily at him. "Paradise," she said. Her head fell forward and hit the table.

Ken deftly scooped the half-empty bottle from the table as it started to fall. He placed the fifty dollars in the slack bosom of her sweat-soaked dress, between her full breasts. He filled her glass once again and then left the shack. He walked down toward the bright lights of the Gulch. Paradise, as he recalled, was northeast of Bisbee, in the Chiricahuas, perhaps fifty or sixty miles as the crow flies. A mining town noted for its roughness and hell raising.

He walked toward the junction of Brewery Gulch and Main Street. It was half past ten. He stopped to let a loaded wagon grind past him and as he did so a thin man, leaning against a porch post across the narrow street, stared at him. Ken rolled a cigarette and lighted it, and as the flare of the match lighted his bearded face the man's eyes narrowed.

When Ken walked up Main toward the plaza, he did not see the man following him. He stopped once more, to restock his supply of Ridgewood, and did not see the curious face of the man outside the dirty windows of the little shop. When he came out, the man was gone, pounding down a side street on his way to the county jail where Deputy Sheriff Max Fremar was holding sway in the absence of Sheriff John Slaughter.

He was dead tired, in mind and body, and wanted a good night's sleep in a comfortable bed. He toyed with the idea as he walked toward the livery stable. At the last moment, something told him to go on. Bisbee was no place for him. He had found out what he had come there for and there was nothing else to hold him there.

The liveryman was gone from his little office. Ken saddled the dun. He left the burro with a note telling the liveryman to keep it until he got back. If he didn't show up in a week, the liveryman could sell it for its keep. Ken had no intention of coming back for the burro. He had no intention of coming back to Bisbee ever again, unless it was as a free man.

He hit the road toward the Whitewater just before midnight, riding steadily, but not pressing the dun. Time and time again he looked back along the dark, echoing road, but there was no sign of life.

All the life at that time was in Brewery Gulch as Max Fremar and the thin, loose-lipped man known as Harry prowled the saloons and the bawdy houses, asking questions about a tall, lean man with a short beard and thick mustache who had been around there that evening. It would be some time before they talked to Delicias, and they damned well would have to sober her up before they got any sense out of her, if ever.

CHAPTER ELEVEN

PARADISE BY NAME, but not by nature, or reputation. The thought was in Ken Sturgis' mind as he saw the lights of the mining town up the canyon. He had crossed the Whitewater in the cold dark hours before the dawn, riding for an hour, then walking the dun for half an hour, driving himself harder than he had the dun. By dawn he had ridden into a shallow canyon where he watered the dun from his canteen, then picketed it far out of sight of the pass road. He had ventured out on the road again in the early afternoon. The dun had bottom after its rest. There was no real rest for Ken Sturgis. The Chiricahuas had been to his left all that long afternoon, and by the time he reached a spring not far from Portal, it was dark, with a cool wind whispering down from the tree-clad heights.

The dun was just about blown as he saw the faint yellow lights of Paradise. The mining boom had faded out of the area, but there was still extensive mining going on. The mountains had seemed to move in on the town at night, and at that altitude the October night was chilly.

The wind shifted and brought the tinny, off-key thumping of a mechanical piano being played far too loud. Bittersweet woodsmoke hung in the canyon, and a scarf of it trailed along the mountainside above the town. Ken tethered the dun to a rack in front of the general store. He walked into the establishment after slapping the trail dust from his clothing.

The thin, bespectacled clerk came from the dim rear of the store. "Your pleasure, sir," he said in a tired voice.

"A dozen Ridgewood," said Ken. "Box of forty-fours. Half a dozen long nines."

The clerk placed the items on the counter. Ken checked the box of cartridges. They seemed fresh. He wasn't so sure about those he had bought from the aged Chinaman in Yuma, weeks ago, although it had begun to seem like years, rather than weeks.

"You carry oats?" said Ken.

"Some," said the clerk. "How much do you need?"

"Half a sack all right with you?"

The clerk nodded. "A sale is a sale, like the boss says. Happens I got a half sack. Need a feedbag?"

Ken shook his head. He lighted one of the long nines and shoved one back toward the clerk. "Help yourself," he said.

"*Gracias,*" said the clerk. He leaned forward as Ken snapped a lucifer into light with his thumbnail. "Passing through?" he added.

Ken nodded. "Horse got tired," he said. "I was heading for Galeyville."

The clerk blew out a cloud of smoke. "Mining man?"

"Yes."

"You look more like a cowman."

Ken grinned. "Went bust on the San Pedro," he said. "Heard one of my old partners was hereabouts.

Galeyville, they said. Figured on touching him up for a grubstake, for old times' sake. Maybe you know him? Goes by the handle of Shorty."

The clerk inspected the end of the cigar. "Like these weeds," he said thoughtfully. "Can't afford 'em, and even if I could, the boss would think I was stealing them from the stock."

"I'll give you a receipt," said Ken.

The clerk looked at him, then grinned. "That's pretty good!" he said. "Never thought of that. Shorty, you say? Shorty Gillis or Short Jaeger? Shorty Patterson?"

Ken blew a smoke ring. "Got a scar on his face," he said. "Fairly fresh."

"But you don't know his last name? Partner of yours, you said, and you don't know his last name?"

Ken glanced toward the door. "Look," he said quietly. "Shorty got into a little trouble down Naco way. Changed his name when he came up here. You know how it is."

The clerk nodded wisely.

Ken placed a five atop another cigar and shoved it toward the clerk. "Your change," he said.

The clerk stared at him. "My change? I didn't buy anything." He studied the expression on Ken's bearded face. "I get you. That'll be Shorty Jaeger."

"He's in town?"

The clerk shook his head as he placed the five in his pants pocket and the long nine in his shirt pocket. "Got a place out on the Galeyville Road. Second place on the right, about a mile and a half. Shorty likes to be right between Galeyville and Paradise, because when they finally cut him off in Paradise he can go back to the Galeyville saloons, starting out with the first and working through all of them, until he can't get a drink in any of them, then he starts all over in Paradise, and so on and so on."

"Shorty ain't changed his habits none."

The clerk nodded. "Beats the hell out of me where he gets his money," he said. "Never seems to work."

Ken relighted his cigar and eyed the clerk above the flare of the match. "A man shouldn't say things like that unless he's got some reason," he said coldly.

The clerk flushed. "Hellsfire, mister! I ain't poking into Shorty Jaeger's business! So, he takes off for weeks at a time and comes back loaded with *dinero*. Maybe he's got a rich relative or something. It's a cinch May ain't got any money."

Ken scratched his beard. "May? She still with him?"

"When she ain't working the saloons in Galeyville. Beats me how she puts up with him. Man, he can get mean. . ." His voice trailed off and he flushed again. "Sorry, mister. Don't say nothing to Shorty, hey?"

"Your opinion of Shorty is your own business," said Ken.

"*Gracias!* I'll get them oats."

Ken left the store, carrying the oat sack. He looked back and saw the store lights blink out one after the other. A few minutes later, as he filled the dun's feedbag, he heard the rear door of the store slam. Then the clerk hurried across the street, puffing on a cigar, headed for the nearest saloon with a fiver burning a hole in his pants pocket.

He slowly rode the dun along the Galeyville Road, in the thick darkness. The name Shorty Jaeger meant nothing to him. All Ken knew was that a man named Shorty had been throwing five-dollar gold pieces around Naco with gay abandon, getting up the light of money lust in all the *putas,* and killing a Mexican because of one of them. It was still a thin thread, but it was better than nothing. A spider starts an intricate web with but one thin thread, and working with incredible patience and knowhow, he weaves a web no man could create. So it must be with Ken, except that time was short. The uneasy feeling kept coming over him that perhaps his escape from Yuma had been found out, and that the battered-faced man who had been buried on Prison Hill had been correctly identified. Maybe Shorty Stiber had told the guards he had not seen Ken Sturgis get killed by a Gatling gun slug at the edge of the empty grave. Maybe they had picked up Carl Mason by now, if the desert hadn't killed him. Maybe he had admitted that he had killed the guard near the grave. Those Yuma guards were slick enough to put two and two together and come up with the name of Ken Sturgis, escaped prisoner.

He saw the dim-lighted windows of the house as he rounded a turn in the road. The odor of woodsmoke drifted toward him. A horse whinnied from a corral behind the low stone house. It wasn't the kind of country where a stranger rode up casually to a house. Both Paradise and Galeyville were just about inaccessible from the western side of the Chiricahuas, and far from the hand of the law. The New Mexico border was just about ten miles due east and Mexico itself was about forty miles due south. A handy, isolated place for men beyond the pale of the law to relax, with a fast horse handy, in case sunlight or moonlight glinted on a star pinned to a lawman's vest. Even if cut off from New Mexico and Mexico, there were always the mountains, a veritable tangle of canyons, caves, hidden trails and hideouts, once well frequented by the Apaches, who had known the value of those mountains as a stronghold. They were hardly more crafty, or deadly, than the Mexican and

American rustlers, thieves and smugglers who had found a home away from home in Galeyville and Paradise.

He looked back along the dark road. Maybe that gabby clerk was talking too much already over the mahogany, with some hard-faced, thoughtful-looking character drinking in his words about a bearded stranger who had been asking questions about Shorty Jaeger. Outlaws worked together, or they hung together. It was as simple as that.

He swung down from the dun and snubbed out his cigarette. He eased the Schofield from its holster and reloaded the cylinder with fresh cartridges. He had never seen Shorty Jaeger, but he knew some of the man's most recent history. *"He got into a fight with a Mexican over a bar girl, was cut up about the face, killed the Mexican, then got back over the border into Arizona. He paid gold for a fast horse and vanished toward the Swisshelms. . . They were freshly minted pieces from the Denver mint. . . This girl, you understand, was Hernan's fiancee. This Shorty came in here, throwing* dinero *around as though he were sowing a field. He wanted Delicias, the girl, to come north with him, into the States. Hernan did not like this, you understand, for Delicias had almost saved up enough money for her dowry. Hernan was quick with the knife, quick enough to scar this man Shorty for life, but not quick enough to escape the bullet, you understand. . . He was very fast, very fast. . . Beats the hell out of me where he gets his money. . . Never seems to work. . . Man, he can get mean. . ."*

He led the dun into the shelter of the trees and tethered it. He walked softly toward the rear of the house, with the wind blowing toward him. He stood for a long time in the shelter of a huge boulder that reared itself up from the ground behind the leaning shed. The lights were on, but there was no sign of life about the house. There was only one horse in the corral, a big gray. The saddle was atop a fence rail. A saddled paint mare was hitched to a scrub tree.

Ken walked along the side of the house. He looked up and down the dark road. It was empty. He could see a faint sprinkling of lights further up the road. That must be Galeyville.

To make an omelette you break eggs. There was no sense in him standing around wondering about Shorty Jaeger. If the man was in the house, Ken would have to confront him. Once more he checked the heavy Schofield. He turned the cylinder with the hammer at half cock, then thrust the six-shooter back into the holster. It had been a long time since he had had to draw in a hurry. He had tried out the Schofield for action and accuracy in the silence of the desert south of the border and had found it good.

He walked to the door and rapped on it. There was no sound from the house. He rapped at it again, hearing the echoes within the house. Maybe Shorty was on a high lonesome in Galeyville, or sleeping off last night's debauch. He rapped at the door for the third time. This time his keen ears caught a sound of movement with the house. He stepped back.

"Who is it?" called out a woman, her voice muffled by the thick stone walls and heavy door of the house.

"Shorty home?" called Ken.

There was a moment's silence. "Who is it?"

"A friend in Bisbee said he lived here."

Ken could hear her talking to someone. "All right," she said. "Who are you?"

"Name of Mike Webster."

The door creaked open. A buxom woman, wearing a faded, stained wrapper, stood there in the dim lamplight, pushing back a loose strand of yellowish hair. The odor of cheap perfume drifted from her, along with some other odors, not quite so pleasant. She surveyed him closely. "I don't know you," she said.

Ken smiled. "You're May, aren't you?"

She nodded, still more puzzled. "Where'd you say you was from?"

"I didn't. Happened to be in Bisbee. Friend said Shorty lived up this way."

She walked toward a door, spitting into the filthy fireplace as she did so. "What was her name?"

"I didn't say it was a woman."

She laughed. "You didn't have to. Tom'll be out in a minute."

"Tom?"

She turned. "Shorty ain't here," she said. She opened the door and entered a rear room, closing the door behind her.

"Mike Webster?" said a dry, cold voice.

Ken turned quickly. A tall man stood framed in another doorway, buttoning a shirt across his broad and hairy chest. He looked at Ken out of the sides of his eyes. His eyes almost startled Ken. They were of an incredibly light blueness.

"I'm Tom Jens," said the man. "Shorty's *amigo*. He never mentioned no Mike Webster to me."

"I knew him along the border."

"What do you want with him?"

'That's between me and him, ain't it?"

Tom shrugged. "I guess so." He walked to a cupboard and took out a bottle. "Shorty's in Galeyville. Set a minute and have a drink. Had a bad night last night. Need a slug of the hair of the dog that bit me. You?"

"Two fingers," said Ken.

Ken glanced around the dim room. The place was a

sty, thick with the accumulated odors of long and unclean occupancy.

"God damn!" said Tom.

Ken turned quickly. The tall man had bumped his head against a hanging brass harp lamp. He placed the bottle on the table and then picked up two glasses. He blew into them to clean them and then filled them. He dropped into a seat on his side of the table. "Set," he said. "May'll go get Shorty."

Ken sat down and moved back the table lamp. He heard a back door open and close and a few minutes later he heard the beating of hoofs on the road. "Shorty hitting the bottle?" he said conversationally.

"No mor'n usual," said Tom. He downed his shot and filled the glass, looking moodily at the front door. "Damned fool!"

Ken grinned. "Shorty gettin' in more scrapes these days?"

"Like what?"

"That cutting down in Naco."

"You knew about that?" Tom laughed. "By Jesus! Nearly ruined his good looks. Who'd you say told you he was up here?"

"I didn't." Ken took out a pair of cigars and shoved one toward Tom. "Woman name of Delicias," he added.

"That *puta?* She got Shorty into nothing but trouble down Naco way. It was on account of her Shorty was cut up."

Ken lighted up. "Well, Shorty paid Hernan off with a Colt, didn't he?"

Tom nodded. He downed another shot. "By Jesus, that's better! I'm beginning to feel human again. That Delicias. I'll have to go down and see her. You know her real well, eh?"

"Happened to do business with her. You know. . ."

Tom grinned and wagged his head. "Hell yes! How's she feelin' toward Shorty?"

"Sore as hell."

Tom glanced sideways at him. He didn't seem to relish looking anyone squarely in the face, keeping his light blue eyes elsewhere. "Why?" he said.

Ken blew a smoke ring and stabbed a finger through it. "Something about gold pieces," he said carelessly.

"So? Drink up."

Ken downed his drink and Tom reached clear across the table with an incredibly long arm, holding the heavy bottle easily as he poured the glass full.

Ken looked toward the door. "Maybe I ought to go into Galeyville after Shorty myself," he said.

"He'll be here. If he ain't in a saloon he's always here."

Ken grinned. "Here or in Galeyville, or Paradise. They cut him off in Paradise?"

"Last week, the dumb sonofabitch. Beat up a miner somethin' awful. Fella asked too many questions how come Shorty always had money and never worked."

"Nice trick if you can do it. No one else's business though."

Tom wagged his head. "Them's my sentiments, *amigo.*"

"Light up," said Ken.

Tom waved a long hand. "Wait'll the booze hits me a little harder," he said. "Cigar smoke is hell on a likker-sick gut."

Ken nodded sympathetically. His ears caught the sound of distant hoofbeats on the Galeyville Road. More than one horse. It would be May and Shorty. He hadn't figured on this Tom. The tall man looked as though he could well take care of himself, but his gunbelt was hanging on a wall peg, ten feet from where he was.

The hoofbeats approached the house and then stopped.

"You didn't say why you wanted to see Shorty," said the tall man.

"No, I didn't," said Ken.

Boots scraped on the hard ground outside the front door.

"That'll be him," said Tom. "He'll be glad to see you, no doubt."

"I think so," said Ken. He downed the liquor. He'd likely need it.

The tall man turned deliberately in his seat to look directly at Ken. He picked up the cigar and leaned forward for a light from Ken. Ken snapped a lucifer on his thumbnail and held it toward the tip of the cigar and as he did so the light of the match revealed a livid scar tracing a course from the top of the tall man's right ear almost to the point of his jaw. The icy blue eyes looked directly into Ken's startled eyes.

"Don't you move, you nosy sonofabitch," said Tom. "I got a cocked forty-four pointing right at your guts under this table. You know Shorty? The hell you do! You ever hear of me, you bastard? Shorty Jaeger? What's your game? Who are you? What do you know about them gold pieces, eh?"

Ken was gut sick. Years ago the saddest man he had ever known had been known as "Happy." The man facing him was at least six feet four inches tall. He heard a rear door open and close. Boots scraped in the kitchen. He knew well enough that it wasn't May, and that someone else was just outside the front door, and that wasn't May either.

Shorty Jaeger blew a cloud of cigar smoke right into Ken's taut face. Ken unfolded like a spring knife, standing up to upset the table against the tall man. Bottle, glasses and lamp went over, the lamp smashing and spilling burning oil across the floor. Shorty's pistol roared against the table. The heavy slug punched a hole through the thick wood of the top.

The door to Ken's right burst open and a man stood there, pistol in hand. Ken hit the floor, drawing and firing as he did so. The man grunted as he folded over in the middle. A second slug hit him on the top of the head, killing him instantly. He fell back into the kitchen.

Shorty cursed viciously, trying to shove the heavy table out of the way. He fired into it twice, as though the soft lead slugs might move it. Ken rolled over and jumped to his feet, firing from hip level. Shorty spun about, his light blue eyes wide, a startling contrast to his tanned, scarred face. He fired as he staggered back against the wall. The slug smashed into Ken's left biceps, driving him back with the impact. There was no pain, but a shocking sickness. He staggered toward the rear door, whirling twice to fire back. Shorty was flat against the wall. The two slugs made his tall body twitch spasmodically. His eyes still stared at approaching death. It was almost as though the bullets were holding him on his feet.

Ken turned as the front door was kicked open and a man jumped in, crouched, pistol at hip level, muzzle weaving back and forth, hard eyes peering through the thick, wreathed gunsmoke. The burning lamp oil had ignited the filthy rug. Shorty fell forward into the leaping flames. The man at the door fired once toward Ken, through the obscuring smoke. Ken staggered into the kitchen, turning to fire the last round from the Schofield. Clearly he saw the man's face. He kicked shut the kitchen door and dropped flat on the floor an instant before bullets smashed through the thin wood, splintering the kitchen side of the door.

Ken snatched up the pistol of the dead man and ran clumsily toward the rear door. He slammed his right shoulder against it. A saddled bay horse stood ground-reined near the shed. He ran toward it, turning once to drive a bullet into the rear door.

There was no time to reach the dun. He swung up into the saddle and kicked the horse with his heels, slashing the reins across the neck of the animal. It buck-jumped in pain and fear, then struck out on the road to Paradise. *The road to Paradise,* thought Ken wryly.

Shots flatted off from near the house. The echoes slammed back and forth between the mountain walls. Ken bent in the saddle, feeling the hot blood running down his left arm. He rounded a turn in the road and looked back. Smoke and flames shone through the trees. Sickness came over him with the first real waves of pain from the wound. He had to get into cover, like a wounded, hunted beast.

He forced the bay into the shelter of the trees, splashing across a shallow stream that bordered the road. Once again, he looked back. The last man alive in that burning house had been Marlin Meyner. There was no doubt in Ken's mind that it had been Meyner standing in the front doorway, looking directly at Ken through the wreathing smoke.

The wind shifted as he rode the bay through the woods, bringing with it the smell of smoke and the faint yelling of men. Killings were nothing new to Galeyville and Paradise. But he was a stranger who had killed two men in a matter of minutes in that burning house, and if Marlin Meyner had recognized Ken, the night would be filled with hard-riding men, weapons ready for quick action and coiled ropes at their saddle horns, looking for a wounded bearded man riding a stolen bay horse, and their justice would be short and swift.

There was a faint touch of moonlight in the eastern sky as he rode deeper into the woods that clothed the lower flank of the tall peak overlooking both Paradise and Galeyville. He stopped long enough in a defile to bind the wound.

The bullet was still in the flesh. He reloaded both pistols. A Winchester was in the saddle scabbard. He rode on, crossing a naked slope. He could see the lights of Paradise below him. "Paradise," he said grimly.

The moon climbed slowly up into the clear sky, shedding silvery light across New Mexico and into Arizona, against the rugged eastern flank of the Chiricahuas, touching tall Cochise Peak, miles to the right, and Fly's Peak, miles to the left, while in between them rode a bearded man, white-faced, swaying now and then in the saddle. Once again Ken Sturgis was on the run, and he had found out nothing in his quest. Nothing except that he had seen and recognized Marlin Meyner, *but had Marlin Meyner seen and recognized Ken Sturgis?*

CHAPTER TWELVE

THIRST CLAWED AT HIS THROAT, the reaction to loss of blood. He had experienced it before and it was a different quality of thirst than that which he had experienced on his lonely walk across most of southern Arizona. He stopped long enough to soak the bandage in stream water and to fill his gut with water, but he spewed most of it out before he reached the bay. The bullet must have lodged close to the bone. He looked down the long tree-stippled slope and saw the lights of both mining towns. Here and there amidst the trees bordering the road between the two towns he saw bobbing lights. He must have dripped blood somewhere. They must have figured he had been hit and had crawled into cover. By the time the moon was fully up they'd be combing the higher slopes for him. By daylight they'd be on his trail. He grinned wryly. They likely had told the local law officer, if there was one, that there had been a double killing on the Galeyville Road. Two outlaws had been killed, but this time the law was on their side. The telegraph wires would hum between Paradise and Bisbee, if they had a line south of the Chiricahuas, or a man on a fast horse might be well on his way to the nearest tele-graph office. Ken had only one choice; to get as deep as he could in the wild Chiricahuas and hole up until the search moved elsewhere and his wound had partially healed. At that he had been damned lucky that he hadn't been hit elsewhere. If it had been a gut wound, or a leg wound, they would have had him by now. Someone would have been able to identify him. If they didn't fit him out with a hemp necktie, he'd be sent back to Yuma. The gibbet would be a better choice than Yuma.

He found reserves of strength to drive himself on. He let the bay pick its way in the more open areas, and guided it when the going got rough. The moonlight was too revealing, and yet he would not have been able to find his way without it. He hardly noticed the beginning of the fantastic scenery that lay spread before him in the clear cold moonlight. A cool wind whispered through the trees and moaned softly through the canyons. Now and then he looked up at the grotesque monoliths that had begun to rear themselves from the cut-up terrain. Great cliffs, curiously carved by water, frost and wind, seemed to hang like fantastic backdrops to some mysterious play, always ready to receive the players, who never appeared.

Now and then he shook his head. He knew his imagi-nation, inflamed by fever, was playing weird tricks on him, changing the shapes of the mountains and canyons to appear like something more suitable for some far-off planet, unknown by man and inconceivable to the wildest of imaginations. Lofty forested domes and pine-edged ridges stood out clearly in the moonlight. Plunging canyons appeared on either hand, their depths unplumbed by the searching moonlight. Even in the light of the moon he could see some of the wild melange of rock coloration of the spires, monoliths and labyrinths of eroded stone. He had never seen country quite like this, and he wasn't even sure he was seeing it now except in his fevered mind.

The moon was on the wane when he reached mountain meadow country, rimmed by soughing pines. Now and then he stopped to rest the bay and to listen, but he heard no sounds of pursuit and hours past he had seen the last lights of the valley far below. Through the night song of the conifers he heard the sound of rushing water, and his thirst seemed to gain intensity. He rode toward the sound. A grass-banked stream rushed down the slope, twisting and turning, glittering in the moonlight. It seemed like an illusion, a cruel mirage, but the bay whinnied, and animals know water when they smell it. Ken slid stiffly from the saddle, wincing in pain as his stiffening wound split and he felt the fresh flow of blood. His undershirt and shirt were thickly pasted to his arm and his left hand had a glove of drying blood on it, black in the moonlight.

He dropped flat on the stream bank and looked into the clear water, the pebbly bottom a foot from his burning face. He plunged his head into the cold water and then withdrew it. He had enough sense to draw his Schofield and lay it on the grass beside him, and then his senses swam and he felt his head strike the ground.

The moon was almost gone when he raised his head. He knew he had better find cover. There was something he had to do and he wasn't sure he could stay conscious after he did it. The bullet had to come out of his arm and there wasn't a doctor for miles, nor could he risk going to one.

He led the tired bay through a moonlight-dappled wood of pines, firs and spruces, until he faced a jumbled mass of eroded rock. He picked his way through it, fighting to keep his senses, until at last he entered a great split in the rock, like a miniature, wedge-shaped canyon, which twisted and turned back on itself, while the walls rose higher and higher until he found himself in thick, wind-murmuring darkness.

To his right he sensed, rather than saw, a wide opening, and this he followed until once more he rose into faint moonlight. The wide mouth of a shallow cave showed to his right and the dying moonlight shone dully on a *tinaja*, inches deep in clear rainwater. This place would have to do. He took the Winchester from its scabbard and rooted in the bulging saddlebags. His luck changed somewhat, for in the bags were a few cans of embalmed beef, beans, a small sack of coffee beans, some flour, cans of preserved tomatoes and peaches. Best of all was the find of two quart bottles of rye. He'd need them before the night was over.

He rounded up scraps of dry wood and carried them to the cave. Inside, it had several rooms, if one could call them that, and one of them turned sharply at a right angle. He built his fire on a rock embedded in the hard-packed dirt floor. He sat there watching the fire until the growing heat allowed him to strip to the waist. He squatted by the fire, taking a nip from one of the bottles now and then, while he patiently honed his clasp knife on a rock. He passed the keen blade through the flames of the fire to cleanse it, then sat there a long time before he formed a tourniquet above the wound, placing a smooth stone over the pressure point, tightening the tourniquet as he did so. He reached for the bottle and then shook his head. He'd need what little sense he had left to get that bullet out. He dipped the knife blade into the rye, then grudgingly poured some of the spirits over the bluish bullet hole. Dark blood still welled from it.

Ken wet his dry lips, then began to cut, steeling himself almost to the breaking point as he probed. Blood streaked the white flesh and ran down his upper arm to mingle with the coagulated blood on his forearm and hand. "Ah, Jesus," he said between set teeth. Pain worked through his arm. Sweat dripped from his white face as he worked. He wanted to stop. Christ, how he wanted to stop, but he knew if he did he'd never have the guts to enter that raw wound again. If he sliced an artery he'd be done. He could stand no more. He dropped the knife, heedless of contaminating it, gripped the rye bottle and raised it, taking a jolt that would have laid a mule low, then gripped the bloody knife again. He slipped it into the wound and pried, the alcohol making a hero, or a bloody damned idiot out of him, and just before he swayed forward to fall he heard the leaden drop of the slug on the ground.

As his senses reeled, he twisted his right fingers inside the tourniquet, then seemed to float off into a whirling void, shot with streaks of bright light, like the staghorn lightning of hot summer nights on the plains.

The woman screamed, far off, but the sound penetrated Ken's unconsciousness. He opened his eyes. He was in darkness. He loosened the tourniquet and sat up, his head reeling. The scream came again, echoing down the canyon. What in God's name was a woman doing in that country?

He pulled himself to his feet and leaned against the cave wall. He shivered in the cold. Slowly he clothed his upper body, then picked up the heavy Schofield. He swayed as he walked to the cave entrance and looked out into the darkness. The haunting, eerie cry came again, and he suddenly realized it wasn't a woman at all, but a mountain lion. Where was that damned bay? He walked toward the *tinaja*. The wind was chilly, sweeping down the narrow canyon, rustling the scant brush, moaning through the rock openings.

The bay whinnied softly. He trotted to Ken. Ken stroked him to quiet him. The lion must have been prowling about for hours, smelling the horse, trying to get up enough nerve to come in close, but picking up the hated man smell as he neared the cave area.

The eastern sky seemed lighter. The false dawn was on the way. Ken led the bay to the cave and inside it, his head barely clearing the roof. The lion would move off when the dawn came.

Ken lighted a small fire and inspected the wound. The hole had been plugged with coagulated blood. There was no pus; not yet anyway. He finger-probed the flesh about the wound but felt no swelling other than that which was normal. All he had to do now to finish the game was develop inflammation, and later gangrene.

He was almighty hungry. He clumsily opened a can of the embalmed beef with his knife, cutting his fingers in the process. "I lose any more blood," he said to the horse, "and I'll be like an empty sack of flesh and bone."

He ate slowly and with relish, washing the stringy beef down with the cold water from the *tinaja*. Whoever he had killed, the owner of the bay had evidently been planning a trip somewhere. He lighted a cigar and sat at the mouth of the cave in the chilly wind, watching the eastern sky light up with the dawn. He knew now that Shorty Jaeger had been mixed up with the Express holdup, but Shorty evidently had not known who Ken really was. Ken had pulled the biggest damned fool stunt of his life in walking into that house and sitting there while May had gone for Shorty's *companeros*. Still, there wasn't much else he could have done. He had had to force a break somewhere, to get a real lead on the bandits who had cracked open the Express. Strange that Shorty Jaeger had been the only one known to have spent freshly minted gold pieces. What had happened to the rest of it? The vast majority of the loot had never been found, nor had anyone been observed spending any of it, outside of Shorty, and he had been smart enough, if that was the correct word, to spend it in Mexico, but stupid enough to spend it too close to the border. There was one question that stood out in Ken's mind: Why had Marlin Meyner stayed in Arizona Territory when he must have known he could be suspected of having had something to do with the robbery? Jim Castleman had told Ruth Harper that he had never bought the story that Ken, Roy and Bobcat had cracked the Express. Max Fremar had sent a man to ask Jim Castleman, at the time of the robbery investigation, if Marlin Meyner was an agent for the Espee. Certainly Jim Castleman must have thought somewhat about Meyner showing up in the pass with an Espee agent's badge.

Ken relighted the cigar and blew out a cloud of smoke. He reached inside the cave and helped himself to a good slug of rye. He shook his head as the rough spirits hit him. A thought suddenly struck him, along with the booze. *Marlin Meyner was still in Arizona Territory because the loot was still hidden there!* None of it had showed up, other than that which Shorty had scattered in Naco. Therefore it was still hidden! Gold was heavy and hard to transport in quantity by horseback. Somewhere, perhaps not far from the scene of the robbery, the bandits might have cached the heavy loot.

Ken looked at the horse. The man who had owned

him had been ready to leave for a long ride; a ride where he could not get immediate supplies, or *perhaps because he did not want to be seen in the area where he was traveling*. He was an *amigo* of Marlin Meyner's. Pieces began to fall into place in Ken's teeming mind. He rubbed the aching wound. It would slow him down, and further, the area around the Chiricahuas would be alive with men looking for a bearded man, likely wounded.

When the sun tipped the mountains to the east, he had erased all signs of his occupancy. Tired and weak as he was, he knew he had to get deeper into cover. He kept to as much shelter as he could as he struck further into the rock wilderness of the Chiricahuas. The Apaches called this area the Big Mountain country, and it had been aptly named. Even in his weakness, and preoccupied as he was with the throbbing pain in his arm, the wonder of the terrain struck him again and again.

Now, with the bright sunlight on the rock formations, the true colors showed in reds, pinks, yellows, buffs and salmon shadings, intermingled or separate, tinting the spires, castellations, monoliths, standing rocks and balanced rocks high overhead, while in the background of this fantasy of rock were great tree-clad heights. Streams flowed in abundance. Deer fled across distant parklike areas. A waddling bear vanished in the waving brush. Banks of fall flowers covered the slopes, clear and sharp as to color and in great and tumbling profusion.

Nature had had a free hand in the Chiricahuas, as though she had tired of standard scenic procedures and had set herself to create something altogether different from the surrounding country. She had not failed. The jumbled geology of the country was incredible to the human eye. Buff-colored rock shaded off into streaks and patches of glowing salmon, and then into bright pink, warm and pleasing to the eye. They seemed to have been daubed with a random paint brush of gigantic proportions. Pines, firs and spruces had been spread with a lavish hand, while here and there were groves of white-stemmed aspens sheltering feathery fern brakes.

He rode across a vast mountain meadow in the bright sunlight, a stranger in a seemingly uninhabited world. A world of nature where man had been left out. Porcupines waddled through sun-dappled clearings. Wild peccaries fled for shelter as they saw him. Somewhere in the shadows of the trees he heard the clear gobbling sound of a turkey. Chickadees and bluejays fluttered among the swaying trees. Once he saw a thick-billed parrot, likely far from the south, sitting on a dead branch, watching with tilted head and bright eyes as the bearded stranger rode below.

He passed from the meadows into an area where time had worked on the softer rock, cracking and shattering it over thousands of years, forming a multitude of towers, turrets, pinnacles, needles and spires of mingled colors, while through it ran a swift clear stream, hurrying past on its journey to softer, lusher lands below, on the western slopes of the Big Mountain.

At noon he stopped, unsaddling the patient bay and rubbing it down with dried grass. He picketed it in a grassy area and slowly and painfully climbed a huge, dome-shaped area of rock until he could look down over the country he had traversed. He lighted the last of his cigars and lay quietly in the warm sunlight, peering out across the beautiful area below him. He was about to go back to the horse when he saw a movement amidst a motte of trees. Five horsemen rode slowly out into the sunlight and toward the huge rock formation upon which Ken lay like a pinned zoological specimen. He did not dare move. His belly ached as he tried to push himself closer to the bare rock.

They rode steadily toward him, turning their heads from side to side, looking now and again at the ground. There wasn't any doubt but that they were searching for something, or somebody, and he knew well enough who it was. The wind was blowing from behind him, over the area where the bay grazed, and if those horses down below scented the bay, he'd never be able to get away from those five men.

The man in the lead was the biggest of them, his hat set squarely on his head, his dark coat flapping in the breeze, his rifle across his thick thighs. Ken studied him. There was something vaguely familiar about that man. The man turned in his saddle. The wind whipped his coat and the sunlight glinted from something bright pinned to his vest. An icy feeling hit Ken in the pit of his stomach. He knew now who the man was. He might have suspected. This was still Cochise County and Max Fremar was still deputy sheriff of that county in the absence of John Slaughter.

They came closer. Ken could distinguish each of their features now. The thin man not far behind Fremar was the man known to Ken as Harry. He had been with Fremar when Roy and Ken had been captured after the Express robbery. Fremar had moved fast, if he had come up there because of the two killings on the Galeyville Road. Still, it wasn't like him to move that fast to investigate the killing of a known outlaw like Shorty Jaeger. An uneasy feeling came over Ken. Maybe Fremar had been on the trail to Paradise and Galeyville *before* Ken had killed those two men.

He seemed to grow in size as he lay there. It was impossible for them not to see him, and yet they rode on, seemingly unconcerned. Maybe they had seen him and were playing that they had not in order to get close enough. They would know he was desperate. Any man who could be trapped in a house such as Shorty's and shoot his way clear, killing two out of three men, good men with a six-shooter, was no man to trifle with, even at odds of five to one.

Fremar drew rein at the bottom of the rock formation, hardly twenty yards from Ken. He did not look up. He sat his sorrel while he lighted a cigar and blew out a puff of bluish smoke. "Beats the hell out of me," he said. "He must have come up this way."

"Might have doubled back, Max," said one of the men. Fremar shook his head. "No chance. He couldn't have worked south or north from where we found that blood. He had to go west."

"Helluva lot of cover in here," said Harry. "No ordinary man could have made it this far between last night and now," said another of the men.

"He ain't no ordinary man," said Fremar. "If it *was* Ken Sturgis." He looked hard at Harry.

Harry shoved back his hat and began to fashion a smoke. "I never bought that business of him being killed in that prison break at Yuma," he said testily. "I seen him in Brewery Gulch, I tell you! Beard and all, it was *him!* Besides, that Mex woman, Delicias, described him pretty well. He was looking for Shorty Jaeger, wasn't he? Something about gold pieces, wasn't it? If Sturgis broke outa Yuma, he'd head back for the loot, because almost all of it is still hidden somewheres. Hell, we never did get a real lead on Jaeger." Fremar spat. "Yeh," he said. "We never could tie Jaeger in with Sturgis' bunch. That other man Sturgis killed, if it *was* Sturgis, had no record. In Arizona, anyways."

Harry shifted in his saddle. "I still think that woman, May, was covering up," he said. "There was someone else mixed up in that shooting."

One of the other men laughed. "You're talking like a Pinkerton man now, Harry. You find some clues, Harry? *Clues!* Hawww!"

Harry slapped a hand on his thigh, raising a little puff of dust. "I seen Sturgis, didn't I! By God, it was him! He's in these mountains somewhere!"

Fremar took his cigar from his mouth. "He won't get away," he said. "I've got men covering every pass out of this area. We warned the rurales in Sonora and Chihuahua. The troopers at Fort Bowie are sending out patrols to cover the country from the New Mexico line to the Dragoons. Posses are working up and down the San Pedro. A posse is heading east from Tombstone toward the Whitewater and the Swisshelms. A damned mouse couldn't get out of these mountains without being seen."

One of the men shoved back his hat and felt for the makings, and as he did so he looked directly at Ken. Ken was completely frozen, not even breathing, looking directly back into the man's face. Maybe he had blended into the rock and maybe he hadn't.

"Come on," said Fremar. "I don't want to stay in these damned mountains tonight if I can help it." He spurred his horse and clattered across a patch of naked rock.

The man who had looked directly in Ken's direction swiftly rolled a smoke, thrust it into his mouth and lighted it. He rode after the others. He turned and looked back once. The huge, domed rock was absolutely bare of life.

CHAPTER THIRTEEN

A FINE RAIN HAD SLANTED off and on across the Big Mountain for two days, filling the streams, bringing a wet freshness to the clear, winey air. A drifting mist hung in the lower areas between showers, and when the rain returned, heralded by the crashing peals hurled by the Thunder People, the mountains seemed to withdraw deeper into their remoteness. At night the air was cold and damp. The bears would soon be looking for a den for the winter. Ghost Face was clearly on the way from the far north.

Ken Sturgis lived like a hunted animal, which indeed he was. He had rationed his store of food and when it had run out, he had rigged snares of woven horsehair in the rabbit runs. There was plenty of water, and in the deep, twisted cave he used for a hideout, he could make his fires of dry wood he had gathered before the start of the fall rains. Pine boughs made a satisfactory bed and the horse blanket was good enough cover. He kept the bay picketed in a grassy box canyon, close to a water pan, half a mile from his hideout.

Ken had had bouts of fever from the effects of the wound, but there had been no inflammation, nothing but laudable pus. He kept the wound scrupulously clean, bathing it with his precious store of rye whiskey, although he would rather have administered it internally. He had plenty of tobacco.

After a week he took the risk of dropping a deer in a lush meadow a mile or more from his hideout. He lay flat in the grass, behind a lichened log, for a long, long time after the echo of the shot had died away in the canyons. It had taken him two days to get up enough courage to shoot, but he had to have the meat. He came back for the carcass at dusk, finding it hardly touched by predators. He buried the refuse in a cleft, covering it with rocks, saving the hide and the good meat.

So busy was he with his hiding, and his gathering of strength, that he had given little thought to his predicament. There had been time, and time enough for the word to spread clear throughout Arizona and the neighboring areas that an escaped prisoner had killed two men on the Galeyville Road. Still, he wasn't sure Meyner had recognized him, and although Fremar's deputy had insisted he had seen Ken, Fremar himself had not seemed sure.

He had to get out of those mountains before the bitter winter came to the heights. It wasn't likely that the Chiricahuas would be watched as they had been the first days after his escape from the burning house and the two dead men he had left behind. But a bearded stranger would be suspect, and reward money was like finding a gold watch after one fell into a privy.

October was almost gone when he decided to make his move. He'd have to strike for New Mexico, a hard night's ride away. The day before he planned to leave, he overhauled his gear, cleaning his guns as best he could, patching his clothing, and getting rid of that which he did not absolutely need. He dumped out the saddlebags to check the contents, and as he did so something clinked on the rocky floor of the cave and rolled out of sight beneath the pine boughs of his bed. He felt about under the boughs and retrieved a shining five-dollar gold piece, freshly minted from the Denver mint. He sat there for a long time, smoking, spinning the gold piece up, catching it in his hand and spinning it upward again. Wherever the owner of the horse and saddlebags had planned to go before Ken had killed him and taken his horse, he had never made it, except perhaps in spirit, but he had come to the house on the Galeyville Road with Marl Meyner, and perhaps he had intended to leave with him. If so, Meyner had had time and aplenty to go to the cache and clean it out. Two of his boys, as Ken figured, had been killed, so the profit of the robbery would be all Meyner's, unless some others had participated in it and were still alive.

He started for the eastern flank of the mountain in the late afternoon, riding through a clammy, drifting mist that shrouded the peaks and hung amidst the trees, filling the lower areas with a cottony-looking blanket. He was heading for the uninhabited region between the Paradise-Galeyville area, and the Southern Pacific line further north. North of the Chiricahuas was Fort Bowie, linked by telegraph line to the outside, and the soldiers had been tipped off weeks past that an escaped killer was loose in the Big Mountain.

It was hard going in the darkness. Twice the bay fell heavily, with Ken just clearing leather in time to avoid a crushed leg. Several hours before dawn he forded the San Simon, bank full from the recent rains, and knew that the

New Mexico line was only a few miles ahead. Through a fine, slanting rain he rode for the unseen Pyramids, crossing the Lordsburg Road in the late afternoon, with the bay hard spent because of the soft, treacherous going. This was sparsely settled country, mountainous and lonely.

He spent the night in a ruined adobe on the flank of the Pyramids, not daring to light a fire, gnawing on the last of his dried venison, fortifying himself with the last slugs left in the second of the two rye bottles. He managed to work up a few limp cigarettes by scraping the bottom of the two saddlebags, complete with lint, dust, and perhaps a dead insect or two. Not that he gave a damn. There had been hardly a day's easy going since he had entered Yuma Pen so many months ago.

Unless there was some break in his quest, the best thing for him to do was head east, toward the Panhandle, and look for work in the Nations. Arizona Territory was nothing but a baited trap for him.

The rain pattered on the leaking roof of the adobe and formed filthy pools on the littered floor. Ken sat in a corner, next to the old beehive fireplace, desiring a fire but not daring to light one. He wasn't quite far enough away from the Arizona line to take unnecessary chances.

During his fitful sleep he saw the face of Ruth Harper, and when he awoke in the pale, clammy light of the dawn, a bitter loneliness was within him. But he couldn't go back to her; not yet, at least. He'd have to be a free man before he could go back to her, and even if he cleared himself of the Express robbery, there were the deaths of two men on his hands. Not that they wouldn't have killed him. Only by God's grace and fast shooting had he managed to get out of that scrape.

The rain had died out during the pre-dawn hours and

was replaced by a wind that rose steadily, until by noon, as he headed east from the Pyramids, it bellowed and raged across the soaked ground, with a honed edge to it that bit through his damp clothing. Sometime around noon, with his bearings lost, he suddenly rode out on a low, windswept ridge and found himself looking down at the Southern Pacific tracks, and he remembered then that the right-of-way made a deep bend between Deming to the east and Lordsburg to the west to take advantage of the more level ground.

He sat the weary bay, eyeing the tracks, remembering all too well that not more than a year ago a westbound Express had roared along those very tracks for a fateful and bloody rendezvous in an Arizona pass. Once again, he had to make his decision to keep on heading east, away from Arizona and Yuma Pen, and the troubles that had beset him like a swarm of wasps, or to return to it and meet his problems face to face. He wanted to return to his old life along the San Miguel, although it would never be the same, but he could not return until he solved the mystery of the real bandits who had wrecked and robbed the Express. He *had* asked *her* to wait for him...

He touched the bay with his heels and rode west toward Lordsburg, thirty miles from the Arizona line.

It was dusk when he saw the distant lights of Lordsburg, and the thought of the hot food, good liquor, warm bed and all the tobacco he could smoke being there within eyeshot, and yet unavailable to him, unless he wanted to risk his neck, was enough to make him want to chew grass.

The wind shifted and brought with it a hint of more icy rain. Now and then the bay stumbled as Ken rode toward Lordsburg. It would likely be a bitter, wet night, not fit for man or beast, and especially for Ken Sturgis and the worn-out bay.

He didn't see the ramshackle house until he turned his head away from the cold, searching wind. It was a composite, of adobe, rock, timber and tin, with a big lean-to behind it. A sagging, peeled-pole corral stood behind the lean-to, with a half-collapsed shed beyond that and a privy that looked as though the wind were about to tear it loose and waft it toward Chihuahua seventy miles to the south. There was no sign of life about the place.

Ken dismounted and eased his crotch. His once-broken leg ached like a sore tooth and the wound in his arm felt like it was on fire. The bay whinnied plaintively. Ken led it to the shed. There was some old feed in it. He covered the bay with an old, musty blanket, took the Winchester from its sheath and walked toward the house. He could see the right-of-way through the gathering darkness. Between the house and the tracks was a long pile of railroad ties, ballast material and other maintenance material.

He turned toward the house. Not a light showed. The place was an uncared-for mess. He tapped on the door with the butt of the Winchester. The door swung open on creaking hinges. He looked inside. "Hello," he said. Something shot past him and he leaped back, levering a round into the rifle. He grinned as he saw the cat streak toward the distant pile of ties.

He snapped a match on his thumbnail and held it inside. The room was furnished. He stepped inside and looked about. Someone had been living there. There was no mistaking signs of recent occupancy. The smell of stale, greasy food hung in the air, mingled with tobacco smoke and un-aired bedding.

The bay whinnied sharply.

Ken blew out the match and stepped outside. A buckboard was being driven from the hard ground beside the right-of-way, directly toward the house. One man was in the vehicle. There was no use in running, Ken realized. He'd have to stand his ground until he knew how he stood with this stranger.

The buckboard was halted. The man leaned forward. "Can I help you, mister?" he said in a pleasant voice.

"I thought the place was empty."

"Looking for a dry place to sleep?"

Ken smiled. "That was the general idea."

"You can put down that Winchester then. I'm Baldy Morris."

"Mike Barker," said Ken. It was easy now to tack a new name on himself whenever he needed it.

"You et yet?" said Morris as he lifted a heavy sack from the back of the buckboard.

"I was figuring someone might have left a few stale beans in this place."

"I usually do," said Baldy with a grin. He walked into the house. "Get a fire started whilst I put up the team."

"I put my horse in the shed."

"I'll corral my team. I can put 'em in the lean-to later on.

Ken leaned his rifle against the wall, lighted a cracked-globe Rochester handlamp, then started a fire in the big, rusty stove. So far so good. When Morris returned, the fire was beginning to roar with the strong wind draft in the chimney.

"Wild night," said Morris. He stuck out a lean hand. "Pleased," he added.

"Railroad man?" said Ken.

Morris shrugged. "Not exactly. Useta be. Lost my job

about a year ago. They let me keep an eye on mainte-nance materials up and down this section. Thieves play hell with them ties and stuff if they ain't watched. Don't pay much, but I get the shack with it, and, until better times, ol' Baldy is content to sit it out."

Ken looked about the low-ceiled room.

"Tobacco over there," said Morris over his shoulder. "Smokin' or chewin'?"

"Smoking," said Ken.

"Sack of Dime Durham somewheres on a shelf over there."

Ken got the makings and rolled a cigarette, lighting it from the lamp. He watched Baldy work with expert skill on the steak and potatoes, the lamplight glistening on his naked skull. He seemed all knobs and angles, like a man toy not quite properly put together, but his pleasant voice and expansive smile made up for his awkwardness and homely ugliness.

"You headin' east or west?" said Baldy as he started the coffee.

Ken blew a smoke ring and watched it get distorted as it flowed toward the updraft from the lamp. "I ain't fussy," he said.

"Cowman?"

Ken nodded. "A little bit of everything. Figured I could get some railroading work in Lordsburg."

"Fat chance," said Baldy. He placed the coffee pot at the back of the stove. "Times ain't too good. Besides, they ain't hiring anybody they can't get a line on."

"They ought to take you back then."

Baldy opened a can of tomatoes. "Hell," he said. "They can keep their gawd-damned railroad. Low pay, hard work, and no appreciation for loyalty."

"So you're waiting for the rainbow?"

Baldy poured the tomatoes into a chipped saucepan. "Sorta," he said. He looked at Ken with his quick smile. "Maybe I'm a damned fool for waiting for it here, eh?" He studied Ken. "*Amigo,* you look downright beat-out, fed up and far from home."

"I am," admitted Ken.

"New Mexico man?"

"When I'm working here," said Ken. "California born and bred. Worked Arizona for a time."

"The border?"

"Mogollon Rim country, the Verde country, and along the Little Colorado for the Hashknife corrida."

"Hashknife boys is mostly Texans," said Baldy.

"That's why I left," said Ken.

Baldy nodded. "I always say: Treat a Texan as nice as you would your dog or your hoss and you *might,* I repeat, just *might* get along with him."

"Yeh," said Ken. "Texans is all right when they ain't full of red-eye, with a loaded cutter in their hands, bawlin' about the Alamo or the Confederacy."

"Nice boys to have in a fight," said Baldy wisely. "On *your* side. Dumb bastards would charge hell with a bucket of water." He studied Ken. "How about a snort before grub?"

"Suits me," said Ken.

Baldy took a bottle out of a cupboard. "Bacanora," he said.

"My favorite poison," said Ken.

Baldy filled a tin cup and placed it in front of Ken. "How about you?" said Ken.

"Never touch the stuff. I got my own special remedy for physical and mental ailments."

There wasn't much conversation during the meal

except: "Pass the ketchup, *amigo*. Shoot the salt, friend. Reach me the coffee pot, *hombre*."

The wind had shifted and a cold wind whined about the shack. Baldy shoved back his plate and stoked up the fire. "By Jesus," he said, "ol' winter is on the way. Gets cold as the ass on a brass monkey out here. No protection. Shoulda gone south to Mexico for this winter."

"What's holding you?" asked Ken as he rolled a cigarette.

Baldy smiled genially and held out his lean hands, palms upward, making a scrabbling motion in the palms with the tips of his fingers. "Scratch. *Dinero*. Mazuma. Cash. Spondulics."

"Smart feller like you ought to get work easy down Mexico way," said Ken. "You headin' that way?"

Ken shrugged. "I'm heading *any* way, Baldy. With the wind at my back, for preference."

Baldy nodded. "Well, I'm still waitin' for that rainbow." Ken looked around the shabby room. "Well, they say you never know where it is. Shows up in the gawd-damnedest places."

Baldy grinned. "As likely to be here as any place else. All I got to do is wait. I'm good at waitin'."

Ken shoved back his plate and cup. "I'll check the hoss," he said. "Privy comfortable?"

Baldy waved a hand. "It'll do. Brace your feet though. It's got a habit of leaning from behind you, durned near shoves a body right through the door with his drawers down."

The bitter wind struck at Ken as he rounded the side of the house. He watered the bay and walked toward the ancient privy. Beyond it, swept by the whining wind, a racetrack for tumbleweeds, he saw low sand dunes, looking rather out of place in that terrain. He walked toward them out of curiosity. A door showed at the front of the first one and as he looked more closely at the others, he saw that they too were fitted with heavy timber doors. He tried the door a the first one and found it locked.

The second one had been locked but the hasp came loose as he pulled at the handle. He peered into the cold, musty darkness. There was a faintly familiar odor in the place. He stepped inside after taking a quick look back at the distant house. He snapped a lucifer on his thumbnail and peered about in the faint, flickering light. Suddenly he blew out the match and a cold shiver ran through him. Damned fool, he thought. The place was stacked with crates of blasting powder in big black corrugated cans. He closed the heavy door behind him and shoved the loose nails back into the half-rotted wood of the door frame. He had been wondering why the railroad would bother to have a man watch a pile of ties and some heaps of ballast material. Baldy was watchman more for the blasting powder needed for railroad work than for the ties and ballast. Certainly, they wouldn't store that amount of explosives in the town, or close to it.

He visited the privy and found out Baldy was right. If you didn't brace your feet at either side of the door, the back boarding would push against you with the force of wind with enough strength to drive you to your feet in a rather unpresentable condition.

He moved Baldy's shivering team into the big lean-to and fed them from a bin. Now and then above the roaring of the wind he could hear Baldy singing in the kitchen-living room combination of the disreputable shack. He grinned. Baldy was all right, and likely glad of the company. The place would do for the night.

Ken closed the door behind him. "You were right about the privy," he said.

"You took a long time," said Baldy. "Ketchin' up like?"

Ken shook his head. "I put up your team."

"*Gracias.* Coffee pot is full again. Bacanora on the shelf. Tobacco is handy. Set and take it easy. I aim to build a couple of dried apple pies tonight. Keeps me occupied. Useta bake quite a bit when I had a hotel at Shakespeare. Mining ran out and the hotel went bust. That's the story of my life."

It was right pleasant in the warm shack. The roaring fire brought out new odors to add to the old, but when the pies began to bake, their tempting aroma drove out the offensive smells, or at least covered them up for the time being.

They covered a lot of ground over the coffee pot. New Mexico, Colorado, the Panhandle and parts of Arizona.

Baldy finally looked at the ancient waggle-tail clock that hung on the wall. "Ten o'clock," he said. "Time for my constitutional. Stoke up the fire, *amigo.* We can get into bed while the shack is still warm. It'll be cold as a well digger's ass in here come mornin'."

Ken walked to the big range and picked up some wood, and as he did so he saw the black lettering on the side of the wood box: "Kepauno Chemical Company Giant Blasting Powder." He recalled that he had seen the same lettering on the side of the crates in the powder magazine behind the house.

He heard Baldy pull out a cork. Ken opened the fire door of the stove and threw in some wood. He could hear Baldy drinking something. He turned and saw the bald-headed man with his head thrown back, pouring something from a bottle into his mouth. The lamplight showed on a blue and white label. Baldy lowered the bottle and a pungent, winey odor drifted from him. He coughed and his eyes glistened with tears.

"I thought you didn't drink," said Ken quietly.

Baldy took another swig and then lowered the bottle. He placed it in a cupboard beside a row of bottles exactly like it. "Abyssinian Desert Companion," he said over his shoulder. He carefully closed the cupboard door. "Good for wind colic, flatulent colic, botts, diarrhea, scouring, dysentery, inflammation of the bowels, bladder and kidney trouble, colds in the head, congestion, fits, the mad staggers, looseness of the bowels, inflammation of the brain and general debility. For botts, in both man and beast, it has no equal."

The wind whined evilly around the house. The fire roared up the chimney. A streamer of smoke arose from the Rochester handlamp. Baldy turned down the wick of the lamp and turned with a friendly grin to look at Ken. His grin faded. His eyes widened. His lower jaw dropped. "What the hell!" he said.

Ken waved the barrel of the Schofield. "Stand back against the wall," he said. "Facing it."

Baldy turned to the wall.

"Reach for the ceiling," said Ken quietly.

The long, lean arms extended so that Baldy could rest his palms against the low ceiling. A hard hand frisked him. Ken took a big Barlow clasp knife from a pocket and tossed it into a corner of the room. "Turn around," he said.

Baldy turned slowly. "Jesus," he said reproachfully. "After I fed yuh, too!"

Ken studied him. "You said you lost your regular job with the Espee," he said. "Why?"

"Like I said: Low pay, hard work, and no appreciation for loyalty. Say! What's this all about?"

"What was your line of work on the railroad?"

Baldy wet his loose lips. "Blasting," he said.

"You're good at that, hey?"

Baldy nodded. "The best in the Southwest. Learned my trade in the mines down Bisbee way."

Ken studied the bald-headed man. He remembered three things: finding a bottle of Abyssinian Desert Companion in the old stagecoach line station; the freshly shattered pieces of wood from a crate or box of Kepauno Chemical Company Giant Blasting Powder; the expert handling of explosives when the Express had been cracked open like a dropped melon in the pass.

Ken picked from his pocket the gold piece he had found in the saddlebag of the man he had killed on the Galeyville Road. He held it out in the palm of his hand, close to the lamp. "Ever see one of them before?"

Baldy's eyes narrowed. "Now and then," he said.

"Like earlier this year when the Espee Express was blown up and robbed in Arizona of eighty thousand dollars' worth?"

"What the hell has that got to do with me?"

Ken rubbed his bearded jaw. It was a cinch Baldy didn't know Ken. Likely had never seen him. Didn't know he had been accused, tried and convicted of the Express robbery. "Where is the loot hidden, Baldy?" he asked quietly.

"I don't know nothing about any loot."

"Where's Marl Meyner, Baldy?"

Baldy's eyes narrowed again. "I don't know him."

"Shorty Jaeger?"

"I don't know no Shorty Jaeger."

Ken grinned. "You ought to," he said. "They're down

in Sonora, living like kings, throwing gold pieces around like chicken feed. Living it up with the booze, the *putas* and the best horseflesh in Mexico."

"The dirty sonsofbitches!"

"We wasn't supposed to use that *dinero* for five years, Marl said! By then it would blow over and we could go back for it together and head for Mexico! Oh, the dirty, double-crossing bastards!" Baldy stopped and stared at Ken. "How come you know all about them? You a lawman? Espee agent?"

"Never mind," said Ken. "Where did they hide the loot?"

"What difference does that make now? It ain't there, according to you. *According to you.* . ." His face changed into a mask of evil hatred. "Hellsfire! You said you knew they had it and you still want to know where it was hid! You tricked me, you coyote!"

"They couldn't have moved the gold very far," said Ken.

Baldy shook his head. "Look," he said quietly. "If I talk, can you get me off easy? Like state's evidence?"

"I think so," said Ken. Lying was getting easier every day for him.

"Where are they?" asked Baldy.

"Shorty is dead."

"What about Meyner?"

"He's still loose."

Baldy paled. "If he finds out I talked!"

"Let *him* take the rap," said Ken. "You want to try the air on Prison Hill in Yuma? There won't be any Abyssinian Desert Companion there."

Baldy nodded. "I trusted them bastards," he said. "How stupid kin a man get? They was likely aimin' to go get it, hey?"

"That was the idea."

Baldy lowered his arms a little. "If a man was to look near the old stagecoach station, he might do some good for hisself," he said.

"Where exactly, Baldy?"

Baldy sniffed the air. "Pies is burning," he said.

"Take them out."

Baldy gratefully lowered his arms. "Well, if they do put me in Yuma they could use a good baker, couldn't they?"

"You're a natural, Baldy. With a light sentence, like say a year or two, working in the bake shop, you'll survive. It's better than digging graves for your cell mates on Prison Hill."

Baldy shivered. He walked to the stove and opened the oven. He picked up a potholder and reached inside the oven, taking out a juicy pie. Suddenly he whirled, hurling the steaming pie at Ken. It glanced from his left shoulder, driving a lance of pain into his wounded arm, splattering hot apples and juice against his bearded face. He staggered back.

"Yieeee!" screamed Baldy. He jerked a butcher knife from a rack, balanced it, then hurled it with deadly accuracy. Ken was half-blinded with the hot juice, but he had the instinct to leap to one side. The knife tore through his right upper sleeve, slicing through the skin, pinning him to the wooden cabinet behind him. Baldy snatched a second knife and hurled it. It whipped past Ken's neck, the handle grazing it. Baldy snatched the last of the knives, a thin sliver of honed steel, a long-bladed boning knife. He kicked a chair out of the way and closed in silently on Ken like a lean hunting cat, sweat dripping from his bald head, and his ugly face twisted into a frozen grimace, the eyes glittering madly in his head.

Ken did the border shift. The Schofield smacked solidly into his left hand, thumb cocking the big spur trigger. He fired at hip level. Baldy spun halfway about but swiped viciously at Ken with the knife. The keen blade ripped through his coat and shirt, tracing a line across his chest. He fired again, catching Baldy in the kidneys. Baldy fell forward, the knife tinkling on the hard-packed earth floor. He twitched spasmodically, his lean fingers clawing through the mess of crushed pastry and hot apple slices on the floor, and then he lay still.

The fire roared in savage delight, leaping up the rusty stovepipe to meet the bitter wind sweeping down from the north, trailing a scarf of smoke and fat sparks across the open ground toward the dark line of railroad tracks.

Ken holstered the smoking pistol and pulled the knife from the cabinet, feeling the hot blood trickle down his right biceps and along the forearm. There was a line of burning pain across his chest where the knife tip had scraped. He walked to the cabinet and felt about on the shelf beneath the neatly ranked rows of Abyssinian Desert Companion until he found gauze and plaster. He bandaged the arm and the chest wounds. Mechanically he removed the second crusty brown apple pie from the oven and placed it on the table.

He couldn't stay in this house of the dead, and yet he was just about at the end of his string. He listened to the bitter whining of the cold wind. There was no choice.

It took him the better part of an hour to ransack the house in his search for gold pieces or a map indicating exactly where the loot had been buried, but he had no luck. The stove fire was dying out by the time he had finished. He gathered a sackful of grub, tobacco, the bottle of Bacanora, and a disreputable, stained and faded sheep-skin coat. He wrapped the cooled pie in some newspapers and slid it into the sack.

The last thing he did was to carry Baldy into the little bedroom off the kitchen and dump him on the bed. He stripped the dead man to his suit of Long Johns and covered him with the sour-smelling bedding. Beside and underneath the bed he piled newspapers and firewood. A can of coal oil was sufficient to soak them thoroughly. The wooden walls of the room had been thickly papered with old newspapers and the shabby furniture was bone dry. Carefully he made sure there would be no signs of his having been there. Every year, when the cold weather came, there were stories about people being burned to death in shacks because of faulty stoves, pipes or flues, or because they smoked in bed. As he worked, he remembered the jacal in Yuma, and of how he had set it afire to cover his escape from Yuma Pen. The shack was far enough from Lordsburg so that it would be well ablaze before anyone spotted it, and besides, they wouldn't be too anxious to close in on a burning shack on a windy night with maybe a ton of blasting powder lying in those earth magazines.

He made a coal-oil-soaked wick out of a strip of bedding, laying it from the bedroom into the kitchen. He rummaged around until he found a stub of candle. He wrapped the end of the improvised wick about it and placed the candle on the floor. The grease would soak into the wick, the flame would burn low enough to set it off in about an hour and a half. It would take maybe half an hour for the fire to get a good hold, and maybe another half hour to an hour before it would be seen.

He picked up the food sack and the rifle, blew out the reeking lamp and looked at the guttering flame of the candle, protected from floor drafts by a shield of greasy cardboard. He closed the door behind him.

Ken used the bay's saddle on one of Baldy's team of mares. He broke the two upper rails of the peeled-pole corral and loosely tethered the other mare in it. When the fire caught hold, she'd break loose and make for the hills. Ken would ride the other mare far to the other side of Lordsburg and give the bay a chance to gain back its strength. He'd turn the other mare loose and she'd likely wander back to the Lordsburg area in a day or two. By that time, he'd be safely into Arizona Territory. "Safely," he said with a dry laugh as he rolled a smoke and lighted it.

He looked back just before the shack was out of sight "You woulda made a helluva fine cook at Yuma Pen, Baldy," he said. "They sure coulda used you."

He turned south from the right-of-way and rode steadily toward the distant hills. The wind roared wildly through the cold night. It was a long, long way to a certain railroad pass in Arizona.

CHAPTER FOURTEEN

TWO THINGS HAD DRAWN Ken Sturgis back into Dragoon Pass: the need for water and a gnawing curiosity that had been within him ever since he had ridden from the east toward the great, hogbacked ridge of rock through which the pass had been cut by nature and improved by man. He had crossed the border between New Mexico and Arizona at night, holing up during the day, then striking west again at night, passing through the dark and eerie Apache Pass, with no sound other than the faint moaning of the cold wind and the striking of the bay's hoofs on the hard-packed road. He had crossed the dry, flat country south of Dos Cabezas until in the distance, beneath the faint light of the moon, he had seen the looming Dragoons, north of which was the railroad pass. In all that time he had not seen a single human being, although he had seen the distant, winking lights of lonely ranches and little settlements through the cold and windy darkness.

The pass was just as lonely and empty as it had been when Ken, along with Roy and Bobcat, had camped there in their hunt for the horse thieves. Come to think of it, they had never had a chance to run down those horse thieves. It was another addition to the score Ken held against those who had wrongfully committed Roy and him to Yuma Pen.

He drew his Winchester from its sheath and loaded the chamber, carrying it in his right hand while he led the bay up the steep and crumbling trail to the water hole. There was no sign of life along the broad shelf where Ken and his companions had camped that night so many months past. The wind moaned eerily, thrashing the dry brush. He watered the bay and scouted about, looking for sign, but the only things he found were horse droppings that crumbled to the touch, a pile of rusted tin cans and the black areas of fires long since extinguished. One of them might have been the very one where Bobcat had buried the bean pot containing the beans concocted according to the "receipt" given Bobcat by the Maine man in Huntsville Pen.

The faint moonlight glistened on the rails far down in the rocky pass. He stood there for a time, leaning on a stunted tree, looking down at the site of the train wreck and robbery. The maintenance crews had cleaned up everything except the smoke stains on the rock walls of the pass. That, and the wrongs that had been committed against three innocent men. No one could do that except Ken Sturgis, and he wasn't sure how much longer his string of luck would stretch. He had stretched it to the snapping point a great many times since he had escaped from Yuma Pen.

He filled his canteen and led the bay along the rock shelf until he found a broken place where he could lead the horse up onto the mesa land north of the pass. He looked down on the flat land east of the pass and saw the dim, crumbling shell of the old stagecoach line station. There was no use in him hunting for the cached loot, if it was down there, until he had some rest and until he could see well enough to make a real hunt out of it. It would be dangerous. If he was seen there he'd have to make a run north toward the Winchesters, a good fifteen to twenty miles away, unless he could double back south of the right-of-way and get into the Dragoons.

Ken picketed the bay in a deep draw and fed him, then he took blanket and food and climbed into a rocky bowl, out of the searching wind. He risked a small fire for his coffee and bacon. When he was done eating he extinguished the fire and wrapped the blanket about himself, settling in a niche from where he could see down to the stagecoach station. He rolled a cigarette and lighted it. As he moved his wounds drew, making him wince in pain. Three times he had had to squeeze the matter out of the arm wound Baldy Morris had given him. He shuddered to think of what would have happened if he hadn't stopped Baldy with a soft-nosed forty-four slug.

Despite his resolution not to kill in his effort to clear himself and the memory of Roy and Bobcat, he had been forced to kill three men. Each of them had been involved in the Express robbery and had let Roy and Ken go to prison. Ken felt no remorse for killing them, other than that it had started a hunt for a bearded stranger whom some suspected *might* be Ken Sturgis.

Maybe he was a fool for coming back to the scene of the crime. It had been weeks since he had left Galeyville a whoop and a holler ahead of those who had been hunting him. In that time Marl Meyner could have returned to the pass area alone and moved out the cached gold, although it would have taken plenty of time and a great deal of risk to transport it elsewhere. That is, if it really had been cached in the area. Baldy was, or *had* been, the type of man who'd tell a whopper with a perfectly straight face. Still, Ken figured neither Shorty Jaeger nor Baldy Morris could have had the shrewdness and the diabolical ability to plan such a crime perfectly, to the last iota, then cover his tracks as Marl Meyner had done. There wasn't any doubt in Ken's mind that Marl was the brain behind the bandit corrida. He had been clever enough to dupe his confederates into caching the gold, for five years, as Baldy had said. In that five years, unless they'd check on Meyner, he could surreptitiously drain off the gold, keeping the greater majority of the loot for himself and then dropping out of sight while his poor fools of confederates would have to be satisfied with a handful of gold pieces. The big mistake Meyner had made was in letting Shorty Jaeger advertise his part in the robbery by throwing around a few gold pieces. On the other hand, Shorty hadn't looked or acted like a man anyone could handle. He had been a ring-tailed roarer, tough as an old boot, with a low boiling point, and even a hardcase like Marl Meyner could have hardly kept Shorty's fingers out of the loot. It was all to Meyner's credit that he had kept Shorty, at least, from doing more than just hen-scratching the mass of gold.

He slept fitfully, off and on, all during the windy night, and it was the sun that awakened him, shining bright from the east, driving off some of the lingering cold. Ken risked a small fire to heat his coffee, eating some of the cold bacon from the night before, and the last slab of Baldy Morris' dried apple pie, crushed, shapeless and slightly stale, but delicious all the same. He kept under cover as he checked the bay.

In any direction he looked from his hideout, there was no sign of life. During the early part of the morning, he was startled to hear the long-drawn-out whistling of a train approaching from the east. It was a freight, laboring up the grade and through the pass at a slow pace, leaving a trail of thick smoke across the clean sky and empty desert country. He heard it for a time until at last it was long gone down into the Valley of the San Pedro.

In the early afternoon he was satisfied there was no one in the immediate area of the pass. He worked his way down the rock-strewn slope and through the tangle of brush until he could approach the old stagecoach station from the rear, taking advantage of every dip and swale of ground, every scrap of sparse cover, until at last he reached the rear of the station. The old corral had completely collapsed and the big rock privy had lost part of its rear wall. The air of desolation, of decay and of utter loneliness hung about the place like a winding sheet.

He darted into the station, looking back over his shoulder to see if he had been spotted by anyone, but the area between the station and the distant railroad tracks was deserted. Not a sign of life showed in the brooding Dragoons south of the right-of-way. Far, far to the south a thin thread of smoke stained the clear sky.

He leaned his rifle in a corner and set about in a systematic search of the place. Likely it would take him days of patient hunting to cover the whole place. Each day would be fraught with danger, for if a single person saw him and carried the news to the law, or the Southern Pacific, he might be trapped in the old ruins and that would be the end of everything.

His first inspection was for outward sign of any digging, or displacement of the thick rock walls. Here and there he did find signs of digging, but this wasn't anything unusual. Treasure-seeking was a legitimate, although as a rule profitless business in the Southwest. Any old ruin was fair target for treasure-seekers. As if the stagecoach company would have hidden "treasure" in a line station.

He checked each empty room in turn and found no sign or clue of any treasure being secreted in it. He was working through the big dining-barroom combination when a thought struck him. "If a man was to look near the old stagecoach station he might do some good for hisself," Baldy had said. *Near* the station, not in it!

Ken stood in the shadow of the big gateway and studied the area. It was all pretty much the same. Rocky, with drifts of windblown sand, stippled with hardy brush, and beyond it to the east the black-looking surface of malpais. The hopelessness of the situation struck him again.

If the loot *was* hidden hereabouts, one could trust Marl Meyner to have done a thorough job of it.

Ken rolled and lighted a cigarette. There was one other solution, dangerous as it was. Find Marl Meyner and force him to reveal the secret. It might be easier at that to hunt through the malpais instead.

As the afternoon lengthened and began to die, he worked thoroughly about the ruins with absolutely no results. The only thing he found was the old bottle of Abyssinian Desert Companion left there by Baldy Morris so long ago. It was already turning purplish from the days of burning sunlight, and the now illegible label was almost gone.

His food would only last another day or two at most. The nights were getting bitter cold. He must either forget the whole thing and strike out for other areas, never to return, or else go for supplies and make a semi-permanent camp near the station until he found that for which he sought. That was dangerous. Someone would see him.

He walked slowly back to his crude, uncomfortable camp. As he did so he heard the far-off whistling of an east-bound train. He was in his hideout when he heard the train labor through the pass and begin the long haul toward the New Mexico line. In the gathering shadows he felt the exquisite loneliness in the mournful whistling of the train. That, and the howling of a coyote on a moonlit night were to Ken the two loneliest sounds in the world. "Moonlight," he said. He looked at the darkening sky. There would be a moon that night, clear and cold.

He stumbled over a rock and the impact lifted it from the ground. He kicked it to one side. The upper portion of it, that which had protruded above the earth, was lighter in color, as compared to that which had been beneath the soil. He recalled something he had learned years ago, from an old Apache tracker who had worked with the Army tracking down bronco Apaches: A displaced rock is darker on that part which was under the soil, lighter on that which was in the open, and the darker, lower portion is usually the heaviest. He rolled a cigarette, eyeing the rock. Something else came to his mind. Disturbed earth is usually different in color and texture from undisturbed earth. He recalled looking down from heights and seeing the outlines of long gone habitations on the lower ground, although if one stood on the very ground, it was almost impossible to see the site unless ridges of earth or rock indicated something had once stood

there. There was another thing he had learned from the Apache tracker: If, in following a faint trail through dense brush, or timber thickly filled with brush, you lost the trail, there was a way to find it. You closed your eyes, then opened them suddenly, facing the direction in which the trail should be. Keen eyesight could spot the faint difference between the undisturbed brush and that which had at one time or another been disturbed.

He looked down at the stage station. It stood out clearly on the bare ground. Beyond it he saw a faint regular pattern on the ground, shaped like a rectangle, perhaps indicating the site of a former building. The stage line had run through the area some years prior to the War between the States, about thirty years past, and the original stage stations had been crude, defenseless shelters for a few men, with a rough corral for the mules and horses. He had walked right across the spot several times, and yet he had not seen any indication that there had been a building there.

He quickly climbed higher on the rough, brushy slope and looked down again. This time the rectangular pattern showed more clearly. There was little light left. He scanned the ground, foot by foot, closing, then suddenly opening his eyes, lining up his visual inspection with the corners of the station, the corral and the old privy. He narrowed his eyes. Beyond the station, between low-rolling humps of stony soil, there was a faintness in the soil texture as though there had been a deposit of a different type of material there. He cut branches from a nearby bush, lashed them together in a crude tripod, and set it up on a flat rock. He lined it up with the faint spot, then scrambled back so that he could peer through the V shape of the tripod top. He set up a second tripod, lining it up with the first by means of a straight branch that pointed directly at the faint spot, just this side of the dark mass of malpais soil. Just as he finished, the light was gone, and along with it, the fainter patch of soil.

He walked down to his camp and rolled a smoke. "Probably the site of an old privy," he said bitterly. He lighted the cigarette. A cold wind searched up the dark slopes. Ken shivered. He couldn't live out there much longer. His strength had taken a terrible beating since he had escaped from Yuma. Long hours on the trail, poor food and little enough of that, harsh, uncomfortable camps and several wounds had not helped his body, and he also felt his determination weakeing as it had before he had met Baldy Morris. How much longer could he go on?

He ate most of the last of his food, then took his rifle and canteen and walked through the darkness over the rough terrain until he could look down into the dark trough of the pass. It seemed deserted. He worked his way down to the water hole, drank deeply, then filled the big canteen. By the time he had smoked three cigarettes and scouted the rock shelf from one end to the other, there was a faint trace of moonlight in the eastern sky.

He walked softly down the trail to the right-of-way and found a tool shed built of thick, rough lumber. He pried off the door lock with a rusty iron bar he had found in the weedy ditch, likely a piece of the wrecked train overlooked by the maintenance crews that had cleaned up the mess. He lighted a match and looked about, selecting a pick and a spade from the tools racked against a wall. He forced the heavy nails of the hasp back into the holes and then climbed swiftly up the trail. As he reached the top of the trail he saw that the eastern sky was lighting with the promise of the moon.

The wind died away and the night became quiet. Ken waited patiently in his hideout until the moon was high above the distant Chiricahuas to the east. He sighted through his crude theodolite, estimating the distances between the low humps of ground, and from the malpais edge to that of the faint spot; then he triangulated from the stage line buildings. It was rough, crude and hardly accurate, but it was the best he could do.

Ken took the tools and his rifle and walked down the slope. The empty loopholes of the stage station stared at him like the eyes of a dead man. The country seemed completely empty of life but as he walked toward the place at which he had selected to dig, he heard the faint, far-off crying of a coyote.

The low hump of ground to the south protected him from the sight of anyone along the right-of-way. He loaded the chamber of the rifle and placed the hammer at half cock, leaning it against a rock. He stripped off coat, gunbelt and shirt, then started to dig. His left arm soon began to ache and throb as he worked down through the upper layer of soil. It seemed hard, well packed, and yet it was at the spot he had sighted from the heights, although he couldn't distinguish it from where he now stood, virtually on top of it.

The moon rose higher and higher, with the heaps of earth on each side of the hole rising too, but slower than the rise of the moon. He stopped often for a rest. Blood leaked from the slash on his arm and his left arm was an aching mass of bone and flesh. Sweat dropped from his lean face despite the coldness of the desert night.

He had been digging for almost two hours when his spade struck something that gave a little. He dropped to his knees and pushed aside the harsh, stony earth with his blistered hands. He cleared a wooden surface of old timbering. "By God," he said between his teeth. "I hope this ain't the old privy. Just the Sturgis luck at that."

He levered up some of the timbers with his pick, then scooped out the earth that flowed into the cavity beneath the timbering. He got down into the hole and peered closely at the wood beneath the timbering. He could see the surfaces of three small, stout wooden boxes, fitted with wing nuts. He wiped the sweat from his face and worked unsteadily at the wing nuts, forcing them around against the resistance of the sand that had packed about the rusting threads.

He pried up the lid of the box with the edge of the pick. The moon had risen high enough to slant its rays down into the hole, and the light glistened on the golden content of the box. He had found at least part of the hidden loot of the Express robbery. His luck *had* kept up.

A shadow fell across the box. Ken looked up. A man stood at the edge of the hole. Ken's blood ran cold as he looked into the broad, impassive face of Max Fremar. The black, unwinking eye of the Winchester muzzle pointed directly at Ken's head. In the taut silence he heard the far-off, wailing cry of a coyote.

CHAPTER FIFTEEN

"**G**ET OUTA THAT HOLE," said Fremar in a flat voice.

Ken climbed out of the hole, feeling the sand run into his worn boots. The wind had begun again, swiftly cooling the sweat on Ken's face and feeling through his damp undershirt for the warm flesh beneath.

Fremar studied Ken. "By God," he said. "Harry was right. It *was* you he seen in Bisbee, wasn't it?"

"How would I know?" said Ken.

"Don't play cozy with me! You hightailed it for Paradise, didn't you?"

There was no use in lying. Ken nodded.

Fremar wet his thin lips. "Killed two men too, hey?"

"*They* would have killed *me.*"

Fremar grinned, but there was no warmth in his flat eyes. "Where's the other one?"

"I don't know."

"Who was he?"

Ken tried to avoid those probing eyes. Once before

he had tried to reason with this law hound. Once before he had tried to involve Marlin Meyner in the robbery.

"You hard of hearing?" asked Fremar. He shifted the rifle in his huge hands.

Ken knew that rifle and he knew Fremar's way with it. He handled it like Bill Savage had handled his iron-wood club, and both of them had used their particular weapons with terrible effect on Roy.

Ken couldn't reach his own rifle. His gunbelt and the Schofield lay at the far side of the gaping hole. "This is the loot," he said, jerking his head toward the hole. "Isn't that enough to clear me?"

"You think this'll free you? You knew it was here all the time. Beats the hell outa me how you hid it so well. We covered damned near every inch of this ground with iron rods, prodding and poking. We had Papago and Tonto trackers in here for days looking for sign. Well, by Jesus, Sturgis, you hung yourself for sure this time. I always knew you had the key to this mystery."

"I swear to God I had nothing to do with that robbery."

Fremar smiled. "That's what you said in court. A jury never believed you, nor do I. How you got out of Yuma is beyond me. They said you was killed and buried there. You're a healthy-looking ghost, Sturgis, beard and all!"

"Let me put on my shirt and coat," said Ken.

"Freeze, you bastard! Me and the boys froze out here many a night this past week or so. We had a feeling you'd be heading this way. I was right."

"Look, Fremar," said Ken quietly. "I'm not the man you want. It was Marlin Meyner who engineered the whole deal. Shorty Jaeger was in on it and likely that other man I killed. Baldy Morris did the blasting. They planned to let the loot lie for years before they came back for it."

Fremar tilted his head to one side. "Sure, sure," he said soothingly. "You got fine witnesses, Sturgis. Jaeger and that other *hombre* been buried for weeks. They say a man named Baldy Morris burned to death in his shack outside of Lordsburg. *Accidentally* ... Or did you have something to do with that too?"

It was no use. Ken could almost feel Yuma Pen closing *in* on him again. He could almost smell the foul odor of the place and the utter hopelessness of it. They'd never let up on him now. He'd die under their punishment, or lose his reason, and the last was worse than the first. It wasn't really death he feared, but the cruel manner of it.

"We had a tracker watching this place," said Fremar, almost as though to himself. "We took turns camping in the Dragoons. Lucky for me, I was at the camp last night when the tracker showed up, saying a bearded stranger was poking around here. Imagine my surprise to find *you* here. Got to buy Harry a drink or two. He was right, for once in his stupid life."

There was no sign of other men behind Fremar. A horse had been tethered in front of the old stagecoach station. Fremar had come alone to savor fully his triumph.

"Git!" said the lawman. He pointed toward the horse.

Ken reached for his shirt and coat and the rifle barrel caught him across the bowed shoulders, driving him sideways into the hole. Rage flashed through his system; a cold, killing rage that upset all reason. He thrust a dirty, blistered hand into the coin box and scooped up a handful of the heavy gold pieces, flinging them in a glittering shower toward Fremar. The big man cursed as the metal stung his face. He jumped to one side. A gun cracked loudly over the hole. Fremar staggered. Ken stared at him. The man had not fired his ready Winchester. Fremar dropped his rifle and fell heavily to one side against the heaped earth. For a moment he stared beyond Ken and then a gush of blood, black in the silvery moonlight, poured from his slack mouth and he lay still. The acrid odor of gunsmoke hung in the hollow.

Ken turned to look up into the set, handsome face of Marlin Meyner, standing at the head of the hole, with a smoking Colt in his gloved hand. Meyner smiled. "When shall we three meet again?" he said quietly. He looked at Fremar and then at Ken. "I didn't expect to find you two *amigos* together on top of *my* gold."

Ken felt a slow draining of his courage. He had been saved by Meyner, just to die at his hand instead of the guards at Yuma.

"By Godfrey," he said, "you've been doing me favors all along, Ken. I owe you something beside a slug in the back. You got rid of Shorty Jaeger and Jim Conroyd for me, and then Baldy Morris suddenly up and burns himself to death."

"That leaves you alone of all the corrida that robbed the Express?"

Meyner nodded. "Sorry to say we lost one of the boys in the robbery. One other was mysteriously murdered between here and Paradise. Another one, by sheer accident, you understand, was shot by Shorty Jaeger. Sad . . ."

Ken looked down at the loot. "You can hardly get this out of here alone." Somewhere, likely within sound of the gunshot, must be some of Fremar's deputies, or the tracker.

"I know what you're thinking, Ken," said Meyner. "I

don't aim to wait here until Fremar's boys show up. Start filling in that hole."

Ken began to heave the earth back into the hole, glancing sideways now and then at his rifle.

Meyner walked to the top of the southern sand hump. "No one in sight yet," he said. He looked down at Ken. "Once you get that hole filled, I've got a proposition for you."

"A shot in the belly or in the back?" grunted Ken.

Meyner laughed. "I'm not such a damned fool as that."

Ken filled the hole in a fraction of the time he had taken to dig it. Under Meyner's direction he smoothed the ground with brush.

"Riders crossing the tracks," said Meyner. He looked at Ken. "Throw in with me, Ken. You've earned a split of this loot. We can ambush those boys and take their horses. By the time a posse starts after us we can be safe in the Chiricahuas. We cache the mass of the loot there, taking enough south of the border to live like *dons* until we can come back for the rest of it. What do you say?"

Ken nodded. "Fair enough," he said quietly. "I've suffered enough to have earned that gold."

"Put on your shirt and coat."

Ken shrugged into the shirt, buttoning it halfway up. He pulled on the coat. "I'll need a gun," he said.

"You'll get it when you need it."

Meyner stepped back and his right boot sank into the soft earth that filled the hole, throwing him off balance. There is an instant when a man of fast reflexes can and must act. Ken snatched up the piece of brush with which he had smoothed the hole, lashing it across Meyner's face. Meyner cursed. His Colt exploded, the slug flicking past Ken's left ear. Ken dived for the rifle, snatched it up and rolled over and over as two slugs slammed into the ground where he had been. He ended belly down, thrusting forward the repeater. He fired upward. Meyner grunted, then fired again, the slug rapping into the ground inches in front of Ken's face, half blinding him with gravel. Ken fired blindly again and again. There were no answering shots. Nothing except the echoes fleeing along the face of the distant ridge and dying hollowly away in the deep pass.

Ken got slowly to his feet. Meyner lay face down, his smoking gun clenched in his right hand, his left hand digging down into the loose earth as though to get the gold lying beneath it. Hoofs thudded on the hard ground south of the station. Meyner was dead, now no one would ever believe Ken's highly improbably story.

Ken dropped the hot rifle. He was through killing, no matter what happened to him from now on. He walked toward the opening between the two humps of sand and rock. He stopped in the opening, raising his blistered hands in the air.

Three horsemen slowed to a walk as they saw him. The moonlight shone dully on rifle barrels and on the badge pinned to the coat of the leading man. It was the thin man known as Harry. He leaned forward in the saddle. "Where's Max?" he called out.

"Dead," said Ken.

"You murderous sonofabitch!" said Harry. "I knew I shoulda come with him. No, he had to do it alone, for all the glory!"

"Take it easy, Harry," said the second rider. It was Jim Castleman.

The three horsemen stopped in front of Ken. The third rider, a dark-faced breed tracker, kept him covered with his rifle.

Castleman whistled softly as he saw the two bodies. He looked at Ken. "So you were really mixed up in it after all?"

Ken opened and then closed his mouth. It wasn't any use. They'd never believe him.

"By God," said Harry. He looked at Max. "Just when he was ready to make a hero outa himself and save his job. John Slaughter come back a week ago and heard some of the stories about Max. He was ready to bust him outa his deputyship when Max asked for a chance to clean this thing up. Well, he done it all right, but it won't do ol' Max any good."

Castleman shoved back his hat. "Where's the loot?" he said.

"Under your feet," said Ken dryly.

"All of it?"

"I can't say."

"You know what this means?" said Castleman quietly

Ken nodded.

Castleman shook his head. "Beats the hell outa me," he said. "I never could believe you and your brother were mixed up in this."

"They weren't," a weak voice said.

Castleman whirled. Marl Meyner had raised his head. He smiled thinly. "It's no go for me," he said weakly. "Ken cut me to pieces with that damned Winchester. Fair enough. I intended to get rid of him anyway after I used him."

Castleman looked at Harry. "You're a witness to this," he said. "Listen carefully! Go on, mister!"

Marl slowly wiped the blood from his mouth. He coughed and a fresh spate of blood darkened the ground. "We killed Bobcat Bates and wounded the kid," he said. "Threw all of you off the trail. One by one the rest of the corrida went. That left me. I knew it was Sturgis who killed Shorty Jaeger and Jim Conroyd back on the Galeyville Road. I had an idea what he was after." Meyner shook spasmodically and coughed thickly.

"Go on, man!" pleaded Castleman.

"Ken had nothing to do with the robbery."

The wind shifted, blowing sand across the hollow.

Meyner looked up at Ken with a bloody smile. "Any man who escaped from Yuma Pen deserves the best in this damned game of life," he said. His head dropped. He was gone.

Castleman looked at Ken. "This clears you," he said.

"What about those killings at Galeyville?"

"That has nothing to do with the Espee," said the agent.

Harry grinned. "Cochise County can afford to lose Shorty Jaeger and Jim Conroyd," he said. He looked at the tracker. "Go get Max Fremar's hoss for Sturgis here."

Ken shook his head. "You'll need it for Fremar's body," he said. "I got a horse hidden in the hills."

"Come on back to the camp," said Castleman. "You look like you need grub and a damned good rest."

Ken picked up his gunbelt and buckled it about his lean waist. "Got any smoking tobacco?" he asked.

"Couple of packs of Bull Durham. You want them?"

Ken nodded. He took the tobacco and rolled a smoke. He snapped a lucifer and lighted the quirley. "You can bury Meyner here," he said quietly. "Use the gold hole. Lonely place, but then Meyner always was a loner."

The two men looked curiously at Ken.

Ken blew a smoke ring. "You got a jumper for the telegraph line?" he asked.

Castleman nodded.

"Send a message both ways that Ken Sturgis is clear

of the Express robbery. Tell them to spread it all over Arizona Territory."

"Aren't you coming with us?" asked Harry.

Ken shook his head. He picked up his rifle. "That pick and shovel are Espee property," he said. He grinned crookedly. "I just *borrowed* them, Castleman." He walked toward the stagecoach station, weaving a little in his weariness.

"Where are you going?" called out Castleman.

Ken turned, with the moon full on his lean, bearded face. His gray eyes peered from deep hollows. "I'm going home to the San Miguel," he said. "You can find me there when you need me for the investigation. *Adios, amigos!*" He turned and struck out for the ridge.

"There goes a man," said Jim Castleman.

"Amen," said Harry.

Somewhere in the sleeping Dragoons a coyote howled.

HANGIN' PARDS

CAST OF CHARACTERS

Cass Riker

He traded fifteen years of his life for eighty thousand dishonest dollars.

Holt Deaver

Because he set out to find a waterhole, he found himself knee deep in a hellhole.

Ernie Carley

He thought the dinero was free for the taking, but it wouldn't take him beyond the grave.

Morg Mills

He engineered an Army payroll robbery, only to find that Army wages weren't enough for him.

Susan Morris

She lied on behalf of a man she believed told the truth.

Trump Foster

Tough and strong, his only weakness was for money.

CHAPTER ONE

H OLT DEAVER squinted his eyes against the glare of the desert sun and looked to the east toward the base of the shimmering Kofas. The whole land seemed ablaze beneath the torrent of heat and light poured down from above. The mountains seemed to lift and waver in the moving air. There was a spiraling thread of saffron dust rising from the desert floor about three or four miles from where Holt Deaver sat his tired sorrel. He slid from his saddle and squatted in the scant shade of the horse, eyeing the mushrooming dust while he felt for the makings and began to roll a smoke.

"Nobody but a damned fool would ride a horse at that speed beneath this sun," said Holt as he lighted up.

He glanced back over his shoulder. The yellow flood of the Colorado was miles behind him now. They had recrossed it in the dark of the moon downriver from Old Ehrenburg and had kept on across the desert all that night and morning. Now it was high noon and the sorrel was in trouble. For that matter so was Holt, for his water had run out and he knew well enough if Alamo Springs was dry he'd probably lose the sorrel and maybe himself. It was a long way to the Gila on foot from Alamo Springs.

Holt sucked in on his cigarette as he teetered on his feet. The heat of the sand and decomposed stone soaked up through his thin boot soles. It was then that he noticed that there was another, thicker rising column of dust several miles behind the first one he had seen. That wasn't unusual in the desert, for he had often seen several wind-devils spiraling upward in the hot air at the same time.

But he saw something glinting at the base of the second dust column, and he saw dark dots moving. Men riding fast and following right on the trail of whatever was causing the first column of dust. Yuma Pen was about fifty miles or so downriver and this desert had seen more than one escaped convict get run down before he could reach the mountains. The Mohaves and the Yumas made quite a business out of tracking down fugitives from the Arizona hellhole. Many times they didn't bother to bring the man in alive; just his head in a gunny sack. The payment was the same and it saved a lot of trouble. The prison officials didn't care either. One less half-mad inmate to deal with. The place was overcrowded anyway.

Holt rubbed his bristly chin. He was damned glad it wasn't him who was running from Yuma. He was *running*, sure enough, but not from bloodthirsty and merciless Indian trackers. Somewhere behind him was Trump Foster and Morgan Mills, who had been following him since he had been involved in a bit of hot gunplay in a grove of cottonwoods not far from Fort Mohave. Holt had been camped there at about the same time Foster and Mills had shown up. He knew them well enough.

Both of them had been evading a stretch in Yuma Pen and the hangman for a good many years. With them had been Mike Mills, younger brother of Morgan, as wild an owlhoot as Holt had ever met.

Foster and the Mills boys had divulged a plan to Holt. Appropriations for army pay had been late, so the paymaster was carrying several months' pay. The outlaws wanted to hit him for the money and had asked Holt, not too politely, to throw in with them. He had refused and had pulled out, only to go back for something he had left behind. Just in time to see the robbery and cold-blooded killing of the paymaster and his small escort. Holt had pulled out again; he had wanted no part of the outlaws or anything to do with robbing the government. But Mike Mills had tried to stop him, and when the gun smoke had cleared the kid was dead and Holt was on the run.

The dust was moving toward Alamo Springs. Holt had to get there first. He needed that water, and if there was any left they'd be welcome to it.

Holt had the edge on distance, but maybe they could travel faster. He spurred the sorrel despite his pity for the weary horse. It was either that, or death in the desert. He looked back toward the Colorado. There was a faint skein of yellow dust rising there too and he wasn't about to sit around on his hunkers waiting to see who *that* was. He had a pretty good idea who was making that dust.

He was concealed by a long, low ridge that rose from the baking desert floor, but he could still see the movement to the east as he drove the sorrel on and on. When he was at last climbing the lower flanks of the Kofas he knew the horse would never make it. They reached the highest point of the shallow pass and Holt slid from the saddle. The sorrel stood straddle-legged, head low, caked with dried lather.

A furnace wind swept steadily around man and horse as they stood there. Then Holt took his rifle and canteen, pulled down the brim of his dusty hat to shade his eyes against the glare of the sun and slogged down toward the springs. He did not look back, for he didn't have the heart to do so.

He made good time on foot and then as he rounded a knoll he saw the springs. After plunging down the slope he saw that there was hardly enough water for one man, let alone those others who were coming toward the springs. He drank sparingly, then filled his canteen, then drank again. There was just about enough water to get him to the Gila, but he'd suffer on the way.

There were horses being ridden by the strangers who were heading for the springs. A hard glint shone in Holt Deaver's eyes. He left the springs and walked slowly up a slope until he could look to the south, and then he saw a lone figure struggling up the incline. A mile and a half more behind the lone man he could see four horsemen walking their horses. Maybe they were sure of their game now. "I wonder why he's running?" he said to himself. He lifted his Winchester and levered a round into the chamber, then slid into a hollow that had the heat of a baker's oven in it. There he could watch to see what happened, and if he was lucky, he could snatch a horse. He had never stolen a horse in his life, but this was no time to be choosy. He had to make Sonora within the next few days and he knew well enough he couldn't make it alone.

The man on foot was making heavy weather of it. Now and then raising an arm to wipe his face he would look back, then flog himself on with a peculiar running, hopping gait until he slowed down again to a stumbling, wavering walk. The hot wind played fitfully with his ragged, grayish-white beard. He was no spring chicken but he had plenty of steam in him for his age. The heat and exertion would have felled many a younger man than him.

Holt touched his dry lips with the tip of his tongue. There was a mouthful or two of water in the spring, no more. Just enough to tease the old-timer when he got there. Certainly there wasn't enough to carry him on to the north to the Wickenburg-Ehrenburg Road; not in that blazing heat at any rate. To the west was the river and plenty of water. To the east was nothing but baking mountains and desert—and death.

There should have been more pity in Holt Deaver than he now felt. But an outlaw had to take care of himself first or he'd lose the bloody game and there'd be no second chance, not for Holt Deaver at least. He had been moving south after a gambling and shooting scrape in Chloride, and for all he knew a posse might be on his trail too. He wasn't too worried about them. He had outridden posses before, but with Trump Foster and Morg Hills it would be another matter. Not only for the killing of Mike Mills, but also for his witnessing the payroll robbery would they want to wipe him out. They'd never let up until they did.

So Holt Deaver had to have a horse. He had his water, and there were four horses being ridden slowly toward the springs. One of those horses was going to be ridden *from* those springs by Holt Deaver.

The strange chase that was being run before his eyes began to intrigue him. The old man wasn't going to win it, of course, and Holt almost felt a twinge of pity for him; but it was a fleeting thought. But you had to give the old man a grudging thought of respect for putting up such a helluva struggle.

Then he saw one of the horsemen leisurely raise a

rifle and then fire it. The slug screamed from the hard earth a few feet from the old man. The rifle flatted off two more times, raising faint spurts of dust from the ground, whipping the old man on and on so that now he was running in a shambling sort of way.

Holt wiped the sweat from his face. There was no need for them to crucify the old man. They had him cold. He could see the man's face plainly now as he tended a little toward Holt's hideout. The horsemen plodded on and the rifleman raised his rifle once more. It cracked and the old man spun about and fell heavily. His left foot had been shorn of its heel. Top-hole shooting, if it had been intended to do what it did.

The old man bellied along the furnace-top ground and Holt could see every one of his agonized features. Bullet after bullet ripped into the ground near him. *Blast them! Why didn't they let him alone?*

Then the old man saw Holt. "For God's sake!" he gasped. "I don't know who you are, but if you hold off them buzzards I'll make you a rich man!"

"Sure, sure," said Holt softly.

"I ain't lyin'! I'll give you five thousand dollars in bills if you hold them back! Word of honor."

Holt grinned. "Yep," he said. "Word of honor. You old coot! Your tack is drove. Five thousand? What the hell! Make it ten thousand!"

The old man nodded. "All right! But hold 'em off!"

The horsemen had drawn rein now and were looking toward the old man. Holt wondered if they had seen him.

"If you're worried about them being lawmen you can forget it," said the fugitive.

Holt glanced quickly at him and an impatient feeling sped through him. He rubbed his bristly jaws. He needed a horse and he was going to get one.

One of the men fired and the shot screamed thinly from the rock near Holt, driving tiny shards against his face. "Gawd dammit!" he snarled. They had seen him now and they were shooting to kill.

He rested the Winchester on the rock, took up the trigger slack, and fired an instant before one of the men did. His slug had whipped through the closest man's hat. He bent low and spurred off. Holt fired again, creasing the horse. It buck-jumped, threw the man heavily, and galloped toward Holt and the old man. Maybe he had smelled the water.

The old man rolled into the hollow and grinned evilly. "Good stuff, *amigo!* Keep shootin'! But aim to kill! Give me that gun! I'll show you!"

Holt turned fiercely. "Shut up!" he snapped.

He fired again and this time one of the men slid from his horse and darted into a hollow. The two other men were dashing madly to the south toward a sheltering ridge. Holt sent a slug whispering over their heads to spur them on.

The horse trotted past Holt and the old man, heading for the springs. Holt spoke out of the side of his mouth. "Go get him! Keep him away from the springs until you get a drink. One more thing." Holt turned. "Don't you take off on that horse, hombre. He's *mine. Comprende?*"

"*Yo comprendo!*"

The old man crawled from the hollow, reached up for the reins of the dun, then grinned at Holt. "You just made yourself ten thousand dollars." Then he was gone.

Holt refilled his rifle magazine and squatted low, wishing for a smoke. The two riders had vanished. The downed man still lay where he had fallen. The man in the hollow was not to be seen, but his horse was trotting back to where the other men had gone.

"Hot as sin," said Holt. He glanced at his canteen, wondering if the loco old coot had found water. There might be a mouthful or two still in the rock water pan.

When he heard a whispering sound coming from the slope, Holt glanced down. The man lay there, grinning like a gargoyle. "Water seepin' in," he said hoarsely. "I dug out a rock or two with my hands. Water seepin' in!"

Holt nodded.

"We can pull out as soon as I water that horse."

"We ain't going anywhere," said Holt dryly. "Leastways, not right now. Those hombres are still waiting out there. Who are they?"

"Sidewinders! They're following me for my money."

"You carrying money in those rags?"

Old Whiskers chuckled. He tapped the side of his head. "No. But it's up here."

Empty of brains. Full of money, thought Holt.

Holt crouched down and lit a cigarette. He never took his eyes from that man in the hollow. The fourth man still lay motionless on the baking ground. It was then that Holt noticed the awkward angle of the man's neck. His neck had been broken. A cold feeling came over him despite the furnace heat. Holt Deaver *killed* again.

Holt sucked in on his cigarette, then raised his rifle and fired across the hollow where the man lay hidden. The man leaped out of it and raced down the slope, trailing his rifle. It was an old dodge to fire across a hollow like that, for the slug would crack over a man's head like a mule skinner's lash, and no matter how safe he was from getting hit, the sound of the slug was enough to put a chill into him.

"There'll be a moon tonight, Old Whiskers," said Holt over his shoulder. "I'll hold them off until dark, then

I'll skin out. And I ain't riding double. You'll be on your own."

"Which way you going?"

"South."

"The money is north."

"Yeh. The North Pole maybe?"

"You made a verbal deal with me, didn'tcha?"

Holt looked at him. The old coot was far gone. "Who are you anyway?" he asked curiously.

"Cass Riker."

Holt stared at him, then grinned. "You lyin' old goat! Cass Riker has been dead for years."

"Nope. I'm Cass Riker all right,"

Holt studied him. He had seen an old Wanted poster in a post office in Tucson some years ago, kept there as a curiosity, and that had been years after Cass Riker had been placed in hot storage at Yuma Pen after his big haul from the Southern Overland Mail. There was a vague resemblance between the hard-bitten face Holt had seen on the poster and the raddled, lined and bewhiskered countenance of the old man.

The old man grinned. "You know the story. Cass Riker got away with the biggest haul in years and went to the pen before he'd confess where it was."

Holt nodded.

"They never did find it," said the old man. "And they never will."

"How so?"

The grin wrinkled up the old face. "Because I'm the only man who knows where it is, that's why!"

"Up north?"

"Up north."

"I'm heading south."

"Go on south," jeered the old man. "Go on! You won't

make it! Sure, you *might* get to the border, but you won't get past the Rurales in Sonora lessn' you pay them off. What're you going to do in Mexico anyways? Punch cows for some ranchero? Come on, boy, help Old Cass Riker get north and I'll pay off what I owe you."

Holt touched his lips with the point of his tongue. The old man was loco, but maybe so was he.

"Say, Old Whiskers," Holt began inquisitively. "How much was in that haul you made from the Southern Overland anyways?"

"Eighty thousand, bub. Eighty thousand."

Holt glanced quickly toward the old man, but Riker had vanished like a gecko lizard. Eighty thousand! A man could live like a king in Mexico with that kind of *dinero*. The best of everything! Horses, food and likker, and *women*. Holt thoughtfully fired another shot toward the south. He had some thinking to do before it grew dark.

CHAPTER TWO

I T WAS intensely dark before the rising of the desert moon. Holt squatted beside a pinnacle of rock with his Winchester across his thighs. Riker had dug out the springs, and they had had their fill of the gamy water.

No chances were taken with the old buzzard. The dun was picketed within fifty feet of Holt. Riker was poking about somewhere in the thick blackness out there. The man was like a cat in the darkness. His past had slowly come back to Holt. He had been a kid when the old man had made his big strike over the barrel of a shotgun in the gunpowder blasted innards of a way station in the Dragoons. That had been in 1870, fifteen years ago, and when Riker had been captured he had been sentenced to Yuma. Both of his *compadres* in the holdup had mysteriously disappeared between the time of the holdup and the capturing of Cass Riker. They had never been found again.

A cold feeling came over Holt as he squatted there in the velvet obscurity. Supposing the old lizard did have it cached away? It might be worth a gamble to go north with Riker. But they'd have to move fast with Riker being followed by that trio, and the two outlaws from up north on his trail. Sonora seemed farther and farther away.

Riker came up the slope. "Got me a rifle," he said.

"Where'd you get it?"

"That dead *hombre* out there didn't need it no longer."

"You might of got a slug through your thick head!"

"You worried?"

"Not about you! I'm worried about that ten thousand bucks that doesn't exist!"

Riker spat. "You'll get it! But you got to help me get up north."

Holt tilted his head to one side. "Yeh," he said softly, "and when we do get up north I might get paid off in lead instead of gold. I oughta take that rifle and that beat-up old sixgun away from you."

"You ain't goin' to take *anything* from me, bub," said Riker softly, as he aimed the Winchester at Holt's belly. "You see?" Riker said. "I can kill you easy. I can take that hoss and the water and dust up a storm getting out of here and I wouldn't have to pay my debt to you."

Holt, breaking out in a cold sweat, could see the set, dim face of the old man. He was right, there wasn't any doubt about that. Him and his blasted ten thousand eagles!

Then Riker lowered the rifle and let down the hammer to half cock. "But I give my word," he said simply.

Holt felt his pulse slow down. "Yeh . . . *gracias,*" he said uneasily.

Something moved in the darkness beyond them. Holt gripped Riker by a shoulder and forced him down while he peered through the darkness with cocked Winchester at hip level, aimed right at the moving patch of shadow.

He was just about to fire when he heard a faint whinny. He stared. "Jesus," he said unbelievingly. "It's my horse."

Holt walked to the sorrel and passed an arm about its neck. "Leastways he don't smell as bad as you do, old man," he said over his shoulder. "Stay here and keep watch while I water him."

He led the sorrel down to the springs and watered him. The horse seemed to be all right now, but he was still pretty well worn out.

There was a faint suggestion of moonlight in the eastern sky. Time to get moving. Holt didn't want to go north, but he couldn't go south now, not with those three men waiting out there. Besides, Foster and Mills would have been making time while Holt had been tapped at the springs. He'd have to go north, for a time at least.

He walked up the slope. Then he stiffened as he heard the voice carry to the springs on the wind. "Hey you, Cass Riker!"

Cass did not move.

"We know you're there, Riker! You and that killer you got with you! We don't know how you arranged meeting him here. Pretty slick, Riker!"

The old man spat in the direction of the voice.

"Look, Riker! We're in a bad way for water! You let us get to those springs and we'll turn back south in the morning!"

"Sure, sure," said Cass *sotto voce*. "You'll turn back all right. In a pigs' butt you will!"

Holt peered through the darkness. He was beginning to distinguish things a little better now, and he realized that in a little while the desert would be silvered with clear light.

"Come on!" he said fiercely to the old man.

"Wait!"

Holt shook a fist at Riker.

"Riker! Let us get some water!"

"O.K., Carley! Come on in, in about ten minutes."

Cass slid down the slope toward the springs.

Holt peered into the darkness again. Carley . . . the name teased his mind. It sounded vaguely familiar.

Riker was fooling around down by the springs. Then he looked at Holt. "You ready?"

"Yes."

"Let's pull out then."

They led the two horses to the north, tending a little easterly, toward the Harquahala Plains. Beyond the plains were more mountains. Holt looked back toward the springs. The wind had shifted, bringing the sound of grating footsteps to the two fleeing men.

Riker turned and fired a shot toward the springs. There was a muffled curse echoing the sound of the shot. "Ten minutes!" the old man yelled.

They moved out faster then, striding through the darkness, with their boot soles husking against the harsh earth. It would be a hell of heat again as soon as the sun came up, and by noon they must have water again. There were other springs and waterholes out there in the darkness, but Holt wasn't quite sure where they were. It had been a long time ago he had been through that country. He had been in the army then as government scout. There were times when he wished he had stayed in that service.

"You know your way to the waterholes?" asked Riker.

"Yes."

"You don't sound very sure of yourself, bub."

"You want to try it alone?" demanded Holt.

Riker did not answer. He knew well enough he had to

depend on this rawboned companion of his, for a time at least. Until they found water again, and he was sure of his way. After that, well, ten thousand was a helluva lot of dinero to pay for a guide.

"Carley," said Holt at last. "Who is he?"

"Ernie Carley. Think hard, *amigo.*"

Holt stared at the old man. "He was one of the two *compadres* you had with you in that holdup!"

Riker cackled. "You recollect the other one?"

"Savvy Harris, wasn't it? Savvy Harris the gunslinger?"

"Keno," said Cass. "He's back there too. The third man is Pete Shalen. You remember who he was?"

Holt shoved back his hat. "There was a Pete Shalen who was a Wells-Fargo guard at the time of the holdup, wasn't there?"

"You're a lot brighter than I thought you was."

"Was he in on the deal too?"

"Keno."

"You played it pretty cosy, didn't you? That is, until they put you away in Yuma."

"You figure they outsmarted me then?"

"Fifteen years' worth, old timer."

"Yeh, but tell me, bub, who knows where the *dinero* is? All eighty thousand of it?"

The new moon was tipping the eastern ranges and Holt could see the sly grin on the face of Cass Riker. "You're joshing me," said Holt.

Riker shook his head. "I paid fifteen years of hell for that money, bub, and I aim to keep it for myself. Less ten thousand of course. That's for you."

"Oh sure, I figgered it was."

"You still don't believe me?"

Holt strode on a few more paces. "I don't know what to believe," he said. He looked back over his shoulder.

Ernie Carley and Savvy Harris! Those two sidewinders were sure death if you crossed them. And Pete Shalen had been known at the time of the robbery as one of the toughest Wells-Fargo agents in the business. "Who was the man I killed," he said at last.

"Oh, *him?* That was Webb Harris, Savvy's kid brother."

Holt looked back again. Now he had Trump Foster, Morg Mills, Ernie Carley, Savvy Harris and Pete Shalen dogging him, and all he had for comfort was a crazy old coot who claimed he owed Holt ten thousand dollars.

"Yup," said Cass. "I figgered it this way: Fifteen years against eighty thousand dollars works out at about five thousand, three hundred and thirty-three dollars a year. Course, I owe you ten thousand. I wisht you'd taken me up on the five thousand offer, but I was in no position to bargain, was I?"

"No," said Holt dryly. "You wasn't."

"Now, that leaves me seventy thousand. Let me figger." Riker looked up, half closed his eyes, wiggled his fingers and his whiskers, then glanced at Holt with gimlet eyes. "That gives me about four thousand, six hundred and sixty-six bucks per annum, don't it?"

Holt stared at Riker. The thought was almost incredible. To trade fifteen years of your life for that kind of money. It didn't make sense, and yet here was Cass Riker, who had certainly been the brains of the Wells-Fargo holdup, and who had never confessed that he knew where the loot was, telling Holt that that was exactly what he had done.

Holt glanced at the old man. He was loco. But Holt hadn't seen any eighty thousand dollars, much less the ten thousand the old rummy said he owed Holt. Still, Holt couldn't get to Sonora for a time, nor could he head west for California. So he'd have to bear north until he could swing back south again. He was twenty-five- years old, dead broke and on the run, and he had shot one man in Chloride and had killed two others in less than a week. Ten thousand bucks! It was worth more than a second thought, unless Cass Riker was playing Holt for the fool. There was always one way out; he could wring the truth out of the old coot if he had to.

The moon now flooded the desert, silvering the hard surface of it, etching shadows of rock and thorny growths against it in fantastic patterns. Holt looked back. "If they get enough water they won't waste any time tailing us," he said.

Riker cackled. "Sure, sure!" He cackled again.

Holt looked closely at the old man. "What's so funny about that?" he demanded.

Riker explored his scraggly beard, scratching vigorously, and then he glanced back over his shoulder. "That water taste sort of gamy to you? Brackish like too?"

"Yes."

The old man grinned. "It'll taste a helluva lot more brackish when they get there. Course they won't really notice it, because they can't afford to be too fussy. Leastways, they won't notice anything for *awhile.*"

"What do you mean?"

Riker yawned. "I dropped a handful of chloral hydrate into that rock pan. I figgered there was enough water to thin it out so's it wouldn't be noticed right away."

"Chloral hydrate? Knockout drops?"

"Yup."

"Why, you dirty old—"

Riker held up a hand. "Maybe you coulda thought of a better way to stop 'em? Hellsfire, all you can think of is shooting, and not too good at that."

"You figured I should have killed them?"

The hard eyes of the old man seemed to bore a hole into Holt's eyes. "Why not? They woulda killed *you.*"

Holt felt for the makings. He was beginning to wonder what kind of a mad partnership he had made with this loony old man. Still, he had been on foot, and had needed a horse.

"For ten thousand bucks, I could do a lot of killings" said Cass Riker. "Give me them makings, *amigo.*"

Holt looked back after he had lighted his cigarette. Chloral hydrate would stop them sure enough, *if* they had imbibed enough of the gamy water from the springs.

He'd have to watch the old man. He was slick as grease and as deadly as a diamondback. Holt had saved him back there at Alamo Springs, and was now helping him to escape. Riker could have gone on alone, of course, but Holt had a feeling that Riker didn't know the country. He needed Holt. For a time at least he wouldn't try any of his tricks on Holt.

"Just where are we heading, Riker?" he asked.

"Northeast, bub, to the next waterhole."

"You know where that is?"

Riker looked quickly at Holt. He drew in on his cigarette and the sudden flareup of light illuminated his face. "No, I don't, bub. But you do."

"Supposing I don't?"

There was a moment's silence, then Riker laughed. "You wouldn't be damned fool enough to come north with me 'less you *did* know where water was. Now, where is it?"

Holt grinned. "Well, Old Whiskers, seems like you *hired* me to find it, so I will, but I ain't telling you where it is until we get there."

"Supposing something happens to you before then? I'd die out here, bub."

"What can happen to me, Old Whiskers?"

The old man did not answer. He sucked in on the last of his cigarette and then dropped it, grinding it under a boot sole. "You mean you don't trust me, bub? Old Cass Riker?"

"Old *Honest* Cass Riker, you mean, don't you?"

The old man stared at him a moment and then he laughed softly. "Keno," he said.

Beyond the desert, to the northeast, were mountains where a man could easily lose himself, or anyone following him. But Holt knew his way through the tangle. He had worked out of Whipple Barracks near Prescott, and also from Camp Verde in the days when the Apaches had been on the warpath. Holt wasn't worried about finding his way through those mountains, and once they were up there, they'd have no water problem. That would be Riker's chance to get rid of Holt.

In all probability, Riker's story of his cache was as nebulous and legendary as the Dutchman's Lost Mine or the Lost Adams Diggings. Now Holt was stuck with the old man until he could make his own getaway to the south, the long way around. But the old coot was so sure of himself!

CHAPTER THREE

HOLT DEAVER lay flat on the ridge top looking down upon the little settlement. He had been there for over an hour, watching the movements of the people down there. He knew the place, for he had passed through often enough when he had been scouting. Yardigan it was called, after old Pop Yardigan, the man who had settled there right after the war, fighting off Apaches to make his place in the mountains. The man had done well enough too. His was the only general store and blacksmithing place for many a mile.

Holt rolled the last of his tobacco into a paper and lighted it. He and the old man needed food, tobacco and cartridges before they plunged further into the mountains. Cass had insisted that Holt go for the stores. The old man had an obsession that everyone in the territory knew he was free from Yuma Pen at last and was on his way to his cache. Holt had been an honest man when he had last been in this area. Even if he was recognized he'd probably be able to carry it off.

The three men who trailed them, if they had recovered from the chloral hydrate in time, would certainly know Riker on sight, but none of them had seen Holt. They didn't worry him half as much as the two men who had been following him from the Colorado. Still, they had no way of knowing which way he had gone from Alamo Springs.

Holt sucked in on his smoke. His belly writhed in hunger. He had wanted to kill some game but Old Whiskers had been against shooting to let anyone know where they were. He was as cautious as an old woman that way.

Holt shrugged. He stood up, eased his Colt in its holster, then led the sorrel down the slope. He had taken Riker's saddle, for a man riding bareback would be a little suspicious-looking. Riker had given Holt ten dollars, profits from Riker's years in Yuma.

Holt tethered his horse to the hitching rail and looked up and down the single street. There was no one in sight. He stepped up onto the warped porch and looked into the store. The place was a jungle of merchandise, stacked against the walls, lining the aisles, hung from wires strung from wall to wall. He walked in and looked toward the rear of the store to where a man was standing behind a battered counter making entries in a thick ledger.

Holt glanced back out of the door once more. The place was on a trail that was used quite a bit. If Holt had been trailing anyone from the area from which he and the old man had come, he would have tried this trail first for results. He'd get his supplies as quickly as he could and then pull out of there.

Holt walked to the back of the store. It was Old Man

Yardigan standing there. He glanced up as he saw Holt. "Howdy? He'p you?"

The young man now gave him his supply order.

"Right." The old man peered at Holt. "You look familiar."

It had been almost four years since Holt had been in that area. He had leaned out a good deal since then and in those days he had sported a short reddish beard.

"You working around here?" asked Yardigan.

"Passing through."

"North or south?"

"North. Say, can I have that stuff now?" Holt placed his penciled list on the counter.

"Sure, sure. You in a hurry?" asked Yardigan a little suspiciously.

"No, but I don't aim to spend the whole day here. Have to make miles before sundown."

"All right." Yardigan began to study the list as though it was some rare medieval hand-illuminated manuscript.

Holt wet his lips. He reached over the counter and snagged a bag of Pride of Durham. "Add this one," he said. He rolled a smoke and lighted it, drawing the smoke deeply into his lungs.

Yardigan moved slowly, placing the articles on the counter. He looked up at Holt. "I got everything here except the cartridges. Just happen to have run out of forty-fours. You know how popular that caliber is. Happens there is a shipment came in last night from Wickenburg and I ain't separated it yet."

"I need them."

"Look, it's going to take some time to get these cartridges. Whyn't you go across the street and have a beer or something?"

"I'm in a hurry, mister."

"Sure. Everyone is in a hurry these days. You want those cartridges or not?"

Holt nodded. He walked to the doorway. He could use a drink. He hadn't had one since Mormon Crossing.

Holt walked across the street to the saloon and pushed through the sagging batwings. The big room was empty except for a bald-headed barkeep reading a newspaper at the end of the long bar. The barkeep looked up. "Your pleasure?"

"Rye."

Bottle and glass slid to a stop in front of Holt. He poured a drink.

The bartender looked up. "Passing through?"

Holt nodded as he raised the glass to his lips.

"Keep an eye open for an old man with a beard. Crusty old coot. He just got sprung out of Yuma so this paper says. Name of Cass Riker."

Holt lowered the glass. How the devil had that gotten into a newspaper so fast? "Cass Riker? Who is he?" he asked quietly.

The bartender eyed him. "You must be a stranger all right. Everyone in this territory knows about Cass Riker. Made a big haul from Wells-Fargo fifteen years ago. Then he got picked up and spent fifteen years in the *juzgado* but they never did find the money. Over a hundred thousand it was they say."

Holt downed his drink. That was a clear profit of twenty thousand if it was true. He refilled his glass.

"Old Cass was too smart for 'em though. Never let on where that money was. They say he was offered a shorter sentence if he'd say where the money was. He never did though."

"So he's loose now?"

"I guess so. This paper doesn't say he was let loose.

Just that he was about to be let loose." The bartender grinned. "I'll bet every hardcase in the territory will be keeping an eye out for him. A hundred thousand! A fortune, friend, a fortune. Cass Riker even double-crossed his partners on the deal. They'll be hot after him, too."

"I seem to remember some of the story now. Didn't the law think that Riker did away with Carley and Harris?"

"Hell, Riker went into the pen to get *away* from Carley and Harris."

"You're sure about that?"

The bartender came down to the end of the bar, took a glass and filled it, then leaned toward Holt. "I am," he said mysteriously. "And I can tell you something else I know." He looked behind him as though a lawman was listening right at his back. "I seen Carley and Harris not more 'an two weeks ago."

"Where?"

"Right here, friend. They come in here with a couple of other *hombres* and drank right there!"

Holt downed his drink. "What do you think they're up to?"

The man grinned. "They wasn't going south for their health. They looked like they'd been in these mountains for some time. I had a feeling they was going down to wait for Cass Riker to get sprung."

Holt nodded. He could feel the liquor warming up his empty gut. There was a cold feeling within him. He was sure now that Riker was heading for his cache, with the bloodhounds hard on his heels, and he had Holt Deaver with him as an almost unwilling ally. But what had Carley and Harris been doing in the mountains? Maybe they had a rough idea of where Riker had hidden the loot.

The batwings swung open and a big, broad-shoul-dered man walked in. "Beer," he said to the bartender. He nodded to Holt and Holt had a cold feeling again. The man had lawman stamped across his broad face. Holt nodded.

"Hello, Stuart," said the bartender.

"Howdy, Baldy. Any news?"

"Cass Riker is out of Yuma."

Stuart nodded. "I knew that."

"You looking for him?"

"No. That's someone else's responsibility. I'm working on something else."

"So?"

Stuart sipped his beer and glanced casually at Holt. "Payroll robbery near Fort Mohave. Paymaster Rascobb and four troopers were shot down from ambush and the payroll was taken. They say four men were in on it. A grave was found in a grove of cottonwoods near the scene of the robbery."

"What was in it? The money?"

Stuart shook his head. "A man shot to death. No name and no identification. The other three were supposed to have headed south along the Colorado. We don't know if they crossed over to the California side or whether they're heading for Sonora. My guess is Sonora."

Holt felt a cold sweat trickle down his sides. He wanted to get out of there in a hurry.

"They got any idea who did the job?"

"Not yet. They think a man by the name of Deaver was mixed up in it. He had been in a shooting scrape in Chloride and had been seen near Fort Mohave."

Holt refilled his glass and held it tightly to keep his hand from shaking.

A boy poked his tousled head beneath the batwing

doors. "Say, mister," he said to Holt, "your things is ready at the store."

He flipped the kid a two-bit piece. "Thanks." He paid his tab and emptied his glass. "See you later," he said with a smile.

Without looking back, he crossed, stepped up onto the store porch and entered the store. He took his sack of supplies and paid for them.

Yardigan leaned back against the shelving behind him. He squinted at Holt. "I'm sure I seen you somewheres, friend."

Holt smiled. "Not likely. First time I've been through here."

"So? You got a twin brother or something like that?"

"No."

"Hmmm ... I never forget a face. I'll think of it after you're gone."

I hope to God you don't, thought Holt. He walked to the door and peered out. His heart sank as he saw three horsemen riding slowly down the slope from the south. He recognized them at once—Ernie Carley, Savvy Harris and Pete Shalen.

Holt stepped back into the store. He walked to the rear. "Say," he said quickly. "There's a man over in the saloon. Name of Stuart. You know him?"

The storekeeper looked curiously at Holt. "Sure. That's Burl Stuart, Deppity United States Marshal for these parts."

"Thanks. I thought he was a lawman. He's looking for three men."

"I know. That Fort Mohave thing."

"Keno! Well, I just looked outside and saw three men riding toward here. Trail-dusty and tired-out looking."

"So?"

"Stuart said he was looking for three men who did the job near Fort Mohave. Get it?"

Yardigan's eyes widened. He reached for his cash box.

"No time for that!" said Holt crisply. "Get over to the saloon and tell Stuart."

"Why don't you go?"

Holt smiled mysteriously. "Because I'm working undercover on the same case. Now git!"

"Sure! Sure!"

Holt followed the storekeeper to the front door. Yardigan hurried across the street. Holt slung his sack of provisions across his saddle cantle and untethered the sorrel, keeping it between him and the three approaching riders. He was leading the sorrel around the side of the store when he heard one of the men yell, then he heard the beating hoofs on the hard ground.

He swung up on his horse and sank the steel into his flanks, racing across an open field for a rail fence at the rear of it. A gun flatted off but he did not look back. They took the fence easily.

Another gun cracked. Holt looked back and saw Burl Stuart standing on the porch of the saloon with a pistol in his hand. The three hardcases were fighting their plunging, rearing horses in the middle of the street.

The man and his horse shot past the pines and was thudding up on a ridge when he heard a faint yelling carried to him on the breeze. "I know who that *hombre* was!" cried Yardigan. "Useta be in the army! Name of Holt Deaver!"

Now Stuart would be after him, as well as Carley, Harris and Shalen, for the last three would know he had been the man with Riker back at Alamo Springs. Now all that had to happen to make things real sporting would be to have Morg Mills and Trump Foster show up.

He circled widely, dismounting to lead the tired sorrel up a steep slope, then down into a ravine which he followed until he reached the road far south of Yardigan. He crossed the road in a hurry, and vanished into the woods. The camp was three miles west of town.

Carley, Harris and Shalen would have a helluva time explaining things to Burl Stuart, but Yardigan had given Holt away, and Stuart would have a hot trail. He'd have a hot trail on Holt, but not on Morg Mills and Trump Foster. If they could have the robbery and the killings pinned on Holt they'd be in the clear. But there was one thing Holt was sure of now. They'd have to kill him to make him keep his mouth shut, in case he might be able to prove that he had had nothing to do with the robbery and the killings.

Holt ground-reined the sorrel a half a mile from the camp, took his Winchester, then padded through the sunlit glades until he could look down upon the camp. Cass Riker was seated on a log, trying to repair one of his boots. There was no sign of anyone else near the camp. Holt whistled softly.

"It's me, Old Whiskers," said Holt.

"Where the hell you been? To a soiree or somethin'?"

"Get your horse. Lead him around this ridge. Get moving. I got news for you, Pop."

"What's up?" he asked.

Holt swiftly explained what had happened in Yardigan, but he eliminated the fact that Stuart had been looking for one Holt Deaver, suspect in the robbery and killing at Fort Mohave. Holt didn't want the old badger to have anything on him. Not yet anyway. Not until Cass led the way to his hidden loot.

They rode slowly toward the north, intending to circle Yardigan and then head up into the canyons toward

Horse Mountain. The sun slanted down through the treetops to heat the ground and the resinous odor of the
pines mingled with that of the dry wind that swept up
from the desert.

"Shoulda got me a smarter partner," said Cass Riker
sourly. "You run right into them boys! Blast and damn
anyway!"

Holt drew rein sharply and leaned toward Riker. "Listen," he said harshly. "I helped you back there at Alamo
Springs. If I hadn't, they would have been still working
over you to make you talk. I got you through that desert
and now I'm taking you through these mountains. If I
ride off and leave you here, you'll get lost in an hour. Now
you shut up that flapping mouth of yours or I'll let you go
it alone!"

"And you lose ten thousand bucks, eh? You loco fool!"

Holt smashed a fist down on his pommel. "You and
your damned ten thousand bucks! I don't believe you
ever had more than the ten dollars you got as a parting
gift from Yuma Pen!"

"Go on then! Leave! In a week I'll be lightin' seegars
with hundred dollar bills, and laughing fit to bust my
belly thinking of you eatin' beans and bacon in the
mountains."

Holt kept a check on his raging temper. He couldn't
go back. Not now. He was shackled to the old man and
he would have to stay that way until he knew whether or
not the old coot was lying in his dirty beard.

"Straightened you out, didn't it?" jeered Riker.

Something made Holt turn in his saddle. Far down
the slope the sun glinted on metal. There was a movement in amongst the trees and he saw a horseman leave
the woods and then look up the tree-stippled slope of
the mountain toward the two fugitives. Then he turned

in his saddle, took off his hat and waved it to someone unseen.

There were no more hot words between Holt Deaver and Cass Riker. They spurred up the slope, heading for a notch. Whoever it was down there was probably no friend to them. Right now it seemed as though every man's hand was against those two.

CHAPTER FOUR

T HEY HAD crossed the Verde River an hour before dusk the day after they had left the Yardigan area. Holt still hadn't been able to worm any information out of Cass Riker as to where their journey would end. The old man was as close-mouthed as a clam, and the further into the mountains they went, the more concerned Holt became. He was getting no closer to Sonora, and Burl Stuart had probably kept the telegraph wires hot, now that one of his suspects had hightailed it out of Yardigan a jump and a holler ahead of Stuart.

Holt rolled a cigarette and automatically passed it on to Cass, then rolled one for himself. They halted their horses to light up. "You reckon Stuart figgered those three tarantulas was clear of that deal at Fort Mohave?" asked Cass. His sharp eyes studied Holt.

"Sure. He's got nothing on them. Besides, I told you that the bartender had told me he had seen Carley and Harris right in Yardigan not too long ago."

Cass blew out a smoke ring. "You don't suppose he told Stuart who they was?"

"He could have, to help them clear themselves of that Fort Mohave thing."

"No," said Cass quietly.

"What do you mean?"

Cass rested a hand on his cantle. "You think Stuart wouldn't have remembered those names? Everybody in Arizona knows that story. Most of them think I done away with Ernie Carley and Savvy Harris. They're still wanted for that robbery, bub. Stuart would remember them."

"So they gave him phoney names?"

"Yell, and unless that barkeep opens his mouth I don't think Stuart could have been any the wiser."

"That barkeep is smart enough to keep his mouth shut, Cass. He wouldn't want two hardcases like Carley and Harris down on him."

"Yup."

They rode on toward the east and then suddenly Cass turned to eye Holt. "You never did tell what you was runnin' from, bub."

"What makes you so sure I'm running from something?"

Cass grinned wickedly. "I got ways of figgering things out."

"You sure do, and most of them wrong."

"I wonder who that was we seen when we was climbing that mountain?"

"*Quien sabe?* Could have been your old *compadres.*"

"Or the boys that been chasing you."

"There you go again!"

Riker's gimlet eyes probed into Holt's eyes. "Sure are a mysterious little fella, ain'tcha?"

Holt ignored the old man. He drew rein. "I'm back-trailing."

"Why?"

"To see if we're being followed. You keep on going. Head for that pinnacle of rock you can see due east. I'll be along soon."

"You'd better be."

Holt waved a hand and then trotted back along the trail. He was getting used to riding bareback, but he sure wished he had left his old saddle on his horse. Maybe Foster and Mills had found that saddle and had known he had made Alamo Springs. He wet his lips. There wasn't a chance that they had trailed Holt up into the mountains —*or was there?*

The sun was low atop the range to the west when Holt halted, slid from his horse, then led him into cover. He took his rifle and padded back along the trail until he could see the narrow Verde flowing lazily between its banks with the late afternoon sun glinting from the clear waters.

Then he saw the movement in the trees a hundred yards back from the far bank of the river. A horseman, riding slowly, with rifle across his thighs, while he looked to right and left through the woods. A moment later another horseman appeared. Holt felt a sickening feeling in the pit of his stomach. He needed no field-glasses to recognize *those* two men. The big, broad-shouldered man in the lead was Trump Foster, wearing his usual cowhide vest and yellowish hat. The other man was Morg Mills, lean and deadly looking, dressed all in gray.

Holt lay still, hardly daring to breathe, while the two men stopped their horses on the far bank and looked across the rippling waters to the bank where Holt was hidden. He could have sworn that Morg Mills was looking directly at him.

There was no chance for him to pull out of there now. If they crossed the river ford, they'd pass within twenty feet of him, and if his horse whinnied there'd be hell to pay.

"This is as good a place as any, Morg," said Trump Foster.

The tall man nodded. He dismounted and led his bay to the water's edge to let it drink, but all the time his eyes flicked through the greenery of the opposite shore. The wind was blowing straight down the valley. If it shifted and the horses scented each other, Holt might have to get out of there two spits and a jump ahead of singing lead.

The big man began to undo his cantle pack. "I figger we'd better forget him, Morg. We keep foolin' around in this country and we might get picked up. You remember what them fellas said back there at Yardigan? That marshal is after Holt Deaver. He ain't after *us*. Right now he ain't anyways. I say we ought to go back and get the money we cached and take off for Sonora and to hell with Holt Deaver."

Morg turned slowly and took the cigarette from his mouth. "You forget one thing, Trump."

"So?"

"He *killed* my brother."

Trump nodded. "Well, maybe we oughta shut him up permanent-like. Why didn't the loco cuss throw in with us?"

"Deaver never did like killing."

Trump spat. "He does a good chore of it when he does. He gunned Mike down so fast it damned near threw me too. That's how he made his break. Then there was that *hombre* he killed back at Alamo Springs. What was his name?"

"Harris. Webb Harris."

"Yeh, the kid brother to that tough-looking galoot Savvy." Trump squatted by his blankets and began to fashion a smoke. "Quite a brother killer, ain't he?"

"Shut up!"

"All right, Morg. Take it easy. I didn't mean nothing."

"You never do."

Trump lighted his smoke. "You still think Deaver is with that old bastard Riker?"

"That's him we saw with Deaver yesterday when they climbed Horse Mountain."

Trump blew a smoke ring. "What the hell are Carley, Shalen, and Harris trailing Riker for?"

Morg traced a pattern on the ground with a stick. "Riker, Harris, Carley and Shalen were all in on the big haul fifteen years ago with the *dinero*. Later on he got caught. No one ever found out what happened to the others. Lot of people thought Riker had done away with 'em. I knew better. I saw Carley down in Sonora some years ago. He didn't tell me, but I got the idea that he and the others were waiting for Riker to get sprung out of Yuma so they could find out where he cached the *dinero*."

Trump whistled softly. "You suppose that's why Deaver is with Riker?"

"He threw in with him back at Alamo Springs, didn't he?"

Trump nodded. "How much loot did Riker get away with?"

"Hundred and twenty thousand, Trump."

Holt stared at the man. The amount got higher every time it got talked about.

"No wonder them three *hombres* are after Riker."

Morg nodded. He stood up and looked across the river. "One hundred and twenty thousand bucks! And we profited by a measly twelve thousand back there on the Colorado. Six thousand lousy bucks!"

Trump shrugged. "I ain't kickin', Morg."

The tall man turned savagely. "No, you wouldn't! You've always been a tinhorn, penny-ante cuss! You can't think big! Supposing we could get our hands on that *dinero* Riker salted away? Sixty thousand dollars apiece, Trump! Sixty thousand dollars!"

"Sixty-six thousand. You forget the payroll money."

Morg squatted beside Trump. "Maybe we could throw in with Carley, Harris and Shalen and give them a hand in running down Deaver and Riker?"

"Hell! That'd cut down the profits, Morg. You divide a hundred and twenty thousand by five and you get only twenty-four thousand apiece."

"A little while ago you were satisfied with six thousand."

Trump flipped his cigarette butt into the river. "Sure, but that was before you got me to thinking." He looked sideways at Morg. "Supposing we did throw in with them? Until we got our hands on that *dinero*. Ain't nothing stopping us from getting rid of them like we done those soldiers at the Colorado.

Morg grinned. "Now, you're talking, Trump!"

Half an hour drifted past and darkness was creeping down into the valley of the Verde when three more horsemen rode up to the campfire beside the Verde. Ernie Carley, Savvy Harris and Pete Shalen. The wind had shifted and the fire crackled, so it was impossible for Holt to hear what they were saying. There was one thing he did know. He had to slow them down. He'd have to take a long chance, for the five of them were as tough a set of hardcases as ever were seen in Arizona Territory, a place noted for such local products.

Holt wriggled back from his lookout and bellied across the open ground to a rock formation. He slid his rifle across the top of it. He had twelve rounds in the magazine. Enough to raise a little hell across the river.

He wet his lips. The five of them were seated, or lying around the campfire, talking in low voices. Beyond the camp the five horses had been tethered to trees.

It would be so easy to drive a slug into one of them and then get at least two more of them before they could break away from the firelight. Who would it be first? It wasn't in him to kill men from ambush, yet he knew any one of the five of them probably wouldn't give a second thought about killing Holt the same way.

He sighted carefully and squeezed off. The forty-four slug struck the big coffee pot that rested beside the fire, smashing it, scattering hot coffee over the men about the fire. They leaped to their feet as the echo of the shot slammed back and forth in the valley of the Verde. They were etched against the bright light. Holt fired again and heard a horse scream in pain and fear. It had been almost as difficult as shooting at a man, but he had to slow those hardcases down.

He fired three more times before one of the yelling men doused the fire with water. The gun flashes dotted the darkness like rubies on velvet and the hungry slugs whipped through the brush not too far from Holt. A horse broke loose and splashed across the river. Holt stood up and pumped his Winchester dry in the general direction of the camp, then grabbed the runaway and swung up into the saddle, slashing at him with the gun barrel.

The moon was just rising when he reached the high land to the east of the Verde. He grinned as he heard an occasional shot. The boys had been pinned down for a little while at least. He rode toward the naked pinnacle of rock that thrust itself up from the ground like an admonishing finger. The old man would be wondering what had happened to him.

The moon lighted the valley of the Verde when Holt reached the rock pinnacle. There was no sign of Cass Riker. Holt rode back and forth, whistling softly. But Cass Riker had vanished like a ghost into the wilderness.

Old Cass had played it smart, getting Holt to save his skin back at Alamo Springs, having him guide the way through desert and mountains, and having him risk arrest by going into Yardigan for supplies. Now the old coot knew the rest of the way and a double-damned fool had gone back to hold off their pursuers while he had skinned out as free as a bird. He had most of the supplies, too.

There was one thing Holt had a good share of though; he had plenty of forty-fours for both Winchester and Colt. The old goat owed him ten thousand dollars, or at least enough money to get him safely to Sonora, and Holt Deaver meant to cash in his six-gun against the old buzzard's head for that *dinero*.

The valley of the Verde was quiet now and the moon glinted on the shallow waters as they purled and rippled along. The wind shifted a little and brought the odor of wet burned wood. Holt reloaded his Winchester, then touched the big buckskin with his spurs. He rode to the east. He really didn't know why, but instinct told him that was the way Cass Riker had gone.

To the east was the Mogollon Rim and the Mogollon Plateau, still haunted by Apaches, the real rimrock boys who hadn't yet been subjugated by the army. Old Cass would take his life in his hands going in there. It was a chance Holt had to take too. He couldn't go back to the west. Those five hard-cases were back there and so was Burl Stuart. There were too many settlements to the north and they'd be looking for Holt Deaver after Burl Stuart had spread the good word. To the south was rough country and Holt wasn't ready yet to go that way.

It was going to be a long ride but there might be ten thousand dollars at the end of it. Or maybe death in a Tonto ambush. High, low or jack, Holt Deaver was on his way, and God help the old man when Holt caught up with him.

CHAPTER FIVE

THE NIGHT wind blew down from Mazatzal Peak and whispered strange forebodings to Holt Deaver as he led the two horses across a small mesa. The moon flooded the country with pure, silvery light by which a man could look for Apaches making damned sure they didn't see him first. They didn't attack at night, or they'd never get into the House of Spirits if they were killed, but they had the patience of spiders and would trail a man for miles, especially a man armed with a fine handgun and a long gun, and two good horses.

Holt wanted to stay holed up until the moon died, but he couldn't take a chance on that. Those five men back at the Verde were just as cruel and vicious as any Apaches, and a lot more capable. Holt had taken care of at least two of their horses, but that had left three mounts, and he knew well enough that those three horses would be used to follow him.

Even after the moon died he'd have to keep on, for he knew he couldn't travel during daylight hours in Tonto country. The big war bands had long ago been subjugated, but there were plenty of broncho Apaches still on the loose, and a lone white man with weapons and two fine horses would be fair game for them. Maybe they'd get Cass Riker too and then no one would ever know where his money, however much it was, could be found.

Somewhere off to the south a coyote howled dismally. A moment later another coyote gave voice to the north, almost as though he was answering right over Holt's head. It wasn't until he was at the east end of the mesa, looking down into a dark canyon, like a trough of ink in the ground, that he heard the third coyote calling from the east, and he knew well enough that those weren't coyotes talking back and forth out there. They were Apaches.

He led the two horses down a long slope, hoping to God that their noise wouldn't give him away. Their shod hoofs struck bright little sparks from the stones, and the cold sweat of fear ran down Holt's body and soaked his shirt, chilling him when the wind blew against him.

He had enough at last. He picketed the horses in a draw on the sloping canyon wall, then walked a quarter of a mile up the canyon until he found a place where he could hide and get some sleep. He wanted a smoke desperately, but those keen noses out there would pick up the blessed odor of the burning weed and travel down it until they found Holt Deaver, and the next smoke he would inhale would be that of brimstone and pitch in the nether regions.

There was no use in driving on through the night with hate as the spur. Holt had to use his head. He had been outsmarted just as Riker had outsmarted Carley, Shalen and Harris. Riker used anyone who got in his clutches. He knew how to play on a man's greed all right.

He had plenty of greed himself for that matter. One hundred and twenty thousand dollars was a lot of *dinero* for one old rascal to play around with. Ten thousand of that was Holt's and now he meant to get it.

It was still dark when he awoke. He raised his head and sniffed the night wind, almost as though it could warn him about his enemies. And he had a lot of them now.

He stood up and picked up his rifle, then crawled out of the hollow to go for his horses. It was so dark he could hardly see the ground to make his way and when he reached the place where he had left the horses he couldn't see, hear or smell them. He rubbed his jaws. They *had* to be there! He had picketed them well enough. One of them might have broken loose, but not *two* of them. Then a cold and evil thought crept into his mind like a worm. He knew well enough they could not have broken loose. Someone had loosed them and driven them off.

He crouched down and looked low across the ground, trying to skyline anyone who might be in the area; he saw nothing but the brush and the rock formations. Slowly he scanned the area and as he did so some of his old scouting skill came back to him. He had been careless in the days since he had left scouting for owlhooting. A man might very well be so in breaking the law, but no man could be negligent in hostile Apache country and live to boast about it.

Holt worked his way down the slope and looked down into the canyon. It was pitch black down there but he knew he had to plunge into that evil ink in order to cross the canyon and gain the heights on the far side. If he was caught on this side of the canyon when daylight came, he'd never have a chance to cross. He had no food and just half a canteen of water, for he had left his big canteen with Cass Riker.

Then an icy calm came over him as he reached the bottom of the canyon and he was no longer afraid. He was halfway across the canyon floor when his eyes picked out a humped shape directly in front of him. For a long moment he stared at it and then he knew what it was. A horse or mule. He moved a little closer and saw that it was a horse, with its throat cut. Then he saw where the flanks and more tender cuts of meat had been sliced from the carcass. It was then that he recognized the horse. It was the sorrel, his own faithful horse.

Holt's hands tightened on his rifle and a sheer flood of hate and killing lust poured over him. Now he was no longer purely concerned with escaping from the Tontos. He wanted them to pay for his fear and what they had done to his horse. It was better for it to have died back there at Alamo Springs after faithfully carrying his master there, rather than to be degraded in death like this.

He padded across the canyon floor and made his way halfway up the slope, then stopped to look and listen. The night brought him nothing but the usual sounds: the dry husking of the wind through the trough of the canyon; the scuttling of nocturnal animals in the brush; the far-off crying of coyotes.

Every fiber in him seemed to cry for him to take off as fast as he could go, to be out of that country before the gray light of dawn, but the hate and determination within him was stronger than that. It was almost as though he was two men instead of one, and the one that wanted vengeance was the one that won out.

As he climbed the canyon wall he found a narrow, winding trail that slanted at an angle toward the top. He did not follow it. More than one white man had died just that way. Apaches knew they tended to follow trails and camp as near to water as possible and they set their ambushes accordingly. He made his way up the steep wall of the canyon, then found a place where he could hide and still see the place where the trail reached the top of the canyon. They might not come this way, but if they did ...

He counted his cartridges and made sure his rifle magazine was full. He checked his Colt and loosened his sheath knife. He allowed himself a mouthful of water and half a handful of cigarette tobacco which he chewed with relish.

Hour after hour he squatted there, a lean lath of a man with a face as hard as flint and with cold death in his gray eyes, until the first faint traces of the false dawn tinged the eastern sky and a cold searching wind swept across the Mogollon Plateau.

He touched his dry lips with the tip of his tongue and hefted his Winchester. Then, as the wind shifted, he heard a faint sound from below the canyon rim. He moved noiselessly, shifting until he could see the place where the trail met the canyon rim. Anyone coming up the trail would be clearly silhouetted there.

Then suddenly as though manipulated by the almost invisible strings of a giant master of marionettes, a mounted figure reached the brink of the canyon, and there was no mistaking his race. The thick mane of hair bound tightly about the forehead with a band of cloth. The naked upper body and the buckskin kilt. The thigh-length, button-toed moccasins turned down about the knotty calves.

One after the other they rose out of the cold depths of the canyon until seven of them were riding right across Holt's field of fire. For a moment he hesitated and the killing fever waned a little, until he saw that the last warrior was leading a saddled horse; the big buckskin Holt had captured at the Verde, and hanging from the saddle were strips and joints of meat. There wasn't any doubt in his mind as to where that meat had been procured.

They had stolen his buckskin and they had killed his sorrel, and they would have killed him too had they been able to find him. Perhaps, if they had had time, they would have played with him, keeping him alive as long as possible for their cold amusement. He had seen some of their work when he had been a scout.

He raised the rifle, sighted calmly on the broad chest of the last brave, then squeezed off the trigger before he had time to reconsider his drastic action. The big slug smashed the warrior back and he slid lifelessly from the back of his calico horse. The first echo had hardly started racing across the canyon when the second shot ripped out and the lead buck went down with a smashed shoulder.

The warriors had little chance now as long as Holt could shoot and as long as he had them panicked. His third, fourth, and fifth shots brought down another buck and two horses. The horses thrashed about and a hoof caught another warrior in the chest, driving him down to die before he could find shelter or reply to Holt's crashing Winchester.

The smoke drifted about the screaming, struggling Apaches, while the soft-nosed forty-fours drove through the smoke and sought flesh until the Winchester clicked dryly.

Then Holt Deaver drew out his Colt, and swiftly reloaded the hot rifle, while watching for an attack. One man did come, racing silently over the rough ground, through the rifting smoke, and the two white bands of clay across his nose and upper cheeks gave him the look of a demon straight from hell. He launched himself from a rock, knife in hand, and was met by two belly shots that killed him before he hit the ground.

Holt finished loading the Winchester and left his hideout, walking coldy and deliberately toward the bloody havoc he had caused. He had no way of knowing whether or not the party he had attacked was all Apaches in that area. He had one advantage if there were more of them, they'd stay away from that ambush after death claimed all of their mates.

Five more shots killed wounded horses, leaving Holt with the big buckskin. The buckskin was frightened until Holt spoke quietly to him and he could smell white man odor instead of Apache.

There was food amongst the scattered bags lying about on the ground. There was even a bottle of good Baconora mezcal, and Holt needed that worse than he did food.

It was quiet now that death had taken over on the mesa. The wind whispered across the canyon and an intense loneliness took over. Holt led the horse to the east. A lone warrior lay beside the trail, face downward, with a knife still clutched in his right hand. He was in a hurry, for he had to make tracks out of that place of death.

It was then that the buck came up off the ground like an uncoiling spring, and he struck hard and viciously for Holt's belly, the honed tip of the blade taking a long cut through jacket, shirt and undershirt, barely scoring the lean belly, but it was enough to make Holt wince in pain and bend down in a reflex action. The return swipe caught him to the left of his nose, tracing a hot course across the cheekbone, through the cheek and down across the lower jaw. A deluge of blood spurted out as Holt managed enough strength to lift the steel-shod butt of the Winchester and strike the brave atop the head, smashing his skull.

Holt grunted in savage pain. The blood poured from his bashed face, and he tried to stanch it with his bandana. "Damned fool!" he raged at himself. "Double-damned fool!"

He should have known better but it was too late now. Another inch or two in that first slash and he would have been disemboweled. Now he'd carry a livid scar on his lean face for the rest of his life, permanent reminder to him for the rest of his life that you can't take chances with these Indians.

He led the buckskin to the east, holding to the reins with his right hand, while keeping the bandana tightly against the wound. A slow thirst crept up into his throat. He had experienced that before when wounded. It wouldn't make it any easier on him in that hellhole of heat, tangled shrubbery and lost canyons. But there was no way back now for Holt Deaver. He was committed again to the long ride.

Even as he slogged along the mesa atop in the first rays of the rising sun the buzzards began to gather like scraps of charred paper floating up there. They'd watch and wait, for they were arrant cowards. But they had plenty of time and they knew there was plenty of fresh meat on which to gorge themselves, and after that, well there was the lone human and his big horse heading into death country. They'd find him when his time came.

CHAPTER SIX

H E HAD MADE it to a large sheltered basin before the fever overtook him. He had tried to cleanse the wound with mezcal, and had fortified himself additionally by drinking some of the strong liquor, but it hadn't helped his lightheadedness at all. Holt made his camp in a cave overlooking the basin, after picketing his horse in a hidden place beside a trickling branch of the stream which watered the basin.

The intense loneliness of the place preyed on his mind, the fever took final hold and in his delirium he saw again people and events of the past.

Suddenly an unearthly scream threaded eerily through the quiet canyon. Cold sweat broke out on him before he realized it was the hunting cry of a mountain lion. This was their stronghold and their domain. You rarely ever saw them but they were always there. You'd see tracks of them and hear their screaming at night, but rare indeed was the man who could say he had seen one.

Holt sat up and wiped the sweat from his face. The bandage was clotted thickly to the slashed flesh of his face and there was a throbbing beneath the bandage. The flesh had puffed up so that his left eye was almost closed. His throat was dry and harsh as though it had been thoroughly sanded. He sipped a little water and crawled to the mouth of the cave. He lay there a long time before he again heard the cry of the lion.

Then he stood up and reached for his rifle. The lion was prowling about the area where his horse was picketed. The big buckskin would be frantic with fright.

Holt walked unsteadily down the slope and through the brush and trees, following the course of the stream, trying to see clearly with his one eye. His head pounded and throbbed like a tom-tom.

He stopped several hundred yards from where he had left the horse. The wind was blowing toward him, so the lion would not scent him. Now it was quiet again except for the soughing of the wind through the trees and the soft murmuring of the stream.

Then the lion struck, driving down on the frightened buckskin with full weight, crushing him down and killing him with swift skill. The buckskin had made one little whinny and the sound was followed by that of thrashing hoofs and the low growling of the killer.

Holt ran forward, raising his rifle for the shot. The lion heard him, turned, crouched, worked his hind legs, then sped forward like a stone hurled from a sling, rising from the ground. The moonlight showed the big beast clearly and Holt fired twice from the hip. The big slugs ripped into the cat but the impetus of its drive carried it forward to strike Holt fully and drive him back into the stream, while the claws, in a last convulsive effort, ripped through Holt's already ragged clothing and played final havoc with it. The tips of the claws raked his chest and belly until the cat was past him and kicking spasmodically in the final throes.

The cold water flowed over Holt's body as he struggled up. The last of the gunshots was still echoing faintly down the long canyon to the west of the basin, far enough to awaken five men who had camped beside the stream.

Holt got to his feet, feeling the hot blood run down mingling with the cold water. He looked at the dead cat, half awash in the stream, then spat thickly upon the carcass.

He walked to the horse and looked down upon it. There'd be no riding out of that canyon for Holt Deaver. What he had feared had happened.

There was nothing to be done. He had his food and ammunition up at the cave. He turned on a heel and walked through the swaying brush beneath the stark shadows of the trees making his way up the slope. Then he entered the cave and peeled off jacket, shirt and undershirt to look at his raked flesh. The claws would be filthy, as they always were, and infection a sure thing. In his weakened condition it might mean death. He had to get out of there right now and head for a settlement and medical care, no matter what would happen to him there. Prison would be better than ending his days in screaming torment in a forgotten canyon, facing death utterly alone.

He bathed the wounds with mezcal, then emptied the last of the strong liquor into his mouth, gasping a little with the ripe stinging of it, and in a little while its strength became his strength, and he left the cave, walking slowly but steadily to the east through the naked moonlight, like a man in a hazy dream.

Far behind Holt Deaver the five men who had heard the shooting had already saddled up, and were riding along the stream, heading east along the canyon as Holt Deaver was heading, and they rode with their rifles across their thighs while the last of the five led a laden burro.

The boy had found the stray and had roped him to bring him back to the little ranch further up the big forked canyon when something made him turn his head, and as he did so his hand dropped to the old Colt which hung holstered at his thigh. He swallowed hard as he stared at the apparition which stood on the far side of the stream staring back at him. A lean lath of a man, wearing tattered, bloodstained clothing, with a filthy and bloody bandage swathing the left side of his face. His toes protruded from the wrecks of boots he wore, and he leaned on a Winchester rifle.

The man opened his mouth and closed it, as though he wanted to speak and could not,

The boy kneed his mare away from the edge of the stream and eased his Colt free from the holster.

The man tried to speak again, raised a hand weakly, then fell face forward into the stream and lay still. The boy slid from his mare and waded into the stream. He hauled the man partway up on the bank and rolled him over. The man opened his eyes, smiled weakly and then said, *"Gracias."* His head lolled to one side and he passed out again.

The boy splashed across the stream and swung up on his mare. He rode swiftly toward the big fork of the canyon with the stray pounding along behind him.

His dreams were peopled again, but this time the actors were different. A freckled boy of about fourteen or fifteen, and a young woman, perhaps of twenty years of age, with dark hair and lovely hazel eyes and hands like healing instruments. Then there was the broth and the

strong tea. The bathings and the fresh bandages. The
warm, soft bed and the crackling of the fire at night,
casting strange shadows on the ceiling of the room and
the chinked log walls.

But he was alive and the fever had been broken,
leaving him as weak as a new born babe. He looked at his
gaunt hands and hardly recognized them. He closed his
eyes a little again and saw the young woman poking up
the fire. She wore a neat gingham dress, and her long
dark hair had been caught up with a bright green ribbon
at the base of her shapely neck. He closed his eyes as she
turned and came back to the table. Then he felt a
wonderously cool hand on his hot forehead and he knew
she was not a dream.

Holt opened his eyes. "Hello," he said in a dry voice.

She smiled. "Hello," she answered. "It's been a long
time for you, hasn't it?"

"How long?"

"Three days."

"Lost forever."

She nodded. "Your wounds were an awful mess. How
did you get them?"

"Mountain lion."

She nodded again, but there was a faint look of suspicion in her lovely hazel eyes. "You'll be all right in a few
days. What happened to you might have killed many
another man. You're all rawhide and steel springs, so my
brother says." She flushed a little as she turned to
measure out some medicine into a glass.

"Not much rawhide and steel left in me," he said
quietly.

"Where have you come from?"

There was no use in lying. "From the Verde."

The spoon clattered against the glass. She turned and

looked down upon him with disbelief on her face. "You must have flown then."

He raised his feet a little and wiggled them. "No," he said. "Partway on a horse and the rest of the way on shank's mare. A lion killed my horse and I killed the lion, but he got a few last licks in on me."

She studied him. "I almost believe you," she said at last.

"Why don't you believe me fully?"

"Do you know where you are?"

He shrugged, wincing as the bandages on his belly and chest drew against the healing flesh. "No."

"You're on the East Fork of the Bandera."

It was his turn to stare at her in disbelief. "How did I get this far?"

She handed him the glass. "You must have walked here after your horse was killed."

"You mean you *found* me *here?*"

"My brother Tim did, but you were only two miles from this house. You must have come through the mountain country west of here if you came from the Verde. Do you know how far that is?"

"It doesn't matter. I won't believe it."

"Over sixty miles," she said quietly. "Another thing: The Tontos have been raiding all around that country. A white man couldn't get through that country. Alone anyway. He'd need at least a company of cavalry with him."

"Aren't *you* afraid of them?"

She shook her head. "They won't bother us."

"You're sure of that?"

"Positive," she said quietly.

He closed his eyes. "Meaning you're too close to a settlement or an army post?"

"No. Why do you ask?"

"Why should they let you alone then?"

"I'll tell you later." She placed a hand on his forehead.

"Is he all right now?" a boyish voice asked from the doorway.

"His fever has broken, Tim."

Holt opened his eyes and looked at the boy. "Hello Tim," he said. "Thanks for helping me."

The boy smiled. "You sure scared me. You looked like Rip Van Winkle standing there."

"Tim!" his sister protested.

Holt grinned. "He's probably right."

She smoothed his pillow. "I'm Susan Morris and this is my brother Timothy."

"Tim!" the boy said.

"Tim is all right with me," said Holt.

"You haven't told us your name," she said.

He hesitated. He'd have to take a chance, for he might have talked in his delirium. "Holt Deaver," he said.

Tim stared at him. "Sis," he said, "this is the man Uncle Cass spoke about!"

A cold feeling broke out in Holt, and his hands gripped the edge of the coverlet. "Uncle Cass?" he asked quietly.

"Sure! You know Uncle Cass! He talked a lot about you, Mister Deaver!"

"Yeh, I know Uncle Cass. Where is he?"

"He only stayed here one night and then he left on business. Said he'd be back in about a week or ten days. Went south, he did."

"On *business?*"

"Yes," said the boy proudly, "and he said we'd never have to worry about money no more, 'cause he was going to take care of us from now on, on account of us bein' orphans. Said he'd send me to school anywhere I wanted to go. I didn't like *that* so much, but he also promised me a silver mounted Winchester and a new saddle."

Holt glanced at the girl. "How long since you saw Uncle Cass?" he asked casually.

"You mean before he came here?"

"Yes."

She turned a little. "How long has it been, Tim? You were a baby then, hardly a few months old. Fifteen years ago I think it was. I was only a child. I could just about remember him."

"Fifteen years would be just about right," said Holt dryly. "What did he say about me?"

Tim came to stand beside the bed. "He said to give you the best of everything until he got back. He said he owed you a debt."

Holt nodded. He remembered the night he had held off the five outlaws back at the Verde only to find out that Cass Riker had vanished like wind driven smoke.

Susan smiled. "He said he didn't think you'd make it, but if you did, you were to have the best of everything. We haven't much, Mister Deaver, but what we have is yours."

He looked about the comfortable room, neat and clean, and then he smiled at her. "To a man like me, Miss Morris, this room itself is enough, and your care is all the reward I ever want."

She flushed a little. "We would have done it for anyone, Mister Deaver. I have some nursing skill. My father was a doctor, formerly a contract surgeon at Fort Apache, and he became interested in treating the Apaches. I can tell you that we are considered their friends. That is why they let us live here, and have done so since Father died two years ago."

"And now Uncle Cass has come back to help you?"

She smiled. "Yes. Isn't it wonderful?"

He nodded. "I suppose you heard from Uncle Cass before he returned?"

She shook her head. "We never knew where he was. I had heard he was in Mexico and had some kind of business down there. My father rarely spoke of him. You see, Uncle Cass was my mother's younger brother, and from the few stories we heard about him he was pretty wild in his younger days. But we'll forget all that now."

"Sure, sure," he said. He found it hard to look at her, knowing that her uncle was as crooked as a stake-and-rider fence. The old coot had probably figured that Holt would be wiped out back at Verde, and if he hadn't been stopped there he would never have passed through the country between the Verde and the Bandera. It was a miracle that he had passed through there with the Tontos raiding all around it. But Old Cass was no fool. He had neatly covered his trail by telling his trusting niece and nephew to expect Holt. Maybe to throw Holt off guard if he did make the Bandera.

There was one thing Holt knew for sure; he meant to be out of that bed before Old Whiskers came back to the Bandera with his saddlebags full of Wells-Fargo money. Holt meant to get his fingers into that pile of loot even if he had to drop down on the old man to do it.

"You'd better sleep now," she said.

He nodded. She snuffed out the candle that guttered on the little table. "The fire will die down soon," she said.

"Thanks, Miss Morris."

"Susan," she said with a smile.

"Susan then." He raised his head. "One thing, Susan: If anyone comes here asking for me, you never saw me."

There was a moment's silence, and then she nodded. "No," she said quietly.

"You're wondering why?"

"A little. But it didn't surprise me."

"How so?"

"Uncle Cass told me the same thing. Good night, Mister Deaver." She closed the door behind her.

He waited a few minutes, then slipped out of the bed, staggering a little in his weakness. He padded over to his gun belt and withdrew his Colt from the sheath. He opened the loading gate and checked it. It was fully loaded. He took it back to the bed with him, sipped a glass of water, then slid the six-shooter beneath his pillow. There was nothing like Samuel Colt and Company for insurance for a man like Holt Deaver.

CHAPTER SEVEN

THE WIND was dry and brisk as it swept across the Mongollon Plateau and moved the pines, picking up their brisk resinous odor and carrying it along. The sky was dotted with fleeting clouds racing ever westward, with their shadows passing up and downhill ahead of them. A thread of smoke rose far down the forked canyon where the little ranch house and its outbuildings were hidden from view.

Holt Deaver sat Tim's mare on an escarpment, studying the land to the west through Doctor Morris' army field glasses. There was no sign of human life to the west. Nothing but a lone hawk hanging high overhead, floating on motionless wings in the strong draft of wind.

Though Holt was still weak he had forced himself from that comfortable bed after three more days of it. Old Cass still had not appeared, nor had there been any sign of the five men riding from the west. Maybe they had lost the trail, maybe . . .

Holt rolled a cigarette and lighted it, then leaned on his saddlehorn to study the country. A man, had he a mind to, could have a fine spread there. The canyon, through which the East Fork of the Bandera flowed, was well watered, protected from the heat of summer and the cold of winter, with plenty of shelter for cattle. There was timber aplenty and rock for building, if a man wanted to build well. The area was out of the way, on the very edge of Apache country, but in time they'd be under complete control, and if a railroad ran a branch line through that country, it would be easy to get in supplies and ship out fat cattle.

But there was a bitter loneliness in Holt Deaver. He was still on the run; in fact, he should have pulled out of there as soon as he was able to, but he had to wait for Old Cass and his loot. There was more to it than just that though. There was Susan Morris. That was the bitter stab, because Holt knew he'd have to leave that country in a hurry, and he knew he'd never be able to come back again, if he was lucky enough to make Sonora.

One good thing at least was the fact that the East Fork of the Bandera was isolated from almost every other settled area within miles. Tim had told Holt that the two of them stayed at the ranch from late spring until late fall, then they moved into town where his sister worked in the small hospital as a nurse. The two of them loved the little ranch, although it hardly afforded them more than a bare living. The boy supplemented the larder by killing deer and other game. They had a small garden and a few head of cattle. But this was to have been their last year on the ranch. Tim had to get more schooling, and his sister had been willing to work to support the two of them until Tim got his education. The boy had told Holt that he wanted to be a doctor as his father had been, and he knew the long and hard road he must follow to achieve that. So they would sell the little spread for whatever they could get. It wouldn't be much, for the Tonto threat cheapened the value to anyone but the two Morrises.

He studied the country spread out beneath the escarpment. Tim had said there was plenty of land adjacent to the ranch that could be homesteaded. Good grazing land, the best range-land in that area. A good rancher could live like a king once he had put down his roots. Trouble was, Holt Deaver was a tumbleweed, with no roots.

Touching the mare with his heels, he rode down the slope. He had made himself useful about the place, suggesting some improvements such as a trough of wooden planking to bring stream water closer to the corral. He had done some rough carpentry about the place and had plastered up the huge outside chimney of the living room fireplace. He had been weak, and had worked slowly, but he had to do something to show these people he appreciated their kindness.

Reaching the canyon floor, he eyed the rippling waters. There must be trout in that water. It was a good place. Deer, bear, fish and other game were plentiful. Cattle would thrive. Horses would flourish.

But now and then as he rode he glanced over his left shoulder at that mysterious and brooding country to the west. It was like a gigantic barrier of silence and mystery. Maybe it was haunted by other beings than the Tontos. Five of them. Maybe the Tontos had taken care of them. It would be no loss to Arizona Territory. But if those five hardcases reached the Bandera and found out that Cass Riker and Holt Deaver had reached that area, there would be gunplay along the East Fork.

Twenty-five years of life lay behind Holt Deaver. A hard life, but not reason enough for him to have turned owlhoot. Still, nothing he had ever done had been more than many another man had done in the Southwest. Sure, he had done a little rustling, some crooked gambling, and had been a hired gun several times. But he had been a drifter, with no home to call his own, no relatives to whom he could return. A cold feeling came over him as he rode toward the ranch buildings. How long could a man go on like that?

Holt looked toward the ranch house and saw Susan feeding her chickens. The wind whipped her neat dress about her long, slim legs, and she held her dark hair back with her free hand as she fed the clucking fowls. It was a picture a man could see many times in a fire in the hidden canyons where he was forced to live until he was free of the law. If he ever got that free. But that picture would never let him be free until the day he died.

It was only after he had corralled the mare and rubbed her down that he saw the late afternoon sun glinting on something up the stream, where the rude log bridge crossed the water. Holt stepped back around the corner of the barn. Susan was walking back toward the house and then she turned and looked back toward the bridge. As she turned again she saw Holt. Their eyes met and then she looked away.

"I'll leave if you want me to," he called out.

"Why?" she asked.

"To keep you from lying."

"How do you know it's you they want?"

He did not answer for a moment. Then he shrugged. "It's logical," he said.

"What is it you have done?"

"Many things," he said dryly.

Her eyes studied him closely. "You don't have to run,"

she said at last. "You couldn't get far. You're not strong enough yet."

"You don't have to lie for me, Susan."

She stepped up onto the porch of the house. "I'm sorry for you, Holt," she said. "Very sorry. I won't say you are here."

Then she was gone. Holt smashed his right fist into his left palm. She had made him feel like a child caught in a wrongdoing—like an utter fool.

But there was no use in taking a chance. He walked to the rear of the barn and up the slope amongst the trees until he found a place where he was well hidden in amongst the rock ledges and brush. He quickly loaded his rifle and then squatted down behind a ledge, to watch whoever was riding toward the house. He uncased the field glasses and focused them on a point near the house. It didn't take long for the three horsemen to ride into his field of vision. They were strangers, but one of them had a star pinned to his vest.

Holt wet his dry lips as he watched them draw rein in front of the house and then dismount. Susan came out on the porch and talked with the man who wore the star. She shook her head several times. Now and then one of the men would look up and down the canyon, passing the place where Holt lay hidden.

Then the three men rode slowly back along the stream and vanished in the trees beyond the bridge. Susan went back into the house. Half an hour passed, and then Tim came out of the house, looked up toward Holt and waved his hat.

Holt turned quickly, raising his rifle, finger on the trigger, ready to shoot and to kill. It was Susan. He lowered the rifle and let the hammer down to half-cock.

"You move like a cat," she said. "How long have you been living like this, Holt?"

He flushed a little. "Too long," he said. "Who were they?"

"Deputy Sheriff Lang Masters and two of his men."

"Who were they looking for?"

"They asked if we had seen a man on the run through here. The description matched you, Holt."

"So? It might have been someone else they were looking for."

She shook her head. "They asked for you by name."

He shoved back his hat. Then Burl Stuart had passed the notice along. They still thought he had had something todo with that mess at the Colorado. And, if anything had happened to end the lives of Morg Mills and Trump Foster after Holt had held them back at the Verde, the whole blame for the paymaster robbery and killings would settle heavily on his shoulders. No jury would believe that he had had nothing to do with it.

She studied him. "It was about a robbery and killing near Fort Mohave," she said.

"I know," he said quietly.

"They'll eventually catch you, Holt. Wouldn't it be easier to give yourself up?"

He rolled a cigarette and lighted it. "Would you believe me if I told you that I had nothing to do with that robbery and those killings?"

She shrugged. "I don't know what to believe, Holt. If you *are* innocent why don't you turn yourself in to be cleared?"

He laughed without mirth. "It's not as easy as all that, Susan. I'm on the run, but not for killing those soldiers. I got in a gun scrape at Chloride and I might have gotten clear of that all right except for my reputation." He looked away from her as he spoke the last words.

"Is it as bad as all that?" she asked.

"It doesn't take much for a man to have a reputation in this country. I had a good one once. I served in the army as a scout. Maybe I should have stayed with them."

"Why did you leave?"

He shrugged. "I had ambitions, ideas, and they couldn't be financed with army pay. I tried a few things, then drifted along until it was easy to break the law. There is one thing you must believe though: I am not a killer."

"But you have killed men?"

"Yes. But it has never been murder, Susan. Those soldiers were killed by two men I knew. I was forced to kill the brother of one of them to escape from them, or they would have killed me to keep my mouth shut. I ran. Maybe that was a mistake, but a man doesn't think clearly at times like that. I killed another man. I dropped his horse and he was killed in the fall."

"You make it sound so innocent."

He dropped his cigarette and stamped on it. "You see?" he demanded. "What chance does a man have to explain once they daub him with the tar brush?"

"You can turn yourself in, Holt."

He shook his head. "No, not until I see your uncle."

Their eyes met and she came closer to him. "What do you have to do with him, Holt?"

He looked away. "It was a business deal."

"What *kind* of business?"

"It has nothing to do with you, Susan." He picked up his rifle. "I'll be pulling out of here tonight," he said. "You can loan me a horse. I'll leave it where Timmie can pick it up."

"Running again?"

"Yes," he said fiercely. "You don't know why! It isn't your way of life! What do you know about men like me? Let me leave here and you'll never be bothered by me again."

She eyed his taut face and the healing scar; the gaunt look of this tired wolf of a man, and her heart could not help but go out to him. "Stay awhile, Holt," she said quietly. "You'll be safe here until you decide to leave." She walked to the far end of the barn and then turned. "We'll eat in twenty minutes. There'll be hot biscuits and venison too." Then she was gone.

He yanked off his hat and slammed it on the ground. Curse the blasted fates that drove a man like him on and on even after he had decided to leave his way of life and try to reform. The desire was within him all right, and he knew he could do it, but the world wouldn't let him go that easily. He was tabbed and marked, and wherever he went his reputation would follow him. It was a marked deck for men like Holt Deaver.

The sickening thing about it all was something that had slowly moved into his mind in the past two days. It was Susan Morris. He had known many women of all kinds, but he had never been fool enough to fall in love; with his way of life it would never pan out. Now, while in the biggest mess of his life, he had the luck to fall in love.

He picked up hat and rifle and walked toward the house. Somewhere along the distant escarpment a coyote howled, and the utter loneliness of that haunting cry cut into Holt Deaver like the bite of a whiplash, for it was a loneliness akin to his own.

CHAPTER EIGHT

THERE WAS no use in him trying to sleep. The thoughts that teemed through his mind drove all sleep away. Holt got up from the bed where he had dropped fully clothed some hours before. He walked to the window and looked out toward the murmuring stream. The moon was on the wane but it was still clear enough to see distant objects, and as he felt for the makings he saw a movement down near the bridge. He eyed the man who was riding slowly along the bank of the stream and then he saw the ragged beard, ruffled by the night wind.

Holt reached for his gun belt and swung it about his lean hips, buckling it swiftly and settling it. He placed his hat on his head and then quietly left the room. The house was silent, and only a few coals showed in the bed of ashes in the huge fireplace. He slipped out of the back door and edged his way around the side of the house farthest away from the direction from which Cass Riker was approaching.

He had made it just in time, for Riker had

dismounted in front of the house and was loosening the girth of his saddle. Holt crossed the patch of ground between them with silent strides, but even so Cass whirled, and his hand dropped to his Colt only for him to see Holt's six-shooter at belly level, and to look into cold gray eyes.

Riker smiled uneasily. "Howdy, bub," he said.

Holt nodded.

Riker tilted his head to one side. "Some filly give you a gouge in the face for gettin' too fresh?"

Holt shook his head.

"Talkative cuss, ain'tcha?"

"Where's the money, Riker?"

Riker grinned. "Oh, *that?*'

"Yeh . .'. *that.*"

"I ain't got it with me, bub."

The Colt muzzle touched Riker's navel. "Where is it, Old Whiskers?" asked Holt coldly.

Riker slowly reached up and scratched in his disreputable beard. "Cached," he said.

"Same place, I suppose?"

"No. I moved it."

"Why didn't you bring it back here? Your niece and nephew been expecting it, *Uncle* Cass. They said they'd never have to worry about money anymore, 'cause Uncle Cass was going to take care of them. High class schooling, a silver mounted Winchester and a new saddle for Timmie. Maybe a rich husband for Susan."

Riker's face darkened. "You talk a helluva lot, bub "

"Not as much as you're going to talk, Old Whiskers."

"I told them to look out for you!"

"Sure, after you jumped up a hell of a lot of dust leaving me behind at the Verde to pull your damned chestnuts out of the fire."

Riker tilted his head. "So you stopped them there anyways?"

"You damned tooting I did!"

"Well, you should have killed them."

"You cold-gutted shark! You don't give a damn who I kill just so long as you keep your shirttail clean, do you? Now, where's that money? I never expected to dun you for that ten thousand bucks. Old Whiskers, but I'm doing it now."

Riker shrugged. "It ain't here, bub."

"Step back!"

Riker obliged.

"Now open those saddlebags and dump them out on the ground!"

The old man shrugged. He unbuckled the bags, opened them and dumped the contents onto the moonlit ground. Holt poked a boot toe amongst the things. An extra shirt, undershirt, a filthy towel, and the usual odds and ends a man would ordinarily carry in saddlebags. Holt eyed the old man. "Peel," he said shortly.

"You double-dammed fool! You think I got all that money on me?" Riker slapped his thighs and his sides. "Look! Or has that scar ruined your eyesight?"

There wasn't any doubt but that the old coot was telling the truth. Holt gripped Riker by the front of the shirt and drew him close. "I'm going to take you out into the barn, Old Whiskers, and pound the truth outa you!"

Riker smirked a little. "Now, bub, take it easy! Lemme tell you what happened."

Riker straightened his shirt as Holt released him. "I seen your old *compadres* at the West Fork of the Bandera. They was camped there. I damned near run into 'em. Sure, I had the *dinero* with me! But I wasn't about to take any chances on them finding me with it, so I cached it."

"Seems like I heard this one before."

"You still think I'm trying to euchre you outa that money I promised you?"

"I haven't seen any money, Riker. I don't even know if you have any money at all. All I know is that if I hadn't showed up to help you, and got you as far as the Verde, you'd be in the hands of those three boys of yours, and if they hadn't squeezed the information out of you as to where you cached that Wells-Fargo money, you'd have been stiff as a poker long ago."

"Well, I got to admit you played the part of the big hero, bub. Real nice of you it was. A real Sir Gallyhad, or whatever his name was."

Holt smiled coldly. "Yeh, Sir Gallyhad and the Robin Hood of the Mogollon country, Old Cass Riker, who robs from the rich to give to the poor. The poor being Old Cass himself!"

"You got me wrong, bub."

"Listen, Old Whiskers: You got those two nice young people in that house thinking you're rich old Uncle Cass come home to give them an early Christmas. Supposing you do give them some of that money and give them all the things you promised them, and then they find out where you got the *dinero?* What then?"

The old man's eyes were as cold as glacier ice. "Now you didn't open that big mouth of yours and tell 'em anything about where the money come from, did you, bub? 'Cause if you did, I'll . . ."

Holt waved his Colt back and forth a little. "You'll *what?*" he asked.

"Well, you got the edge now, but I know you ain't the type to work over an old man like me to take out your spite. Look, I ain't lyin' about that money, bub. You'll get your ten thousand quick as I find out that those rattlesnakes followin' me ain't wise to where I got it hid."

Holt nodded. He let down the hammer of his Colt to half-cock, and slid the weapon into its holster. "Fair enough. How soon do we start?"

"Couple of days."

Holt smiled and shook his head. "Tomorrow."

"Now, bub"

"Tomorrow, Old Whiskers! And just to make sure you don't get any ideas to the contrary you can bunk with me tonight, though I'd rather bunk with an old billy goat."

"Well, you ain't no rose."

Riker took his horse to the corral and unsaddled it while Holt leaned against the fence smoking. The old coot could sure weave a mess of lies but this time Holt had him cold.

They walked back to the house and eased into it. When they were in the room, Holt jerked a thumb at the far side of the big bed, then watched Riker peel to his long Johns and hop into the bed.

Holt pulled off boots and gun belt, scaled his hat at a wall peg, then took his Colt from its sheath. "I don't sleep well, Old Whiskers," he said "I'm nervous as hell. One time I come up out of a sound sleep and planted a bullet right through the skull of my partner's pack mule."

"Remarkable," said Cass dryly.

"Come to think of it, that danged mule looked a lot like you, but he had a little edge as to looks."

"Stop, you're killing me, bub."

Holt rolled a cigarette and lighted it. "Maybe I will one of these days, Old Whiskers, maybe I will . . ."

It was a quiet and taciturn Holt who sat at breakfast the morning after the old buzzard had returned to the ranch. Riker could play a part with ease. He was as slick as varnish, and he had those two young people a little dewy-eyed with his conversation. Yet it seemed to Holt that every now and then he caught a feeling of tenseness, and a little tinge of fear in Riker's eyes.

"Sure, sure," the old man was saying. "Holt here and me is old *compadres*. I knew he'd be coming through this way."

"How come the two of you didn't travel together to get here?" asked Tim. "Uncle Cass leave you somewhere, Holt?"

"Yes," said Holt, "he left me somewhere, all right."

Cass Riker stood up and looked at Holt. Maybe you'd like to come along?"

"Maybe I would."

"I'll get the horses."

"Do that," said Holt politely.

"I'll give you a hand, Uncle Cass," said Tim quickly.

"Sure, sure, boy, glad to have you!"

Susan leaned over and refilled Holt's coffee cup after they left. "What were the two of you talking about last night in front of the house?"

"Odds and ends. I didn't know we had an audience."

"Do you always talk with your old *compadre* with a pistol in your hand?"

Holt felt for the makings, took them out, then looked at Susan. She nodded. He rolled a smoke and lighted it.

"You didn't answer me, Holt."

"There isn't anything for me to tell you."

"You're lying!"

"Maybe I am. There are some things that don't concern you, Susan."

"Uncle Cass does."

He eyed her. "I didn't know you loved him that much."

"It isn't him, Holt. It's Tim I'm concerned about. He has no father and no mother and I've had to fill in for both of them. We were happy enough until Uncle Cass came along. Now he's filled that boy up with big ideas, talking about money, gifts, the whole world to be placed at his feet."

"So? I don't see anything wrong with that."

"With dirty money, Holt?"

He flushed. "What do you mean by that?"

She leaned closer to him. "I'm not such a fool as you might think, Holt. Your stories don't quite hang together. He shows up here after fifteen years looking like a saddle tramp, talking about money, money until I wondered if he was in his right mind. Then he vanishes to somewhere, never saying where he was going, and then *you* show up, on the run from the law, practically cut to ribbons."

"I almost believed that story of yours that you had nothing to do with those killings on the Colorado."

He stood up and snubbed out his cigarette. "You still believe me," he said.

"Why do you say that?"

"You wouldn't have covered up for me yesterday if you hadn't believed me."

She looked away. "I want to believe you," she said.

"Well, in any case, I'll be out of your way before too long."

"On the run again?"

He looked down at her. "What difference does it make?"

"It might make a difference to me, Holt."

Then an impulse made him bend down, lift her chin with his hand, and kiss her on the lips. She did not resist. He walked to the door and looked back at her. "Forget about me, Susan," he said. "I'm nothing but a long rider. Here today and gone tomorrow."

"Caring little about yourself and less about other people, is that it?"

"I suppose so. I don't like it any better than you do, Susan."

She stood up and began to clear the table. "Tim thinks a lot of you, Holt."

"I'm glad to hear that."

She studied him. "Don't let him down, Holt. Whatever Uncle Cass has done, and wherever he got the money might hurt Tim for the rest of his life. I don't want to know. But you know, and somehow I believe that you'll work this thing out so that Tim doesn't get hurt."

"And you?"

She turned away. "When you said you were leaving that was hurt enough."

"Holt!" called Cass from the corral.

"Coming!"

He walked back to Susan and took her in his arms. He kissed her gently and she lightly touched the livid scar on his face, then kissed him in return, placing her head against his chest when she took her lips from his. He held her close, then released her and walked to the door. There was nothing he could say although his mind was confused and filled with teeming thoughts. She knew Cass Riker had not made his fortune in Mexico, or anywhere else. But with a deep feminine intuition she had seemed to cast aside Holt Deaver's faults and had called upon him to show his virtues.

He walked to the corral and swung up onto his horse.

Cass pulled down his disreputable hat. "You might need your rifle, Holt," he said casually. "Might run into a deer or two, and I'm partial to fresh venison."

"I'll get it!" said Tim. He ran toward the house.

Riker fiddled with his right stirrup. "Well?" he asked.

"She's on to you, Cass."

"I'm beginning to think so."

"So?"

The old man shrugged. "I earned that money. Fifteen years it cost me."

"And you're going to give most of it to them, is that it?"

said Holt sarcastically. "You make me sick! You *ever* tell the truth?"

"Maybe I am this time."

Holt grunted. "I'll believe it when I see it."

"Stick around."

Holt swiveled his eyes and held the old man's attention. "I aim to do just that, Old Whiskers."

Tim came from the house and handed Holt the rifle. *"Gracias,"* said Holt as he slid the Winchester into its sheath.

They kneed their horses away from the boy and rode down the canyon. Susan Morris came out on the front porch and watched them as they rode. Holt glanced back. He seemed still to taste the soft freshness of her lips and her words came back to him. *When you said you were leaving that was hurt enough.*

"Nice girl that," said Cass.

"For once you're telling the truth."

"I don't want nothin' to happen to her, Holt."

"Meaning?"

The hard old eyes flicked at Holt. "You know what I mean, bub. You'll get your money. I promise you that. But that's *all* you'll take away from the Bandera country. Understand?"

Holt looked away from the old man. He knew Cass

meant what he said. Maybe the old man *did* have a virtue or two left, although it was almost impossible to believe.

Holt looked back at the house. She was gone.

"You know where we're heading?" asked Riker.

"For the *dinero?*"

"Not yet."

Holt eyed him.

"I want to take a look at those boys on the West Fork."

"Fair enough, but no killing, Riker."

They rode downstream until they rounded a huge shoulder of rock, which cut off the view of the ranch buildings. Cass turned his horse and began to ride up a long slanting fault in the canyon wall, hardly wide enough for a horse. He glanced back. "We can come out on the West Fork about half a mile from where they are by going this way."

"A real highway, ain't it?"

"If you're scared, bub, you can go back. This is *man's* work."

Holt only grunted. The old man had more than his share of guts. You had to give him credit for that at least. Holt couldn't help but wonder what it had been like in the old days to ride behind Cass Riker. The old coot would have to show a little more guts if they ever ran face on into the boys on the West Fork of the Bandera. He had been running at Alamo Springs, and he had run from Verde. Maybe he aimed to run again and leave Holt Deaver to face their enemies. Well, he could try,but Holt was going to stick to him like a cockleburr on a saddle blanket, and never give him another chance.

CHAPTER NINE

T HE EARLY afternoon sun slanted down into the canyon of the Bandera and glinted from the swiftly running waters of the stream. The wind swayed the trees and made them form dappled patches of shade on the clear waters. The two men lay belly flat on a ridge overlooking most of the canyon, watching the simple camp far below them. Cass Riker handed the field glasses to Holt. "I can see only one of them down there. It's Pete Shalen I think. Got his left arm in a sling. Maybe it's a memento of the Verde."

Holt focused the glasses and studied the camp. There was only one man there as Cass had said. A horse and a mule grazed not far away. And there was no sign of any of the others. "I wonder where they are?" he said.

Cass rested his bearded chin on his crossed forearms. "That's a good question. Looking for you, I guess."

"Only two of them are interested in me. But all five of them are interested in *you*."

"How so?"

Holt told him of how Morg Mills and Trump Foster

had thrown in with the others back on the Verde. "Between me and you, Old Whiskers, if those five buzzards ever get their hands on that money, won't any of them sleep easy as long as they're in each other's company."

Cass grunted deep in his throat. "Gives me an idea," he said with a queer glint in his hard eyes. "Why not let 'em get their hands on the money? Then after two or three of 'em get killed off by their *compadres,* we can move in on the survivors and wipe them out. We get rid of them and we get the money."

"You sure think big!"

The old man grinned. "You have to admit it's not a bad idea."

Holt raised the field glasses again. He wasn't as much worried about the outlaws as he was about the law being after him. "What about Wells-Fargo?" asked Holt. "Don't you think they might be interested in where you hid that loot?"

"I suppose so. I never saw any of their agents waiting around Yuma for me. 'Course, I was in one helluva big rush to get outa there before those three *ex-compadres* of mine threw a loop on me."

"That figures. One thing bothers me though. Supposing Wells-Fargo agents come to the ranch looking for you? Or our five friends go there. What happens then?"

Cass grinned. "Wells-Fargo don't know about them two kids and neither does my three *ex-compadres.*"

"Sure, sure, but you came back and shot off your mouth to them about all that money. Supposing they talk about it?"

"Who's going to find out where the money come from?"

"You dumb-block! They'll find you some day, won't they?"

Cass Riker spat. "No," he said quietly. "They won't ever find me, Holt, 'cause I ain't goin' to be around."

Holt lowered the glasses and looked at him. "You mean you're going to give them the money and then pull out?"

"You figure right, bub."

"What makes you think they'll want that kind of money?"

"A blasted fortune in their hands and they're goin' to ask where it comes from?"

"Maybe they will," said Holt quietly. "Maybe they won't want it."

The old man stared at him. "Maybe you're loco," he said.

"Look, Old Whiskers! Maybe some people don't figure the way you do. Maybe some people are honest. 'Course, how would *you* know? You ain't been around anyone that's honest for so long you wouldn't know one if you saw one."

"I know you, bub," said Cass coldly.

"What I said still goes. Don't judge other people by me, Old Whiskers." Holt looked down on the camp again. "It wouldn't surprise me none if your niece and nephew didn't turn that money in to Wells-Fargo."

"Who's going to tell 'em it's Wells-Fargo money? You?"

"I ain't crazy. They'll find out by themselves likely enough. By that time I'll be in Sonora dickering for my own rancho with that ten thousand you owe me."

"Yeh," said Cass dryly.

Holt looked at him. "There's only one big thing bothering me, Cass. If any of those buzzards get to the ranch they won't go easy on those two there. They'll try to get them to talk."

"They don't know nothing about the money."

"Maybe not, but Carley and the others don't know that." Holt cased the glasses. "They sure could make it rough on them if they had a mind to."

Cass Riker wet his thin lips and looked uncertainly at Holt. "I never thought of that."

"Well, you'd better think of it!"

"Yeh . . . yeh . . . Mebbe we'd better take a look back there?"

Holt sat up and gently fingered his healing scar. "We were going after the money, Old Whiskers. Maybe I ain't changed my mind about that."

Cass stood up and began to scratch his lean stomach and when he took his hand away it held a double-barreled derringer in it, and the little gun with the big bite was pointed right at Holt's belly. "I don't know about you, Deaver," said the old man, "but I'm going back to the ranch."

Holt looked down at the gun and then into the hard eyes of the old man. "Your argument is most convincing, Old Whiskers," he said dryly. "Maybe I'd better go along with you."

"Ahead of me, *amigo*. Ahead of me!"

Holt shrugged. He led the way to the horses. They mounted and rode back toward the dangerous trail by which they had approached the West Fork of the Bandera, and this time the young man was in the lead.

They had left the horses behind the huge shoulder of rock that jutted out into the canyon, and had made their way on foot through the thick brush and trees that bordered the west side of the canyon until the ranch was in view. A scarf of smoke drifted up from the chimney but there was no sign of life about the place.

The two of them squatted down in the brush and studied the house. "Looks peaceful enough," said Cass. There was a worried note in his voice.

Holt nodded. He uncased the field glasses and focused them, sighting them on the house. There were no strange horses around the place. There were two horses in the corral and one of them was Tim's sprightly little mare, while the other was an old timer, practically retired, that used to haul the doctor's buggy in the days when he had had his practice.

"What do you think?" asked the old man.

Holt shrugged. "I know one thing: I'm not going to ride up to that house as a prime target for someone."

"Ain't no one there other than the kids," said Cass. "You can see the boy's hoss and you got Susan's hoss."

Holt nodded. "Well, let's Indian up on the place."

"We'll sure look silly if Susan and Tim see us."

"We'll look a lot sillier if those four hardcases are waiting down there for us."

"You sure are nervous, bub."

Holt spat. "You weren't exactly calm and collected this morning when you were eating breakfast."

The old man did not answer. They kept to the woods until they were up behind the ranch buildings. Still no sign of life. Cass tapped Holt on the shoulder and pointed toward the house. A fresh puff of smoke had drifted up from the chimney. "It's all right," said the old man. "Susan just fed the fire."

Holt rubbed his jaw. "You can see through those log walls, Old Whiskers?"

"I ain't a-scared to go down and make sure," said Cass.

Holt shrugged. They walked down the slope to the back of the barn, looked up and down the winding stream, then walked toward the house. "Susan!" called out Cass.

"Yes, Uncle Cass!" she called from a kitchen window.

"You all right, honey?"

"Certainly, Uncle Cass!"

"See? said the old man to Holt. "You and yer ideas!"

They walked toward the back door of the house feeling a little foolish. "We can send Tim for the hosses," said Cass.

Holt nodded. He was tired, for he had not yet fully recovered his strength. Beyond that he was getting weary of the whole business. He had been living with it too long.

The kitchen door swung open and Susan stood there looking at them. Her face was a little pale. Something warned Holt. He dropped behind the old man, turned his head quickly from side to side, and as he looked toward the south wall of the house, saw a lean shadow move. "Look out, Cass!" he yelled.

There was Ernie Carley standing behind Susan. The tall man shoved the girl aside and raised a six-shooter. Morg Mills came around the side of the house. "Get Deaver!" he yelled.

Holt dare not fire toward the girl. He swung and drew, facing Morgan Mills. It was then that he saw Savvy Harris framed in the barn door with a Colt in his hand. Holt whirled and fired from the hip even as Harris fired. Harris' slug whipped through the slack of Holt's shirt. The gunman staggered a little and pumped out two more shots which went wild as Holt slammed another slug into him. He went down and lay still.

Morgan Mills fired twice at Holt from the shelter of

the side of the house, but Holt had hit the ground an instant before the first shot and fired from the ground a bullet which struck the log closest to Mills' face, scattering bark against it, temporarily blinding the man.

Ernie Carley dodged to one side to avoid hitting Cass and tried to get a shot in at Holt, but Susan shoved the tall man and his shot whispered past Holt's left ear.

Cass had turned and ran. He gripped the top rail of the corral and vaulted over it as cleanly as an athlete, striking the soft ground inside the corral. He dashed across the corral and over the far fence to vanish into the woods.

Holt jumped for cover inside the barn, rapping out a shot toward Morg Mills, who was clutching his face. The gunman vanished from Holt's view.

Then Ernie Carley jumped back inside the house, shoving Susan ahead of him. Holt raised his pistol, and as he did so a rifle flatted off from across the creek and the slug smashed into the framing of the barn door. He dropped flat. Now he knew where Trump Foster was. Holt and Cass had been neatly suckered in by the four outlaws.

Holt crawled across the barn floor until he could peer through an unchinked place. Gun smoke still drifted about the rear of the house. There was no sign of Morg Mills or Ernie Carley. Trump Foster was not to be seen but Holt knew the big man was better than most men with the long gun and he'd have a bead on that barn door right now.

One of the five would never trouble Holt again. Savvy Harris had died as he had lived, fast and violently. It had been a near thing out there, and if it hadn't been for Susan, Holt might be lying out there beside Savvy Harris. The old man had been a big help. He had broken all records getting out of bullet range and hadn't fired a shot. Morg Mills had yelled to get Holt. They wanted him out of the way. They wanted the old man alive to find out where he had cached the loot. Now they had Susan as a hostage and quite likely they had Tim, too.

Holt opened the loading gate of his Colt and refilled the cylinder, mentally cursing himself for leaving his rifle on his horse.

"Deaver!" called Carley from inside the house.

"Yes?" answered Holt. He quickly moved his position so as not to be pinpointed.

"We don't want you, we want Riker."

"That's not what Mills said."

"Hell! You've been nothing but trouble for us. I don't know how you're still alive, but that can't be helped."

"Thanks."

Holt crawled to the far side of the barn and stood up justbeyond a narrow window. He could see the back of the house and the place about where Trump Foster should be.

"We've got the woman and the boy here, Deaver! We know who they are! Now we want that old sidewinder to come along peaceful like. We got some talking to do."

"You saw him take off, Carley."

"Yes. But it's up to you to get him back."

"Why me?"

There was a few minutes of silence and then Morg Mills spoke from somewhere inside the house. "You want these people to get killed, Deaver?" he said in his cold, toneless voice.

The man meant it. He was as cold-gutted as a shark. They had all the aces. Trouble was Holt had little faith in Cass Riker, and he wasn't at all sure the old coot would come back peaceful like as Carley would want him to.

"You hear me, Deaver?" called Morg Mills.

"Go ahead and kill them," said Holt on a long shot.

It was quiet again for a time, then Mills called out again. "I know you better than that, Deaver. You always had a soft spot in your head for other people. That's why you didn't pitch in with me and the boys back at the Colorado."

Holt knew then that Susan Morris would know that he had spoken the truth. Susan didn't know men like Morg Mills and Trump Foster.

Mills laughed. "Trouble for you is that the story is out that you were in on the deal, Deaver. Fact is, no one seems to know the names or descriptions of any of the others mixed up in it."

I do ... thought Holt.

"Now, Deaver," said Carley clearly, "you just go and get that old goat and bring him back. We want him delivered or these two people here will die. That's clear enough. As for you, you can beat it. Webb Harris died of a busted neck and it was Savvy who wanted to make you pay for it, not me and Pete. Well, you got Savvy too. That's one less for the big payoff."

"What about Morg Mills? It was his brother I killed. Morg won't ever forget that!"

Again a long silence although Holt could have sworn he heard low voices in the house.

"Deaver?" It was Morg Mills.

"Shoot!"

"Mike is gone. Ain't no use in digging up the dead. I got to look out for myself from now on. You bring in Riker and I'll forget you killed Mike."

"All right! What's the deal?"

There might be time for Holt to get into town and bring out the sheriff and some of his boys.

Carley spoke up. "You pull out after we leave. You won't shoot, for we'll have the woman and the boy with us. You get the old man and bring him to Slide Rock on the West Fork of the Bandera."

"Where will you be?"

Carley laughed. "Wouldn't you like to know? You figure we don't know you're thinking of bringing down the law?"

Holt crawled to the other side of the barn to spot Trump Foster. He saw a horse toss its head amongst the trees of a basket across the river, and the sun glinted on something else —the barrel of a rifle.

"When you get to Slide Rock we'll let you know what to do, Deaver."

They'd let him know all right, with a bullet through the back. But there was nothing else he could do, not now, in any case. He had to play their game and wait for a break. He knew well enough that once they got their hands on Riker and made him talk, neither Riker or his kind would ever be found again. They'd get Holt too if they had a chance.

"Agreed, Deaver?" called out Carley.

"All right. How much time do I have?"

"Twenty-four hours."

"Give me a break, Carley!"

"He said twenty-four hours," said Morg Mills in his flat voice. "You have Riker at Slide Rock in twenty-four hours. You have him there by three o'clock tomorrow afternoon. That's final."

There was nothing for him to do but watch them take Susan and Tim as living shields until they reached the bridge and vanished into the woods.

Holt wiped the cold sweat from his face. He walked

outside and rolled a cigarette, then remembered Trump Foster, and jumped back behind the house.

The wind ruffled the bloodstained shirt of Savvy Harris. "The least they could have done was to bury their own carrion," said Holt.

He dragged the body to a hollow several hundred yards from the house, rolled it in a ragged tarpaulin, then covered the body with boards, and piled rocks atop that. It would do until a better burial could be arranged.

He rolled a smoke and walked downstream until he reached the place where he and Cass had left the horses. The horse Holt had been riding was still there, grazing peacefully. But there was no sign of the horse Cass Riker had ridden.

Holt rode slowly back to the ranch. He tried to figure out where the old man might have gone. He drew rein behind the house and looked up at the west canyon wall, already deep in shadow as the sun sank. He wouldn't have gone west into Tonto country. That left north, east and south. Maybe he had gone south to get his money.

CHAPTER TEN

I T WAS dusk when he headed away from the ranch. He had done a little hard and fast thinking too, trying to fit the odd-shaped pieces of the jigsaw puzzle together. Susan had told him that Uncle Cass had gone south for a week or ten day's journey, yet it had been less than a week when he had showed up at the ranch. Then, by great fortune, he had spotted the outlaws on the West Fork of the Bandera when he was on his way back with the money. He said he had cached it for fear that they might see him and capture him. Therefore the money at least was on the West Fork. And if Holt Deaver knew Old Whiskers as he thought he did, the old coot would have headed for the West Fork as well as the others.

It would be real cosy there. The four hardcases, Susan and Tim, Cass Riker, thousands of dollars in stolen money, and Holt Deaver, riding into trouble with a ranch girl's apron as his guerdon. Meanwhile, somewhere out in the blue might be Burl Stuart, U.S. Marshal and Deputy-Sheriff Lang Masters, all with a special interest in him.

With only twenty-one hours left in which to deliver
Cass Riker, Holt Deaver drew rein at the foot of the
insanely dangerous trail. It wasn't in the cards for Holt
Deaver to die from a fall. The Fates had other plans, not
quite ready as yet, but probably just as violent and just as
final. Thinking this, he ascended the treacherous slope.

The moon had not yet risen when he reached the
ridge that overlooked the West Fork of the Bandera and
the camp they had spotted earlier in the day.

He led the horse quietly down the ridge and along the
canyon floor, half expecting a hoarse challenge out of the
night. Would they fire upon him? They expected him to
find Cass Riker, so perhaps they would be content to let
the full twenty-four hours pass; *but they knew he was
there now.*

He found the place where the camp had been. The
ground was still warm from the fire. Slide Rock was
further upstream; Cass Riker had mentioned it earlier
that day. The whole area in that stretch of the canyon
was known as Slide Rock, but the huge mass of detritus
that formed the wide talus slope and gave the area its
name was not in sight from the camp area.

Holt felt a touch of panic creep up in his mind. So
little time! He followed the stream toward the slide area.
A thought came to him. Cass had said he had *seen* the
outlaws camp, then had cached the loot for the second
time, so the place where he had seen the camp could not
be too far. Holt stopped at a point where the canyon
trended northeast, then looked back. Dark as it was he
knew that no one could see the camp once he passed
around the canyon bend. But if a man was up high he
might be able to see *over* it.

The rock formations of the area were deteriorating,
and many places had decayed. It was outright insanity to

try and scale those walls even in daylight. The moon would be up before long to give him plenty of light, but he couldn't wait. If he only knew that country better!

He led the horse into a box canyon and picketed it near a pool of water, took his Winchester, some food, his reata, then he formed a rifle sling from several saddle straps and slung the weapon on his back.

There was a faint suggestion of moonlight to the east when he started his climb. It was easy enough until he reachedthe first naked shoulder of rock. By the time he was halfway up the canyon wall, great shards hung by the weakest of joints to the massive rock.

He scouted gingerly along the base of the decomposed rock formations, thrusting a hand into catclaw now and then, and feeling the stinging whip of cholla through the thin material of his levis. The moon was making a silvered path of the West Fork of the Bandera when he found a place that looked less risky than any other place. There was no other choice.

Feeling his way step by step, he dared not look down. The sweat ran down his gaunt body and stung his freshly-healing cuts. His temples throbbed and his guts became queasy. He knew he might never make it.

Then he felt a little surge of triumph, for he could see the lip of the canyon about twenty feet above him. He reached for a hold and got a firm grip when suddenly his footing sank beneath him, and with a roaring, rushing and grating of tons of rock the whole formation let go to pour in a dusty mass down to the canyon below. As he hung there, fighting with fingertips and toes for claw holds, he heard the last pitiful whinnying of his horse as it was crushed and buried beneath the rock.

He was unable to go up or down, and the racing

seconds of doom-pattered through his mind like the final pattering of bits and shards on the slope.

With his leg and arm muscles tiring, Holt cautiously felt along the thin line of a rock ledge above him until his strong fingers felt a groove. He thrust out his right foot and tapped with it along the rock until it found a hold. After breathing a short prayer, he swung himself until he could grip the groove with both hands and let his full weight depend on them until his boot toes scrabbled into holds.

Then inch by inch he worked up the rock face; it seemed as though that twenty feet were more like twenty miles. Suddenly the strange and horrible delusion came over him that the rock was leaning out toward him and that he was scaling further and further back, until it seemed he would be hanging there in space.

Staring at the rock inches from his nose, he worked slowly and steadily upward until at last his questing right hand struck the top. He paused, then exerted the last of his strength, swung his whole body upward and rolled away from that damnable edge.

The surface of the rocky ground seemed to float and heave beneath him and his hands remained clawed and tense as he lay there fighting nausea and panic. It was a long time until he could raise his head, then his body, to look about him.

The moon was flooding the country with light now, lending a cold-looking and eerie pattern to the rock formations and stunted trees, making it into an imitation of a lunar landscape; he had the odd impression that perhaps he had climbed from the earth into some alien land.

There was nothing to be gained by sitting there. He rose and rolled a cigarette, studying the terrain until the cigarette was finished. Then he walked off with long easy strides to the north. Now and then he walked almost to the edge of the canyon brink and peered down, but there was no place that looked any easier than the place he had scaled. Now, if he had climbed to a place where there was no trail in or out, he'd have to descend the canyon wall—and that could be more dangerous than climbing it. He shuddered a little as he thought of the tons and tons of rock that had broken loose back there to almost bury the horse.

He glanced ahead and to his right. The wide shelf had narrowed somewhat and had curved to follow the rock face to his right with still no indication of opening or passage through the brooding wall of rock. But the formation had changed to a rather odd-looking conglomeration of geometrically patterned rock, much darker than the rest of the rock facing. It was a curious sort of a country, with continual surprises for a man, but this beat all.

Staring at the formation with squinted eyes, he walked on, and then suddenly he stopped and opened his eyes widely. "By God," he said hoarsely, "that ain't rock! It's buildings!"

He reached back for his Winchester and pulled it forward to lever a round into the chamber. He let the hammer down to half cock then paced forward slowly and softly with his head turning from side to side to scan each foot of ground. He was within two hundred yards of them when he realized what they were. Someone, probably years ago, had built those buildings about a mine. But how had they managed to get in there to bring in building materials and mining machinery and how did they get the ore out of there? It was an unanswered question but he did know one thing for sure; there was a way in and out of that dangerous rock shelf, and he aimed to find it.

When he was closer he noticed the red scaling rust on the metal structures and the silvery-gray of the unpainted, warped wood. Shreds of tattered canvas waved back and forth in the wind and somewhere within the group of buildings a door suddenly banged, slammed shut by the invisible hand of the wind. The ruins were imposing even against the great backdrop of the rock wall towering behind them. The shaky metal and wood scaffolding etched angles and triangles against the lighter-colored rock. It had been a Paul Bunyan feat to bring in material to construct such buildings and other structures. But the men who had built the place and had worked it had left long ago and now it was the haunt of bats, mice, rattlesnakes and utter loneliness.

But it was no time to admire the guts of the men who had built such a place in the almost inaccessible canyon of the West Fork of the Bandera in a hard search for fortune. Holt Deaver was looking for a man who had found, or rather appropriated, a fortune not by sweating blood in a hellhole of a canyon, but by cashing in his six-shooters at Wells-Fargo. Time was running as swiftly as it always did when a big game was in progress and the chips were down.

Holt wiped the sweat from his face and grounded his rifle. He looked to his left, along the great rock shelf and saw that wheels and hoofs of bygone days had etched a roadway there. So there was a way out and it was plain enough to see, but somehow or another he could not drag himself away from the great rusty and decaying ghost town that squatted on the rock before him.

He walked between two buildings and halted to eye the sort of street that ran from left to right in front of him, littered with rusted tin cans, broken bottles, pieces of rusted machinery almost impossible to identify. The buildings all had the same hangdog, forlorn look of the ghost town, almost as though furtively hoping they'd be used again, but knowing they never would.

He looked up the slope toward the mine machinery set against the face of the rock wall and it almost seemed to him there was a quick, almost unseen movement in the darkness of the base structure. He wet his lips and raised his rifle. He waited and watched with the spidery patience he had learned in his scouting days. Then, as so often happened, his eyes began to play their little tricks engendered by the shifting moonlight, the movements of canvas, tin or wood actuated by the wind.

He tried an old trick. He closed his eyes, waited, then quickly opened them and this time he was sure he saw something move. A whitish, grayish sort of substance, moved by the wind.

Holt eased back, passed behind the building, avoided walking on a rusted sheet of metal, then walked between the next two buildings, taking off his hat as he did so. He got down on his knees and peered around the side of the building, knowing he was in thick shadow. This time he could see the base structure from a different angle. Once again he closed and opened his eyes and again he saw the fluttering object.

He moved back once more. He wasn't sure what it was but his instinct probed him to take a closer look.

He was within fifty yards of the base structure, close by the low wall of a vat, flat on his lean belly, when he saw the movement again. *I'll be double-damned,* he thought, *it ain't possible!*

Holt inched backward, then crawled around the base of the vat until he could again peer at the structure. This time he was sure. He faded into the shadows near the base of the rock wall, then padded forward. His silence seemed impossible for a man of his size, but he went as softly as the night-hunting owl he had seen a little while back.

He was within twenty feet of the object when it moved slowly, fluttering in the wind. He froze, then as the object moved into the thicker shadows he cat-footed forward like a puma. Just as the object turned and looked at him, hisrifle muzzle moved out and rested comfortably on a lean gut and the hammer was thumbed back to full cock. "Hello, Old Whiskers," said Holt coldly. "I might of knowed this would be a good place for you to hole up in."

The grayish-white whiskers thrust out toward Holt and moved pugnaciously in the wind. "Why?" asked Cass Riker sourly.

Holt jerked his head. "The bat, the rat, the snake and the hootie owl like these places, and by godfrey, Old Whiskers, I do believe you found yourself a real home with your furred and feathered kin."

"Gawddamn you, boy, take that rifle muzzle outa my navel!"

Holt grinned evilly. "You old snake. Why'd you run off like that?"

Cass Riker looked away. "Well, I didn't see no sense in standing there like a damned ol' wooden Indian to get shot full of lead."

"It was all right for *me* to stand there though, wasn't it?"

"Well, you got to allow you ain't too bright, bub." The bright old eyes glittered in the cold moonlight. "You got more luck than brains, I gotta admit. They hit you at all?"

"No."

"Well, we can't expect *everything*. You get any of them?"

"One."

"Only *one?* Boy, you oughta stay outa gun scrapes, if that's the best you can do," jeered Cass. "Who'd you do in?"

"Savvy Harris."

Riker paled a little. "That was him in the barn, weren't it, bub?"

"It were, bub."

The old man nodded. He rubbed his whiskery jaw. "He fired first though?"

Holt nodded.

"That's what I thought. By godfrey I woulda never believed it, bub. You know something?"

"No."

"You're damned near as fast as me. Now I . . ."

Holt leaned on the rifle a little. "Shut up," he said. "We've talked long enough. We're going to take a little trip, Cass."

"Where to?" asked the old man suspiciously.

"Down to Slide Rock."

Riker laughed. "You loco, bub? I know them boys are down there somewheres. I didn't see 'em but I heard 'em. They got a gal with 'em too. Probably figurin' on a real blowout down there. Likker and a woman. Might be interestin' to go at that. Haww!" His face changed. "Where'd they get a filly in this damned country?"

"Don't you know, Cass?" asked Holt softly.

The hard eyes narrowed. "God's sake! I never thought of that!"

"They got the boy too, Cass."

Riker paled. "You let 'em? I oughta . . ."

"You oughta what?" jeered Holt. "Old Footloose, you

left there fast and furious like the devil beating tanbark! Now keep that waggin' jaw still while I tell you the story."

Riker listened quietly while Holt told him of the deal he had been forced to make. "They mean it too, Cass," said Holt. "They'd kill those two like a man drowns unwanted kittens, if you don't show up and pay off."

Riker shook his head as though to clear it. "You know what will happen to me, and maybe them anyways if I pay off?"

Holt nodded. "And we can't go to the law."

"Hell no! You plumb loco to think that? We'd lose the whole damned kit and caboodle, lock, stock and barrel!"

"Meaning the money?"

The wind sighed softly through the ironwork of the structure over them and what it sighed about sent a cold chill through Holt Deaver and he wondered suspiciously if Cass Riker felt the same way.

"Well," said Cass, "we can't stand here like two crows on an outhouse roof, leastways, not with a rifle in my belly." He placed a hand on the barrel and tried to move it away but it was as rigid as a girder. "How come?" demanded Riker.

"This may strike you as a bellybuster, Old Whiskers, but I don't exactly trust you."

"Sho, bub, but we got to work *together* now to figger a plan."

Holt stepped back and let the hammer down to half cock. "Walk," he said quietly. *"Ahead* of me."

They walked down to one of the buildings and sat down on the porch. Holt rolled a smoke and passed the makings to Riker. They lighted up and sat there silently for a time.

"Three o'clock you said?" asked Riker at last.

"Yes. I hope to God you got your cache not too far from here."

"I ain't sayin' *where* it is!"

Holt tapped the knuckles of his right hand with the fingertips of his left hand. "You will, bub, *you will.*"

Riker held his head in his gnarled hands. "I just can't think of a way outa this, Holt."

"We have no choice."

The wind soughed through the great canyon and whispered dryly around the buildings and mine structures. Holt leaned back against a post and suddenly a thought came tohim. The old man had been hiding there. Damned if he wouldn't have the loot there too! Holt was slow on the brain, quick on the trigger.

Riker sighed, flipped away his cigarette, then reached for the makings. "All right," he said quietly. "The cache is here at the mine. Slide Rock ain't no more than three miles from here. We got plenty time to make that. All we need is time to think of a plan." He rolled a second smoke and lighted it and his hard little eyes studied Holt over the flare of the match. "We got some advantages and they got others. We got the money and they got the kids. Now all we have to do is to get the money to them four buzzards and get them two lambs outa their hands, without them gettin' killed."

"And us," said Holt.

Riker spat to one side. "I ain't thinkin' about myself no more, Holt."

He sounded so utterly sincere that Holt *almost* believed him.

CHAPTER ELEVEN

T HEY SAT there as the moon waned, slowly eating the food brought from the ranch by Holt, sipping at the water, and not looking at each other. No inspiration had come to them, and yet they knew right well that in a matter of hours they would have to have some solution.

Holt finished his meal and then rolled a cigarette. "There's one thing we can do, Cass," he said thoughtfully. "They told me to bring you to Slide Rock, but they didn't say anything about bringing the money there too."

"Figgered you might be tempted," said Riker slyly.

Holt ignored him. "They said I should bring you there, but I won't go."

"Meaning?"

Holt sucked in on his cigarette and blew a smoke ring. "Maybe they expect me too, but I won't get there."

Riker eyed him suspiciously. "They might not like that. They might raise hell, Holt."

"Let them! What do they really want? Me or you? Hell no! They want that money. When they seen you they figure you'll have to lead them to the money, and they'll damned quick forget about me."

"That don't make sense when I tell them you found me."

Holt spat. "How you ever engineered that Wells-Fargo deal is beyond me. Dumb luck I call it. You don't tell them I found you! You just say you saw them with the two prisoners and figured they were using them as hostages, and you, being the kindly old Uncle Cass, come in to give yourself up."

"They won't buy that bill of goods!"

Holt nodded slowly. "Yes they will, because I'm going to be dead, Old Whiskers."

"I'm for it, bub, but ain't that the *hard* way to do it?"

Holt looked up at the sky in silent prayer, as though asking for strength to go on. "I won't be dead! I'll be where the loot is cached, and I'll make my play when you bring them here for it. It will be touch and go and the devil will get the hindmost, but I can't think of any other way out."

"You think they'll believe you're dead?"

Holt smiled indulgently. "You poor old man. I got to tell you everything? We're going to make it *look* as though I died. You remember hearing a helluva rock fall some hours before I got here?"

"Yes."

"I made that rock slide! I swear, Cass, it sounded as though the whole canyon wall fell in, and my hoss is down there, with his legs sticking up out of the fallen rock. Now you're going to go to that slide pile and plant enough stuff around that hoss to make it look as though I was caught under it too."

"You think they'll buy that pig in a poke?"

Rolling a smoke for himself, Holt grinned. "Look, Old

Whiskers, whether they but that pig in a poke or not, it's the only plan we got."

Holt walked softly through the ruins until he managed to kill a large rat with a blow from his Winchester butt. He stripped off his hat band and ripped off a shirt sleeve, tore at the hat and crushed it, and then opened the rat with his sheath knife and dabbled the blood on the articles. He carried the things to Cass Riker who sniffed suspiciously.

"We have until three o'clock tomorrow afternoon," said Holt. "You'd better get out of here before daylight and get to the fallen rock before the dawn. Plant the stuff, then get out of there and go the long way around before you reach Slide Rock. Get there around noon. Now, you make it look like you just happened to see them with their prisoners and came in by yourself."

"Supposing they split up? Leave the kids somewheres with a guard whilst I bring the others up here for the *dinero?* That would fox *us*, bub."

Holt shrugged. "It's another risk. Between thee and me, Old Whiskers, I think the four of them will stay together. There ain't no honor amongst thieves, like the book says."

Riker squinted a little as he studied Holt. "Yeh, I been thinking about that."

"Well look at someone else then."

They discussed their plan for another half-hour. It would be touch and go and the lead would fly and maybe the two of them might not make it; maybe the young woman and the boy might not make it either. But there was nothing else to do unless they stalked the four outlaws and their captives, trying to pick them off one by one; but the risks in such an action would be greater than what they had planned.

Holt looked at the dying moon. "One more thing to do, Cass."

"So?"

"Show me where the loot is."

There was a tense silence from the old man.

"Well?"

Riker tugged at his beard, spat leisurely, squinted at the sky, then at the ground.

"Riker!"

Cass stood up. "How will I know whether you'll be here or not when I bring 'em back?"

"Meaning?"

"All that money left here with a broke saddle bum whilst Old Whiskers trots down into the canyon and gives hisself up to them sidewinders? What proof do I have that you'll be here?"

"My word."

They stood there eyeing each other. Then Holt reached inside his shirt and took out Susan's apron. He silently handed it to Riker.

Riker fingered the material, then looked at Holt.

"I get the message, Holt. You win. Let's go."

Holt followed the old man toward the mining structure over the mine itself. It was getting darker now with the death of the moon and a colder wind sighed through the canyon. Holt shivered a little.

Riker walked like a cat through the litter and beneath the lower part of the structure. He felt about, then Holt heard the creaking of hinges and felt a draft of cool, earthy-smelling air flow about him.

"Here," said Cass. "Strike a light."

He handed Holt a candle lantern. Holt lighted it and held it up. The guttering, yellow light revealed a thick door that had been set neatly into the chiseled rock of the mine entrance.

Holt leaned the rifle against the side of the mine entrance and then followed Cass. He held the lantern up high as they walked. The old man was right. The going was rough. Rock had fallen as well as a pit prop; rusting machinery, balks of wood and abandoned gear littered the narrow passageway. On and on they went into the echoing darkness until Cass turned sharply right into a drift and walked steadily onward. The drift was narrower and just as cluttered. A cold draft poured about them.

Then Cass Riker stopped, rested a hand against a sagging prop and simply said, "Here, bub."

Holt held the lantern up higher. A number of leathern bags with brass fittings, now green with verdigris, lay on the floor of the drift.

"Take a look," said Cass quietly. "You never did believe me, did you?"

Holt hooked the lantern to a rusted spike, wiped his sweating hands on his thin levis, and went down on one knee beside the first sack. He struggled a little with the leather straps thickened with dampness and age, until at last he raised the flap and thrust in a questing hand. It struck something thick and wadded. He withdrew it and stared at a wad of bills, neatly bound with paper and elastic bands. The top bill was a one hundred dollar bill. Holt riffled through the wad. They were *all* one hundred dollar bills. The real sugar!

"There's eighty thousand eagles in them dirty *old* bags, bub. When we settle this business, you get ten of them like I agreed," said Cass. His voice seemed further away, for Holt was in a vague, almost dreamlike state.

"Go ahead, bub! Count 'em!"

But just then he remembered something. Cass had

said he had made a haul of eighty thousand. The saloon-keeper in Yardigan had said it had been one hundred thousand, and Morg Mills, in the conversation that Holt had overheard at the Verde, had claimed it had been one hundred and twenty thousand!

After counting the eighty thousand, he spoke over his shoulder. "This is all of it, Cass?"

There was no answer.

"You hear me, Old Whiskers?"

No answer.

He looked behind himself. There was no one there. He jumped to his feet and reached for the lantern, kicking aside several wads of the stolen money. "Cass Riker!" he called out.

"Cass Riker . . . Cass Ri . . ." The echo died tauntingly away.

Holt ran through the narrow drift, heedless of the obstructions. "Damn you, Cass!" he yelled.

He hurled himself down the main tunnel toward the doorway and just in time he saw it close and heard the rattling of metal against metal. He slammed a shoulder into the massive door and winced with cruel pain. "Riker!" he yelled hoarsely.

Then it was deathly silent except for the distant dripping of water far down the tunnel.

Holt placed the lantern on the floor and rested an ear against the damp wood of the door.

"Deaver?" came the thin faint voice of the old man.

"Damn you! Where'd you think I was?"

Riker chuckled. "Countin that *dinero!* Was it all there, bub?"

"Ill wring your skinny neck!"

Riker laughed again, "No, you won't, 'cause you can't get outa there, bub."

"I'll smash this door down!"

"Hear him," jeered Riker. Then his voice changed and became cold and hard. "Listen, and keep that big mouth of yours shut for once! You think I was goin' to go down in that canyon and leave you up here nice and cosy with eighty thousand dollars? I ain't *that* loco."

"What's your dirty game, Riker?"

Silence again. Then Riker spoke steadily. "I'm going down there like we planned. I'm going to bring 'em up here like we planned. Only instead of finding you gone with the loot, I'll have you safe and sound in there, standing guard over it like a *pat inn*. You get it, bub?"

A cold feeling raised the flesh on Holt's body. The old Spanish miners used to close a mine and hide it, planning to come back some day, and as a guard they would slay one of their Indian laborers so that his ghost would guard the treasure.

Riker laughed. "You'll live! Now, when we get back here, it's up to you to take care of them. I got you spotted, bub, guarding Old Whisker's loot like a good little boy."

Holt wiped the cold sweat from his face. "Supposing you *don't* come back, Riker?"

This time there was no answer from the old man. Nothing but the dying echoes fleeing down the cold dank tunnel.

The candle was getting low, and he still had not found any way of getting out of that tomb-like mine. The main tunnel ended in a massive rock fall. It would take him days to dig through it, and even if he succeeded, he still didn't know whether it led to freedom or death. He explored drift after drift to find them ending in blank rock faces. He went back to the place where the money littered the floor of the drift and sat down on a timber to think.

What if the old coot kept on going? He'd wait until he was sure Holt was dead, then come back for the loot. Riker had outwitted three partners fifteen years ago when he had made the haul. He liked the idea of running alone through those lovely green leaves.

But Susan and Timmie were still in horrible danger down in the canyon. Maybe the old billy goat did have a sense of responsibility and maybe he planned to get rid of his pursuers alone. That would take some doing!

Hours had ticked past like the sound of a death-watch beetle. That damned door sealed the mine like the lid on a tomb and the simile was not pleasant. He rested his head in his hands and stared at his worn boot toes.

Holt idly kicked at a wad of the money. He grinned coldly. Well, the old billy goat had kept his word. Holt had his ten thousand. In fact he had *eighty* thousand, but a million times that number couldn't buy his way to freedom now.

He thought back on the days when he had worked as a miner. He had been with a blasting crew then, working under a skilled young engineer, and some of his lore had rubbed off on Holt. It was a subject he had liked, but his feet had gotten itchy and the long ride had beckoned as it usually did.

One stinking stick of dynamite might loosen that ponderous door. One stick might just make it, and he had eighty thousand dollars to pay for it. He thought back on Yardigan's and the powder house the old storekeeper kept at a safe distance behind his store.

Idly he picked up one of the decks of greasy playing cards and began to play solitaire, and as he handled the pasteboards something began to plague his mind. Something that young engineer had told him so many years ago. Something that began to work in his mind like a ferment. He slapped down the cards. Something to do with explosives! Something to do with playing cards! But what was the connection?

He reached for the bottle of liquor and pulled the cork out. The rich, fruity odor filled his nostrils. He drank deeply and felt the welcome warmth in his gut, then he played on while his mind tried to race ahead of him, to tell him something.

Then he remembered that playing cards are made of cellulose. The red ink used on the hearts and diamonds is made of glycerin and silver nitrate. A wet mass of this, tamped solidly into a pipe and capped, then heated, will form steam and gas. Glycerin and nitrate together with cellulose, under heat and compression, should form pressure enough to explode.

"Yeh," grunted Holt, "but how much of an explosion? Maybe not enough to blow my big nose."

Then he took the red cards from both sets, tearing the red spots from each card and placing them in a tin can. With a trickle of water he was able to make mush of the pasteboard. Then he searched for and found a piece of pipe capped at one end. After pouring the mess into it, he stopped the pipe up with a small piece of wood.

Anxiously, he hurried to the mouth of the tunnel. He placed the pipe upright in the angle between the wall and door, then wedged it tightly, leaving enough space to place the lantern beneath the pipe. There might just be enough heat, but it would take time, and the candle didn't have long to go. He placed heavy articles about the pipe, slid the lantern beneath it, then wedged more material into place.

He uncorked the bottle and got up on his knees to

drink. The candle had almost gutted out, and his heart sank within him. He raised the bottle and took a good slug. Just as it hit his throat the blast roared along the tunnel, and a wall of gas hit him as well as a melon-sized chunk of rock.

CHAPTER TWELVE

I T WAS later than two o'clock in the afternoon by the angle of the sun when Holt Deaver finished with his preparations. He had taken the money from the drift and had recached it, then he had reset the huge door, which the blast had driven forward at the bottom and off the great hinge.

The thing he wanted to do was to get Cass to lead the outlaws into the mine, hoping that they might, in their greed and excitement at the proximity of the money, just leave Susan and Timmie outside of the mine. The odds were high against that, of course, but Holt had been faced with high odds ever since he had left Chloride.

What was holding them back? He had told Cass to reach them about noon, but then you couldn't depend on the old buck. His mind worked in devious ways like the book said. Holt had no rifle, but he had his six-shooter. Six slugs against four, fast gunslingers who would have twenty-four shots from their six-guns aimed at one target.

Maybe they'd been suspicious of the old man's story

about Holt Deaver being beneath that rock fall. Maybe they had dug into it. Maybe they had been suspicious of him returning alone. Morg Mills and Trump Foster didn't know the old bat too well, but Ernie Carley and Pete Shalen sure did.

The sweat of indecision ran down his body. He took a long chance and trotted to the canyon brink to look down. There was no sign of human life, but he could have sworn he saw a thin wreath of wood smoke drifting up from the trees far below. Someone was down there.

Maybe they had heard the explosion of the improvised charge Holt had devised and had become too suspicious. But the money was the lodestar. It would make them charge hell with a bucket of water.

Holt walked slowly back to the mine keeping an eye out toward the only way up to the rock shelf. No sign of life there either. Then a cold thought raced through his head. He looked up at the ragged escarpment high above the mine. Maybe they were up there watching the mine! But there was nothing to see except a tattered fringe of pines and a lone hawk floating easily in the updraft from the deep canyon. That wary bird would have been long gone had anyone been up there.

Retreating into one of the buildings away from the warm sun, he could see the narrow shelf where the rutted road came around a rock shoulder toward the mine. Where were they? It was getting close to four o'clock by now and still no sign nor sound of them.

He risked a smoke and lay flat on his belly peering through a crack in the thin siding of the building. It was so—that a man's luck would run out. In some things at least. Some men were lucky in cards and others in love. An odd, but lingering thought entered his mind. He smashed a fist down on the warped flooring. "By godfrey," he said softly. He had almost forgotten *one* thing: The love that Susan Morris had for Holt Deaver, the long rider! He felt inside his shirt and touched the apron, no longer crisp and fresh, but crumpled and stained with dirt and sweat.

"Susan!" he said aloud.

What was it she had said to him? *When you said you were leaving that was hurt enough.*

Then to hell with Cass Riker and his ill-gotten loot, and to hell with Ernie Carley, Pete Shalen, Morg Mills and Trump Foster! It was Susan he was fighting for now and the sudden wonder of the revelation filled him with a faith and courage he had never experienced before. He *had* to win now!

Then it was darker and darker. Somewhere off in the tangled brush of the mesa top a coyote howled mournfully.

Holt Deaver cursed. A man could hardly see his hand in front of his face now and if they came at that time it would be touch and go. It would be some hours before the full moon arose.

He paced about like a lean lobo with his hand resting on the butt of his Colt, peering into the darkness, testing the night with all his senses, straining his hearing at each sound.

Then slowly the faint light came from the east, ever so slowly, and it was then that he could distinguish objects that had vanished with the departure of the sunlight.

Yet there was nothing to warn him of their coming. No sound of hoof striking stone, or creak of saddle leather; no muted voices; no sudden whickering of a horse. Nothing . . .

At least Holt Deaver had two advantages over and

above his native skills with gun, fists and boots. He had the advantage of surprise—if they believed he lay stark beneath the rock fall; he had the advantage, earned through hours of nervous wandering, of knowing the mine area like the palms of his dirty, calloused hands. Every building, structure, machine and rise or fall of ground was etched in his memory.

He paced behind a row of sagging buildings, then stopped just behind the last of them, while he raised his head and sharply drew in his breath. It had come to him at last. He had seen nothing and had heard nothing and his keen nostrils had scented nothing alien to the night, but it was there just the same!

Crouching behind a rusted pile of gears and cogs, he could watch that double ribbon of ruts worn into the soft rock. He stayed there for a long time until he saw a faint, furtive movement at the rock shoulder. He wet his dry lips with the tip of his tongue and became more conscious of the steady beating of his heart.

The movement came again. Then suddenly a man moved along the road with a rifle held in his hands, and there was no mistaking Morgan Mills, the human timber wolf. He moved as quietly as the vagrant night breeze.

Holt raised his head and looked up at the rock facing above the road. It didn't take long to spot another movement up there. A rock fell and bounced on the roadway. Trump Foster was deadly with the long gun, but he moved as softly and as cautiously as an ox. The big man went along the top of the wall, keeping pace with Mills. Holt couldn't help but grin, scared as he was. He could just imagine what Morg Mills had thought when Trump had kicked that rock over the side.

Mills reached the first of the buildings, set between the road and the rock wall, with just about enough space to make it. He peered along the line of buildings. Then he waved a hand.

A moment later two more men appeared. One of them walking ahead of the other and stumbled as he walked, for his hands were tied behind his back. There was no doubt about who he was. Just behind Riker was Ernie Carley, walking with a Colt in his right hand, while his left held a rope attached about Riker's neck in a noose which could be tightened swiftly with a pull. They weren't taking any chances with Old Whiskers, for the old ram could butt viciously if he had a chance.

Then Holt felt a tightening in his throat as he saw three more people coming slowly up the center of the moonlit road. Timmie was first, just ahead of his sister, and his face was white in the moonlight. The wind toyed with Susan's dark, lustrous hair. She held her head high, for there was the air of a thoroughbred about that girl, who was now mixed in with a pack of curs and mongrels. Holt numbered himself amongst the last. Pete Shalen, with his left arm still in a sling, walked just behind the girl. She had not been bound because she'd never be able to outrun or dodge a slug from the pistol he carried in his right hand.

While Trump Foster found a place to work his way down the rock wall, Holt lay flat. The big man joined Morgan Mills and they walked softly past the first of the buildings with cocked rifles swinging steadily back and forth, covering each door and window as they peered about.

Holt dared not move until they had passed him. He saw Susan's face clearly in the moonlight, with her lovely hazel eyes and soft mouth. Her face was set and taut as she passed. He heard the grating of their feet on the gravelly surface of the road. None of them had spoken. It had almost been like a procession of ghosts.

When next he saw them they were beneath the rusted iron structure built about the mine entrance. Then he heard the creaking of the huge door and wondered if Old Whiskers had noticed that the door didn't swing quite so easily as it had when he had closed it on Holt.

Then all of them but Trump Foster entered the mine. Foster stood in the shadows, betrayed only by the dull light of the moon on his rifle barrel. Holt inched along the shadowed side of the vat. Trump had ears and eyes like an Apache and could shoot by sound as well as by sight. A man didn't take chances with him.

There was a place beside the vat where rain water had softened the ground. It was a whitish deposit of soft earth.

Holt moved his hands around in it then smeared it over his face. He cleaned his hands on his shirt, then inched along until he could stand up in the shadows of the rock wall. He freed his Colt, then walked like a cat closer and closer to Trump. If Trump turned . . . But Holt was within a few feet of him before the big man turned quickly and stared at Holt.

"Trump . . . Trump Foster," said Holt in a hollow voice.

Trump's mouth opened and his eyes widened and he seemed to freeze in position. "You're dead, Deaver," he said hoarsely.

"Come with me, Trump Foster."

"No—no."

Then Holt swung swiftly and viciously like a striking copperhead and the heavy pistol barrel caught Trump on the left temple. He swayed toward the rock face, and

Holt caught the rifle from his limp hands. Trump sagged to the ground. Holt wasted not a second. He gripped the big man and dragged him roughly along the harsh ground to a place behind the cyanide vat. He had just ripped off Trump's pants belt and bandanna to bind him when he heard voices in the tunnel. There was no time to pinion Trump now. He jerked the big man's holster gun free from the leather and ran like an antelope to duck in behind a building from which he could still see the mine entrance. Maybe he should have slid a knife between the man's ribs, but that wasn't Holt Deaver's way.

"Trump!" called out Morg Mills.

"Trump . . . Trump . . . Trump . . ." answered the echoes.

"He's gone," said Morg.

They all came out from beneath the rusted structure. Something black had etched itself on Cass Riker's face, something like ink, but it wasn't ink, it was blood. Riker stumbled as Ernie Carley viciously jerked the noose about the old man's neck yanking him to and fro. "Where's that loot, you damned old goat?" he snarled.

Susan reached out a hand and Morg Mills shoved her back. Tim struck at the man, but a backhand from Mills struck the boy and drove him to the ground where he lay still.

Holt felt the hot blood rush through him. Raw courage and hate wouldn't beat those men; not yet in any case. Other weapons had to be used and Holt thought he had the answer.

Holt eased into the building beside him. He padded through it, feeling his way carefully. Then he stopped beside one of the leathern bags which he had taken from the drift. He could hear the harsh voices of the three outlaws as they lashed out at Cass Riker.

"Let him alone!" said Susan. "He doesn't know anything about money! He's never had any!"

Ernie Carley laughed. "Helluva lot you know about it! Don't let this old devil fool you. Uncle Cass! That's rich!"

"Where is the loot?" yelled Morg Mills.

"Talk, Riker, or we'll break your skinny neck," snarled Pete Shalen.

Holt peered through a window. He had them easily in his sights. He didn't give a tinker's damn for the old man, but Susan would be in the line of fire. That group had to be split up.

Holt framed himself in the window. "You looking for money, *hombres?*" he called out. "Look!" He reached inside his shirt and took out one of the wads, snapping the band with a thumbnail, then hurled the loose bills out into the street.

"Come and git it!" Morg Mills snapped a shot at him. He darted behind the building and into the next one, snatching up a wad from the pile he had left there in the middle of the floor. He broke the band and hurled the wad through the window. "Look!" he yelled. "Free *dinero* for the taking!"

Then he was gone again, running like hell past one building and into the next where he again hurled bills out into the bright moonlight. He could hear yelling and cursing, but above all the old man's voice was the clearest.

"He's gone plumb loco! Throwing my money away like that! Plumb loco I tell you!"

He reached the last building and rounded the end of it in time to see Pete Shalen leaping up on the porch of the closest building. "Shalen," yelled Holt.

Pete had his Colt in his free hand and he snapped a shot at Holt. Holt fired twice from the hip and the second shot caught Shalen in the belly, driving him back off the porch to crash lifelessly on the moonlit ground.

Powder smoke drifted across the street as Holt ran toward the' next building. Ernie Carley was framed in the doorway. He fired twice at Holt, but Holt had hit the ground and he fired twice too, almost like an echo. One of Carley's slugs spurted dirt against Holt's face. Carley had been hit. He reeled out into the middle of the street, doing the border shift from wounded right to good left hand, but a forty-four drove upward into his chest and he fell flat on his back while his Colt skidded across the ground. Blood gushed from his mouth and flooded down onto the ground, staining it blackly.

Holt leaped to his feet and darted behind a building. "Hide, Susan!" he yelled. A shot splintered the wood near his face and he fired at the flash.

"I can't leave Tim!" she cried.

"Stay low then!"

A shot answered his command.

Then it was quiet except for the rustling of the wind. The powder smoke drifted across the street in sheets rifted by the wind. Two dead men stared up at the moonlit sky with wide open eyes that did not see. Two down, two to go, and maybe Trump Foster was ready for battle. But the toughest of them all would be Morgan Mills.

Holt wet his dry lips as he scanned the street. It was quiet; it was too damned quiet. Morg Mills must be stalking Holt, for he knew he'd never have another chance if Holt was still free with a hot rifle in his hands. This was the final hand. But where the hell was Trump Foster?

Minutes ticked past. Holt padded softly behind a shed and peered around the corner in time to see a swift movement close by the biggest building across the street. Someone dressed all in gray. That would be Morgan Mills.

Quiet again. Holt looked toward the mine structures and caught sight of a beard bobbing up and down in there. So, the old billy goat was alive anyway and so were Susan and Tim. The wind fluttered her loose skirt, and he knew she was lying flat beside her brother behind some timber balks. But Trump Foster was closer to them than he was to Holt and if he came to life ...

Holt eased behind one building after another until he was beyond the building in which Morgan Mills was hiding and closer to the mine. He eyed each building in turn on the far side of the street, then took a chance and walked toward the mine. He was halfway across the street when something made him turn quickly. Trump Foster was standing near the body of Pete Shalen with Pete's six-shooter in his hand. He fired at Holt and Holt felt the whip of lead through the slack of his shirt. He fired but Trump, swift for one of his size, had darted for cover.

Holt heard a noise behind him. He whirled, rifle at hip level, in time to see Morg Mills standing in a door-way. Mills fired once and the slug struck savagely. The forty-four had ripped into Holt's left shoulder, high up, but enough to drive him reeling back. Pain and faintness flooded through him and he knew he couldn't stay long on his feet.

Mills snapped another shot and it skinned along Holt's left forearm like a red-hot iron. Still Holt kept his feet peering dazedly at Mills while blood dripped from his left hand and stained the earth at his feet. Once more Mills fired, and this time he missed. His Colt clicked dryly and he vanished from sight to reload.

Holt steadied his rifle, held it at about the waist level of a man who'd be standing inside that building and with the last of his strength fired, levered and fired again and again until the Winchester clicked dryly. Splinters flew from the thin wood. There was a sharp cry just once and then a man was framed in the doorway. A man in gray, but the waist of shirt and vest was black with blood. He held his hands to his belly and stepped out onto the porch, one step at a time, then stepped down into the street. He walked slowly through the rifting smoke and his eyes looked as though they were peering from a smoky window of hell itself. Step by step until he was ten feet from Holt Deaver. Then he stopped.

"You killed Mike," said Morgan Mills slowly and distinctly. "You can't kill me too, Deaver."

Holt was bracing himself on the empty rifle and the street seemed to reel and waver. Blood was soaking through his clothing and running warmly down his body.

"You can't kill me too, Deaver," repeated Morgan Mills.

Then he pitched forward on his face, stiffened spasmodically and lay still forever.

"Holt!" cried Susan.

He turned slowly and saw Trump Foster walking slowly toward him with cocked Colt in a paw of a hand. "How do you want it, Deaver?" taunted Trump. "Head or belly?"

Holt dropped the rifle and clawed for his Colt, but he knew he'd never make it.

"Head or belly, Deaver?"

The big man was hardly moving now and there was a wide grin on his loose face. "Thanks," he said. "That was a nice job you done. You got rid of all the shareholders. Thanks again, Deaver." He raised the Colt.

But something moved swiftly across the moonlit street. A skinny old man with a fluttering beard and a large rusted piece of machinery which he bore like a medieval mace. It didn't seem possible Cass Riker could lift it, much less run with it.

Trump grinned again. "Ready?" he said.

"Sure as hell am, Foster!" screamed Cass Riker.

As Trump whirled in surprise the gear came down with all the power Cass had in his body, and the mass of metal flattened the big man like a poleaxe.

That was the last, or almost the last thing Holt Deaver remembered as he fell slowly. The last thing was the cry of a woman. "You can't die, Holt! You just can't die! I won't let you!"

CHAPTER THIRTEEN

HOLT DEAVER opened his eyes and knew at once where he was. It was the pleasant room where he had recuperated once before, in the Morris ranch house. It was bright daylight. He moved a little, then winced in pain as his shoulder and arm objected to the movement. He looked curiously down at them. They were swathed in neat clean bandages.

A shadow caught the corner of his left eye and he turned a little to see Susan Morris coming toward him.

"He's awake!" she called over her shoulder. She placed a deliciously cool hand on his forehead. "And no fever!" She kissed him gently.

He smiled. "That'll bring the fever right back," he said.

"Are you strong enough to talk?" she asked.

"With you? Always!"

She shook her head. "There is a gentleman here to see you."

Holt had a peculiar feeling as though she was holding back something. "All right," he said.

"You may come in. Marshal," she said.

Oh Christ, thought Holt. Where in hell were his pants and horse? But he knew he was trapped at last.

Burl Stuart came to the bedside and looked down at Holt. "How are you, Deaver?" he asked. , "Not well enough to travel to Yuma yet."

"No. But what makes you think you're going there?"

Holt eyed him. "You didn't come here to ask about my health."

"Happens I did . . . today, anyway."

Tim Morris came into the room and stood beside his sister, grinning at Holt.

Burl Stuart hooked a thumb beneath his belt. "You've been cleared of that paymaster robbery and killing, Deaver."

"How so?"

"Trump Foster lived long enough to ask us to take his boots off and tell his story. Said he didn't want to die with it on his conscience."

Holt closed his eyes. "Thank God," he said. "What about the other mess?"

"Wells-Fargo has their money back if that's what you mean."

Holt nodded. "How much was it anyway?"

"Eighty thousand, or close to it anyway."

"There was eighty thousand when I last remember," said Holt. He grinned weakly. "I ought to know. I counted it three times."

"Eighty thousand when *you* counted it. Seventy-five thousand when *we* counted it."

Holt opened his eyes. "I haven't got it, Stuart, I'm clean."

"Well, we have an idea who got it."

"Not dead men."

"No. A real live one. Ex-outlaw by the name of Cass Riker."

Holt moved so quickly that he felt a rush of pain through his left side. "Where is he?"

Stuart shrugged. "Where are the snows of yesteryear? He skinned out after he helped Susan and Tim here get you back to the ranch. I don't know how you're alive, Deaver."

Holt smiled at the two Morrisses.

Stuart held out an envelope. "This is for you."

Holt took it and opened it. A thousand dollars was in it. "What's this for?"

"The government had offered it for the men who robbed the paymaster and did those killings. Dead or alive, Deaver."

Holt fingered the bills. He hated blood money.

"Don't feel badly. You did the country a service."

"I suppose so." Holt looked up at the marshal. "How about that Chloride business?"

Stuart looked surprised. *"What* Chloride business?" He winked broadly.

"Gracias!"

"It is nothing." Stuart gripped Holt's hand. "I'm leaving now, Deaver. You'll be all right before too long. Who wouldn't be in these pleasant surroundings?" He bent close to Holt's ear and whispered something and Holt's face nearly split with a wide grin.

After Stuart was gone Susan came to sit by Holt's bedside. "What was that last thing he told you, Holt?" she asked curiously.

He shook his head. "I'd rather not tell you right now. I will later. It will be improved by the keeping."

She kissed him gently. "What are your plans, Holt?"

He looked up at her. "I'd like to know yours first."

She held his gaunt face in her lovely hands. "I think we can talk about them together, Holt, because I think we will be discussing our plans for many years to come."

It was Holt Deaver, ex-long rider, who did the kissing that time.

The winter had passed, although snow still lay in the passes and high on the mountain sides. Holt Deaver, rancher, rode south along the East Fork of the Bandera looking for strays.

He breathed. deeply of the windy, cold air. This was his home now. He shrugged his sheepskin collar higher about his neck and felt for the makings. He rolled a smoke and lighted it, eyeing with pleasure the swift and clear racing of the East Fork. It was a good land and in time it would open up so Susan could have the company of other ranch women. Tim had gone to school and wouldn't be back until summer.

He splashed through the stream and rode south along a rock face, not far from the dangerous trail he had last taken to hunt for Cass Riker. He shook his head as he thought of the old coot who had dropped out of sight as though spirited to another planet.

Although Holt was no longer a scout and the last of the rim-rock Tontos had been herded onto reservations, there was still that keen intuition in him, that feeling for the warnings that came to men with hand-honed senses. That was what now made him suddenly scan the broken ledge of rock, thickly stippled with scrub trees, not fifty yards to his left.

Something fluttered amongst the trees, and it wasn't moss. This mass of material had a pair of gimlet-sharp eyes peering just above it.

"Hello, Old Whiskers," said Holt with a grin.

Cass Riker stood up and looked quickly up and down the canyon. "We alone?" he demanded.

"Yes. Where you been, you old billy goat?"

"Running like hell. Bub, as much as I hate to admit it, I ain't got the snap and spring like I had when I took care of all them sidewinders that night up at the mine."

"*All* of them?"

"Well, what the hell, I got a *little* help from you."

"*Gracias,*" said Holt dryly.

"Can I come stay at the place for awhile?"

"Sure. Lose all your money?"

Cass looked furtive. "Well, not *all* of it."

"Climb up behind, then. The law won't be around."

Cass clambered up behind Holt like a whiskered little tin monkey. "How come?" Cass demanded suspiciously.

Holt grinned as he remembered what he had told Susan not so long ago. "They ain't interested in you, old-timer."

"I got away with five thousand bucks!"

Holt turned. "Sure, you damned old fool, but Wells-Fargo had offered that for reward, and they agreed you had it coming! They figured you served fifteen years for that robbery and were useful in getting the money back to them. So you were in the clear all the time!"

"You big dumb-block! How come you never told me?"

Holt laughed so hard his shoulder pained him. "Because you never let us know where you were, you old billy goat!"

Cass swore under his breath. "You mean I been running all over Arizona and Sonora thinking they wanted me while I was a free man all the time?"

"You got it right, old timer. Now Missus Deaver will be right glad to see you."

"Missus Deaver?"

"Missus *Susan* Deaver!"

"I always thought that girl had more brains than that!"

Holt shook his head. "She didn't." He paused, then passed the makings back to the old man. "Welcome home, Old Whiskers."

They rode slowly home beside the East Fork of the Bandera, and both of them felt as though a piece that had been lost from each of them had at last been found.

TAKE A LOOK AT: JACK OF SPADES AND AMBUSH ON THE MESA

Two Full Length Western Novels

A blazing shoot-out waited for them South of Sonora...

In this classic western double, Hugh Kinzie and Holt Deaver have one thing in common: they've both found themselves in tough circumstances that may turn fatal.

A regiment was needed but they sent only one man, Hugh Kinzie – he saddled his dun and rode west. He found the party of men and women ambushed by Red Sleeves, the maniacal chief who hated the white man more than he feared death itself. Hugh counted on one thing to get them out—his old, battered, still-deadly rifle.

Holt Deaver, a young man who has drifted onto the wrong side of the law on occasion is running from trouble. After the men he was riding with robbed and murdered an army paymaster they agreed they would need to kill Holt to keep him quiet.

"If you're a fan of tough-minded Westerns, I highly recommend it and just about anything else by Gordon D. Shirreffs." –James Reasoner, author of Rattler's Law

COMING MARCH 2022

ABOUT THE AUTHOR

Gordon D. Shirreffs published more than 80 western novels, 20 of them juvenile books, and John Wayne bought his book title, Rio Bravo, during the 1950s for a motion picture, which Shirreffs said constituted *"the most money I ever earned for two words."* Four of his novels were adapted to motion pictures, and he wrote a Playhouse 90 and the Boots and Saddles TV series pilot in 1957.

A former pulp magazine writer, he survived the transition to western novels without undue trauma, earning the admiration of his peers along the way. The novelist saw life a bit cynically from the edge of his funny bone and described himself as looking like a slightly parboiled owl. Despite his multifarious quips, he was dead serious about the writing profession.

Gordon D. Shirreffs was the 1995 recipient of the Owen Wister Award, given by the Western Writers of America for "a living individual who has made an outstanding contribution to the American West."

He passed in 1996.

www.ingramcontent.com/pod-product-compliance
Lightning Source LLC
Chambersburg PA
CBHW010823250626

47169CB00010B/2936